PRAISE FOR 'A POLAROID OF 1 EGGY

"I loved it. Funny. Revealing. Wonderful. His voice is authentic, his prose dynamic, his evocation of an era is pinpoint accurate and the whole hilarious fiction deserves an effing 'OLOGY'."

Maureen Lipman

"Richard Phillips is good on nostalgia, guilt, the emotional messes people make, and the play-acting involved in both the building up or breaking down of a relationship, but the main strength of his book lies in the portrayal of the central character, a superficially shallow man desperately trying to paper over the black holes appearing through the old wallpaper of his life.

"Cynic and romantic, confident adman, bag of nerves, he is believably ambiguous and skilfully realised, as is the slow build of his obsession with the eponymous Peggy, whose twenty-year-old photograph, randomly found in the pocket of an old jacket, triggers a crisis on levels both existential and material."

Carol Birch, author of 'Jamrach's Menagerie', shortlisted for the Booker Prize 2012

apolaroidofpeggy.com

apolaroidofpeggy@gmail.com

A Polaroid of Peggy

RICHARD PHILLIPS

First published in the UK in 2015 by Small and Greene, London

@smallandgreene1
smallandgreene@gmail.com

ISBN 978-0-9930910-6-3

Produced by whitefox

www.wearewhitefox.com

Printed and bound by Clays Ltd, St Ives plc.

FOR HANNAH

PART ONE

CHAPTER 1

LONDON, MARCH 1999

On the E to P scale, as I am sure you will come to agree, I scored pretty well.

Haven't the foggiest what the E to P scale is? Well, don't feel too badly about it. Seeing as I'm the one who came up with the idea and have only ever previously mentioned it to two people – my partners Geoff Bradley and Vince Dutton – during an insanely alcoholic lunch on the third Friday in March 1999, the only way you'd have a clue is if you had been sitting at the next table and overheard me, which, let's face it, doesn't seem very likely. True, we were a bit pissed – possibly more than a bit – and conceivably a little over excited and consequently speaking in unnaturally loud voices, so, if you really want to be picky about it, I suppose you could have been on the next table but one, but even so. (Actually, now I think about it, it might have been Geoff or Vince who first came up with the E to P scale, and not me, but isn't that always the way with really good ideas? Everyone in the room is convinced that theirs was the head in which the switch was first thrown.)

To be absolutely honest, it really wasn't that great an idea but at the time – a couple of bottles of Chateau Petrus in – alright, maybe three – we all loved it. (Correction for the sake of absolute accuracy: probably not Chateau Petrus but definitely something not too shabby.)

We loved it because we were all feeling terrifically pleased with ourselves – as pleased with ourselves as only the founding partners of rather a successful advertising agency can be, and that was because we had just landed an exceptionally juicy piece of business, the name of which now escapes me. (I have a particular talent for obliterating certain bits of the past, as you will see.) But at the time we were exultant. It was yet another feather in the already densely feathered cap of BWD, the acronym by which our agency was known, standing for Bradley, Williams, Dutton; Williams being me, Andrew Williams, Creative Director extraordinaire. As extraordinaire as I needed to be anyway, at least until I got the Peggy thing, but we'll come to that soon enough.

I should say that being pleased with yourself is an essential prerequisite for appreciating the genius of the E to P concept. If you weren't, you'd think that only smug tossers like the founding partners of BWD would ever come up with something so shallow and trivial, even in jest. And I have to say you'd be absolutely right, so if you're a BET – that stands for Bitter and Envious Type – one up to you.

BETs, by the way, are essential to the E to P scale. It is, you see, a wholly unscientific method of measuring one's success relative to that of one's peers. And obviously the more of one's peers who are bitter and envious of one, then, ipso facto, the better one is doing. Any set of peers will do – other people in the industry for instance, or chums from university – if you went to University that is, which, of us, only Vince did, and that was in Australia so it barely counts. But ideally, it should be the peers from your teens. Those are the days when your life standards are truly set, and against which you measure yourself for evermore.

So the way it works is this. You imagine a school reunion: everyone is there. The brainboxes who went to Oxford and LSE, the sporty types whose Saturday afternoon heroics you ignored to the rafters when announced at Monday morning assembly, the prefects, about whom nothing more damning could be said than that is what they were. And you.

And you have to work out where on the E to P scale you sit. Having nonchalantly let slip to the assembled company what you are doing and how well you are doing at it, you simply have to fantasise about how much you will be Envied or Pitied.

If you are B, W or D having a well lubricated lunch at a smart Soho hostelry to celebrate hauling in a socking great account, then you are not in the slightest doubt that all those pimply arsed twats who thought that getting As at A level was the same as being clever, who mistook scoring a 50 for the first XI for being a winner, who thought that being a prison trusty was a path to a golden future, will all be BETs to a man.

The idea that you, B, W or D, work in something as fashionable – and as full of gorgeous women – as advertising and, what's more, seem to be making a packet out of it – naturally you park the company Porsche where it can't be missed – will be guaranteed to get the bile rising in every throat in the class. Always assuming Bryan Ferry or Richard Branson weren't at school with you, it would be all E and no P.

Now here's the sobering thing. (Not that we let it impose on us that day we won the thingummy account.) We did, or at least I did, and what went for W, I am pretty sure went for B and D as well, yes, we really did measure ourselves on the E to P scale. I mean all the hilarious – to us – riffing on the idea of the E to P that we did over the pudding Yquem was obviously done with a lorry load of ironic nods and knowing winks but the tragic and inescapable truth is that, as much as were joking, we were deadly serious.

To my everlasting shame – but I am determined to admit all here so it can't be ignored – I remember that after we had gone on to Grouchos and I had finally fallen into a cab at about midnight to be disgorged in my dishevelled – but still unmistakably Prada – suit outside my recently restored stucco Westbourne Park semi, and after

I had fumbled for my keys and tripped over the cat − didn't have a cat but you get the idea − I sprawled in my Conran recliner with a bottle of Calvados − I must have been pissed because I cannot bear the stuff − and considered my life in the round. And yes, mortified though I am to say it, I remember quite distinctly that I used the E to P scale to measure it. (Probably having a jokey conversation in my head with Geoff and Vince, but still, definitely, using it.) And, let me be clear: if, which I very much doubt, I appeared at any time to be blushing, that was the drink, not any kind of modesty.

I considered my family asleep upstairs. I thought about Alison, my Titian-haired (real, well, once anyway) market research executive wife (met her at a group discussion about a lager campaign I was doing) who was forty-two but looked thirty-five. And a bloody fit thirty-five at that. I thought about my two exquisitely pretty tweenie daughters, Florence and India − could have been worse: if India had been a boy we were toying with Paris − and I thought about our recent Christmas in the Seychelles, our forthcoming Easter skiing holiday in Val d'Isere, my week in Cannes at the Film Festival in June − no, alright, not the real one, just the advertising one, but still a week in Cannes is a week in Cannes. I didn't have any idea where our family summer holiday would be but I knew it would be three weeks in a villa in the South of France or in Italy or on a Greek island or somewhere like that and we'd take the nanny too − if memory serves me right it was the South African girl at the time, sweet face, nice arse − because let's face it, it was a holiday for Alison too and it would hardly make sense if she was having to do more work when she was on holiday than when she wasn't.

I had got to the bottom of this page of the ledger and given it a nice fat tick − I'll bet Stephen Wilkinson, left half for South of England Grammar Schools circa 1970, the freckly bloke with the massive Adam's apple who came directly after me on the class register, didn't take his family on holiday half the bloody year − when I twisted my knee rather painfully, incurred various other minor injuries and damaged about £1000 of Prada suit – at 1999 prices! – beyond repair.

This happened because, having totted up my good fortune in the family and chattels column, I then unwisely decided to move on to property and cars. I can't recall the exact sequence of events that led to the accident but it was something like this: I was reclining in my recliner to get a good shufty at the sumptuousness of the living room – lounge was a word I had left behind with Stephen Wilkinson long ago. It was reassuringly swaggy – modernist minimalism was not yet upon us in 1999 – with vases stuffed full of bright early tulips by Alison. (Or possibly by Mrs Whoeverit-was-at-the-time, the daily.)

Of course, the swagginess was appropriately alleviated by semiotically correct works of art: a couple of Hockneys and a Warhol – prints only but still worth a bob or two even then – and some nicely challenging South African pieces done by a Zulu artist which were, as far as one could tell, montages of township life in Soweto or somewhere like that. They worked a treat in swaggy Westbourne Park.

Having made a mental note of all that, I then got it into my head – and here was the error – to survey the magnificence of 'New Pemberley' from the outside. (We really had called it 'New Pemberley' and had had it tastefully painted on the front door. Or rather I had. Colin Firth and Jane Austen had been all over the television the year before we had bought the house, and 'New Pemberley' had been borne of the same obviously-not-meaning-it-but-actually-really-meaning-it mindset as the E to P scale – and very possibly at the same restaurant. I thought it was fucking hilarious.)

So, still holding the Calvados bottle – more for effect than for drinking because, as I said, I can't abide the stuff – I staggered down the front steps. (Effect on who? The imaginary Geoff and Vince, I suppose. Wouldn't want them thinking I was the sort of chap who didn't appreciate a good digestif.)

Now, to get a really good look at the house, I needed to get back from it, and, as the pavement obviously wasn't deep enough, this involved wandering backwards into the road. On the one hand this was good, because it did enable me to get the full effect of the finely proportioned sash windows — all remade and double glazed but to the exact spec of the originals including the critically narrow width of the glazing bars which, as any nouveau riche media type knows, is so difficult to achieve it can only be done with the soon-to-die-out skills of the ancient and eye-wateringly expensive joiners whose number only your architect knows.

And not only that, but having stepped back far enough, I was able to simultaneously observe the full range of the family cars. Parked in front of the newly painted glossy black railings that separated 'New Pemberley' from the riff raff were my 911 — two years old, time for a new one? — Alison's brand new Grand Cherokee — black, tinted windows, natch — and a second-hand Golf that we'd bought for the Nanny. (For personal use only. When she was driving to and from the girls' school, whose already stratospheric fees were exponentially increasing by the nanosecond — as I was only too happy to jocularly remind the notional Geoff and Vince — we insisted on the higher riding safety of the Cherokee. And so did the girls. You wouldn't catch Florence and India being seen getting out of a second hand Golf!)

Alright, alright, I hear you. Not exactly a collection to strike fear into the hearts of Jay Kay or Rowan Atkinson, but then they didn't go to my school. The point was that I'd have bet five Park Drive to a Sherbert Dab that my modest little motorcade would have had Stephen Wilkinson's Adam's apple gulping in horror.

Yes, no doubt about it. Es all round. So, as I say, stepping back into the road to survey all that was mine had paid dividends. But, as you will long ago have foreseen, pride was about to come before a fall. Roads aren't principally there for drunks to lurch about in whilst having self-congratulatory conversations with their imaginary mates, but for vehicles to drive down. And, yes, one duly did.

I vaguely heard an engine noise break through my self-reverie but I didn't want to be disturbed. So it took a sharp squealing of breaks to prompt evasive action, which in turn led to a dropping of the unloved Calvados bottle, a shattering of glass, a falling to the ground, a cutting of the hand, a tearing of the left Prada trouser leg, a wrenching of the left Williams knee and a lot of unjustified effing and blinding at the young driver who might, not entirely without cause, have got out of the car and remonstrated with me with violence.

Fortunately – joyriding perhaps? – he contented himself with a sharp up and down movement of the loosely closed right fist (with matching epithet) and drove off. Which left me with the unavoidable task of hauling myself to my feet in the deserted street as best I could, and dragging myself up the steps. Carelessly, but once again fortunately, I had left the front door open so a single push got me through it. Unthinkingly I used my cut hand to do the pushing and left a bloody, crimson smear across the white cursive script of 'New Pemberley'.

(See Gods; signs from.)

*

The afternoon of the following day, a rare, sunny, early spring Saturday, found me propped up in a comfy chair in the orangerie, my damaged leg resting on what, in my long-deceased parents' day, was called, without sniggering, a pouffe.

They certainly wouldn't have called the orangerie an orangerie. To Syd (heart failure) and Mavis (pneumonia) it would have been a sun lounge. Or Mavis – but definitely not Syd – might possibly have opted for sun 'loggia'. I am sure loggia was a word that was big back in their day. And frankly, left to my own devices, I probably wouldn't have called it an orangerie either. I'd have gone for conservatory. But Alison, a dedicated Interiors disciple, had, in her limitless wisdom, decreed that it should be an orangerie. Perhaps 'orangerie' was the 1999 version of 'sun loggia'.

Perhaps Alison was the 1999 version of Mavis.

Having introduced them to you, this seems an appropriate place to say a word or two about Mavis and Syd, though their part in this story is only small. By and large, I feel nothing but gratitude to my parents, my only serious quibble being their failure to bequeath me better genes longevity-wise, and I still fervently hope to be proved wrong on that point. They did what they saw as their best for me, that I have never doubted. And if some of their ideas seem a little wrong-headed by today's standards, well wasn't that bound to be the way, and won't it always? Until I was nearly old enough to vote, you could be sent to prison for being a practising homosexual or for having an abortion, and parents allowed virtual strangers – and some teachers of my acquaintance were very strange indeed – to beat the living daylights of their children. I am not saying Mavis and Syd went along with any of that but those were the prevailing ideas of the day. Who knows what people will regard as equally morally repugnant in fifty years? Eating vegetables, keeping pets, having cut flowers in the house? I am sure that by the time I reach my dotage – not that long – Florence and India will look back at some of the things I banged on about during their childhood and sadly shake their heads.

As it happens, Mavis and Syd – Syd particularly – were, I think, rather enlightened for their time, but they had their little foibles. One of Mavis's was her refusal to countenance the use of diminutives. Except in Syd's case, which I suppose was the exception that proved the rule. But I was Andrew, always Andrew, and never anything else.

Except that, at the very outset, I wasn't. My given names were, God help me, and I am not a believer, Cyril Andrew – Cyril after Mavis's late father. This was only done in my grandfather's honour, and not because they had any intention of calling me Cyril, and for that mercy I am truly grateful. I don't know how old I can have been when I discovered I was a Cyril, but I do know I sensed immediately that I did not want to be one. By the time I was seven, I was already telling schoolmates who were nosey enough to ask, that the C in my name stood for Colin or Christopher – unlikely being Jewish but better than Cyril – or Keith. (At that age, nobody's spelling is good enough to argue.) By the time I had reached Grammar School, it was Charles, if anyone noticed a document with a C on it, and it has stayed that way. Almost. Because, so much did I hate the whole business, that at the age of twenty-two, I went to a solicitor and paid – using money I had saved up as soon as I was working – to have my name changed, or at least, reordered, by deed poll. I became Andrew Charles Williams. That is how I have been ever since. It is on my passport, on my National Insurance records, driving license, everything. I have never told this to my partners, my wife, my children, to anyone. Mavis and Syd, sadly, are no longer in a position to grass me up. I have very, very nearly forgotten that I was ever anything else.

You may think this legal change rather odd, in the light of another conviction I have about my name. I have always considered Andrew Williams about the dullest name a person could have. When I was about ten, I went to Mavis and Syd, and complained bitterly about it, and with the kind of indulgent parental smiles you would expect, they asked me what I would like to be called instead. I came up with Floyd Meccano. Floyd Patterson was the World Heavyweight Boxing Champion at the time, a time when there were only about six sports to know about, so that explains that, and every small boy in those days had a Meccano set. I showed not the slightest interest in engineering, but even then I could appreciate a good brand name.

'What's in a name? That which we call a rose, By any other name would smell as sweet.' Well that may be Juliet's opinion but it's never been mine. What's in a name? Why did Cary Grant dump

Archibald Leach? Ask Lady Gaga why she doesn't call herself Stephanie Germanotta. Names matter. Names can be worth money. And it's always seemed to me that having a name with a bit of a ring to it, providing you have a modicum of ability to back it up, can do you no harm. So why didn't I go for something more exotic when I went to law? I honestly don't know. Maybe I felt it would be some kind of betrayal of Mavis and Syd. Anyway, Andrew Charles Williams was the farthest I was prepared to go. And that, despite it still being as boring as it ever was, is how I remain to this day.

I had woken on that Saturday morning, head and knee apparently locked in competition to see which could throb more agonisingly, to find Alison standing over me, hair swishing meaningfully from side to side and eyes rolling.

"For Christ's sake, Andrew, you could at least have taken your bloody clothes off."

"Er, yes … well, you see …"

"And what have you done to your suit. You've ruined it!"

"Er, yes … well, I fell and twisted my knee. Dunno what I've done to it. Hurts like buggery."

"Didn't I buy you that suit? It's Prada – do you have any idea how much that cost?"

"Well, um, a lot I expect. But my knee – aargh."

"And your hand – what the hell have you – didn't slip while you were trying to slash your wrists, did you?"

Cue convulsive laughter at own joke. Personally, I found it a struggle to join in but it did seem to have the benefit of lightening her mood.

After a perfunctory attempt at cleaning up, and the donning of shorts – hideous and unseasonable but the only thing I could get over my knee without giving away the name of every member of the French Resistance – we went off to Casualty. (Or had it already become A and E by then?) Into the Cherokee we climbed, the three of us, Alison and I and India, all sweet nine-year-old concern for

17

poor Daddy, leaving Florence, all door-slamming-twelve-year-old contempt for just about anybody, to take care of Spot. As if.

(Spot was our all-black, utterly spot-free, French bulldog whom the six-year-old Florence had, entirely without irony, insisted on so naming.)

A few hours, a losing argument with a triage nurse, three bloody painful stitches and a reassuringly clear X-ray later, we drove back home, with me constantly repeating Sister's stricture that my knee needed complete rest.

Thus my place in the comfy chair in the orangerie. And thus one more fork in the road taken to – well, that will become apparent very soon.

The point is that my enforced inactivity meant that I couldn't be dragooned into accompanying (meaning chauffeuring) Alison on her usual weekend shopping expedition and that she had to think of something else to do. And it must have been my torn trousers I think, that served as the catalyst that sent Alison into one of her 'let's chuck everything out' moods.

If there was one thing Alison loved almost as much as buying new stuff, it was chucking out the old. It was one of the many ways in which she and I were complete opposites. I, the squirreling hoarder, she, the compulsive clearer of decks. And, beginning with those torn trousers, and without bothering to ask if I was agreeable – for the simple reason that she knew I wouldn't be – it was my stuff that she had decided to chuck out.

So I happily sat and watched 'Grease' for the twelve hundredth time with India and Spot, blissfully unaware that, all the while, Alison was gleefully filling black bin bags with the old shirts and shoes and trousers and sweaters that she decided I didn't want. And yes, jackets too. And one jacket in particular, a short denim jacket in the style that had been de rigueur in the late seventies and which I probably hadn't worn since, but from which I would never have voluntarily parted.

And now we come to the nub of the matter, the crucial, life changing moment. Alison, deck clearing, methodical Alison, naturally decided to methodically check the pockets of any garment before it was dispatched Oxfam-wards. And into the inside pocket of my de rigueur seventies denim jacket she reached and found there, as I was about to discover when she tapped me on the shoulder and thrust it into my line of a sight, the butterfly whose flapping wings would set off the earthquake. It came in the guise of a shiny-feeling, squarish, sort of but not quite cardboardy thing which, when she pulled it out, turned out to be a dog-eared Polaroid of a young woman; rather pretty, dark haired, with almond-shaped eyes, slightly Italianate or possibly Jewish, or maybe even Puerto Rican – it was hard to tell, Polaroids fade – but definitely pretty.

"Andrew?" she asked, all sweetness and light – almost. "Who is this?"

CHAPTER 2

NEW YORK, 1979

Peggy and I wandered back down Fifth Avenue with the rest of the crowd dribbling out of the Robert Palmer concert that had just reached its exhausted finale in Central Park. It was part of the annual Dr Pepper Central Park Music Festival and whatever Robert Palmer may have thought, I, for one, was extremely grateful for their sponsorship, because it was one of those unbearable summer nights in Manhattan – very late summer, it was already September – when the humidity is a thousand per cent and even the most refined of ladies glistens buckets. We grabbed the ice-cold cans that were being handed out as we left the arena and not just because they were free. On a night like that, an ice-cold anything is a lifeline. With my de rigueur denim jacket slung over my shoulder – don't know why I'd bought it, far too hot to wear, but once a fashionista always a fashionista, I suppose – I tossed back my head and drained the lot.

"You like this stuff?" asked Peggy.

"Actually, I've never had it before. We don't get it in England."

"We don't get it here either," said Peggy. "I mean, we do, but I don't know anyone who ever, like, gets it."

"Somebody must," I said.

"Yup. Somebody must. I guess somebody must."

Yes, you're right. An utterly unremarkable, nothingy, so-what exchange and yet, for me, intoxicating. It was the rhythm of Peggy's voice that I swooned over. The little staccato bursts, the subtlest of inflections, the bone dry delivery. It was pure essence of New York. Not the 'On The Waterfront', Hell's Kitchen, Hey-Youse-Gimme-A-Cawfee Noo Yawk. But something else; sharp, smart, sassy, seductive. Yes, all those clichés that, when put together, beget another whole alliterating string of them: Manhattan, Martinis, Madison Avenue. It was all there in Peggy's voice, every time she spoke.

So maybe you're thinking it was the idea of Peggy that I was so infatuated with. That any pretty uptown girl might have done just as well. It's a legitimate debating point, and I will admit that maybe there's the tiniest scintilla of truth that I was, indeed, in love with the idea of a girl like Peggy. After all, I was, with one or two minor caveats, in love with everything 'New York'. But inside Peggy's New York wrapper was someone who rang so many bells for me, I would have become every bit as besotted with her if she'd come from Nanking or Narnia.

I had the not very original idea – still do – that love is a wavelength thing. It's just a question of finding someone who is on the same one as you. Nobody that I have ever met – not before nor since – received my signal and sent back hers so clearly, with so little interference, as Peggy. No moody dropout. No emotional static. It was, for those few short months, such an unburdening relief to find someone to whom I could get through and who came through to me. As I had had so little real hope of finding someone like that – never got remotely close to it before so why should I ever? – I was simply amazed. And even more amazing was Peggy's often given and never solicited – well, only very rarely solicited – assurance that the feeling was entirely mutual. There was Peggy in this relationship, there was me, and for the first, and perhaps only, time in my life, there was a real, almost tangible 'us', the sum that was greater than the parts.

So, given all this, how on earth had we managed to get ourselves into a situation where tonight would be our last?

*

It had begun in the lift. Or the elevator. Two countries separated by one language as Churchill said, and he wasn't wrong.

I had come to New York a few weeks before to work for an agency called McConnell Martin. They had a majority holding in the place I'd been at in London, and Todd Zwiebel, McConnell's senior VP and ECD (that's senior Vice President and Executive Creative Director to the uninitiated) had 'flown over the pond', as was his wont to say, to supervise a pitch (ad jargon for 'presentation') for a big piece of international business that the two agencies, successful pitch permitting, would both get a slice of. The product in question, was a not very revolutionary new kind of sanitary towel produced by a vast multinational shampoo-to-savoury snacks conglomerate, and I, with all my experience of the wonderful world of menstruation, had been chosen to work as a copywriter on the project. (Why, you might ask, would they pick a 29-year-old unmarried, single bloke with neither a regular girlfriend nor even a sister, whose main experience had been on tyre and margarine accounts, to work on a campaign for a sanitary towel? As I say, you might ask. Just so long as you're not expecting a sensible answer.)

Anyway, being this 29-year-old single bloke, I had been delighted to get the gig – it was after all, a product connected with that area of a woman's body in which … oh well, you know what I mean – and I had actually had what Todd Zwiebel thought was a rather witty idea for the campaign. Not so the client, a company man of German Swiss origin who, prior to his recently being appointed to head up the vast multinational conglomerate's sanitary products operation in Europe and North America, had spent the previous dozen years managing its chewing gum division in South East Asia.

Sadly, but not entirely surprisingly perhaps, the wit of my campaign failed to raise a Swiss German smile.

Nevertheless, Todd, who was soon to be made company President and Chief Creative Officer of the World – a title conferred without a hint of irony, I am certain – had taken something of a shine to me and before he traversed the pond in the reverse direction, he was kind enough to facilitate my transfer to the New York office.

Hence my stepping in to the lift/elevator in the McConnell Martin building on Madison and 38th.

I was wearing a white tee-shirt with a specially personalised printed front. Clothes maketh the man, or, as Shakespeare might have said had he been in marketing, clothing is personal packaging and it can make all the difference to whether a punter buys or not. That's something I've always known – Mavis and Syd were in the fashion business and they drummed it into me – but I can safely say that no item I have ever worn has had such an impact. Few things change your life, but that tee-shirt changed mine.

In order to explain further, a short historical note is necessary here: Remember, if you will, that we are talking about the late seventies. Long before Al Qaida. Long before identity theft. Long before security was the consuming obsession of every corporation and government department, the world over. In London at that time – despite the activities of the IRA – security at your place of work was, as like as not, in the hands of a chain smoking old geezer called Alf who would man the front desk of the building on those rare occasions when he wasn't down the betting shop, and even during the brief spells when he was actually present, he was so engrossed in the Racing Post he wouldn't have noticed if Ronnie Biggs and Charles Manson had strolled past him holding hands. So when I got to New York, I was dumbfounded to find that all employees of McConnell Martin had to be issued with special ID cards, with name, employee number and photograph printed on them.

I was not alone in my dumbfoundment. With my old schoolboy habit of naturally gravitating towards the nearest troublemaker, I had, within days of my arrival, become pally with a couple of home grown 'creatives', whose working days were largely spent with their office door locked and their bong filled. And these two mavericks were not averse, once they had done their daily deep breathing exercises, to a spot of mischief making at the management's expense. The ID cards provided an ideal opportunity.

I can't remember whether it was Brett or Bart who came up with the wheeze – it may even have been me – but what we did was to have each of our ID cards enlarged several times over and then to have it printed on the front of a white tee-shirt, thereby creating a sort of prisoner inmate look. The genius of the idea was that while the powers that be would understand that this was clearly intended to be a subversive act, they wouldn't be able to put the corporate finger on exactly what we were doing that broke any rules.

The effect of wearing my prisoner-esque tee-shirt was illuminating. Not a single word was said. Many was the surreptitious glance, occasionally came a nervous tight lipped rictus, but neither humble colleague nor lofty VP ever said a dickybird to me.

Except for one person. In the elevator. (Enough of this lift business – we're in America now.) And that person was a short, slight, curly dark-haired girl with slightly almond-shaped eyes, Jewish perhaps, or Italian, perhaps even Puerto Rican – I wasn't wearing my glasses so it was hard to tell – but pretty, definitely pretty. And she took one look at my tee-shirt and laughed like a drain. She saw it. She got it. And she wasn't the least bit concerned about showing what she thought about it. We stopped at the ninth floor and out she stepped, still laughing.

"What's your name?" I called out after her.

"Peggy," she said. And then, after a brief pause, she threw this titbit over her departing shoulder, "Casting."

'Casting'. Not CARsting with the long, dreary English 'A', but the short, snappy American version. The short, snappy, SEXY American version. And why had she said it? Well, why else would she have said it? What could it be but the abridged version of 'come up and see me sometime'?

Needless to say, having let about twenty minutes pass – didn't want her to think I was too keen – I went sniffing about the second floor trying to pick up the scent. I found a group of girls stationed at a row of desks and click-clacking away at golf-ball typewriters.

"Excuse me," I said, laying on the diffident English politeness and drawing out my vowels like a poor man's Bertie Wooster. "Would you happen to know if there is someone called Peggy working in this department?" (I had already discovered, of course, that if a girl with an American accent could get my juices flowing, that was as nothing to the knee-weakening power that an English accent seemed to have over the average American girl.)

"Sure," someone said. "You mean Peggy Lee."

Did I? Peggy Lee? Peggy LEE? As in the famous American, platinum-blonde, jazz/big-band songstress Peggy Lee? Or rather, and rather weirdly, as in someone definitely not platinum blonde or anything else fitting that Peggy Lee's description but having the same name as her. That was who I meant?

"Is she the only Peggy in casting?"

"I'll just check. Hey girls, is she the only Peggy in CARsting?"

"I'm called Peggy."

"Me too."

"And me."

"Well thank you, ladies," I said. "It's nice to know we can cast all the comedy parts in-house."

No, I didn't. I went slightly red and decided that it would be wiser to retire and pursue the matter by phone.

Which I duly did and, after the slightly self-conscious hi-I'm-the-guy-in-the-tee-shirt-you-met-in-the-lift-sorry-I-mean-elevator intro, it all proceeded relatively smoothly and we arranged to meet for a drink the following evening after work. I put the phone down feeling pretty damn pleased with myself. (It was always a feeling that came too naturally to me.)

At the very least I hadn't had to deal with the humiliation of rejection before we had even got past GO – not likely, I accept, given that she hadn't exactly tried to cover her spoor but you know women, so always a possibility. And, at the most, it could mean romance, sex – with luck, not in that order – marriage, children, grandchildren, a lifetime's blissful partnership. Who knew? Maybe she really would turn out to be the one.

When I got into the bar and after I had battled my way through the usual frenzy of high fiving and inane yelling – my greatest creative effort ever was a two line poem: 'Noo Yorkers, Too Raucous' – I spotted Peggy, wedged into a corner by another girl whom I recognised as being one of those golf-ball bashers I had tangled with the day before.

"Hi Peggy," I tried. Basic, straightforward Pawn to King Four opening.

"Hi-ie" they both sang back and then dissolved into laughter.

"I think," I said, "at least one of you is pulling my plonker." (A little bit of rather forced Del Boy to leaven the Wooster. Bad move.)

"Pulling your what?" asked not-Peggy.

A ham-fisted attempt to explain its literal and vernacular meanings followed. Followed by a pause. Aka a hiatus. Aka a sign that things suddenly seemed to be not going that well.

"Um, can I get either of you another drink?" Not, it's true, the witty game changer with which one would have liked to halt the worrying slide, but the tried and trusted basic holding tactic if one can't think of anything better.

"Not for me," said not-Peggy, draining her whatever-it-was. "Gotta TV show to catch."

Now my whole future suddenly teetered on a knife-edge. Was this remark by not-Peggy a reference to some duty that her role in 'casting' might oblige her to undertake? Had she been asked to check out the ability of a supposed actor to simultaneously walk and chew gum? Or was her connection to 'the business' entirely coincidental and was this just a throwaway to indicate that she had nothing much to do but that she knew that we two lovebirds would much rather be left to our own devices?

The world stopped turning. Would not-not-Peggy stay for a drink and who knew what after that, or had she already decided that yesterday's tee-shirt had been the funniest thing about me and that this whole drink thing with the weird Limey copywriter was just one big mistake? Milliseconds turned into light years. The inane yellers were frozen mid high-five. And then –

"Sure, I'll have an orange juice."

Bang. The billion decibels of bar noise instantly came back on. A thousand people stopped playing statues. Palm to palm slapping machine-gunned all around. And I suddenly remembered to breathe again.

"So" I said, when I'd finally managed to battle my way back from the bar. "Peggy Lee. That's, er, pretty unusual."

"Hmm," said Peggy Lee. "Do you prefer usual? You don't look the type that goes for usual."

"God no, no I don't—"

"Not that it is unusual. Not really. I mean it IS totally unoriginal. Right?"

"Well, er, yes, if you look at it like that—"

"You're telling me I'm totally unoriginal? You buy me one lousy orange juice—"

And so it went on. All the while her gently teasing me and me a half step behind, unable to get back in control of the conversation. And all the while that almost imperceptible twinkle in the eyes, the enormous, dark brown – dark almost to the point of being black – eyes.

"Your eyes. They're very dark. I don't think I've ever seen eyes so dark."

"Ah yes, well that's my ancestry, the Chinese part."

"Really? Actually your eyes are quite almond-shaped."

"Uhuh. You see, now it's Lee, L-E-E, but when my great-great … um … well, you know, came over from their shtetl in, ah, Beijing it was spelt L-I."

"Shtetl? I thought you only got those in Russia."

"They were Jewish, Andrew. Where else would they live?"

Of course I knew it couldn't be true. Could it? As I've mentioned, I am Jewish myself – in a vague, uncommitted, very British kind of way – and I'd never heard of Chinese Jews. But on the other hand, they'd had Jews everywhere else, so why not China? And that L-I thing. That sounded plausible enough. I decided not to make a challenge. Stupidly, I went back to the name business.

"But Peggy? Is that a nickname?"

"How did you guess that?"

I had a foothold. At last.

"Well, um, it's pretty obvious I suppose. I mean who would do that – I mean name their child after a person with such a distinctive name, you know after a really famous star?"

All wide-eyed innocence, she said, "You mean like Andy Williams?"

Like I said: stupid. Of course, I'd heard it before, plenty of times. But like I also said, my mother, for some inexplicable reason – probably deciding it was 'common' – flatly forbade it, and, without thinking, I'd taken her lead. Even at school I'd just refused to along with it. Without encouragement, and perhaps because of the stony reception I gave 'Andy' whenever someone tried it on me, it never stuck. Could have gone the other way I suppose, and led to remorseless piss taking, but for whatever reason, it never did. I was Andrew, always identified myself as Andrew, and that was the end of it. Until now.

"Peggy Lee and Andy Williams, kinda goes together, don't you think?"

I could see there was a certain apt symmetry but I wasn't ready to admit it, not without my first putting up some kind of a fight. I rose to my mother's defence. (Neglecting to offer, of course, the most convincing piece of evidence, that Andrew was not the first name I had been originally given.)

"Number one," I said. "Even Andy Williams wasn't Andy Williams when I was born, so for that reason alone my parents could never have named me after him, and number two, I've never answered to anything but Andrew."

I was, almost immediately, wishing I hadn't said it quite like that because Peggy was looking straight at me, like she was asking herself a very fundamental question about who I really was. And I was pretty sure I knew what that question was: is this the slightly-less-predictable-than-usual, little-bit-more-interesting-than-your-usual-ad-agency kind of a guy that I thought he might be yesterday when I saw him wearing that tee-shirt? Or is he a broom-up-the-ass, uptight English prig who thinks he's just too important to have his name shortened?

She decided to ascertain the answer by first repeating my own pompous phrasing back to me.

"So you never answer to anything but Androo."

And then, without missing a beat, she added a question, on the answer to which, I rapidly realised, our future depended.

"Is that right – Andy?"

She'd given me my chance, and I wasn't going to miss it.

"For you," I said, "I am prepared to make an exception."

So to Peggy and to Peggy alone, Andrew became Andy, and then Andy asked Peggy if she'd like to get something to eat, and they transferred to a not very salubrious Italian place near the subway on 53rd and Lex.

We talked about a lot of other things, we must have done, because two or three hours raced by before, just after I had asked for the check, I couldn't stop myself from bringing the conversation full circle.

(With any other American girl by the way, I probably would have made a point of asking for 'the bill' just to emphasise my irresistible Britishness. But already with Peggy, I knew it couldn't be like that.)

So, as we sipped at that stewed-for-hours black stuff that, for some reason, Americans call coffee, I asked her, "If Peggy's your nickname, what's your proper name then? Or is it a secret?"

"No, it's not a secret," she said cheerfully, "it's Brenda."

"Brenda," I repeated as non-committally as I could, but thinking to myself, 'Brenda! With a name like Brenda I'm not surprised you're happy to be called something else.'

And it wasn't until I had seen her back to the subway station from where she would ride to her apartment on the Upper West Side – I didn't even try to kiss her that first night, by the way – that the penny dropped. First Peggy Lee, now Brenda Lee! How gullible did she think I was? Not that I minded in the least – I wasn't in a mood to mind anything that night.

As I walked home I felt like Don Lockwood 'Singin' In The Rain'. Except it wasn't raining and it was 'Let's Jump The Broomstick' that kept running through my head.

CHAPTER 3

LONDON, 1999

It should have been an all-hands-to-the-ground, hit-the-pump-running kind of a day. Or something like that. I was very confused that morning.

Usually, the adrenalin rush of being flat out gets my thinking Sabatier-sharp and already the new client had been on the phone to Vince telling him that he wanted a dozen things done. A dozen things done in addition to the hundred and one things we were already doing for our old clients. But I was never daunted by pressure – just bring it on! As a rule I'd be fizzing with ideas, firing out instructions to all and sundry, whipping everyone up into a lather of enthusiasm.

But not that day. That day was different. I was subdued, I was distracted, and, frankly, all over the place.

"Are you feeling okay?" asked Vince, not very solicitously, as he barged into my office.

"Ever heard of knocking," I said, not even bothering to swivel back to face him. I was in my state of the art, ergonomically efficient, king-of-the-world office chair looking through the rain-spattered window at the Fitzrovia street scene half a dozen floors below. For some reason, I remember – I mean I don't remember the reason, I just remember doing it – I was fixating on a bloke trying to get a floor lamp through the back of his hatchback. However many times he tried, and at whichever angle he tried to fit it in, he couldn't get the door to close. Perhaps I felt there must be some kind of symbolism in this, but I have no idea what I thought it might have been.

"I have heard of knocking, yes," said Vince, "and for what it's worth Julia threw herself bodily in front of me to stop me disturbing you, but we were supposed to be having a meeting in Delibes twenty minutes ago, and everyone was there but you. Thought I'd enquire why."

(FYI: Julia was my uber-loyal, faux-posh PA and she'd thrown herself bodily in front of a lot of people but not usually to stop them from entering. Quite the reverse, boom, boom. Delibes was the name we had given to one of our four meeting rooms, each of which had just been redecorated and named after an iconic figure of the wider creative world – it's the sort of absurdly self-aggrandising thing that advertising agencies do. You cannot believe the time we wasted over this. As this room was to have a musical theme, we'd first considered Mozart. Thumbs down. Too obvious. Likewise Presley, Beethoven and Lennon. We were keen on Armstrong for a while – added ethnic 'cool' – but then rejected him because someone said it might look like tokenism. We settled on Delibes on the basis that he wrote that famous British Airways music which we could all hum and because he was certainly *not* obvious. So not-obvious that none of us had ever heard of Delibes until someone told us about the BA thing, and that, of course, did make him a bit dubious icon-wise. But by this point we were too exhausted to care. The other rooms were Twain, Magritte, and Kurosawa. Isn't posterity marvellous?)

"Sorry about the meeting, Vince, but – I dunno – I just didn't feel like it. Anyway, I've twisted my knee. I can hardly walk."

"You've twisted your knee?! There's still a room full of people, Andrew – all waiting for the oracle to speak. Come on mate, we need you down there. I'll carry you if your leg's that bad."

But for reasons I couldn't have explained – or at least I wasn't ready to – no, I was right the first time, I couldn't have, because I really didn't have the faintest idea what they were – I was determined not to go. I stayed steadfastly looking out of the window.

"For fuck's sake, Andrew, what's the matter? Has somebody died?"

I didn't reply.

"For fuck's sake!" Vince said again, and turned on his heel and slammed the door shut behind him.

But I hadn't been ignoring him; I'd been thinking about what he'd said.

Had somebody died?

*

I was sufficiently long in the tooth to know that when you are accused of something, or asked a question which might lead you to being accused of something, truth should always be your first line of defence. Not only is the weaving of tangled webs neatly avoided, but I have always found that it is far easier to face someone down when you use the truth to do so, even if, as in this case, you are using it to conceal a greater truth that lies behind. So when Alison demanded to know who the girl in the Polaroid was, and after I had got over the shock of seeing the face of someone whom I had once worshipped, suddenly snatched out of the past and dumped into a very, very different present, I answered with what I hoped was an air of total unconcern: "That's Peggy. I knew her in New York about a hundred years ago. Where did you find that?"

So: About this air of total unconcern I was trying for. Did I pull it off? How could I? If you were one of those Indian holy men who's given away all his worldly goods and wears nothing but a loin cloth, I'll bet you'd still have 'guilty as hell' written all over your face every time you walked through customs. It's human nature. And if a customs officer or one of those community support chaps who's not even a proper policeman can make an innocent man feel like that, it's as nothing compared to what a wife can do.

So Alison carefully weighed my answer and then gave me one of those looks that only a wife can give. She did nothing but raise her eyebrows a half smidgeon but the message was clear. Peggy might have been someone I'd known a hundred years before in New York but there *had* to be more to it than that. I fought back by making an assault on the moral high ground; what the hell did she think she was doing going through my things – never mind *throwing them out* – without asking me first? Schoolboy error; in complaining – or pretending to complain – about her going through my things, I was implying that there might be something in there I didn't want her to see. And she'd just found out what, hadn't she?

Peggy indeed! The fact that I hadn't seen her for the last twenty years, and hadn't even met Alison until half a dozen after that, made me just as guilty as if I'd been caught red handed in a three-way with the South African nanny and Spot.

There was only one way to deal with this – go back to watching the television. My reluctance to engage was, in Alison's eyes, tantamount to accepting the charge and asking for a hundred and fifty-four other offences to be taken into account, but it seemed to draw the matter to a close. I stuffed the photo into my jacket pocket and might, conceivably, have never given the matter another thought but for two things.

One, I wore the same jacket again on Monday morning. Two, India went into Florence's room and tried on her new top from Gap. Florence duly went ballistic. Alison then went into her room to find out what the fuss was about, saw what a Godawful mess Florence's room was in, and *she* went ballistic. Florence burst into tears and ran to me in the orangerie for consolation which, of course, I provided. Alison then followed Florence into the orangerie and accused me of taking her side as always.

Alison's sense of grievance was now well and truly stoked up and she was going to find one pretext or another to pick a fight, no matter what evasive action I took. I could bury my head in 'Grease', I could plead a poorly leg, I could do what the hell I liked – it mattered not. War would be declared!

So what was the invasion of Poland that set it all off? Well Alison didn't have much to go on, given that I had spent the day injured, immobile and silent in front of the telly. So, in the absence of anything better, it was, as you may have guessed, back to the Polaroid of Peggy. That night, as we were undressing for bed (for sleep only, I hardly need add) she brought it up again. Who exactly was Peggy, precisely *how* had I known her a hundred years ago, and why, yes, pray tell why, why had I kept her photograph for all this time?

A furious slanging match followed, punctuated by some foundation-shaking door slamming as Alison marched in and out of the bathroom in order to remove the day's slap and apply her regimen of mentally expensive, only available from Harvey Nicks, de-wrinkling face creams. (Probably not very effective wrinkle-wise but jolly useful for frightening off night-time intruders.)

As usual my feeble weapons of logic and common sense proved useless in the face of Alison's remorseless onslaught – yes, yes I know there are two sides to every story but *I'm* writing this one – and with a final "Oh for fuck's sake!" – what a splendidly serviceable expression that is – I turned over and pretended to go to sleep.

After the day's events, Peggy's image, not unsurprisingly, floated into my mind and, even less surprisingly, given the sub-arctic temperature of my current relations with Alison, I was bound to look back at our time together through the very rosiest of rose-tinted glasses. I drifted off that night watching this lovely movie in my head – Peggy and I, the way we were. Or perhaps the way we weren't, but, as with every movie, whatever bad bits there may have been were left on the cutting room floor.

But by Sunday, Peggy seemed to have faded into the background once more. The gammy leg prevented me from playing in my regular ten o' clock tennis match with Geoff and a couple of fellow hackers, but I went to watch them and have the usual latte and croissant afterwards. The rest of the daylight hours were filled with the weekly routine of ferrying the girls to and from birthday parties, play dates, shopping malls, whatever. Bad leg or no, I wasn't excused, but I quite liked that part of Dadship, so I really didn't mind. Glenda and Vic, Alison's parents, came round for an early supper, so Alison and I gave our normal competent performances in the parts of a happily married couple. Sometimes, if you act well enough, you can seem convincing even to yourself – so, by the end of the evening, after the getting-ready-for-the-new-week ritual of bathing and hair washing and finishing off the girls' homework for them, Alison and I were being quite civil to each other. At one point, as we were watching 'Antiques Roadshow' or something similarly Sunday nightish, she even cuddled up on the sofa and gave me a kiss. From the outside, which, remember, is the place where you are measured on the E to P scale, Andrew Williams might not have looked like he had that much to complain about.

But then came Monday, and the realisation of just how much of my wardrobe Alison had culled. She hadn't just thinned the herd, she'd practically wiped it out, and I couldn't find a single thing I wanted to put on. So I muttered the usual string of pointless profanities, grabbed the jacket I had been wearing on Saturday and limped out of the house in a huff. Then, when I got into the Porsche to drive to work, one of those really blinding early spring suns came out, so I reached into my pocket in the vain hope of finding my Ray-Bans and instead, what should I come across but the Polaroid of Peggy. I suppose I could have foreseen where all this might lead and torn the Polaroid into little pieces and thrown them out of the window, letting the little pieces of Peggy be blown away on the wind. But I didn't. Instead, I pulled the picture out and looked at her Jewish/ Italianate/could-almost-be-Puerto Rican face once more, with the inevitable result that the movie that I had been watching in my head under the duvet on Saturday night began running again. And again. And again. And then the replay button got stuck, and nothing I could think of or do would distract me from it. And even when the day came in the not too distant future when India insisted I sit down to watch 'Grease' with her for the twelfth hundred and first time, it wasn't John and Olivia I saw but Peggy and me.

*

I never did go to that meeting. I told Julia that she'd be summarily defenestrated if she ever allowed Vince or Geoff or anyone else into my office again before I had given my express permission.

"Golly, that sounds rather exciting," she said, with her trademark ooh-you-are-a-one look, but whether she did or didn't know what I was talking about, she got the message and I was left in peace to gaze out of the window at blokes trying to fit standard lamps into the back of hatchbacks or similar.

After a couple of days of this, and some intense negotiations between Julia and Vince's PA, Maxine, I agreed to let him back in.

"Got something to tell you mate." Vince's Aussie accent had a soupçon of extra Strine in it that day, which, experience had taught me, was an unmistakable sign that he was going to tell me something I didn't want to hear.

I tipped back in my chair, steepled my fingers and raised my eyebrows.

"And that would be?"

"Just that the meeting on Monday went fine without you—"

"Pleased to hear it."

"—and that I've put Will and Lucille on the account. Hope you don't mind."

Mind? Mind! You hope I don't fucking well mind!!! On any other such occasion these words, or something less subtle, would have shot from my mouth like the venom from a very, very angry viper's tongue. Will and Lucille were a senior, early thirties – that's senior in advertising – creative team at BWD (meaning Art Director and Copywriter) and the sort of people who would have been asked to come up with the campaign for this new piece of business. I say 'sort of' because they were one of several teams who might have been picked for the job and – this is the point – or rather would have been the point – it was the Creative Director's job, that is to say it was MY job, that is to say my RIGHT, that is to say my INALIENABLE right to be the one to do the picking. Not the job of the Head of Account Management – Vince – not even the job of the MD – Geoff – but mine! Unarguably, indisputably, incontestably – and any other word meaning exactly the same thing – mine!

Normally – not that there could have been a normally because it was frankly unimaginable that anyone would usurp the authority of the Creative Director on such a fundamental issue of principle – but if there had been a normally – I would have responded by following up my first round of expletives by making it absolutely clear that Will and Lucille would only be given the job over my dead body. And not just dead but pickled in lime, padlocked in chains, weighted down in concrete and dropped into the deepest point of the ocean. Not that Will and Lucille, nakedly ambitious (particularly her), and a bit too smug for my liking, weren't otherwise perfectly qualified and would, in all probability, have been first my choice anyway.

No, it was the principle of the fucking thing. Or rather, as I keep saying, it would have been. But on this matter, at this time, given the place in which my head was presently at, I really had nothing to say, negative or otherwise. I couldn't have summoned the energy to give a twopenny shit about matters of principle regarding lines of authority or anything else.

So I continued to steeple my fingers, looked blankly at Vince, semi-shrugged my shoulders to indicate my utter passivity in the face of such news and wheeled around and back to my vigil by the window. I didn't mean to be rude you understand; I had wanted to speak to him. I had wanted to say to him, "Why have you come into my office to talk to me about this completely meaningless shit, when I was having such a nice time thinking about Peggy?"

It was just that I wasn't convinced he'd fully understand why the fate of a seven-million-pound account was of less importance than daydreams about a girl I had gone out with for a few months twenty years ago.

A few seconds passed and then I heard a quietly resigned, "Bloody hell" and the careful shutting of my office door behind him.

Later Vince would tell me that he had gone straight to see Geoff after leaving me, and that, even at that early stage, they had begun to discuss the possibility that they might have to do without me. Vince and Geoff and I had been friends for the best part of twenty years – well, more or less since I came back from the States – and partners in BWD for nearly ten. But, as with the Corleones, this was business, and there was no room for sentiment. They had no idea what the problem was at first – he told me they suspected it was some kind of breakdown, whatever that meant – but they weren't going to let the small matter of the mental health of a close friend stand in the way of business. If I had to play Tessio to their Michael and Tom and be garrotted with a cheesewire, then so be it. And, let me make it clear, if I had been in their position, I would have acted no differently.

As it happened that's not quite how things worked out – but I'm getting ahead of myself. My leg was rapidly improving – actually it was fine by Wednesday – but I carried on limping, hoping that the ostensible need to rest might seem to legitimise my being chairbound in my office. For the rest of that first week, I continued to hide there and ponder. Ponder, without really thinking about anything in any focused way. I pondered on Peggy. I pondered on Alison. I pondered on blokes in the street trying to cram things into cars.

When I left the office in the evening, after saying a brief goodnight to an increasingly anxious looking Julia, and ignoring all the other quizzical eyes upon me – the answer to the "What the fuck's up with Andrew?" question was obviously a matter for all-staff conjecture and no-one was buying the dodgy knee excuse – I would drive towards home and then, at a place in between, in Bayswater or somewhere, I would find a pub where I could safely count on not being recognised. Then I'd spend the evening drinking some not too terrible red and mooning over the Polaroid of Peggy.

There was nothing unusual to arouse Alison's suspicions about my getting back late from the office slightly the worse for wear – she quite often did the same herself. If she was already in, I would give her a perfunctory peck, ask her how her day had been without listening to the reply, grab something from the fridge, and plonk myself in front of Newsnight. If she wasn't back, I'd ask the Nanny how the girls had been – without listening to the reply, politely dismiss her, and then go through my fridge/Newsnight routine. On the way up to bed, I'd look in on the girls – feeling vaguely tearful I seem to remember – and then get into bed with as little contact or conversation as could be managed without forcing a conflict. As Alison seemed as disinterested in me as I was in her, this was all accomplished fairly smoothly.

Come the weekend and I was happy enough to get back to chauffeuring Alison round the shops; while I sat in the driver's seat waiting for her to emerge from Joseph or Jigsaw or wherever, I had time to concentrate on Peggy. I busked my way through the evening and then it was Sunday again and tennis and being a dad and another chance to see 'Grease' and before you knew it, it was bedtime and somehow I had survived.

And then I woke up on the Monday morning and the fog at last seemed to have lifted. I finally realised that I could not go on like this. After a week of fretting over my ancient lost romance, something approaching common sense had focused my dewy eyes and my dilemma was clear before me.

However much the passage of time might have softened the reality of the past, I was in no doubt that I'd had a certain something with Peggy that I'd never had with anyone before or since. And that certain something had somehow, idiotically and regrettably – perhaps even tragically – been allowed to slip through my fingers. Incontrovertible fact: I only had one life. Didn't I owe it to myself to find – or at least try to find – that something again?

Yes.

But.

But those same hands through whose fingers I had let my once-in-a-lifetime something with Peggy slip, were now full to overflowing with another life: with children I loved, with a wife who I – well, let's come back to that – with a business and partners and employees who depended on me. And yes, with a house and cars and holidays and all the other stuff that is measured on the E to P scale – meaningless shit, unquestionably, but, in all honesty, would I really want to be without it?

So there was my dilemma. Except it wasn't really a dilemma. Because, by any accepted definition of reality, Peggy was out of the frame – she'd been out of the frame for twenty years – so all I had to do was force myself to stop running the movie in my head.

That's what I told myself that Monday morning. Then I climbed into the Porsche, put on my Ray-Bans, hit the gas, and roared off to work, resolved to apologise to Vince and Geoff, and get back to real life. If it had been the proverbial midlife crisis, well, at least it had only lasted a week. I was going to be a man and forget about Peggy once and for all. Cold turkey, I told myself, cold turkey.

Then I turned on the radio to my favourite Golden Oldie station, and out came Roxy Music. They were playing 'Love is the Drug.'

Love is the drug. Yes, indeed.

CHAPTER 4

NEW YORK, 1979

It doesn't matter whether you're sixteen or sixty-four – as I now know from too much personal experience – after the euphoria of that rare first date, the one that goes well, comes the sudden onset of anxious doubt. Did it really go as well as all that? Or have you flipped through the runes but totally misread them?

Sometimes I have memories of events which cannot possibly be as I remember them. A picture comes to mind which includes me bodily – in other words I am looking at myself in whatever scenario it is – and clearly that cannot have been the way it was. These misremembered events usually take vaguely cinematic form – once, for instance, I hitchhiked in the back of a red pickup truck up the Interstate to San Francisco, and what I see in my mind's eye when I recollect that day is a kind of helicopter shot of the truck travelling a hundred feet below with the small figures of me – and the girl I was with – in the back.

When I think back to the morning after that first evening out with Peggy, the camera is looking down from the ceiling in my rather tatty sublet on 2nd Avenue and 9th, and I am lying on my bed with my hands behind my head resting on the pillow. We are shooting through the ancient ceiling fan which, out of focus, is slicing through the picture in the foreground. Shades of 'Apocalypse Now' perhaps, but this is a very different movie. Though awake, my eyes are closed and there is a dreamy expression on my face, implying such beatific happiness that, compared with me, Larry wouldn't have been at the races.

Then my eyes open, my forehead furrows, and I sit bolt upright. Larry needn't have worried. I am worried enough for both of us.

Could I have got it wrong? I must have got it wrong. (Maybe I slap my forehead with the heel of my palm here.) Things like this – things like Peggy – don't happen to me!

Like most people, all but the really dull I am sure, I am a mass of contradictions. One is that I am, in some ways, absurdly, completely unjustifiably, self-confident and in others, a frightened rabbit. Ask me to do a presentation to a bunch of complete strangers – ten, twenty, fifty, doesn't matter how many – and I know I am going to be absolutely brilliant. But when it comes to women, I am often headfirst straight down the nearest burrow. I'm pretty relaxed at the chat-up stage, but I never believe it is ultimately going to work. At bottom, I suppose, I don't really believe I'm lovable. Mavis, what the fuck did you do to me?

So this incredible feeling of oneness that I had sensed the night before with Peggy, seemed, in the cold light of day – and it was cold, April but not remotely spring-like – frankly, incredible. (Now I think about it, why on earth was that fan switched on in my moviemory?)

I was still turning things over in my mind and never getting them settled, as I ate my breakfast – two eggs sunny side up, bacon, home fries, unbeatable – in the diner next door. I was, as always, flicking through 'The New York Times' – I'm a news and sports junkie wherever I am – but that day I was taking nothing in. When I got to work I went straight in to see Brett or Bart, one or the other, and allowed myself to be persuaded to suck on a little loosener. Usually, it would set off the predictable fit of the giggles but it just wound me up even more.

I went back to my own office and brooded. What should I do? Should I casually pass by her desk and make like I just happened to be down on her floor and thought I'd say hi? Except that I'd never been down on her floor apart from when I went to find her the other day, so how embarrassingly unconvincing would that be? Should I call her and solicitously ask if she got home safely? That seemed like a more promising line to take except wouldn't it make me look a bit too keen? Did anything kill passion more quickly than being too keen? Except possibly being solicitous. What girl wanted a guy whose old fashioned ways would impress her mother? I wondered what time she went to lunch. I wondered if I hung about in the entrance lobby I could spot her coming out of the elevator and just happen to run into her. Even I could see that not only was that a plan fraught with potential disaster, but possibly even less convincing than pretending to casually pass by her desk. But I was seriously turning over it in my mind, and trying to work out where I might stand to get a full view of all the elevator doors – tricky, so perhaps I should wait outside instead so I'd catch her as she came of out of the revolving door onto the street, but then it would seem like I was going back in, so how would I manufacture a reason for coming back out with her? – when my phone rang.

"Hello, is that Andy?"

My God, could it really be—

"This is Peggy."

—it could, it could, and not only it could, it WAS. My ego suddenly re-inflated like an airbag in a head-on collision. How could I have ever doubted me?

*

That Saturday night we went to a movie, a Woody Allen movie. She was a major Woody-phile, as most were back then, and I was very excited: What could have been more appropriate than going to see a Woody Allen film in New York? It was all a bit surreal really. Going to the movies in Manhattan with a New York girl like Peggy was pretty much like being in a Woody Allen film – and within that movie-like scenario I was going to see a Woody film.

I put this to her as we stood in line waiting to buy our tickets.

"Just imagine," she said, picking up on the idea, "if the Woody Allen movie we are going to see had a scene in it in which we are going to the movies to see a Woody Allen film."

"Right," I said, "and imagine if, in that scene, the movie we are going to see is the movie we are going to see."

"Oh my God, yes," said Peggy, "it would be like infinity! You know, like when you're standing in a room full of mirrors so your reflection just keeps bouncing backwards and forwards."

Look, it wasn't the most brilliant or original exchange but it was that wavelength thing I've been on about – and the comfort you get from realising that you're not out there in deep space alone. That there is someone who gets you – and who you get – standing right there beside you.

"Have you ever seen those Escher drawings?" I asked.

"What, you mean those staircase drawings that never end? And you can't work out whether the people are supposed to be going up or down. I love those. I had one on my wall in my room when I was in High School—"

"'Ascending and Descending'," I said quietly, a little nonplussed because I now knew something slightly amazing that she was about to find out.

She looked at me carefully.

"That was the one. Yeah, that was definitely the one. How did you know that?"

"I had it on my wall too."

We stood in silence, absorbing the significance of this. I wasn't a believer in fate or destiny or anything like that but there seemed to be a message here.

"That's freaky," she said.

"Weird," I said.

But I don't think either Peggy or I thought it was freaky or weird. We didn't say it, but I am pretty sure we both secretly thought it was, in the argot of the time and place, pretty neat.

She put her arm through mine and we walked into the cinema.

*

After the movie came the small questions: Are you hungry? Fancy a drink? Just a coffee maybe? (We settled on just a coffee.) And then over the coffee I began to contemplate the big question: We'd seen the movie, we'd very soon have had the coffee, what happened then?

Yes, sex was about to come into the equation. (By the way, if you're thinking that it's only girls who think like this, you're obviously a girl.)

Options: I play it extremely cool, don't even try to kiss her, and let things build a little longer. Or: I go for the kiss – the way things had been going I was pretty sure she wasn't going to do the last minute turn of the head thing and catch it on the cheek – but then leave it at that for tonight. Or: I go for the big one, invitation to come up, view etchings, etc. First option – safe – possibly too safe, actually maybe just cowardly. Second one, pretty safe, but still, conceivably, with the suggestion of smouldering passion to come. Third, obviously risky but potential ecstasy, movement of earth, explosion of stars, creation of universe, start of Williams/ Lee dynasty, future member of which goes on to win Nobel prize.

Really, a moment's serious thought told you it was a no-brainer – as they didn't used to say in 1979. Go for option two – to begin with. If she responds in a big way – enthusiastic tongue engagement, willing participation in embrace, even hint of pelvic thrust – then you switch to option three. If you just get back a non-committal so-so probe between your teeth, you should probably

46

go for a neat finish, pull away, promise to call her and go home to put the best construction on her reaction you possibly can: something like – she's a nice girl who's not the type to jump into bed before she's had a chance to get to know you. Emphasise the positives. She kissed back, didn't she? She didn't try to pull away. And if you start worrying that was because you went for the neat finish before she had the chance to pull away, remember that was why you went for the neat finish. To make sure you could tell yourself afterwards that you honestly didn't know whether she might or might not have pulled out, thus keeping open the possibility that she might have wanted to continue onward – and upward – and who knows whereward! – which would mean in turn, that you can go off to sleep believing that somewhere down the yet-to-be-established line there might still be a Nobel prize in the offing.

Okay, strategy sorted. But now for the tactics. Where to do the kissing? I could lean across now – still in the coffee place – and go for it. But that might be clumsy – bound to be when you're sitting in separate chairs. You lean towards her, your chair tips forwards, weight plus momentum etc., and before you know it you're in free-fall, head first into lap. Not cool.

Instead I make the sensible call. I ask for the check and pay, noting, appreciating but refusing to accept her offer to stump up for her half – though also hoping that won't be taken as setting a pattern – and walk Peggy towards the subway station. I reach for her hand. She takes mine. So far so good. I give her hand a little squeeze. She returns squeeze. As Peggy herself might say, better yet. We get to the subway station. I put my arm around her waist, gently pull her towards me, and project my lips in the direction of hers. She tilts her chin upward to me. Lips meet, lips open – teeth don't clash, hooray! – tongues mingle, tongues explore, saliva is exchanged. Meanwhile the concomitant reaction elsewhere. Nerve endings tingle, blood flows, member stirs, hips thrust – nothing too aggressive, just the natural order of things – and, blow me down – I use the words advisedly – if her hips aren't pushing back. Houston, we are go!

I pull my head away and look her in the eye. Making it sound as deep and meaningful as I can and not at all connected with the needle on the lustometer which is now well into the red zone, I say, "Peggy, do you want to come back to my place?"

And she says, "Oh Andy, I'd love too, I really would – but I don't think I can."

And I say, as I obviously would, "Why not?" and then trying to seem playfully ironic but more probably just sounding desperate, I add, "The night is young."

And she says, "No, I really can't. Miller will start worrying if I don't get back."

And I say, with an uneasy, creeping premonition, "Miller?"

And she says, "Yeah, Miller. I guess I should have told you about Miller. We ah … we ah … kind of live together."

There is a tiny, delusional bit of me that is hanging on to the improbable idea that this is one of Peggy's jokes, and that I am about to discover Miller is her pet goldfish.

"Miller's kind of possessive."

A possessive goldfish? Seems unlikely. Could still be a dog though? Or maybe a Siamese cat.

"Might start phoning round."

Probably not a dog then, or a Siamese, no matter how uncannily intelligent they are supposed to be. All not lost yet however. Could still be just a roommate, could even be a girl. This was America after all, and you kept coming across girls with surnames for first names – like Cameron or Porter or yes, maybe, Miller.

"Look I know I should have told you about him—"

Miller obviously wasn't one of those girls.

"—but you see, these days we're mostly more like roommates."

Last possible escape route cut off. And now the worm is finally beginning to turn. Miller? Miller! Apart from anything else, what sort of poncey, pretentious name is that? I was casting around for a weapon; that would have to do.

"Sorry Peggy, there's something I don't quite understand. 'These days he's more like a roommate' indicates to me that at some point Mill-er, was slightly more than just a roommate. And 'mostly' kind of suggests that occasionally at least, Mill-er still is. In which case, can you possibly explain what all this is about?"

"Why are you saying Miller like that? You don't have to be nasty about him. You don't even know him."

"No, you're right, I don't know him. I thought I might be getting to know you, but clearly I was woefully mistaken." She opened her mouth to say something but I cut her off. "And don't you think it's a bit rich to be questioning my – my – my attitude towards Mill-er when you're the one with some fucking explaining to do?"

It was the end of a beautiful evening.

*

I got back to my grubby little apartment at about two in the morning, fell face down on the bed and passed out fully clothed, window blinds still up, neon signs blinking from across the street and intermittently lighting up my bedroom.

Furious, without another word to Peggy, I'd turned on my heel and stomped off in a self-righteous paddy, walking the forty-odd blocks between the midtown subway station where I'd left her, and my place downtown. But I didn't get home before finding a bar or two along the way – the first was in Gramercy Park, I think, the second, who knows – where I got into serious set-em-up-Joe mode. Whiskey is an acquired taste which I've never acquired but I managed to grimace and shiver my way through a succession of neat shots of Jack Daniels. It was the only brand of American whiskey I'd ever heard of so that was the one I ordered. (Who says advertising doesn't work?) I have to confess I wallowed in my role of jilted, heartsick loner – I'd gone from being in a Woody Allen romantic comedy to some sort of film noir: shades of Ray Milland in 'The Lost Weekend', tie loosened, hat tipped back. Not that I was wearing a tie or a hat, and actually, I'm not at all sure Ray Milland was either or whether he was even sitting in a bar in 'The Lost Weekend', but you get the general idea. In a certain, masochistic way I probably rather enjoyed it, or at least, on some level felt a slightly warped satisfaction. Didn't it just go to show that the inner, inner, inner me was right all along? That I was a no-hope loser doomed forever not to get the girl?

When I abandoned Peggy I was incredulous – how could she have just sprung it on me like that? – and I felt entirely within my rights to be as livid as I was. But even as I slumped on the stool at the bar I was beginning to question whether I hadn't over reacted. Of course, it wouldn't have been me if I hadn't been beset by self-doubt, but when I tried to properly review what had happened I just couldn't make sense of it. It seemed that Peggy had, by any standards, behaved appallingly in encouraging me to think she was single and fancy free, and what's more, fancied me – when all the time she was concealing the fact that she was living with another bloke. And yet, against that, there had been absolutely no necessity for her to have mentioned him at all. She could have just found a polite way to decline my offer and gone home. I might even have 'respected' her for that – as I said before, I could have looked at it from the 'she's a nice girl who's not the type to jump into bed before she's had a chance to get know you' angle. So either it was just a sort of casual cruelty or … or I didn't really know, but maybe she just felt she needed to be honest with me. And hadn't everything I'd seen in Peggy, everything I intuited – all the vibes I got from her – up until the moment of her confession at the subway station, been so totally positive? She liked to kid around, yes, that much I knew – but that was a mile away from the apparent duplicity over Miller.

Miller. Miller! Mill-er! Just bringing his ridiculous name to mind set me off again. Apparent duplicity? Apparent! It was apparent because what it looked like was exactly what it was. "Barman, gimme another Jacque Dannulls." (I never said please. People in American bars never do.) Besides, the fact that I had so totally bought into her being a decent sort proved precisely what? Since when had I been such a great judge of character? "Barmannuther Jacquesdannulls." And so it went on.

On Sunday, it was no better. I surfaced – that is to say, had my eyes forced open by the blinding sunlight now streaming in – to discover the proverbial jackhammer between my ears. I got out of bed long enough to pull down the blinds, tear off my jacket and trousers, get a glass of water, locate some Tylenol, have a pee, and turn on the TV. Then I went back to bed in my underwear and shirt – disgusting but true, I didn't take it off until I fell into the shower on Monday morning – and socks! – and watched reruns of 'The Honeymooners' and 'I Love Lucy' until I fell asleep with the lights still on at goodness knows what time. If it had been today, I would undoubtedly have spent the day with my cellphone – I would have been in America so I wouldn't have called it a mobile – never out of my sight or hearing. I would have been hoping against hope that Peggy would call, and been fighting the urge to call her. But this was 1979 so mobile phones were no more of a reality than jetpacks. At least, that was one agony from which I was mercifully spared.

Of course, unless you're paying absolutely no attention to the timeline here, you will have realised that it was all eventually resolved. Eventually was in about twelve hours, first thing Monday morning. Peggy knocked politely on my office door, and stood before my desk – I didn't ask her to sit down – from which position she offered this explanation.

"Andy, you had a perfect right to get shitty with me, I'm sorry, I really am. I know I should have mentioned Miller and everything before but it's been falling apart for months, a year maybe, well maybe not quite a year but anyway. It was only a matter of time before one of us – well, you get the picture. Anyway, I run into you and we go for a drink and we have such a good time and you ask me out and I think why not? What am I going to do, say no, I've got to stay in and spend another Saturday night not talking to a guy who I'm really not that into anymore, and who's certainly not into me?"

"I thought you said he was possessive?"

"Yeah, well … that's except when I'm with him, I guess … Anyway, where was I? Oh yeah … look … I just never thought ahead, I suppose. Dumb. But whoever said I was smart? Anyway I just wanted to say I was sorry, and you know what, I totally like you. I really do. That was the reason I came along. You were the reason."

I may not have that absolutely word perfect and got all the phrasing and half-a-beat New York pauses and what have you in exactly the right places but, as near as dammit, that was it. She really did say – I totally like you – you were the reason. For a perfect score she could have added 'I went straight home, packed my things, and moved out and spent the rest of the weekend huddled in your doorway praying for your forgiveness,' but she didn't and being the magnanimous guy I am, I was prepared to overlook it.

So that was it. A storm in a teacup. Hardly worth mentioning you might think. But if that was it, it was only it for now. Because what seemed to characterise our relationship from the very beginning – or at least one of the things that did – was that we had to weather a whole series of storms in teacups. I am not going to bother to record them all here, but, staying with the meteorological theme, it was as though our relationship was centred somewhere near Haiti in the middle of the hurricane season. No, it wasn't. That's going much too far. No, it was situated in a place where most of the time it's a perfect temperature and the sun is always on your face and you'd never want to be anywhere else except on those too frequent occasions when these black clouds suddenly appear and explode above your head. In other words, mostly utterly glorious but sometimes, for short bursts, anything but.

52

Why this was, whose fault it was, I really can't say. Looking back, it seems to me that we were never really able to get past that; we never seemed to get on an even keel for long enough. Maybe that was the reason, or one of them, why just sailing serenely on for ever and ever was never going to be our thing.

Anyway, after Peggy had given her little speech of contrition, I came round to her side of the desk and kissed her. It was, bar none, the most fabulous snog of my life. Slow, lingering, wet and wonderful. If you're thinking I'm going to tell you that some perfectly appropriate piece of music just happened to start coming through the wall from the office next door, you'd be wrong. My moviemory of that scene is a two shot of Peggy and I clinging and kissing, and as the camera slowly pushes in closer and closer, we hear nothing but the white noise of the air conditioning and the occasional muffled beep from the Manhattan traffic outside.

CHAPTER 5

LONDON, 1999

I tried. I really did. For the next few weeks the Polaroid of Peggy stayed locked away. I dropped it into the top left hand drawer of my office desk and turned the key. And whenever I was tempted to look at it – and dive into the warm waters of the past – I willed myself not to, or found some sort of distraction. I didn't exactly take the Baden Powell option and nip off for a cold shower whenever I felt the blood rise, but it was that kind of thing. Denial – and the masochistic satisfaction one takes from it – were the order of the day. The trouble with denial is that the more you try to deny whatever it happens to be that you're denying, the more you think about it. Which sort of defeats the object.

I pretended to throw myself into work. I really didn't feel the genuine pull of it, the way I had pre-PP, but I made a decent fist of pretending that I did. I went to all the meetings I was asked to, and a few that I wasn't. I manufactured a fake enthusiasm that I was sure looked just like the real thing. I made a point of randomly pitching up in the offices of all my people, not to keep them on their toes but to give them the impression that I was on mine. To all intents and purposes, I was back to being the relentlessly upbeat, company cheerleader that they expected me to be. Eeyore was out. Tigger was back in.

I suppose I hoped that if I carried on like this, sooner or later I would begin to feel the way I was pretending to feel, that the act would become the reality. Only it didn't. I was Sally at Katz's Deli and not a wet patch anywhere.

I tried to get involved with the work Will and Lucille were doing on the new business we'd won. (It was a breakfast cereal account – our initial project for which was to be the launch of some new kind of chocolatey (but not actual chocolate, of course) wheaty something or others.) I got Julia to fix a time with them, and, at the appointed hour, they came to my office with some ideas for TV commercials. Normally I would have seen them alone, but Vince had popped in to waste ten minutes, and he was still there. He was leaning back on my desk, right beside my chair, in which I, not unnaturally, was seated.

"I'll leave you to it," Vince said, as Will and Lucille came in but, possibly because it slightly rankled – despite my previously denial – that Vince had appointed them to the account in the first place, I said something like, "No, stay Vince. We're all friends here."

So he stayed, still leaning on my desk; in other words right beside me, or, after I swivelled in my chair to face them, perhaps just behind and, as he was standing, above me.

"So," I said, ushering them towards the repro Eileen Gray leather sofa that my office guests were expected to perch on – bloody uncomfortable really, "What have you got?"

Will, a rather rangy, dress-down (but properly labelled) Mancunian was the Art Director, and, for whatever reason, it's usually the case, as it was in this, that the Art Director nods along while his work-partner, the Copywriter, does the talking.

One of my very favourite words in all dictionary-dom is 'pulchritudinous' and it might have been invented for Lucille. (Lucille Wood to give her some family context. 'Lucille Wood – and so would I!' as some office wag once had it, and which all the boys – being boys – would chorus whenever her full name was said.) Lucille liked to wear tight pencil skirts to emphasise her swervy hips and would sit with her legs pinned together – possibly to get you thinking about what it might be like if they weren't – and tucked slightly at an angle to her body. She favoured men's shirts not, shall we say, buttoned all the way to the very top, and would lean forward in such a way that her impossible to ignore, and wonderfully supported bosoms – another of my favourite words – were, well, impossible to ignore.

She was, as, of course, she would have to have been, from Bristol, and had that slightly childish Julie Burchill-like voice, with just a hint of a lisp thrown in. To complete the effect was a torrent of loosely arranged blondish hair and a pair of thick, black, men's glasses kept on the edge of her nicely turned-up nose. She thought that everyone fancied the pants off her, and she was usually right. She was ruthless in using this to advantage, and, by the way, we weren't above it either. If we had an excuse to squeeze her into a new business pitch, particularly if none of the prospective clients were women, we had been known to do it.

Lucille consulted her script, cleared her throat and started reading. I couldn't tell you what she said – I remember it sounded decent enough to me but not world-shattering which is probably why I can't remember it – and then, having finished, glanced up at me.

I said something like "Yeah, that sounds like you're on the right track," throwing in some minor suggestion which I knew full well they would do their best to ignore, and that was it. Except that on the way out of the door, Will first, Lucille following, she glanced towards me and offered just the very briefest of smiley farewell-for-nows, a look which, I couldn't help feeling, was more than a tad on the coquettish side. I couldn't remember her having done this – at least not quite so unambiguously – before.

Now, I think you will have deduced from the detail of my description of Lucille, that a) I was not entirely unappreciative of her charms and b) that she looked not one whit, not in any way at all, like Peggy.

And possibly – no, almost certainly I would say – because Peggy had been so much on my mind, and I had been reliving the glories of our time together, Lucille's inviting little glance, did not, as it might at any other time, have me figuratively twiddling the ends of my waxed moustache. It left the lounge lizard in me disinterestedly curled up on a rock.

But then, as I was much later to reflect, perhaps that look was not meant for me at all. Was not Vince right beside me, and effectively in the same line of sight? And did I not mention a little earlier in the piece that Lucille was a girl with naked ambition?

*

I tried at home too. I made an effort to get back by eight so I could see India before she went to sleep. I started reading to her again, something I hadn't done much of since she was four or five. Glenda and Vic had given her some Tracey Beaker books for Christmas so we started working our way through those, and on about the second or third night, Florence wandered into India's room and sat on the end of her bed while I was reading. After that she came in most nights to listen, and though, theoretically, a little beyond the Tracy Beaker stage – she was chalking off the days to teenhood like a prisoner waiting for release – it didn't seem to bother her in the least.

Perhaps because Alison noticed me coming home earlier, she started to do the same, and one evening, for the first time in goodness knows how long, we made a point of sitting down together for dinner. I don't think we said a lot but the time passed pleasantly enough – and, compared to the way things had been recently, pleasantly enough was half way to paradise.

We even enjoyed 'marital relations' once or twice during this period of calm, though perhaps 'enjoyed' is stretching a point. It was your basic rolling on, rolling off kind of thing, without too much preamble and no more than the minimum acceptable amount of post coitus cuddling. I'm pretty sure it didn't do a lot for Alison and I'm not altogether sure what it did for me. Did it allow me to fool myself for a little longer that we had something approaching a working marriage? Or did the evident lack of passion or romance or anything except the half-hearted desire for release have precisely the opposite effect? Was this just one more piece in a jigsaw which, sooner or later, would inevitably reveal itself to be a picture of a relationship dying on its feet?

Anyway, we soldiered on, sometimes, I'm sure, genuinely believing that the battle to save Alison and Andrew could be won. It was Alison who came up with the idea of a 'project'.

"I was thinking," she said, as we meandered round Kensington Gardens one Sunday, following Spot with little plastic bags at the ready, and fervently hoping that India, wobbling on her roller blades, wasn't going to lead us straight to Casualty. (Florence, as usual, was ten pin bowling or ice-skating or some such with her mates.)

"Why don't we do something with the basement? We could get rid of the guest bedroom – we haven't used it for ages – and open it all up and make a kind of rumpus room or something for the kids. Florence will want somewhere to hang out with her friends soon and how long will it be before India does too? And," she added brightly, now reaching the climax of her clearly well-rehearsed speech, "because it's for them, we can all be involved, all four of us."

"A 'rumpus' room you say? You don't mean a rumpy-pumpus room do you?" Ever the adman – the slick line was my stock-in-trade after all – I was rather pleased with that.

Alison correctly took my self-satisfied smirk as a sign that I was willing to go along with her plan, and she laughed and put her arm through mine.

"For God's sake, Andrew, she's not even thirteen yet."

"I know," I said, "that's what I'm worried about."

But I wasn't really worried. It was just the sort of thing you say,

58

something that sounds vaguely meaningful but is actually just froth – a bit of babble to move things along. Alison and I had agreed upon something, we now had a plan, and that seemed like progress of a sort. I didn't want to talk about it anymore; I wanted to finish the conversation, to run after Spot and throw a stick for him to fetch, and to get home – to draw a line under the day while we were still ahead. This little bit of goodwill could be entered in the credit column of the ledger of our marriage, and it was the first such entry for a long time. I wanted to record it before something on the debit side cancelled it out. Or to put it another way, I just wanted everything to be alright despite all the evidence there might be to the contrary; if I could avoid facing the truth and thus prevent the flimsy edifice of our lives from crashing down for just a little bit longer, then I would. The truth hurts – in a marriage it can be fatal – and isn't that why we would so often rather go on living a lie?

*

"Well, at first glance, I don't think it looks that complicated," said Dougal Harris. Dougal – 'please call me Doug, everyone does' – was the thirty-fiveish architect-cum-designer who had revamped Geoff's fund manager brother-in-law's place in Wandsworth, and whose excellent credentials had thus been brought to my attention. He took a stroll around our basement with Alison and I in tow, Florence slouching, and India bouncing along behind.

It wasn't too difficult to guess the lines along which he was thinking – knock a wall down here, put an RSJ in there, add some discreet downlighting, or possibly some discreet uplighting, one of the two, possibly even both, maybe put in some of those clever Danish or Swiss or whatever sweetly sliding doors to replace those fucking awful French windows – or not – all depending how much Alison and I were prepared to run to. Yes, it didn't look like a bad little job – not going to be as lucrative as Geoff's brother-in-law's but these people seem to have a bob or two, and aren't they just the kind of people who are bound to know other people who might like something done too?

"Could we have a table tennis table?" Florence suddenly asked.

I had to laugh – though I was careful not to. I had never witnessed Florence, who considered all sports seriously uncool, so much as lift a table tennis bat.

"Table tennis?" I said, all pretend naivety. "Doesn't sound very girly to me."

Florence turned to me, and raised her eyebrows in her precocious, knowing way. Alison laughed. And India was baffled.

"What? What? What is it? Tell me."

It was Dougal-call-him-Doug who obliged.

"I believe some boys are quite keen on table tennis," he said.

"Boys?" I said. "Why would you want a table tennis table because boys—"

"Very funny, Daddy." said Florence, and she turned to Dougal Harris and gave him the expected sorry-about-that-he's-my-father-look. India grimaced at the very idea of boys, as nine-year-old girls are obliged to do. And Alison looked on, smiling warmly, the very picture of the glamorous but family-first nineties mother. Everyone had played their part to perfection. Except, in my opinion, our new architect friend, who had slightly annoyed me by his intervention. Completely irrationally perhaps, I just didn't feel he should have had a speaking part in this little family tableau.

After he had gone, we all sat down to review the meeting.

"He was nice, wasn't he, Daddy?" offered India, eyes shining, so that there wasn't much else I could do but seem to agree.

"Yes, he was. Doug really seemed to get it," said Florence.

I wanted to ask her where she had got 'really seemed to get it' from, but I knew that would just provoke her, so I said, "Well, that's a world first. You two agreeing." And then I asked Alison what her opinion was. At first she didn't answer. She seemed miles away. "Alison? Come in."

"Oh, what? Sorry. Yes, yes, I thought he was very nice. I liked him a lot."

So the girls liked him, and Alison liked him a lot. What could I say? In the fullness of time, after a bit of toing and froing about design details and colour schemes – and costs of course – Doug – Doug, even then his name was beginning to stick in my craw – got the job.

*

So it went on for several weeks. 'Twas all peace and harmony in the Williams household notwithstanding the odd tantrum from one or other of the girls. On one shopping Saturday, things were so convivial that Alison treated me to a new suit to replace the torn Prada. She decided that Ozwald Boateng was the thing now. Since I was tallish and thinnish, I was able to squeeze into his trademark tight cut and I got a sort of greeny-blue job, with a scarlet lining. Very sharp. I squeezed her hand in genuine gratitude as we left the shop, and we walked back into Savile Row, for all the world like a couple who could stand the sight of each other.

But it couldn't last – the old lull/storm thing, I suppose. It was, in fact, just after we'd finally given Doug the job that relations between Alison and me took a turn for the worse again. We were using a building contractor that he had recommended – and was supposedly supervising – but within days of the work starting, the costs started to creep up. Alison was managing affairs from our side, and so it was she who would have the meetings with Doug, at which he would routinely explain that because of this or that unforeseen circumstance, what they thought had been going to cost X would now cost X+. She would then report this to me. I was not impressed.

"But I thought we'd signed a contract, Alison."

"Yes, but building is not a precision science. There always has to be a bit of leeway and if you want to get the best out of people you have to be fair."

"What! They gave us a price down to the last screw. That's what Doug told us. That was his exact phrase."

"Nail."

"What?"

"He said 'down to the last nail', not 'screw'."

"Oh well, that makes all the bloody difference! Nail, screw, who gives a fuck! What I want to know is why they are asking for more money, a week into the job."

"Well you never know what's underneath until you get the plaster off the walls."

"Alison, is this you talking or is it Doug?"

"Can you see Doug in the room?"

And then came the descent from mild sarcasm into an increasingly bitter confrontation. What I could not understand is why Alison seemed to be so supine in the face of this pressure from Doug. Part of her job as a commercials producer was to keep costs down, and professionally, she had the reputation of being a pretty hard-arsed negotiator. So what the hell was going on with our 'project'?

It didn't take long for the ill-feeling from these arguments about the building work to infect the rest of our relationship. Walls might be coming down in the basement, but not as fast as the barriers between Alison and me were being rebuilt.

One day in late June, soon after the building work began, Geoff and I had to fly to Paris to attend a marketing conference at the headquarters of one of our biggest clients and then go onto the big boozy dinner that would follow. Vince, who was also meant to go, cried off with a virus. When I heard this, all I could think was that it would have taken more than a virus to stop me from going. Not because I was any more dedicated to the job than Vince – far from it these days – but because I was desperate to get away from the poisonous atmosphere of 'New Pemberley'. If I'd had rabies, dengue fever and necrotising fasciitis all at the same time, I think I would still have found a way to go.

All I had to do was find my passport. I gave my pockets a perfunctory pat but I knew it couldn't be there because I had the Ozwald Boateng on and I was sure I hadn't been out of the country since Alison bought it for me. It wasn't in any of my other jackets either or in any of my trousers or in a pair of plaid Bermudas that I hadn't worn since Cannes about five years ago. (And which Alison, in her ruthless de-cluttering, had somehow missed.) But I was getting more desperate by the minute, and now I was furiously hunting anywhere and everywhere. The passport hadn't somehow fallen on the floor of my wardrobe or been kicked under the bed. Or been stuffed in the back of the bathroom cupboard. Or left on top of the fridge. I turned the house upside down looking for it but all to no avail, and, feeling completely hacked off and with only about five minutes left before I was due to meet Geoff to leave for the airport, I marched into the office and totally unfairly accused Julia of having lost it. She promptly burst into tears, I was stricken by remorse, and as I was casting around my office for a tissue to give her, my eyes fell upon my desk and more particularly upon its top left hand drawer. It was then I remembered where I'd last seen my passport – in this very drawer, the same one in which I had locked the Polaroid of Peggy.

I scrabbled in the pocket of my jacket for the keyring – put my hand on a small packet of tissues I didn't know I had, thrust one at Julia, and then having finally located my keys, stared at them blankly trying to remember which was the right one for this particular drawer. Frantically I tried about five before I found it and, with a flood of relief, was reunited with my passport. But not, since the passport was lying under the Polaroid, until I had looked once more upon Peggy's face. For one frozen moment, thoughts of the plane flew out of the window as I gazed at her wistfully. Then, at last hearing Julia's slightly choked-up but, as ever, piercing voice – "Andrew! Andrew, you've got to go! Now!" – I grabbed my passport, and, inadvertently, the Polaroid with it, and tore out of the office, shouting a promise to Julia as I pushed past her that I would bring her back something gorgeous from Paris to make up for my boorish behaviour.

Julia never did get anything from Paris, gorgeous or otherwise, because when we got to Heathrow we found out that both Charles de Gaulle and Orly airports were fogbound and we were unable to take off for either. But it was hours and hours before we were finally told that all Paris departures would be cancelled, and, in the meantime, Geoff and I installed ourselves in the BA Executive Lounge.

As Geoff chomped through his second or third stale but complimentary BA croissant – he was one of those wiry little guys who eats like a horse but never puts on an ounce – he casually asked me how things were going with Doug. For a moment I had to stop to think who he was talking about as I'd almost forgotten the connection.

"Oh, Doug," I said, finally understanding. "Yeah, seems okay. Bit of a cocky sod if you ask me and a bit too cosy with the bloody builders, but Alison seems to rate him."

Neutral enough, nothing really to give anything away, but there must have been something in my voice – perhaps I was unwittingly sounding as downbeat as I was feeling – that prompted him to say in a slightly more engaged way, "You alright Andrew? Everything okay at home?"

Which was when the first of the dams burst. I suppose I was just waiting for the opportunity to tell someone how shitty I was feeling, how fucked-up things were with Alison, how – and this was not a wise thing to mention to Geoff but I was in full flow – how work, well, work just seemed like work these days.

He stopped eating for a moment, and slowly nodded his head.

"Yeah well, it's not always as easy as it looks. Don't I know it." He accompanied the rhetorical question with a rueful look – Geoff was on his third marriage. And I thought that was what he was referring to but he went on, "It's a young man's game, we all know that Andrew. You've got to pace yourself old mate. How old are you now, forty-five?"

"Forty-nine." I replied, stupidly taking the bait. But I wasn't really sure I liked where this was going – I was the oldest of the three of us by several years and it was a slightly touchy subject – and, besides, Geoff knew exactly how old I was.

"Forty-nine? Are you now?" he said, grinning. "No, but seriously – all these young blokes you've never heard of opening agencies every ten minutes – we all know it's bloody tough. And the clients, they're all about twelve too!"

I realised I should never have mentioned the work part of it – he was bound to dwell on that – and I felt I needed to defend myself.

"You needn't worry about it, Geoff. I'm still a five times a night kind of a guy."

"Are you Andrew?" he said, more seriously, thoughtfully stirring his coffee.

"Didn't seem to be what you were saying a minute ago."

Maybe it was this sudden switch back to the subject of my marriage, maybe it was the meaningful look he gave me as he finished speaking, maybe it was the fact that I was just falling to pieces, but out of nowhere I felt tears pricking my eyes, and in a panic, I reached into my pocket to grab one of those tissues, and clumsily pulled out my passport, and with it, the Polaroid of Peggy which fell on the floor.

Geoff reached down to pick it up, looked at it, nodded to himself as though a penny had suddenly dropped and said, "Haven't seen one of these for a while. Pretty girl. Who is she?"

And, in my utterly discombobulated state, dam number two

broke. I told him about Peggy and how Alison had come upon the Polaroid, and, well, all of it. When I'd finished he looked at me open mouthed. And then, instead of offering the sympathy and understanding I had somehow been expecting, he let loose.

"Are you telling me you have fallen for a picture of some girl you knew for a – for a – I dunno, a fucking nanosecond—"

"It was four or five months—"

"I repeat, a fucking NANOsecond, and that was half a lifetime ago – a picture you didn't even know you had! – of a girl you've never spoken to since! – and that that is what is behind all this fucking craziness! Jesus, Andrew, you need a fucking shrink!"

Put like that I had to agree that he had a point.

*

I probably should have called Alison to tell her that I wasn't going to Paris and that I would be coming home after all. But in all my 'fucking craziness', to use Geoff's nicely turned phrase, Alison wasn't uppermost in my mind. When we were finally told we weren't even going to be able to get to Paris in time to make a late appearance at the boozy dinner, it was after five, and, once in the cab out of Heathrow, I decided the ideal compensation for missing it was to visit one of those pubs around Bayswater of which I had recently been an habitué. Whether the landlord was pleased to see me again I cannot say, nor indeed can I tell you much more about the evening, beyond the fact that I got home and fell into bed at about eleven to find that Alison still wasn't back.

My memory of the following morning is, however, slightly clearer. When I awoke, Alison still wasn't back.

CHAPTER 6

NEW YORK, 1979

Not surprisingly, the first thing I wanted to clarify with Peggy after our reconciliatory snog was what the deal with this guy, Miller, really was.

"It's over I guess ... we just haven't gotten round to finishing it."

"But if it's over, it is finished."

"It's not that easy."

"Why don't you just leave him?"

"Well, for one thing, I don't have a place to go."

We had known each other for not much more than a week, and been out for drinks after work once, and had one proper date that had ended in disaster. So I didn't feel able to say, "Yes, you do. You can come and live with me." It would obviously have been absurdly impulsive and, knowing the sensible, practical girl Peggy was – or, at least, the crazily impractical girl she wasn't – any such offer would almost certainly have been met with a derisory "Get outta here." (A favourite expression of hers.) But almost as soon as the words weren't out of my mouth, I began to regret that I hadn't said them. If you want someone to believe in you, you have to show you believe in them. There is a power in commitment; it's an act of faith and some people believe that acts of faith can move mountains. Perhaps if, there and then, even at that ridiculously early stage, I'd had the balls to lean down, grab hold of Peggy by the waist and pull her up on to my horse, she would have been prepared to ride off into the sunset with me. A long shot. A million to one shot. But you never know. That's the thing; you never know. And you do hear of such things. Not just of love at first sight, but of people acting on it, dropping everything for each other, eloping, getting married, backing their hunch against all the odds that this is the person, and now is the time.

I, however, said, "Don't you have a friend you can stay with?" – which, let's face it, was not, as acts of faith go, a nailed-on mountain mover.

"I dunno. Maybe I could stay with Noreen for a while." (Noreen turned out to be not-Peggy from casting.)

For the time being I left it there. Not because I was worried any more about seeming too keen – I didn't think she could have been in the slightest doubt about how keen I was – but because I didn't want to push it. I could survive for a while on the knowledge that it was over with Miller – for the most part I chose to believe that it must be true – and I could lie in my bed and stare dreamily at the ceiling, feasting at midnight and way into the small hours on 'I totally like you.'

'I totally like you.' Surely, it could only be the tiniest of steps from there to 'I love you'?

*

In the next week or so, Peggy and I had lunch a couple of times, went for dinner in Chinatown once, took a Sunday walk in the park, and saw another movie – some sort of horror film which I suggested. It was the kind of thing I normally didn't go for but I thought she might need someone to cling on to. Yes, we kissed and cuddled whenever I could contrive the opportunity – in the movie, on a bench or two in Central Park, in any doorway near the subway station where there wasn't a down-and-out inconveniently trying to sleep – in short, wherever I could manoeuvre her; and however unsubtle in going about it I was, I never noticed her complaining. It was a little less than I might have hoped for – she fended off all my suggestions to spend a night away from her own place, which, you will need no reminding, wasn't just her place, but Miller's too – and though I seriously resented this, I neatly compartmentalised my feelings. For Peggy, I reserved all my uncritical adoration. The bad stuff, the frustration and anger I felt every time she took the subway back uptown, I hung on Miller.

Then Peggy was suddenly absent. When I called down to her desk in casting and she didn't pick up, I went to see what was wrong. I was a copywriter – I was paid to have a lively imagination – and all sorts of ghastly possibilities went through my mind as I rode the eight stories down. Had she been mugged? Kidnapped? Murdered? But the worst was that she'd made up with Miller and that they'd run off to get married.

But Noreen was able to comfort me.

"She called in sick. Her throat's all swollen and she's got this, like, funny, thick voice. She says they think it might be Mono."

I looked at her blankly.

"Mono. Mo-noe. What, you don't have Mono in England? Perhaps you pronounce it different there: MOE-NOE."

"Not as far as I'm aware."

I mentioned this to Bart and Brett, as I ingested a lungful of Colombian Gold or Peruvian Purple or whatever. They seemed alarmed.

"Shit that stuff is real contagious," said Bart, refusing the joint that I was passing back to him. "You've like … er … you've er … with her, right?"

I thought I knew what he was driving at, and pride forbade for me from disabusing him. So he decided to roll another rather than risk catching the Mono that I might have caught from Peggy.

Still, it was only when I found out from an English secretary, who worked for some bigwig on the executive floor and who I bumped into by the water-cooler, that we did, in fact, have Mono in England, only we called it Glandular Fever, that I began to take it seriously. There was good news in that I'd had it as a teenager and I knew that you could seldom, if ever, catch it twice, but the bad was that I knew that it could keep Peggy off work – and away from me – for months. I thought I should send her a get well card.

In the advertising world it is a matter of creative honour that you create your own cards rather than send store-bought, so I enlisted Bart's Art Directorial help and he and I made a card that we thought was screamingly funny (although the Peruvian Purple may have had something to do with that) and the next day I went to ask Noreen for Peggy's address. But her desk was empty. I guessed that she too must have the dreaded signs of Mono, and, judging by the eerie emptiness of the casting department, it seemed that most of the other not-Peggys were probably similarly afflicted. So where to send my screamingly funny card?

I called Personnel or HR or whatever they called it then but they refused to reveal any details. And so I was stuck. I didn't have her home number and even if I had, I wouldn't have called it for fear of speaking to Miller. (Fear of the manly things I might say to him, I mean.) Remember this was 1979. No e-mail, no Facebook, no mobile phone. No chance of communicating with Peggy until she came back to work.

The upshot of all this was that I fretted and pined for her helplessly in the week that we were apart. Yes, only a week because it turned out not to be Mono at all, but just a passing bug, yet time enough for the heart's fondness to increase by the bucketload and for the thought that she was spending that week with Miller to niggle, and wiggle and jiggle inside me and drive me bloody bananas. As soon as she got back, I dropped everything and went down to see her with my unsent card. I can't say she screamed quite as heartily as Bart and I but she seemed to genuinely appreciate the effort I had made and we arranged another date. In fact, Peggy did the asking. A friend of hers had given her tickets for some off-off-off-Broadway play and she was keen to go. She felt it might be useful for her job in casting if she got around more and saw some new acting talent; she wasn't remotely senior enough to be allowed to make any serious casting recommendations herself but she thought that making this sort of extra-mural effort might win her a few brownie points with her boss. Although the play sounded as though it would be unutterably tedious – some sort of reworking of Uncle Vanya with the setting transferred to contemporary Nicaragua, just the sort of thing any advertising person would instinctively loathe – I was happy enough to tag along. I thought it might earn me some brownie points with Peggy.

The play was as dreary and worthy and as everything-I-hated as I'd expected. I spent the whole of the second half trying to imagine the various players acting in fantasy TV commercials that I was writing in my head. None of them looked liked they had what it would take, apart from Uncle Vanya himself who I could possibly see doing something for Roach Motel. ('Roach Motel – roaches check in but they don't check out.' My favourite product and line ever.) I thought Uncle Vanya might be useful if they ever wanted anthropomorphised cockroaches. I shared these ideas with Peggy when, to my intense relief, the final curtain came down.

"Not good, huh?" she said.

"Whoever gave you those tickets should be made to sit through it themselves."

"He already did," she said.

"He must really dislike you then. Who was it?"

A short pause followed – as though Peggy was thinking better of something.

"Oh, just a guy."

My antennae waggled.

"What guy?"

"What difference what guy? You don't know him."

Yes, I did.

"It was Miller wasn't it?"

A hesitation, then the inevitable admission, although without much remorse.

"Yes, alright, if you must know, it was Miller. Actors get given tickets for this kind of thing all the time, and anyway he'd seen it, so he gave them to me. What difference does it make that it was Miller? He wasn't here. You were."

Well. Well, well, well! Quite a lot to unpack there. First, what difference did it make that it was Miller? ALL the fucking difference, that was the difference that it made. Just the very fact that Mill-er had been my benefactor made me feel physically ill. Second, she had once again kept me in the dark – it seemed we'd only just got things straight from the last time, when here she was, deliberately concealing something else from me. Third, he WAS there. In a sense. I wasn't sure in what sense, but somehow, in some sneaky, underhanded, metaphysical way he had definitely been there.

And fourth, and much the most disconcerting, was the fact that –

"Miller is an actor?"

Peggy raised an eyebrow. This wasn't quite the bitter recrimination she may have been expecting.

"Yes, he's an actor."

"How did you meet him? Did you meet him at the office?"

"I really don't see this is your business, Andy."

"Did you? Did you meet him at the office? Did he come in for a casting?"

"Yes, if you must know, he did. So wh—"

"What was the casting for?"

"What? What difference can that poss—"

All the difference in the world. Pray that it wasn't for a hair gel – deep-set blue eyes, dead straight nose, a mane of thick, shiny, bouncy – at twenty-nine, I was already thinning noticeably.

"Really this is absurd—"

"Tell me! Please. You have to tell me."

"Okay, okay, it was a shaving cream. Satisfied now?"

OH MY GOD! A shaving cream! That was worse than a hair gel – a shaving cream – granite jaw, exposed torso – bound to be – rippling pecs!

"Are you okay Andrew? You look a little pale."

*

I recovered enough for us to round off the evening at a bar in the West Village – somewhere near Bleecker Street, which was where the converted studio/theatre had been. Peggy just had a coffee – she wasn't much of a drinker – but I felt I needed something stronger. I needed to be fortified for what was to come. No matter what the cost to my health, I was determined to get to the bottom of this once and for all, and, when we were seated at our table by the window, I pressed on with my inquisition. There was a red neon sign in the window, advertising some brand of drink – I couldn't see which because it faced outwards onto the street, as it would have to if it was to lure any customers in, so the lettering read back to front from where we were. But I remember the hot light it reflected back on us, and Peggy commenting, "That kind of works don't you think? Adds to the atmosphere. Makes it feel like a real interrogation."

She seemed to have decided to take all this nonsense in her stride. She was, after her initial defensiveness, rather amused by it, and probably a little flattered. So on I went. And I relaxed a little when I received the answer to my next question: no, she told me, he hadn't got the part. And I brightened up considerably when, unbidden, she added that he hadn't even made the short list. To have an actor – and one obviously photogenic enough to go up for a shaving cream commercial – for a love rival was bad enough. To have had one good looking enough to get the part, and therefore, an actor who was that extreme rarity, one who was successful and earning, would have been very, very hard to bear.

Not that Peggy would concede for a second that he was a rival to me in any way.

"Will you just knock it off, Andy? I keep telling you Miller and I are history." (Tiny pause.) "Almost history. No, no. Not almost. We are. We just haven't you know – formalised it – yet."

That was reassuring, but to someone with my extra-heightened levels of insecurity, not quite reassuring enough. So I pressed on.

"Does he have a surname? Or is Mill-er one of those actors with only one name? You know – like Topol."

"For the last time, enough with the 'ers' already! No, he is not like Topol. Yes, he does have a surname."

"Which is?"

"Prince. Miller Prince. Happy?"

Was I happy? No, I was not. Miller Prince. I didn't like the sound of that one bit. In a sexy name contest, Miller Prince v. Andrew Williams would have been too obviously one sided for the Sexy Names Board of Control to have ever allowed it to take place.

"Miller Prince," I repeated back disconsolately. "Really?"

"Well no" she said, "Since you ask, not really. He changed it. He didn't think his real name kind of worked for an actor. Wouldn't have looked good on the movie posters – yeah, right! – he should have such problems."

"So his name isn't really Miller at all?"

"Yeah, yeah," Peggy said, "Miller is his real name. But the Prince part – well, that does have elements of his real name but that's all."

"What elements?"

"Er, let's see now. The P. And the R. And like the, um, 'nce' sound."

"The what sound?"

"The 'nce' sound."

"So what's his real name?"

"You're not going to laugh if I tell you, are you?"

"I don't know."

"Well, we'll see I guess. It's Pronski. Miller Pronski."

"Miller Pronski? Are you serious?"

"I am serious."

And, as you may have guessed, and Peggy had anticipated, this revelation did provoke a quiet chuckle. Or two, or more. Miller Pronski v. Andrew Williams seemed to be a much more even contest.

I finished my drink in a much improved mood and left the bar, hand in hand with Peggy, and with a veritable spring in my step. I might have bounced all the way home had I not turned to quickly check what hair that I had left, by inspecting my reflection in the bar window. It was then, as I brushed my hair first this way and then that, vainly – in both senses of the word – trying to cover the increasingly threadbare spaces, that I noticed the red neon sign again, and this time, being outside, I was able to read it.

Those of you who know anything about American alcohol brands, or who have ever walked down any downtown street in just about any American city, will, surely, have long ago correctly anticipated the jolt I was about to receive. And I, too, particularly since I was in the ad biz and acutely conscious of brand names in a way that ordinary, usefully employed folk are not, would, even in the short time I had been in the States, certainly have seen and registered this same red neon sign, or rather exact replicas of it, innumerable times.

And yet, somehow, I had never before made the connection between

Miller –

– and Miller.

Miller, the no.2 beer brand in America, whose red neon name stared out from half the bars in America.

And Miller – Miller – Miller Prince, nay Pronski, the actor

75

handsome enough to go up for a shaving-gel casting and therefore, inevitably with a full head of gleaming hair, hair so healthy it would be bound so tight to the scalp, not a single strand would ever fall out.

If I had gone into the bar and stuck my fingers into the socket in which the neon sign was plugged, I could hardly have received a more sickening shock to the system.

I am not a religious fellow, not remotely spiritual, not the least bit superstitious – well, I may have been known to touch wood, but only when no-one can see me do it. I see nothing in clairvoyants, am unstirred by tealeaves, and say crystal balls to tarot cards.

But this – even I could not deny – was a sign!

A less insecure man, a more self-assured man, a man with maturity, might have seen the funny side. But, as we have discussed, I was not he.

Peggy saw it though. She creased up. Ah, the pleasure I gave that girl.

*

Is there anything more absurd, more destructive, more completely pointless, more self-defeating than jealousy? But, as motivational tools go, it's unbeatable.

I adored Peggy from the first – within seconds of clapping eyes on her in the elevator in McDonnell Martin, I was utterly besotted. She had exactly the looks – black, glossy, wavy hair, long lashes, sweetheart lips, wry smile, but, above all, those dark, deep eyes – that, for some reason, I thought of as my ideal. (Curious that I ended up marrying a carrot-top. Although it's true, that, at the time, I thought I loved her too.)

And then there was Peggy's neat figure, her tight little body, her perky, pointy tits – it added up to just about the perfect package as far as I was concerned. But then, you might say, yes, but there are a million girls like that in New York and you probably wouldn't be more than a few hundred thousand out.

Looks matter, you can't deny it – when you first see someone across the room, what else is there? – but, once I knew her a little, it was much more than that. It was Peggy's very particular take on life, her quiet independence, her sparky irreverence, her amused scepticism, her capacity to surprise, her sudden invention, her unreproducible Pegginess, that so entranced me. And let's not forget that she laughed at my tee-shirt, got all my jokes, and totally liked me. That may have helped too.

But as much as I worshipped the ground she walked on, and needed no added incentive to place Peggy front and centre of my life, I had one: my jealousy of Miller.

It was, I realise, looking back, ridiculous – beyond ridiculous. Yes, she had had a relationship that I knew, if I cared to think about it, must have had its carnal side. And I knew that it had lasted for a year or two – actually more like two than one. And yes, one had to assume, that, at the beginning there had to have been a certain enthusiasm on her part.

Now, if you look at this logically, deductively, where do you end up? Peggy is a truly wonderful person who says she totally likes you. But once upon a time she must have felt something similar for Miller. You trust Peggy's judgement implicitly. Q.E.D: Miller must have his good points. She probably got his jokes, just as she gets yours. And if she got his jokes and she gets your jokes, then probably you'd get his jokes also. If you only got to know him, you'd very possibly end up in a close, meaningful relationship with Miller, which, if things had gone a different way in or around puberty might even –

Only that isn't the way it works. Not with a love rival. You don't think, if she liked him he can't be all bad. You think what a total, utter slimeball he is. You think he's an untrustworthy, scheming Svengali who's somehow gulled this sweet, sensible girl into behaving completely out of character and into falling, like a drugged-up Moonie, for his devious, dastardly ways. How else to explain what she ever saw in him?

And you think something else too. You think, 'I must save her from Miller's evil clutches'. Even if you don't actually think it, in quite those terms. And even if, by this time, she's pretty much got out of Miller's evil clutches all on her own.

Actually you don't think that. You don't think at all.

What you do is leave work early on a day you haven't arranged to see Peggy, and hang around outside the office – but not too close, on the next corner in fact – until she comes out of the revolving doors. Then, doing what you imagine a gumshoe would do – keeping your distance, holding a newspaper that you pretend to be reading, making sure you're near a pillar you can stand behind or a doorway you can nip into – you follow Peggy down onto the subway and get on to her train. Then, hoping you've correctly remembered which stop she mentioned that she gets off at, you wait until the very last second before you get off the train. Then you sneak a look around the emptying platform, pray you don't walk straight into her, and, would you believe it, you catch sight of the back of her as she pushes through the turnstile.

You follow her out of the station, across the lights, up the street and then stop about twenty yards away and carefully observe – whilst hoping like hell that Miller isn't watching you out of the window – as she turns the key in the brownstone and walks in. Then, feeling slightly soiled and ashamed of yourself, but also slightly elated and a bit like you're drunk, you turn round and go home, and you spend the evening watching telly, during which time you have to sit through about six Miller commercials – "It's Millertime!" – as though the great media buyer in the sky – not that you believe in any great thing in the sky – has deliberately gone out of his way to cause you deep psychological pain.

And then the next day, you take the morning off, take the subway back up to Peggy's place, figuring that that slimeball Miller is an actor, and we all know what actors are like, the lazy bastards, they don't have regular jobs so they sleep all day. Then you ring every buzzer by the door and ask if Miller Prince is there – you're gagging to say Miller Pronski but you manage to restrain yourself – until somebody with a very deep, dark brown voice says, pleasantly enough, "Yes, I'm Miller Prince."

And then, although you'd had some vague, half-arsed plan to ask Miller Prince/Pronski to come out and be a man, and tell him that you loved Peggy and that he was nothing to her anymore and, and, well, you didn't quite know what after that, you suddenly realise in the yawning silence after he's said 'Yes, I'm Miller Prince' that you've taken complete leave of your senses and that you need to get out of there pronto.

And then you run off down the street and keep running for about six blocks until you're knackered and sweating and wheezing like a man of eighty and you realise how unfit you are, and you make a brief mental note to do something about it, not that you ever do. And then, having got your breath back, thinking 'well, that told him' while at the same time feeling like a complete pillock because it clearly hadn't, you find yourself muttering, in some weird, meant-to-be-menacing Clint Eastwood-y whisper, "Just you wait, pal. Soon it really will be Miller-time!"

And then you go back to the office, make some feeble excuse for being late and disappear into Brett and Bart's office, persuade them to get the bong out, not that that takes a lot of persuasion, and get as high as a kite.

*

That night Bart and Brett dragged me off to a party at a photographer's loft somewhere in the meat packing district. I was already several sheets to the wind or whatever the druggie equivalent of that is. Now – I want to set the record straight here;

despite the impression I may have been giving, drugs aren't and never have been my thing. Despite being a teenager in the sixties, I was one of those who remember it well, and thus, as they say, couldn't have been there. I didn't have a joint until I was twenty-three, never took LSD or any chemical drug as I was unshakable in my conviction that if anyone was going to attempt to fly off a building it would be me, and although I was, later, to attempt to snort a line of coke, it did sod all for me and I never tried it again. In London, prior to my going to New York, I did used to enjoy a spliff with some friends in Hammersmith who grew their own and dried it in an airing cupboard, but it was nothing more than the mildest sort of giggle prompter and munchie inducer.

When I came to New York and was drawn into the orbit of Brett and Bart and one or two others, my intake did increase a notch or two, and the stuff was a whole lot stronger than I'd been used to. But, frankly, compared with most people I have known in the media world – of which advertising is, I suppose, a bit – I was, and am, and have always been, a total amateur.

So when we rode up in the big industrial elevator into the party in the photographer's loft, I was as the proverbial babe in the woods. Actually, having already had a good go at Bart and Brett's bong I wasn't even possessed of the danger sniffing faculties that even the most innocent and unsuspecting of babes would have had upon entering the world, never mind the woods.

Beer in hand – I was so out of it, it might even have been a Miller – I launched myself into the blurry groups of models and fashion people and hairdressers and hangers on. I was ready for anything and prepared for nothing. Someone handed me a joint and I took it. In all, I suppose – I really wasn't counting – I had about half a dozen puffs and then I began to feel absolutely terrified. I staggered out into a corridor, found some steps and slumped on them. The world was turning through its axis and for the next six or eight hours the bubble in my personal spirit level zipped up and down like a pinball. Eventually, somehow, I found my way back home, and fell asleep, totally shattered.

To this day, I have no idea what was in that joint – I suspect it was laced with something called PCP which I believe is a pig tranquilliser – but I do know that if that was the case, and I were a pig, I would make damn sure that no pig psychiatrist ever came near me with it.

I awoke the next day, sweating and scared, but with just enough brainpower left to realise that I had to get a grip and fast. The problem wasn't Brett or Bart or the bong. It was me. It was New York. Or rather it was me *in* New York. New York is a city of extremes. Extreme buildings. Extreme weather. Extreme noise. New York is a place to set the pulse racing, so if you want to stay sane and in control, you want to start off nice and slow. But I hadn't, and I was seriously concerned that I had begun to lose my bearings.

I got up and showered, and struggled down to the diner. As I sat on the bar stool at the counter drinking the so-called coffee and waiting for my very late breakfast to be plonked down in front of me, I started to think about Peggy and wondered if she wasn't part of it too. No, not quite that. I wondered if my extreme reaction to Peggy wasn't part of it too. Was this intensity of feeling that I had for her not partly, at least, due to the effect of being in New York? If I had been anywhere else – certainly in London – wouldn't I have been much more measured? Context is everything, isn't that what they say? On the other hand, when I tried to concentrate on her and only her, and zone in on what I truly felt about her and shut out everything else, I still felt the same. I was nuts about her. Simple as that.

And that's what I remember about that day. Drinking this foul coffee. Batting these ideas around and around. And never being sure what I really thought.

I also remember a line I read somewhere around this time:

If you're going to get carried away, New York is the place where they are going to come and get you.

81

CHAPTER 7

MID-AIR, COTE D'AZUR AND RICHMOND
UPON THAMES, 1999

The air hostess or flight stewardess or cabin attendant or whatever they called them in 1999 smiled at me sweetly as she stretched down and across the empty seat next to me to hand me my complimentary pretzels.

"I like your suit, Monsieur," she said, eyebrows arching slightly as she caught sight of the scarlet lining of my unbuttoned jacket. "Tres chic."

"Thank you," I said, and was about to generously add 'it was a present from my wife', when I stopped myself. First, why was I telling this to a complete stranger? And second, well, because I suddenly became acutely conscious that I was travelling alone – i.e. without my wife. Somehow that seemed significant.

This time the Air France plane had managed to get off the ground and would carry me, I sincerely hoped, to the South of France. (Is there any place anywhere with a name more evocative of glamour and privilege? Just to say you are going the South of France makes you feel all jetsetty inside. If you want bonus points on the E to P scale, there's no better place to be seen to be going.)

It was early June, and that meant it was time for the world's greatest freebie – also known as the annual advertising festival in Cannes. I say 'freebie' because I was a one third shareholder in BWD and so, technically if indirectly, would be putting my hand deep into my Ozwald Boateng pocket to pay for the very splendid junket that I and quite a few other BWDers would be on this week. But it always felt like a freebie; perhaps it was because, to ad folk of my generation, this was the 'Cannes' that was embedded into your subconscious when you first went. Invariably, as happened with me, you would be sent off there at a juniorish stage in your career as a reward for some good work you had done. (I don't mean 'good work' as in 'good works', I mean 'good work' as in a good press campaign or TV commercial.) It amused one's world weary superiors to see young Andrew's eyes opened to the free lunches and free dinners and free hotel rooms – with room service! – and to the non-stop parties and the waterskiing and to the waiters in bow ties bringing champagne to your sunbed – always assuming you could take any more champagne – citron presse if you couldn't. ("Don't know what it is but I'll have it anyway, it's free isn't it?") A few free days in Cannes gave you a brief glimpse of the goodies that might really be available behind the golden doors of the inner sanctum, and acted as a useful incentive for you to give the agency just a few extra drops of your blood. And not to be sneezed at was the added bonus that it made all the other young wannabees in the Creative Department as jealous as hell that you'd been chosen to go and they hadn't.

The official purpose of the Cannes Film Festival was to offer delegates a chance to see the best television commercials from around the world made in the previous year, and from these, the very best would be selected to win prizes – a noble purpose I am sure you will agree. The prizes, known as Cannes Lions – Bronze, Silver or Gold – would be handed out in the Palais de something on the closing Saturday evening before a packed crowd of paralytic Finns, South Koreans, Egyptians, Luxemburgers, Venezuelans and, for all I know, Inuits, who would cheer or hurl abuse depending on whether or not they approved of the Judges' choices. The judges would be a small group of people, none of whom, as a rule, could speak the same language, who had the great good fortune to be stuck in a basement from dawn 'til dusk, from Monday to Friday, yawning their way through a gazillion indecipherable spots from Burkino Faso to the Faroe Islands while the rest of us of were gallivanting about the Croisette. Having the esteemed honour of being asked to be a judge at Cannes was, I always felt, to draw the very shortest of short straws, and was a damn good reason to be nice to your PA lest she should decide to take revenge on you by accepting such an invitation on your behalf.

Of course, in today's world of the Internet and instant digital communications etc., you can, at the bash of a button, see all the commercials from Burkino Faso to the Faroe Islands that you might care to, and it is a measure of the true value of Cannes to advertising people that they still flock to the festival in their pissed-up thousands, global economic meltdown or no. (Sadly, I am no longer in a position to get my snout into the trough.)

Cannes marks the end – in so far as it ever ends – of the advertising awards season, and this year had been a humdinger for BWD. We had picked up the usual horrendous bits of perspex and fake brass at 'Creative Circle', and the 'British Television Advertising Awards' – and oh, I forget most of the rest, but those too. One I could never forget was the Oscar of the advertising awards world – a 'DADA', an acronym for Designers and Art Directors Association, a stodgy sounding bunch to the uninitiated perhaps, but a 'DADA' was the crème de la crème. And "this year, the Silver Pencil for best thirty second television commercial" – yes, they awarded pencilly shaped prizes, like Cannes gave out Lion shaped thingies – "goes to Bradley Williams Dutton for …" – Do you know, I cannot, for the life of me remember the name of the product? Still, that's advertising for you.

What I can remember is that it was a cat food of some kind,

that Will and Lucille had come up with the idea and written it, and that, as a result, their star in the London advertising firmament was waxing powerful strong, and that they were becoming increasingly poachable by our competitor agencies. This meant that sooner or later, we knew – and they knew – we would have to bung them a few extra thou to keep them. Rules of the game – we didn't really mind.

But by the time Cannes came around – possibly even because I had become a little distracted by the Polaroid of Peggy and associated personal matters – there were quite a few things I hadn't yet got around to doing, and giving them their rise was one of them. This was an error, one smallish reason being that, having won a DADA Silver Pencil (hugely prestigious) they were hot favourites to pick up a Gold Lion (goldier but less prestigious), and this would give them another arrow in their cough-up-or-we-fuck-off quiver. Naturally, Will and Lucille would be amongst the BWD people swanning about Cannes this year, as they were all but certain to be called up for a gong and a bow.

Being principally a festival about 'creativity', the 'suits' – the poor fools who were forced to deal with an agency's clients – did not usually get to go to Cannes and were made to remain, embittered and muttering, in London. But should a piece of work – I use the phrase advisedly – which had been done for one of their clients win one of those coveted Lions, then they would be permitted to call the said client or clients – you would be amazed how many there turned out to be when there was a chance of a free trip to Cannes – and accompany them, whooping and hollering, to the glorious S of F to join us. Therefore, as the rules should have applied, we would, if things went as expected, get an advance call with the good news, and then transmit the signal to the relevant suit in London to grab the cat food clients and bring 'em on down.

But, for a reason I was not yet to fully appreciate, Vince, who was not the relevant suit in this case, but, as Head of Account Management, the chief suit, as you might say, on all BWD accounts, had decided to come to Cannes, having unilaterally decided that he would be the one to do the requisite feting of the cat food clients. This was odd because a) he had never done this before, b) it was counting our cat food chickens before they had hatched, and c) the guy who was the relevant suit would, understandably, be more than a little teed off, and why upset him?

And there was another rather rum thing about Vince's decision to come to Cannes. He was coming without his wife. What self-respecting wife of an adman would ever refuse a free week in Cannes? Yes, alright, I know mine would, and had, but I think I have set out some of the background for her decision. So far as I was aware, Vince and his wife Carol, who had only been married for a couple of years, were still at the two bugs in a rug stage, so to know that he was sitting a couple of rows back from me in the Air France plane might have made me scratch my chin a little harder had I not been so engrossed.

Yes, engrossed in Peggy. Because for much of the flight I sat there taking the Polaroid of Peggy in and out of my pocket and gazing and reflecting upon it. I was thinking not just about her or the 'us' that I supposed she and I once to have been, but trying to examine what was really going in my head. What were the forces – even sub-conscious ones, perhaps – that really were driving me in all this?

I wasn't aware of having deliberately brought the Polaroid with me – it had stayed in the pocket of this suit since I had found it there on my aborted trip to Paris with Geoff – but, I asked myself, was I actually surprised to find that I had it to hand? Perhaps I could even have subconsciously chosen to wear the Ozwald Boateng – as a matter of fact, it really should have been more of a tee-shirt and jeans kind of a trip – in order that I would be able to unwittingly put my hand in my pocket and go, oops, gosh what do I have here? – Would you believe it, it's the Polaroid of Peggy? And if such a thing were possible, then why bother with such self-deceit? Was it that I felt guilty that I was, in merely thinking about Peggy, betraying Alison just as she had implied? Alright, not just thinking about, but obsessing over, but even so, nothing had actually happened – how could it when my co-respondent was only a fading image on a twenty-year-old Polaroid? And besides, why should I feel any guilt towards Alison when she was increasingly and deliberately distancing herself from me; wasn't her refusal to come to Cannes just that attitude made manifest?

And so there I sat on the plane, thinking, thinking, thinking. And not looking up, in case I caught Vince's eye should he pass my row on the way to the loo or wherever. I had told him at the check-in I didn't want to sit next to him because I had work to do and needed space to spread out. But what I really wanted was space to think – and now I thought about it, we'd had that slightly awkward conversation at the check-in desk before I had 'found' the Polaroid of Peggy. Increasingly, this finding looked like less and less of an accidental discovery. In which case ...

*

I had entered into this phase of deep self-examination – or would-be but not very deep self-examination – when I went to see Donald McEwan.

Geoff's thoughtful response to my blubbing confession in the BA Executive Lounge had not been ignored. "You need a fucking shrink!" he had kindly counselled and I saw his point. So I went to see Dr Donald McEwan MD MAPsych PHD at his basement consulting room near Richmond Hill. Or to be more accurate, I went back to see him. For Dr Donald McEwan and I were old sparring chums. I don't think anything could describe our relationship better than that. He had first been recommended to me some years before, and I'd had spells of – well, not exactly treatment, and not analysis, so, let's just say 'appointments' – after various dodgy periods of my life.

The pattern that developed was: I would get in a neurotic tizz about something or other – the emptiness of my life, the black holes I sank into in the dead of night, the usual kind of thing – and I would call Donald. He would then kindly and unfailingly make time for me, and I'd rush off to receive the balm that only he could ever supply. He wasn't exactly a Freudian, nor a Jungian nor an Adlerian, at least, not I think, with me. He knew all the theory backwards I am sure – had indeed written lots of learned books and lectured for years at London teaching hospitals – but with me he practised what I came to think of as a uniquely Donaldian form of therapy. He knew I would never survive the rigours of analysis, and never tried to push me into it. What I really wanted was a mixture of cosy reassurance and a bit of an argument – usually about something abstract like the nature of feeling or what is instinct and what is intuition? – in other words, anything to distract me from my real problems – and he played his part to a tee. After each group of these sessions – sometimes lasting a few months, sometimes maybe a year or so – I would decide I didn't really need Donald any more, and then summarily end our relationship until the next time. He never made any objection to being so casually treated, always seemed to welcome me back, and he was never – no matter what I brought up from the darkest depths of my imagination – the least bit judgemental. When I was with him, he seemed to think his only purpose was to make me feel better, which, in my experience, is not an idea that has much currency with other medics. My bottom line on shrinks – and I make no distinction between psychologists, psychiatrists, analysts, therapists, whatever – is that they are, essentially, secular priests and most of them are as unconvincing as the religious kind. Donald was the exception that proved the rule.

It took more than a few hesitant minutes but I finally finished telling Donald the story of the Polaroid of Peggy, of its discovery and of my obsession with it, of the worrying disintegration of my relations with Alison, of my loss of interest in my work, and of whatever else it was from which my chest demanded to be unburdened. Donald, who had listened carefully throughout but with no more apparent reaction than the occasional raising of a wise old cove's eyebrow, then sat in thoughtful silence for several moments while he arranged his response. It gave me the chance to steep myself in the atmosphere of his cosy little consulting room, which, with its pair of mismatched woolly armchairs (tartan throws to cover the threadbare bits) and its heatless real-flame gas fire that never seemed to be turned off, was such a peaceful contrast to the early-adopter chic of New Pemberley or the relentless funkiness of the BWD offices. Whenever I entered it, I felt as though I were stepping into some sort of retreat. (Not that I would ever set foot in a proper retreat. Ten minutes of monastic silence would do my head in.)

"Do you not think," he asked in his soft Aberdonian burr, such a reassuringly solid, WASPy sound to flighty Jewish neurotics like me, "that this, eh, business with the photo might not, eh, be symptom rather than cause?"

"You mean, I am totally fucked up and sooner or later I was going to have a major crisis and the picture was just one of any number of things that might have set it off?"

"I'm not sure I would put it in, eh, quite those terms, Andrew, but yes, something like that."

"Well, is that what you think?"

Fortunately, Donald was not one of those bloody annoying shrinky types who insist on answering every 'what do you think?' question with a 'what do you think?' back. Instead, having planted that idea – or rather, having watered it, because, of course, the same thought had already occurred to me – he tried another line.

"And why do you think it is, that in all the years we've known each other, Andrew, you've never mentioned Peggy before. My memory may not be quite what it was when I was younger, but, eh, we've spoken a lot about your past Andrew, a lot, but I cannot ever recall you telling me about this girl, Peggy."

Hadn't I?

"Haven't I?"

"No."

"Oh."

Hmm. I pondered. I have the sort of mind that has a superficial knowledge about a lot of things – politics, art, books, music, sport, whatever is in the news today – and could write about one hundred seemingly salient words, but no more, on pretty well anything. It's exactly the sort of mind you need to write an ad, but not so useful for profound introspection. However it is my default position, and, having spent half my adult life talking to shrinks of one colour or another, psychostuff is another of those subjects that I am glibly versed in. And from this not very deep well of knowledge, I came up with this inspired line of argument.

"Are you suggesting that if Peggy had had real importance in my life, I would have mentioned her at some other point during the past ten years?"

"Eh yes, something like that."

"But could it not mean the very opposite. That it – my time with Peggy I mean – was so important I was repressing it?"

"Repressing it, you say?" Donald didn't look convinced.

"Yes, couldn't it be that this is a sort of 'recovered memory' – you know like you hear about victims of childhood abuse having? Something buried so deep because I wanted to deny it. But, no, Donald hear me out—"

He was shifting in his seat and beginning to smile.

"But Donald, but – could it not be that when I saw her picture, I simply couldn't deny it any longer?"

"We-hell," said Donald, "theoretically, I don't suppose one could categorically rule it out but—"

But I wasn't thinking about the buts. I was feeling tremendously cheered up. I had scored a debating point – tendentious, true, but not entirely implausible – and as had often happened in my sessions with Donald I was content with that. Rather than actually suffer the pain of seriously trying to get to the bottom of whatever my problem was, I would manoeuvre us into a sort of verbal fencing match, the sort of thing I really enjoyed, and challenge myself to come up with a point that might have this brilliant man, with his dozens of degrees and doctorates, scratching his head. In other words, I could show him – as I always wanted to show everyone – I'm a fucking adman aren't I? – how clever I was.

And, for the rest of the session, as sceptical as he obviously was about my repressed/recovered memory theory, Donald was unable to convincingly, entirely, one hundred per cent, beyond all possible doubt, rule it out. (That's one of the best things about shrinkery; it's all basically guesswork. None of them can really prove – really prove, as in show it under a microscope – a damn thing.)

As I walked out of the door and back up the steps to street level and what passed for my real life, his farewell address, accompanied by a wry smile and a rueful shake of the head, was:

"I will say this, Andrew. If you had my job, you'd make a bloody fortune."

That, of course, was exactly what I wanted to hear from him. I told you he knew how to make me feel better.

*

Cannes went exactly as anticipated. Until the last moment. Of the last evening, of the last day.

We had done all the usual things; eaten confit de this and drunk chateau de that at Michelin starred restaurants (two minimum) in Mougin and St. Paul de Vence. (Insanely expensive naturellement, but, whenever possible, and that was almost all the time, at somebody else's expense.) We had partied the night away with luscious young floozies and pushed them into swimming pools (and jumped in after them) at sumptuous villas hired for the week by film production companies or music companies or post-production companies or whomever else might have something to flog and surmised that we might be the poor suckers who could be conned into paying for it. We had drunk ourselves into a stupor, night after night, in the Martinez bar, gladhanding all the freeloaders from Serbia to Surinam who had made the pilgrimage to the Cote d'Azure for this glorious gathering of the international brotherhood of advertising.

And, as expected, we, BWD, had picked up a whole pride of Cannes Lions, Bronze, Silver and Gold, culminating in the award to Will and Lucille's cat food commercial, which won the Gold Lion for best thirty-second commercial in the highly competitive groceries/non-food category. (Food for animals didn't count as proper food.) The top cat food client, the Marketing Director, who last year had been in the beer business, and next year would move onto savoury snacks, a sweating, paunchy thirty-five-year-old who already looked fifty, wept tears of pride or envy or pure alcohol as Will and Lucille went on stage at the packed Palais de wotsit to claim their prize.

After that, BWD, having hired a fleet of black limos, took everyone from the agency and all the cat food clients and all the people from the production company and all their wives, husbands, partners, and one night stands back to our hotel – the coolest place to stay in Cannes except it wasn't in Cannes, it was the art deco palace, La Belle Rive, along the coast in Juans Les Pins. There, in the balmy open air on a clear, starry night, we held a banquet – nothing less – for fifty or sixty, however many we could squeeze on to the table in the walled terrace overlooking the gleaming black ocean. We, BWD, were the toast of Cannes, or pretended we were, and seemed intent on celebrating by drowning in champagne and choking to death on foie gras and courgette flowers. So far, so good.

Although I had spent the week without Alison and, in the occasional moments of downtime between freebies, had lain alone on my sunbed by the Med, and spent a fair bit of time dwelling on the true significance of the Polaroid of Peggy, I could not, in the end, fail to be caught up in the spirit of things. I sat in the middle of one side of the table, basking in the reflected glory of our success, whilst modestly declaiming to anyone who would listen that, really, it was nothing to do with me – as indeed, most of it wasn't. Opposite sat Vince, his left arm around the shoulder of the top cat food client who was getting drunker and sweatier by the minute, and with his other arm, his right, around the shoulder – the satiny, bronzed, bare shoulder – of Lucille, who, dressed in flowing white diaphanous floor length dress, and high on the drug of public acclaim, looked nothing less than ravishing. And, as one couldn't fail to notice, she seemed to radiate happiness; she was positively beaming.

After dessert we called for yet more champagne. We toasted Will, we toasted Lucille. We toasted the cat food clients. And the cat food clients toasted us. And then, as the army of waiters arrived with the coffee, came the first sign that something might be going awry. Will tapped me on the shoulder and asked if he might have a word. In private.

"Of course," I said, grabbing a bottle of champagne and a couple of glasses and beckoning him to follow me down the steps. I thought we might have our private chat at one of the empty tables down by the beach bar.

The chat didn't take long. Will told me he had been offered a position as Creative Director at one of our rival agencies and that he planned to take it. My first reaction, predictably, was to ask him if we could do anything to keep him, but he shook his head, smiled, and assured me that he had told nobody about this apart from Lucille, who had known for a couple of days, but that his new agency would be briefing 'Campaign' – the advertising trade rag – on Monday. He then rose from the table, thanked me for all that BWD had done for him, and walked away, leaving me there to regret that I hadn't given him the rise he should have had after the previous cat food commercial awards triumphs. Not that I imagined my oversight had really made all that much difference, but it couldn't have helped. I then started to vacantly muse about the scene in 'The Godfather', one of my all time faves, when Marlon Brando returns from the meeting with the Mafia bosses and says, referring to Sonny's murder at the toll booth, 'Until this night, I never knew it was Barzini, all along.' That was kind of how I felt about Will. All the time I'd been thinking it was Lucille whose ambition we should be wary of, and now, it was Will who had completely blindsided us. And then I got to thinking about Lucille, and how we had better act fast now to buy her off, before somebody came in with an offer for her too. It wouldn't look too clever that we were losing one of our two biggest creative stars at the moment of their greatest success – thus allowing Will's new agency to grab the 'Campaign' headlines and tap into the cat food glory that should have been BWD's alone – but to lose both of them, would smack not just of carelessness but of downright incompetence.

And then I started to think about Lucille, and it was then that I started to get an uneasy feeling that maybe there was a bigger, uglier picture that I wasn't yet seeing. If Lucille had known since before dinner about Will's leaving, how come she had looked so deliriously happy? If she was half as ruthlessly competitive as I'd always believed her to be, then surely, she would be absolutely fuming that Will had landed a job like that before her?

I tried to examine all the possible explanations. Maybe she too had a piece of news for me that I wouldn't want to hear – maybe my failure to give Will and Lucille their post DADA rises really had upset them, and they were going to take spectacular revenge with a lethal one-two. Or, maybe, she was playing it ultra-cool and was going to let me do all the worrying, in the belief that this was the way to screw a really good deal out of BWD. (The mild panic I was getting into suggested that, if this was the case, she was right.) Or maybe she appeared to be so happy because she was genuinely pleased for Will and thoroughly content with her lot and … and …

and I discounted that possible explanation pretty well immediately.

As it happened I wasn't even close. I went back up to rejoin the party and to tell Vince what was going on, but when I pulled him aside, I got another shock.

"Actually mate, I already knew."

"What! How?"

"Lucille told me."

"Lucille told you? Why the fuck didn't you tell me?"

"Well, I dunno mate, you've been so remote lately – you know like on the plane out and everything and down by the beach – kind of into yourself – that I didn't think I should bother you."

"Didn't think you should bother me? I'm your fucking partner. I'm the Creative Director. Will works in my department – did work in my department. I need to sort Lucille out."

"Oh I don't think you need to worry about Lucille. Lucille and I get on pretty well, you know Andrew—"

"No, I don't fucking well know—"

"And I've come up with a package—"

"YOU'VE DONE WHAT!"

"—that I think she's gonna buy."

Something inside told me that if the steam coming out of my ears wasn't going to be the prelude to a full scale nuclear melt-down, I had better try to be a little calmer. So between clenched teeth, I said as evenly I could, "And what precisely is in this package?"

"We-ell, more money of course—" He paused as though he had something to add.

"Yes. And?"

"And a week's extra holiday. And—" He paused again.

"And?"

"—a seat on the board."

"A seat on the fucking board?! Are you fucking insane? You can't offer someone a seat on the board without asking Geoff and me!" My internal plutonium rods were in serious overload again.

"Er yeah, well, I did ask Geoff."

"And he was in agreement, was he?"

That wasn't intended as a rhetorical question but even before the words were out of my mouth, I realised it might as well have been. I sat down, utterly deflated and looked up at Vince like a beaten dog.

He sat beside me and rested his hand gently on my arm.

"Look mate, you know you haven't been on top of things recently. Lucille came to see me and said she and Will were really upset that you'd let the DADA thing go by with barely a by your leave—"

"What do you mean? I sent a memo round the office—"

"Yeah, well, she said they'd had about enough and I was going to speak to you and then the next thing I know, we're here, and she tells me Will's off and I thought, you know what, we really can't afford to lose her. Even forgetting all these awards, she's special Andrew, she really is."

Special? Really special? For the first time, the precise shape of the 'package' was beginning to take shape in my mind. But I said nothing, just nodding meekly. Perhaps taking this as a signal that I was beginning to see things from his point of view, he went on, "Look mate, think about it. She's winning every fucking award known to man. She's getting a serious profile now. Did you know 'The Times' want to do a piece on her? Well, no, you wouldn't but they do. Andrew, she's a woman, a fucking beautiful woman, she's whip smart and she's young. This is 1999 mate. We're three guys and we're all in our forties—"

Here he paused and gave me a meaningful look, very possibly to remind me that in a very few months one of we three guys would not be in our forties. And then he continued, and I was soon to realise that all the other bombshells he'd dropped were just to soften me up, because now came Hiroshima.

"Just think Andrew, with Lucille as Deputy Creative Director, BWD can really kick on."

At last I found the strength to speak.

"So, am I to understand that you and Geoff have agreed that Lucille will be appointed to the board as Deputy Creative Director."

Vince took his hand off my arm and looked me straight in the eye. He was all business now.

"Yes Andrew, we have."

"Don't we need a board meeting to decide that sort of thing?"

"Do you really want us to have a board meeting to do it? Do you?"

He didn't wait for my answer because that really was a rhetorical question. He stood up and walked away from the table. And then after a few steps, he turned and came back, and leaned down and whispered in my ear.

"And listen mate, you know the rules. What happens in Vegas, stays in Vegas. Okay?"

And then he walked away again and up to Lucille who was talking to the top cat food client, both of them with their backs to where I sat. Vince put his right arm round her satiny bronzed shoulders just as he had been doing earlier, but this time, he didn't put the other arm round the top cat food client. The picture was quite different and crystal clear.

Predictably, I was feeling very sorry for myself. And, despite the fact that it was well after midnight in London, pathetically, I pulled out my mobile phone and called home to speak to Alison. A sleepy voice answered; it was the South African nanny. Alison wasn't at home.

CHAPTER 8

NEW YORK, 1979

"You mean anal?" asked Peggy over the lemon cheesecake.

And she wasn't using the word in any metaphorical sense, as in someone being anal. She meant anal as in directly connected with the anus, as in someone doing anal. And she seemed not to bat an eyelid as she said it, as sunnily unconcerned as if she had been discussing the possibility of having a cup of tea. Which, as it happens, at the time I was. Or rather, I was having not a cup of tea, but a glass. We were in the Russian Tearoom on West 57th, a week or so after the madness with Miller, and my subsequent unhinging at the photographers party. (I had, after the sound morning-after talking-to I had given myself, managed to take things a little more steadily – except where Peggy was concerned. I was as infatuated as ever.)

I can't recall exactly what I had said that had led to her asking the question, but, whatever it was, I am pretty sure that wasn't what I'd meant and Peggy had, to coin an appropriate phrase, got things completely arse about face. I can remember that my response was, in best comedy fashion, to spit half of my mouthful of tea straight out and to choke on the rest. This was 1979 remember, and the world was not quite as anally aware as it is in 2015. I don't mean to sound like a prude, it wasn't a subject that I was disinterested in, just one that I couldn't have imagined broaching – at least not over tea and cheesecake, and certainly not in the Russian Tearoom where the average age of the clientele seemed to be about eighty – for some inexplicable reason Peggy loved the place – and, I imagined, not the sort of people who were in the habit of hearing the word anal much used in public. (Bowels on the other hand would have been a different matter. They looked like exactly the sort of people who talked about bowels non-stop.)

While I struggled for life, Peggy casually added a rider, "'Cos you can't just do it, you know. You've got to prepare for it."

I chose not to go into precisely what she meant by that, though I have to confess I have always rather regretted that I didn't – I can't be certain that it wouldn't have led to an opportunity forever lost; it was a subject that we never did get back to. Instead, I made a half-hearted attempt to mop the tea off my shirt, muttering something like "No, no, I didn't mean that at all, what on earth are you on about?" and abruptly suggested we get the check. Peggy thought my embarrassment hilarious.

What this little scene shows is first, that we had, by this stage, got around to talking about sex, if not yet engaging in it, and second, that Peggy was much more than the nice Jewish girl one might have taken her to be. At least, that was the way I looked at it. If I was a little shocked at the implication that she might have indulged in such practises, I didn't think of her as being in the least bit diminished by it. Quite the reverse. To begin with, I have always liked the idea of a woman with a past – and this suggested she might have had one. And I was more than a little impressed by how unfazed she had seemed to be. It was that American thing, which I so envied, of seemingly being entirely at ease with everything to do with sex, so unlike we repressed Brits. Or, despite the popular myth – popular in America anyway – maybe I am doing a disservice to my fellow countrymen. Maybe it was just me.

*

99

Sex. We were moving towards it. Slowly, by the standards of 2015, I will grant you. Glacially even. And not too sharpish even by the standards of 1979. But, in mitigation, let me remind you yet again that I did have the Miller problem to contend with. 'Carpe diem' is all very well but you have to have somewhere for the action to happen. What was wrong with my place, you may ask? Pretty much everything is the answer. The Playboy Mansion it wasn't. I had, you may remember, made a half-hearted attempt to lure her back there on the night of our first date, but in view of the state of the place, it was probably no bad thing that she declined.

But a man can take only so much. Caution was about to be thrown to the wind. After our hurried exit from the Russian Tearooms, and some sort of equilibrium had been restored after a stroll through Central Park and a bite to eat somewhere, I did for a second time, at long last, ask Peggy to come back to my place.

But sometimes a man should take a little more. (Usually at the times when he can only take so much.) Caution should be kept firmly in hand. As I'd suspected would be the case, Peggy wasn't much impressed with my sub-fusc sub-let and its faded furnishings and who could blame her? I wasn't the most fastidious of housekeepers – I really did no more than maintain an uneasy truce with the cockroaches squatting in the kitchen – and then there was the cat. Part of the sub-letting deal was that I should look after the landlord's manky (tom)cat. I'd never much cared for cats and I found this one particularly unappealing – never even bothered to learn his name then so I can't share it with you now – but the apartment came with the cat or the apartment didn't come at all, and it came a lot cheaper than most. However, possibly because I wasn't the most diligent carer, his litter tray was sniffable from the moment you had turned the six locks on the front door. This didn't enhance the romantic atmosphere. Though Peggy was willing to do some heavy petting on the sagging sofa she refused – as we used to say when I was a boy – to go all the way. (Younger readers may find this part of the story stretches their credulity.) Ever the optimist, I chose to believe that she was saving herself for a more convivial setting or at least until she was free to spend the night, but when this was to be I had no idea.

It was Jerry Seinfeld who solved the problem. Indirectly perhaps, but he played the pivotal role.

*

Shortly after the tea-room incident, I was sent off to the Chicago office for a few days – I was needed to "help put out a fire on a hot chilli sauce", as my Creative Supervisor, thrilled with his own joke, put it – and so Peggy and I had a little break from each other. Absence, as in the case of the Mono affair, did just what they say it does. My conviction that she was *the one* grew deeper every moment I was away from her, and as soon as I returned, I rushed straight down to her office to present her with a little gift I had brought her. I had spent hours trudging round O'Hare looking for just the right thing – nothing too corny. As usual I couldn't make up my mind and eventually heard the tannoy announcer insist that 'Andrew Williams go to Gate 24 immediately.' So, in my panic, I flung a few dollars at the hapless sales girl and grabbed something I had seen and unequivocally rejected two or three tours around the airport before, but which now seemed to be the only thing to hand. It was a novelty cigarette table lighter, a miniature Marlboro cowboy whose ten gallon hat you tipped from the back. This engaged the flywheel, which in turn caused the spark that sent a flame roaring out the back of his horse, its tail rising just in time to avoid conflagration. On a plaque on the little plastic plinth, it said 'A Gift From The Windy City.' I fretted on the plane all the way back to New York that it really wasn't Peggy's kind of thing, and not only because she didn't smoke. But, having nothing else to give her and hoping, I suppose, that it really would be the thought that counts, I duly presented it. She seemed absolutely thrilled, declared it 'just hilarious' and insisted on running around demonstrating it to all the not-Peggys in the casting department. I did suspect that maybe she was laughing just a little too hard, but the possibility that she might be faking it – and the kindness that implied – made me love her all the more.

She was still enthusing about the Marlboro man and his horse at the coffee shop where we had lunch later that day.

"Jerry would love this," she mused, as she ignited the lighter for the thousandth time. "He would absolutely love it."

"Who is Jerry?"

She looked up at me, somehow surprised that I hadn't divined who she meant.

"Jerry," she repeated. "Jerry Seinfeld."

"Who's Jerry Seinfeld?"

She set the cowboy and his horse on the table.

"You don't know who Jerry Seinfeld is?"

Hard to believe now, but at that time I, along with just about every other living Englishman, had never heard of Jerry Seinfeld. But Peggy, along with a growing band of in-the-know aficionados, was already a major league fan.

"Jerry Seinfeld," she patiently explained, "is this incredibly amazing new comedian. I mean he's not *that* new, he's been around a couple years, I think. But he is funny, I mean *really* funny. He just like talks about everyday stuff, stuff he just comes across. Andy you have to see him. Check out the 'Voice'. He's doing all the comedy clubs."

To this day, I have never managed to work out why Peggy thought the cowboy with the farting horse would have proved so irresistible to Jerry – in some post-modern, ironic way, I have always assumed, without quite knowing how – but I didn't pursue the point and it didn't matter. What her remark did do was inspire me to look in that week's 'Village Voice' to see where he might be playing, and what I discovered was that, one week hence, on Saturday night at

9 p.m., Jerry Seinfeld, the hottest new comedian in America, would be playing at The Blue Mongoose in Stamford, Connecticut.

A plan began to be hatched. I asked Bart or Brett where Stamford was, and they confirmed what I had thought, that it was about an hour or so from Manhattan, about fifty miles away, close to the Connecticut, New York State border. At the next free moment, which just happened to be the very next moment, I took a break from the office – telling Laverne, the receptionist on my floor, that I was going to Barnes and Noble to get a book about something I was working on. And in a sense, all senses really apart from the critical one, I wasn't deceiving her. Because I was indeed going to Barnes and Noble to get a book, and it was for something I was working on: the most important thing I was working on, in fact. The seduction of Peggy.

The book I chose was 'Country Inns of the Tri-state Area' by Karen Brown. Not a title to set the heart racing you might think, but in my case, in this case, you would have been wrong. The sales assistant at Barnes and Noble had told me that if I was looking for a really nice place to stay near Stamford – "not too big, something a little intimate" were my exact words to him, and with a slightly camp, semi-leer he got my meaning exactly – then this was the book that I would be sure to find it in.

I took it back to the office and with Bart or Brett's advice to assist me – "hey man, check that place out!" – I selected the Gardner Inn, a few miles away in a place called Pound Ridge, just across the state border in New York. The illustration in Karen Brown's book showed a big, white clapboard house, a 'colonial' something they called it in the blurb, with a lawn that ran down to a small lake, where there was a little jetty and a boat you could take out for a row. It had six rooms, all with their own everything, and their 'celebrated award winning Sunday brunches' included 'locally smoked river trout accompanied by horseradish scrambled eggs and home-baked corn bread and Bloody Mary's mixed to Dan Gardner's secret recipe – a bracing walk afterwards strongly advised!'

Faint heart never won fair maiden and there is a tide in the affairs of men which if taken at the flood and all that kind of thing and for once, I did seize the moment. I called the Blue Mongoose and booked two tickets, and I called The Gardner Inn and booked the second best double room. (The price would normally have made me blanche but having already been told the price of the very best double room it somehow seemed quite reasonable.)

I then told Laverne that the book I had wasn't the right one and I needed to change it and I left the office again, but this time I went to Grand Central, where I bought two return tickets to Stamford for the required date.

With the complete dirty deed done – well, not the complete dirty deed but the complete preliminary part of the dirty deed that I intended should lead to the ultimate dirty deed – I called down to Peggy and asked her to meet me for a drink that evening, an invitation which she seemed happy enough to accept.

"Peggy," I asked, as the waitress set our drinks down, "are you sitting comfortably?"

"Am I *what?*" she said, clearly not familiar with the phrase.

"Never mind," I said and proceeded to lay out the plan that I had for the forthcoming weekend – the plan for the two of us. And, for added drama, I produced, and laid on the table and turned around so she could read them, the 'Village Voice' open at the page with the ad for Jerry Seinfeld's gig, 'Country Inns of the Tri-state Area' by Karen Brown open at the page with the Gardner Inn on it, and the two rail tickets to Stamford. 'Voice' first, Karen Brown on top of that, and then the tickets placed, first one and then, with a flourish, the other, on top of that.

"Wow," she said, silently studying them. "Nice work."

Then she looked up at me and with a shrug and a little smile said, "Okay." (Brief pause.) "Okay."

*

The rest of the week I actually made a point of not seeing Peggy. She called up one day to suggest going to a movie, but I asked if she minded if we took a raincheck – I was beginning to get into the lingo – because I had too much work to do. This was totally untrue, but I didn't want anything to go wrong between now and the weekend and I figured that the less we saw of each other, the less chance of a misunderstanding that could lead to a wrong word that could lead to a row that would bring the carefully constructed architecture of our weekend away crashing down.

What I did do, however, was make sure that our arrangements for Saturday were beyond misunderstanding. I constantly took the rail tickets out of my wallet to check and recheck that I had booked to the right place and on the right date. And then I checked in my wallet again to make sure that I had safely put the tickets back in it. I called the The Blue Mongoose to make certain that Jerry Seinfeld had not been laid low by Mono or some other itinerant germ and that the performance was due to proceed as planned. I called the Gardners in Pound Ridge on at least four separate occasions to make absolutely certain that for this coming Saturday night, the second best double bedroom in the house had my name on it and that it was written in unmistakeably clear, capital letters in indelible ink. On the first occasion this involved no more than a polite enquiry that there had been no confusion.

"No Mr Williams, it's all done. Looking forward to seeing you Saturday."

On the second, my pretext was to enquire as to the checking-in times.

"Oh, any time after midday is fine with us Mr Williams."

On the third, I called back with apologies, but I had forgotten to ask about the checking-out times.

"Oh no hurry on a Sunday, Mr Williams. Eleven would be good but you can leave your bags at reception and spend the whole day here if you like."

By the fourth time I was struggling, but I just needed to make absolutely, completely, beyond-any-room-for-the-slightest-doubt certain that Jerry Seinfeld's management hadn't come in at the last moment with an unrefusable offer to book out the entire place for his family and friends.

"Er, awfully sorry to bother you, Mrs Gardner," – I always laid on the English-ness at times like these – "but I wonder if you would just confirm that pets aren't allowed?"

"Why no, Mr Williams, I am afraid they're not. Oh dear, did you have a dog you wanted to bring? It's a little late to cancel for tomorrow."

"Oh good Lord, no. No. Bit of a fur allergy, that's all."

"Oh really? Oh I am afraid we do have an old cat about the place."

"A cat? Oh that's fine. Just dogs with me. Just dogs. No, not cat fur. Love cats, got one myself."

*

By the day before I was beginning to feel a certain excited anticipation – or perhaps apprehension is a more appropriate word. I spent most of that Friday afternoon in the dubious company of Brett and Bart. After my experience at the photographer's party I had foresworn the bong but they certainly hadn't, and passive smoking ensured that my emotions were heightened. Unwisely, but in need of reassurance, I chose to reveal my insecurities.

"Man, you mean you haven't laid her yet? I thought you told us you were way past that like months ago," said Bart.

"Well, no, I didn't. I don't think I actually said anything specific."

"Jeez, you Brits – you are so gal-*lant*," said Brett.

"Yeh, right, gal-*lant*," echoed Bart, finding this enormously amusing. And then he and Brett spent the rest of the afternoon, riffing, between draws, on the theme of my old world courtesy, enquiring variously if I clicked my heels whenever I greeted Peggy prior to kissing her hand, if I had lain down my cloak so that she might not have to step in a puddle, whether, whenever we went out together, a team of ancient female chaperones followed ten yards behind etc., etc. Being Americans, and stoned Americans at that, they got countries and eras hideously confused but, unconcerned about such niceties, they laughed like drains. And I, being British, bore it all with stiff, good humour.

At home that evening, I swore at the cat, paced up and down, tried to watch a bit of telly to calm my nerves. But I took nothing in. So I decided the best course would be to go to bed early with a good book. Predictably I discovered that I could neither read nor sleep and eventually got up again at about two to make myself a cheese sandwich, but then discovered that there were too many butterflies in my stomach to cope with food as well. I went back to bed and laid there, snoozing fitfully and fretfully, until finally, at around six I accepted defeat and rose to prepare myself for all that might come to be.

Have I mentioned my earring before? A few months before I had left England, I had 'celebrated' my twenty-ninth birthday – the year before is always worse than the actual marking of the next decade – and I had decided that what I needed to make the unambiguous statement that I was still a funky young rebel, was an earring. So I went to Selfridges, insisted upon receiving umpteen reassurances that I was not set upon an irrevocable course towards gangrene and certain death and then bit my lip and held my breath and the hand of the hole-puncher's assistant while her boss mutilated my left ear. (At the time, I seem to remember, there was some received wisdom that left was hetero, right wasn't.)

I will skip the full story of the bleeding, the disinfecting, the endless twirling of the ring to prevent sticking, the constant removing and reinserting with left lobe cocked towards the bathroom mirror, the preening and self-congratulating on how terrifically Keith Richards I now looked. Suffice to say that many was the time my earring fell from my fumbling hands and I could be found on my hands and knees feeling for the bloody thing behind the lavatory.

By today, on this day that was to be the day of days, I had long ago switched to a gold stud (with the usual butterfly back) feeling that it was slightly subtler and cooler than the original more piratical look, and indeed, much to my satisfaction, several people – Peggy I think, definitely Brett and Bart – had more than once complementarily remarked upon it.

I think it perfectly understandable, given the importance I placed upon the events of the weekend, that I would, in the very early morning, lower East Side light, carefully inspect myself in the mirror above the bathroom sink, for signs of any blemishes that I might be able to eradicate or mask. And given my self-consciousness about my rapidly retreating hairline and the thinness of what remained behind it, no surprise that I turned my head this way and that to check out my head from all angles. But as to why I chose to unscrew the butterfly back of my gold ear stud, I can think of not one sensible reason. All I know is that I did it, and then, distracted by the cat suddenly announcing its entry into the bathroom by unaccountably brushing itself against my as-yet-untrousered legs – not a sign of friendliness I am sure, it knew exactly what it was doing – I somehow contrived to drop said butterfly into the unplugged sink. I looked down aghast to see it bounce – clink, clink and down and away into the sewers of New York.

This was not the best of starts to the day.

*

By ten o' clock I had recovered my composure sufficiently to choose, pack, and re-choose and repack a bag – the choice of which was itself a matter of considerable conjecture – and then shave, shower and, minus my earring but with a hole in my ear which I was sure would be noticed and pointed at by every passenger on the subway, to get myself to Grand Central. The fact that I wasn't due to meet Peggy until midday did not overly concern me. Better much, much too early than too late. I wandered about Grand Central looking in bookshops, stopping at coffee shops, grabbing a bagel from Zabars and generally filling in time; at one point I suddenly realised that I did not have my bag in my hand and, panic-stricken, I had to rush back along the barely remembered route until I found the coffee-shop, in which, miraculously, it still was. But mainly the time was taken up watching the minute hand on the Grand Central clock tick slowly round. Given Peggy's ready acquiescence to the weekend plans, I wasn't overly worried that there would be some last minute hitch – like Miller suddenly falling on his knees and imploring her not to leave – but with all that hinged on this, even being unduly worried was enough to make me extremely antsy. (On the subject of Miller, by the way, I had said not one further word to her, and I pledged myself, no matter what the temptation, to maintain my silence through the weekend.)

In the event, Peggy showed up not just on time, but five minutes early, right by the enquiry counter, in the centre of the main concourse just like we'd arranged. As I walked up to her, she reached up, pulled me towards her, kissed me full on the lips for a good few seconds and then said, "You've taken your earring out. Better."

"Yeah, well. You know. I thought it was a bit last year."

And off we went.

CHAPTER 9

MID-AIR AND RICHMOND UPON THAMES, 1999

LONDON, 1979–1989

I flew back to London as preoccupied as on the way out. But, for the first time in months it was not Peggy I was dwelling upon. It was those treacherous bastards, Vince and Geoff.

My association with Vince had begun nearly twenty years previously, just after I had come back from New York. McConnell Martin had, by then, fully absorbed the old London agency I had worked for, and having done a stint on Madison Avenue, and having once received the benediction of Todd Zwiebel – even if our relationship had later cooled – I had returned, if not yet a made man, then certainly a coming one.

*

Vince was a young account executive, who had done a few months in the Sydney office straight out of 'Uni' as he called it – it was not then a term that had been adopted in the motherland – and then, with a burning desire to see Earls Court, had handed in his notice, climbed on a plane, had a quick gander at the Acropolis, irritated the bulls in Pamplona, chundered at the Munich Beer Festival, and, according to him, fucked half the women from the Atlantic to the Aegean, before completing the de rigueur six-week, Kombi-borne dash around Europe. Having run out of money, he had then thrown himself on the mercy of McConnell Martin, London, and – probably because the guy who interviewed him was gay and took a fancy to this stocky sun bleached little chap who sat eagerly before him – a fancy which Vince, ever with the eye for the main chance, would have done nothing to discourage – he was taken on.

Professionally speaking, Vince was wet behind the ears but, being Australian, not entirely without self-confidence, and, being Vince, had a keen sense of which stars it might be useful to hitch his wagon to – he was always far too shrewd to gamble on just one. Amongst others, he chose mine. I don't know quite when I began to notice him, but he was soon hanging about the office bar in the early evenings (converted from its daytime role as canteen) and was a keen participant on the quarter size snooker table and on the football table. Now I think about it, the football table was probably the fawning ground that he quite deliberately chose.

I wouldn't claim to have the world's greatest eye-to-hand coordination and, when at the snooker table, pot white was, as often as not, my game. But on the football table I was a whiz. I had spent hours, days, weeks, forever, in my local youth club picking up all the flash little tricks and feints from the older kids and whenever, as an adult, I saw a table, I felt bound to bung in my 20p or whatever, and take on all-comers if playing singles, or if it was doubles, then find a stooge who was prepared to play defence while I dazzled in attack. One evening Vince volunteered to be that stooge, and soon he seemed to have the job on a semi-permanent basis.

Having just returned from the States once more unattached, and only too aware of the fact, I was never too willing to go home after work and sit in front of the telly brooding about my lonely life. Vince, who was not only a quick learner on the football table but also had the wry Australian take on life which I have always found bloody funny, would, as often as not, join me and some of the other guys when we went on to the The Jolly Brewers – the pub around the corner from the agency – after the office bar had been shut, and after that come on with us to the Greek or Italian or Indian restaurant, wherever it was we chose to round off the evening. Frequently he and I would be the last patrons to be shepherded out of the door by Vassos or Vittorio or Vikram. Yes, Vince was five years younger than I – quite a lot in your twenties – and yes, he was an account guy – a role normally considered to be strictly below stairs by us aristos of the creative department – but, soon, I had come to accept that Vince was, more or less, my best mate.

And if we were mates after work, then it was bound to follow, I suppose, that we would see more and more of each other during the day. He'd drop by my office for a chat, and I by his, and then bit by bit – I really have no idea how – he somehow ended up being the junior bag carrier (dismissive term for account handlers used by creatives) on some of the accounts I was working on, and then, as I had a couple of successes and the awards and promotions followed, he became a more senior bag carrier. It seemed inevitable that when I first became first deputy, and then, finally reaching the pinnacle, executive Creative Director of McConnell Martin, I would find Vince, too, supping at the top table.

It was about the time that I got 'the big office' that Geoff joined the agency.

He was the same sort of age as Vince, actually a couple of years younger, but he already had a growing reputation in the business and, much to Vince's initial annoyance which he didn't do a lot to hide, came in at a higher level than Vince, as the agency's Senior Account Director on its biggest piece of business. But though only in his late twenties, Geoff was prematurely grey – always useful if you're young and ambitious – and evinced a cool solidity to enhance the effect.

Although now officially 'management' and running the creative department of McConnell Martin London, I was still writing my own stuff too, and, in '88, I had my own big years at DADA and at Cannes and at all the other innumerable 'and the award goes to' dinner and dances. I had written a couple of campaigns, one for a vacuum cleaner and one for a brand of jeans, that had floated the boats of the various juries, and I was becoming a hottish property in London, frequently quoted in 'Campaign' with accompanying photograph, always unsmiling and intense as is considered appropriate for creative types. And always too, with my shaven head first laboriously dabbed with panstick to make sure that it didn't shine too brightly in the camera lights. (Having conceded the lost battle with baldness I had by now decided to assume control of the situation by the daily removal of the remaining fringe around the sides.) Several other agencies tried to tempt me away with all manner of goodies on offer, but after accepting all the invitations to lunch at Le Gavroche and breakfast at the Connaught, I always decided that McConnell Martin was the place where my bread was buttered the best.

And then one day, or rather one evening, at the McConnell Martin Christmas party in '89, Vince asked me to step outside for a moment, and there, on the steps of the Park Lane hotel where our shindig was in full swing, I found Geoff drawing deep on a B and H in the chilly night air. It was Geoff who, without even the most perfunctory of near-bush beatings, stubbed the butt out under his black brogued foot, and then made me the offer I was to discover I couldn't refuse: to start a new agency, just me and the pair of them, all as equal partners. And, with Vince looking on approvingly, Geoff added that Charles Mullins, chief executive of McConnell Martin's biggest client, whose business, of course, he looked after, had made him a personal promise that the account for a new range of products that they were about to launch would be awarded not to McConnell Martin but to Williams, Dutton, Bradley. (I always remember, that when making that first pitch to me, outside the hotel entrance, he put my name first.)

113

If you were writing a textbook on gob-smacking and wanted a picture to illustrate the front cover, mine would surely have been a shoo-in. I don't know which surprised me more, the up-front, no fucking about delivery of the offer, or the fact that Geoff and Vince had never before demonstrated the slightest attachment for each other and yet, here they were, side by side, hatching a plan that must have taken months of careful gestation. Or, even more astonishing, the incredibly risky – but, as it proved, correct – assumption that I wouldn't walk straight back in to the do and spill the beans to Gerry. (Gerry Morgan, CEO of McConnell Martin.) If I'd done that, there would have been no new agency to get the new account and they would have both been summarily slung out on their respective ears. (Of course, had I done that, they would have immediately been on the phone, scrabbling about for someone else to be the Creative Director of the new outfit, but I am pretty sure that it was me, out of whose creative arse, Charles Mullins, for some reason, thought the sun shone, who had served as the shiny bit of mirror that had dazzled him into submission and that, without me, they would never have got off the ground.) Not that, as the whole advertising world now knows, it ever got to that. And it was, in fact, this, their willingness to take the bungee jump without a safety net, their sheer fucking chutzpah, that was, I think, the clincher for me. They had shown that they had the cojones – and if you're going to bust out and start an agency on your own, and be, from day one, in no-holds-barred competition with the agency you have just quit, at war, to the death if necessary, with the mothership, then cojones – above talent, application, cash flow, and all the other things that count – cojones are what you need the most.

Once he had finished his initial stunning speech, Geoff, said not another word, and neither did Vince. They simply stood there, watching me, waiting for what must have seemed an eternity to them, to see if the gamble of their lives – the gamble that I would forsake the cushiest of creative billets from which I would not, despite the blandishments of so many, previously be budged, to join them in the cold, cold world outside. It was a moment so significant in my life that I don't have one of my usual can't-have-been-the way-it-really-was moviemories of it. I am sure that I snapped it in my mind and retained the image exactly as it was: my subjective view of them standing there, the collars of their DJs turned up against the cold; and, as I re-examine the picture closely, I see not a single bead of perspiration on their brows. Cojones, yes, they had all you would need, and they were the coolest of customers too. Not bad qualities to have in your business partners.

Eventually, I managed to speak, and after the opening stuttering overture of something like 'Jesus! Fuck me! Christ! Well, I wasn't fucking expecting that!' I finally had the composure to ask a few sensible questions.

"Are you telling me you have told Charles I am on for this without even fucking asking me?'

"No" said Geoff. "We told Charles that without the business you'd never do it, but with it, we'd bet our lives – professional lives anyway – that you would. And we've just bet our professional lives haven't we?"

(Was this the truth, or had he told Charles Mullins that I was in from the beginning? I chose to believe him but I wouldn't bet my life – professional or any other version of it – that he wasn't lying through his teeth.)

My second question was:

"So what's in it for Charles?"

"Well, we haven't promised him some kind of hidden interest in the agency, if that's what you mean." (It wasn't, it hadn't crossed my mind. I suppose such things happen, but the advertising business, in my experience, despite what people may think, isn't that crudely corrupt.)

"No," continued Geoff, "what's in it for him is that he likes what he gets from McConnell Martin, but he doesn't want all his eggs in one basket. This way he gets another agency but he's also getting McConnells – in his mind that's who we are – all over again. It's what he knows and what he likes. And he's got a stick to beat them with when he needs it."

My third question was this, and I remember the words precisely:

"Isn't Gerry just going to sue the arse off us? Sorry, I'll rephrase that; *wouldn't* Gerry just sue the arse off us? Surely there must be something in a board director's contract that stops him from doing something like this?"

(Note 1. In the very act of drawing attention to the fact that I had first said 'isn't', had I not indicated that I was already half way down the slippery slope to buying into their scheme? I am pretty sure I can recall seeing Vince steal a sideways look – just the smallest of smiles – at Geoff at exactly this point.)

(Note 2. I had never bothered to read a word of my own board director's contract.)

Vince spoke now, the first time he had said anything.

"Gerry's not going to do a fucking thing. You think he's going to call Charles Mullins out on this? Yeah, right. McConnell's biggest fucking client! They're twenty per cent of the agency's billing. No mate, he won't like it, he'll kick up seven kinds of shit, he'll call us treacherous bastards, but in the end, he's got no option, he'll wear it."

And Vince was right. He wore it. In public, Gerry even pretended to claim that we were starting the new agency with McConnell Martin's blessing. Not a bad tactic; always best to look big if you can.

And Vince was right too about how Gerry would react in private. He did threaten us, he did kick up seven kinds of shit, and he did call us treacherous bastards.

And as I sipped thoughtfully from my second glass of complimentary Air France Chablis, I couldn't help but reflect that, as far as Geoff and Vince were concerned, he'd had a damned good point.

On Geoff's recommendation we hired a firm of solicitors to sort out the paperwork. Some piggy-eyed, thin-lipped assassin they put on the job drew everything up and in due course, it was off to their offices in Mayfair for the ceremonial cutting of palms and mingling of blood. Then it was all about business plans and getting the start-up money from the bank. Of course, a business plan, no matter how good, doesn't actually get you any money. It just gets you through the door. Once through the door, you have to show them the colour of *your* money. That bit is called providing collateral. To get the readies needed to get our agency off the ground we had, quite literally, to put our houses on it, or at least that part of them that one bank or another didn't already own. After three months of insanely frenetic activity, during which period there were also a couple of personal milestones, the birth of my second child, India, and my fortieth birthday, we opened our agency in the spring of 1990. The picture in 'Campaign' showed the three of us leaning on a fire-escape of our new office in Frith Street. (Fire escapes, for some inexplicable reason, were the kind of background favoured by 'Campaign' photographers.) Geoff, short and lean, on the left, Vince, no taller and already thickening on the right, and me, by at least half a head – half a gleaming, shaven head – the tallest, in the middle. It was the logical way for the photographer to arrange us and it carried a symbolic significance too. In terms of public perception, I was the main man, the one with the reputation, the one on whose coat-tails the others were riding to success. How soon they forget!

The pictures had already been taken before that first 'Campaign' article announcing the launch had been written, and we had the proofs in front of us during the interview with the journalist. Scrawled across the bottom were our names as we appeared in the shot, running from left to right. The journalist assumed that would be our agency name, Bradley, Williams, Dutton, and when neither Geoff nor Vince contradicted him, I, though slightly taken aback, said nothing, thinking it would be a little immodest and rather uncool to announce that my name should have been first; that was most definitely not the kind of impression I wanted to create. So Bradley, Williams, Dutton we became, soon to be commonly referred to as BWD, the W never to completely forget that he should have come before the B and always nurturing the tiniest of grudges as a result.

As the Airbus crossed back across the channel that tiniest of grudges was recalled and considerably amplified along with all the other little slights and small broken promises of which I imagined I had been the victim over the years. Treacherous bastards, yes, indeed. But who did I really have to blame but myself? Hadn't the signs been there from the very beginning?

But at the beginning it was all such a whirlwind – who had time to notice? We had offices to find, and interior design to bicker about, and finances to organise, and cash flow to fret over, and staff to hire, not to mention trying to do the work we were actually supposed to be doing: dreaming up the new campaigns for the business that Charles Mullins had, as promised, delivered to us. One thing we weren't doing a lot of was cold-calling, touting for business. Because the phones never seemed to stop ringing with potential clients calling us! As much as anything it was pure luck, but our timing seemed to have been incredibly propitious. In 1990, the country was on the verge of going to hell in a handcart, driven there by poll tax protesters who would soon have Mrs Thatcher dead in the water. But, despite the trouble the country was in, BWD had somehow caught a wave that would carry us on to a sun-drenched beach where caskets of pirate treasure lay open and ready for us to plunder.

I won't say we didn't put in the hours – we seemed to be in the office night and day, weekends not excluded – and I think we played our hand pretty shrewdly, but from day one, almost nothing seemed to go wrong and virtually everything went right. For the next nine and whatever it was years, right up to the point where the new breakfast cereal client had come through our door bearing the weight of his seven-million-pound account of which we had gladly relieved him, we had stayed on the same path, unstoppably onward and upward. No longer were we in the original boutiquey little office in Frith Street but now, via two intermediate moves to places bigger and better, we were comfortably ensconced in our gleaming bought and paid for (okay, mortgaged, but still) eight-storey building in Fitzrovia. We had bought a couple of companies, a design place and a PR outfit, so we could claim to offer a broader all-in-one client service, and we were talking about going public in a minor way, by listing on the AIM market on the Stock Exchange. It was either that or fatten up even more and then sell out to someone bigger for a small – no, who I am kidding – a seriously sizable fortune. We'd already had two or three serious offers but had decided we were in no rush, and if we hung on for a while longer we could become even richer. The bottom line – a bottom line with rows of lovely noughts all in the black – was this: if there were an E to P scale for agency start-ups, which, if not quite expressed in those terms, believe me, there most definitely was – to our intense satisfaction our rivals absolutely hated us – then BWD would have had nearly ten years of straight Es, all picked out in the very deepest shade of envious green.

Looked at like that, despite my current difficulties with Vince and Geoff and sodding Lucille, I still had a lot – and a lot to lose. So as I bade the Air France lovelies 'à bientôt' and stepped off the plane, I resolved to meet underhandedness with underhandedness and to take a leaf out of Gerry Morgan's book. I too would appear to accept the situation with good grace and embrace the idea of Lucille's promotion as if it had been my own. Better, far better, to look big than bitter. Then I would kill – no, perhaps not kill, but, shall we say, slowly stifle her, with kindness.

*

A few days later – it was Thursday, I believe, that had become shrink day – I was back in Donald McEwan's comfy mole hole in Richmond. I began, naturally, by sharing with him the happy events of Cannes. (If it surprises you that this was the kind of thing we discussed and consider that I should have been examining instead the long term effects of my potty training or similar, then I can only say that you may well be right, and it might have done me more good if we had. But, as I have indicated, I used Donald as a father confessor as much as anything and with my wife's shoulder unavailable – of which more later – it was inevitable that it would be his that I would cry on.)

Donald heard me out and then said, "Well, that doesn't sound too bad at all."

"I'm sorry Donald, did you not hear what I've been saying for the past ten minutes?" (I glanced at the clock. Shit. As usual, I'd been late arriving and it was already twenty past.)

"Yes, you told me your company won lots of awards [somehow his precise Scottish enunciation made 'awards' sound as meretricious as they really were] and that your colleagues want to give you more support by sanctioning the appointment of a deputy – at considerable expense I would imagine – to lighten your workload."

My mouth was already half way open in preparation for saying something like 'I didn't say anything of the sort' when I shut it again.

Now, of course, anyone with half a brain might have turned my words around and presented them back to me in the way that Donald had done. It didn't need his dozen degrees and PhD and years of shrinkery to have that kind of insight – if insight it was. But if it had been anyone else, I would probably have dismissed what they had said out of hand. Instead, because it was Donald, and I was in his little basement hideaway, the one place I came to for some inner reflection – even if I did do all I could to avoid it when I got there – what he said sometimes made me reconsider. That is the value of going to shrinks I suppose, or at least, it was the value

I got from going to see Donald. Occasionally, it gave me pause and in that pause I had a moment or two to steady the ship.

But if what he seemed to be implying was right, that I might be just being a teensy weensy bit paranoid, then why? And if the answer to that was the obvious one, that I was, for some reason, feeling particularly insecure, then why? And that always seems to be the downside of going to see people like Donald; the endless introspection, the never ending whys. Because after every why, there is always another one, and where do they lead in the end? Perhaps, I suppose, if I ever let them, yes, back to my potty training but what, to coin a glib but appropriate phrase, really is the use of all that shit? I think, I hope – goodness, I spent enough – that what I may have got from all this, was that, in some mysterious way, all the little promptings from Donald somehow affected the workings of my mind – slightly recalibrated the speed of the whirling cogs – so that afterwards I functioned that little bit more smoothly.

Eventually Donald broke the silence with an unexpected question that threw me.

"How old are you now, Andrew?"

"I think you know that. Forty-nine."

"Ah."

I got defensive.

"Well, what's that got to do with the price of fish? Surely you're not going to hand me the old midlife crisis line. If I'd wanted the platitudes of an agony uncle I'd have written to the 'Sun'."

I winced even as I said it. But Donald remained as serene as ever, apparently unmoved by my gratuitous rudeness. (As I've said he never seemed to judge; never even checked his watch or made a comment when I was – as I habitually was – late for my session.)

"What I would say Andrew is that sometimes people use a forthcoming birthday – especially those they think of as a 'big one' – as being a moment to do a kind of personal stocktaking. But I'm not sure they always place the proper value on what they find."

"Are you talking about Peggy?"

"Peggy, yes, and Alison—"

"Alison?"

"Alison, yes, and everyone – and everything – else. Time alters perspective, doesn't it? That's all I'm saying."

"I thought hindsight was a wonderful thing."

He didn't respond to that so I managed to have the last word, but today, I had to concede, Donald had shaded it.

Afterwards, in the back of the cab that took me back to the office, I wondered: perhaps it did have something to do with the price of fish.

CHAPTER 10

POUND RIDGE, NEW YORK AND NEW YORK, NEW YORK, 1979

We took the Metro North railroad – so much more glamorous a word to my English ears than 'railway' – silly I admit, but there it is – to Stamford and from there we would get a cab to Pound Ridge. I was as excited as a kid going to the seaside. It was the first time I'd been on a train in America, and if it wasn't quite like it was in the movies – I had some vague forties image in my mind, black and white, fellows in trilbies and Katherine Hepburn types in New Look clothes – I was thrilled to discover we were going through places that the movies had made famous. The first station we came to was Harlem, and then a couple of stops later came Pelham.

"This is *the* Pelham?" I asked Peggy.

"Only one I know."

"As in 'The Taking of Pelham 123'?"

"The very same."

"With Walter Matthau. And Robert Shaw."

"Well, I don't believe they're here all the time."

"Blimey!" I said, star struck like a tourist being taken around Bel Air. But when I looked out of the window, and I saw what a dreary looking place Pelham was, I sort of wished I hadn't seen it.

But the next stop really did get me going. New Rochelle. It wasn't actually until I heard the announcer say we were approaching Nooroeshel that I realised its true significance.

"You don't mean—" I said, breathlessly.

"What now?" asked Peggy, who was trying to read 'The New York Times' or, at least, a very small portion of it, the tonnage of the Saturday edition being such that you wouldn't make a serious dent in it in a year. Her tone suggested that my childlike wonder might have begun to wear a little thin.

"Well, I never realised until now that Nooroeshel was actually New Rochelle – in fact, I never realised it was an actual place."

"What the hell are you talking about Andy?"

"Nooroeshel!" I said. "It's where they lived in 'The Dick Van Dyke Show' … Dick Van Dyke and Mary Tyler Moore … with their twin beds … what were their names in the show now? … Rob … Rob and—"

"Laura."

"That's it. Rob and Laura. Rob and Laura … PETRIE! Got it. Rob and Laura Petrie and little Richie."

She grinned and made a little noise, a sort of 'oh boy!' sound.

"You know who else lives here?" she asked.

"Who?"

"My parents."

"Rob and Laura Petrie lived in the same town as your parents?"

"For years. Rob and Laura dropped in all the time."

"Now," I said "I am seriously impressed." And, slightly tragically perhaps, I really was.

On we went, me playing the wide-eyed naïf and her the savvy New Yorker, all the way to Stamford.

During one of my calls to the Gardner Inn we had discussed how Peggy and I were to get there from the station at Stamford, and Mrs Gardner – she and I had got quite pally after so many conversations – very kindly volunteered her husband to pick us up.

"Oh that's good of you, Mrs Gardner, but I'm sure we can get a cab or something," I replied, hoping that I sounded just helpless enough that she wouldn't take me at my word.

"No way, Mr Williams! Dan's always in Stamford. He'll be glad to do it."

Result!

Dan Gardner turned out to be a florid, chubby but muscly looking chap of about fifty with an unimpressively sparse beard. He was waiting outside the station as promised, standing by an enormous estate car, one of those gas guzzlers with fake 'woody' side panels, beloved of suburban America.

"Jeep Wagoneer" he proudly told me in response to my polite enquiry – made not because I was particularly interested in the answer so much as to break the slightly awkward silence in which we were travelling.

"'75 model. Eighty thousand miles and runs like new," he added, affectionately tapping the steering wheel like he might the neck of a favourite steed. There then followed one of the usual 'you from England? I have a cousin in Lye-cester' conversations which left me wishing I'd never opened my mouth and Peggy suppressing a giggle in the back seat. (I had sat in the front, not wanting to make Mr Gardner feel like a chauffeur.)

Soon, we pulled on to a gravelly drive and the photo in Karen Brown's book came to life. I don't know from which colony this 'colonial' something or other took its architectural cues – it didn't seem very likely that the Pilgrim Fathers would have had anything similar – but it was absolutely perfect to my eyes, the very picture of Technicolor America. If Doris Day or Rock Hudson had come strolling out of the front door, I wouldn't have been the least surprised. The lawns of the so called front yard, bordered by flowers bigger and brighter than anything you get in England – just like everything in America is – were perfectly manicured and from one corner of them sprang the essential stars and stripes, billowing gently in the breeze.

We stepped into a wood-panelled hallway out of which grew a wide staircase, which if it wasn't quite sweeping was certainly the next best thing and up which our bags were promptly whisked by a young chap who had appeared from nowhere before the door was closed behind us. Also there, with beaming smile and hand outstretched, was Mrs Gardner, a curious mixture of the chunkily sexy and slightly grand – sort of Shelley Winters meets Barbara Bush.

"Hi," she said, "I'm Nancy Gardner, welcome to the Gardner Inn. Once you've signed in, Dan will make you one of his famous Bloody Marys – first one on the house!"

"You're really very kind," I remember saying because Peggy leaned up and whispered in my ear *"You're really very kind?"* – her way of gently enquiring why I was sounding as though I had suddenly jumped into a play by Noel Coward. My excuse for unthinkingly switching on my Brit-in-America autopilot – had I not been too embarrassed to give it – would have been that I was now completely pre-occupied with the upcoming perils of registration. How *were we* supposed to sign in? I wasn't quite as gauche as Benjamin Braddock but I understood how he felt. In the event, Peggy became an unlikely Mrs Robinson by taking hold of the form and signing – with our real names – and then smiling sweetly but directly at Nancy Gardner and challenging her to raise an eyebrow if she dared. Which, of course, being the wise-in-the-ways-of-the-world innkeeper she was, she didn't.

Peggy and I were then invited to take our seats for brunch. Did we have the smoked trout with the horseradish scrambled eggs? The constantly replenished jug of Bloody Mary, the secret of whose legendary recipe, was, I would guess, about ten parts vodka to one part the rest, ensured that I haven't got the foggiest idea. After that, we attempted to regain our balance by taking some fresh air and strolled hand in hand down to the lake.

There cannot be a Brit who has spent any time in the States who hasn't periodically felt that they were living through a movie.

Having been weaned on American film and sitcom, the sights and sounds of the place are so familiar, that reality and the cinematic often become almost indistinguishable. My description of that weekend may seem like an endless series of allusions to film stars and movies but every ten minutes something came up that reminded me of one Hollywood moment or another. And the next two names to spring to mind were Bing Crosby and Grace Kelly as they appeared in 'High Society'. It was clambering into the boat by the jetty, where the billiard table lawn – *backyard*? per-lease! – met the rippling water, that set me off. You remember the bit where Bing sings 'True Love' to Grace? I know that scene took place in a yacht on the open sea, rather than in a rowing boat on a smallish lake, but as Peggy dangled her hand in the water and I pulled on the oars – or was it the other way around? – it still felt like we'd been cast in a remake. I don't believe I was so foolish as to try to sing to Peggy, but it was no less a serenade.

The afternoon wore on. We just about managed to get the boat back to land – being a natural oarsman is another of those gifts with which I have not been blessed – and, after a couple of near catastrophes, we were somehow able to clamber back on to the jetty without falling in and tie the boat up without it drifting back into the middle of the lake.

Feeling rather smug about this successful demonstration of my seamanship – our manoeuvres were closely scrutinised by a couple of other guests in deckchairs as well as the Gardner's enormous marmalade cat from its position in the sunniest spot on the lawn – I took Peggy's hand and led her up to the patio where a couple of comely waitresses were serving what they fondly imagined was English afternoon tea. An elderly man with a pencil moustache and a bowtie sat at a baby grand positioned just inside the open French doors of the house, and was accompanying the proceedings with slightly jazzy interpretations of tunes from what has since become known as the Great American Songbook.

It was when he started to play "Let's Fall in Love" that I started to feel an incipient queasiness about proceedings. While Peggy was spreading Boysenberry jam or something equally American on a scone the size of a landmine she began absentmindedly singing along and it was when she got to the bit about the doings of birds, bees and educated fleas that I was suddenly reminded of what was expected of me when the sun went down. Now, I suppose there are some blokes who are so secure in their blokeishness that it never occurs to them that homo erectus might not always do what it says on the tin. But on this day of days, which more to the point, was to be followed by this night of nights, I began, despite all my best efforts to distract myself, to imagine the unimaginable. And, as we all know, when a doubt creeps in, it usually adamantly refuses to creep out again. And if one is sufficiently neurotic – and the sufficiency of my neuroses has never been questioned – then it is not unknown for a creeping doubt to metamorphose into a full-blown self-fulfilling fucking prophecy. In golf, this phenomenon, which has been known to afflict some of the greatest ever to have played the game – the double Masters winner, Bernhard Langer is perhaps the best known victim – is called the 'yips'. Despite the fact that you may be able to drive the ball with unerring accuracy and perform all the other golfing feats of derring do that only prodigious natural talent and years of mind-numbing practice and the very latest computer designed equipment can bring about, when you have the 'yips' you can find yourself unable to do something your half blind granny could do with her walking stick; namely get it in the hole from two feet away. I don't know if there is a name for the sexual version of the yips, but we all know what happens when you can't get it in. And the last bloody thing I wanted that night, was a consoling arm from Peggy around my slumped shoulders and to hear her utter the dreaded words, 'Really, it's nothing to worry about, it happens to everyone.'

Sensing that all wasn't as it should be, Peggy broke out of her scone-spreading song-singing reverie to look at me, frown, and say, "What?" And then, when she saw I was still lost in space, more insistently she repeated, "*What*?!"

I realised I was staring straight ahead, with my mouth open, my face, I imagine, appearing to be as transfixed with horror as my thoughts were. Thinking that her question was best avoided, I attempted to reconfigure my expression into something approaching a casual smile, and said, "More tea?"

"Tea?" she said. "That's what you were thinking about? More tea?"

She didn't seem remotely convinced. She looked at me thoughtfully for a moment, shook her head, then picked up her scone and boysenberry jam, and then brought it towards her mouth before suddenly changing her mind. She set the scone back on the plate, stood up and said to me, "C'mon. Is this what we've come for? Tea?"

And she took my hand, walked me back to reception, asked for the room key, won another eyeball to eyeball challenge with Nancy Gardner and led me upstairs to the second best room in the house.

*

With reference to what went on that night in the second best room in the house, and this not being *that* kind of book, I am only going to mention what is strictly dramatically necessary.

I am able to report – with relief – that none of the misgivings I had at the tea table proved to have any foundation. I cannot say that this was all or even in part due to Peggy's rapid response to my fit of the vapours over the boysenberry jam. Everything might have gone swimmingly anyway, though her intervention could hardly have done any harm. We never discussed what demons were at work in my head that afternoon, so what she knew or what she thought she knew, I have absolutely no idea. What is certain is that by osmosis or intuition or whatever, she divined that this was the moment to drop the scone and carpe diem pronto.

This demonstrates two of the characteristics in Peggy that I found most wonderful. One was this wavelength thing I've mentioned. Somehow, unlike any other girl or woman I have ever known, she had this uncanny understanding of where I was coming from – and of where I was trying to get to. The other, as I was to realise more and more – in this case to my benefit but sometimes to my cost – was that she not only knew my mind, she knew her own, and she was never afraid to act upon it. I began by fancying Peggy, then I found out that I liked her, then that I loved her, and, in the end, on top of all this, I discovered how much I admired her.

A couple of other things to mention about our night under the gabled roof of the Gardner Inn. And here, I am – just this once – going to describe a physical detail of what went on. As with most couples I suspect, not that I can possibly know such a thing for certain of course, when Peggy and I first advanced bedward we found ourselves in what is rather unerotically referred to as the missionary position. Whatever its reputation for unadventurousness, the one overwhelming advantage of this old favourite is that, at the critical moment, you are looking straight into each other's eyes. (Unless, that is, you are trying to deliberately avoid them, which only serves to underline how much truth about your feelings it reveals.)

I should emphasise at this point that I am not big on souls. As I've mentioned before, I am not a religious person, and neither do I claim to be a spiritual one. Really, I have no idea what that even means. If I can't see and touch it, if it can't be proved under a microscope, than by and large, I choose not to believe it. I have no difficulty in following the Douglas Adams line that 42 is the answer to everything.

Except.

Except that when I looked into Peggy's eyes that night – and I believe she felt the same looking into mine – it really did seem as if

I was seeing something beyond the physical and yes, if such a thing exists, which, of course, I know for absolutely certain – almost – that it doesn't, then I was looking deep into the proverbial windows of the soul. There is nothing on earth so thrilling as that feeling and I have never known that feeling so strongly as I did that night with Peggy.

And that is all that I have to say on this matter. Except this: we didn't leave the second best room in the house at all that evening. We ordered room service, watched a bit of telly, and the rest will have to be left to your imagination. When we awoke the next morning, the two tickets for the 9 p.m. show at The Blue Mongoose in Stamford were still, unused, in my wallet.

Over breakfast Peggy said, "A pity. You'd have really loved Jerry."

To which I should have answered, "Not as much as I love you."

But I didn't.

'Coulda, Woulda, Shoulda'. Isn't that how the song goes?

*

On that warm and sunny Sunday morning – it could have been overcast and freezing for all I know, but, inevitably, warm and sunny is how I remember it – we elected to take a walk into town: 'The historic hamlet of Pound Ridge' as it was described in the little publicity brochure that was left in our room and which Peggy pored over amongst the detritus of the enormous breakfast we had been served.

As we walked out of the dining room cum library in which we'd eaten, I felt that all eyes were upon us. I certainly hoped they were; after my overnight heroics there was definitely a give-away swagger in my step. I'd hate to think it was wasted.

Peggy kept quoting from the brochure as we took the leafy lane into the 'hamlet' – actually a dangerously bendy road with no thought of a pavement. Americans don't expect to walk.

"You related to people called Tarleton?" she asked.

"Tarleton?" I said, and having no idea where this was going, flippantly added, "Doesn't sound Jewish."

"Well neither does Williams, does it? What's that all about? Which shtetl did the Williams come from?"

The 'Williams' had come about because, according to family legend, my illiterate great grandfather had taken the name of the immigration official at Tilbury who, speaking as much Lithuanian or Yiddish as my great-grandfather spoke English, had given up trying to get any sense out of him, and, for want of anything better, and seeing the scrawled mark that was the best the old boy could come up with by way of a signature, put his own name down on his immigration papers. The family has always been grateful. It has probably served us better than being called X. I told Peggy this, but she didn't seem satisfied. Like many New Yorkers, she simply could not get her head around the fact that there were such things as English Jews at all. To Americans, Jewishness and Englishness are polar opposites, the one all wise-cracking and smart business, the other sang froid and snottiness. In America, English equals WASP. And the idea of a Jewish White Anglo Saxon Protestant doesn't make a lot of sense.

"Yeah, well, whatever," she said, "I am pretty sure *Ban-As-tre* – Jesus, what sort of name is that? – Banastre Tarleton wasn't Jewish anyway. But if he had been an ancestor of yours, I was going to suggest you keep quiet about it. He was some kind of English colonel who burnt Pound Ridge down before George kicked your British asses outta town. Says here he was called 'The Butcher'."

"But not the kosher butcher."

"Seems unlikely."

"Who knows? A historical detail lost in the mist of time."

"I don't think they've lost any of the historical details. They're all here. Lovingly preserved. Wonder what happened to the Siwanoy and Kitchawong Indians."

"No idea. Any theories?"

"We-hell, it says they were a sub-group of the Algonquins."

"Obviously they went for drinks with Dorothy Parker."

"Obviously."

On we walked. And on we bantered. And if it sounds like we were completely, self-indulgently wrapped up in our own wit and wonderfulness, well, so we were. That's the joy of the wavelength thing for you. Once or twice in a lifetime you hit paydirt and you just can't get enough of the sum being greater than the parts. If you're on the outside looking in – as least to someone with my meagre generosity of spirit – it always looks nauseatingly smug and you can't wait for the happy couple to come to blows. But if it's you and your beloved, then the outside world might as well be Mars. You just don't give a shit what anybody thinks.

It took about ten minutes to walk into one side of the cutesy little white clapboard town and out of the other. As we were about to turn on our heels, the heavens opened – perhaps it had been overcast after all – and we ran for cover. We found a little coffee shop, and it was there, through my stupidity and clumsiness, that I broke the spell. Having come so far, I couldn't help but wonder what came next. Although, I managed to stick to my pre-weekend vow to myself not to mention him by name, Miller inevitably came between us.

"What do you mean what comes next?" asked Peggy. If it had been possible to show some sort of infra-red image of her voice, and the warmth in it was a great big glowing red blob which before this moment had encompassed the whole picture, you would, in the space of about half a dozen words, have seen it suddenly shrink to nothing.

Softly, softly, catchee monkey. All good things come to he who waits. Dah di dah di dah di dah. But, although I could clearly see even then that putting pressure on Peggy was not the answer, I just couldn't help myself. And besides, wasn't it a question I was perfectly entitled to ask? Were we supposed to run off and have the most romantic weekend of our lives – of my life anyway – and then simply return to New York and our separate existences, me in my shabby sublet and her – her with Mill-*er*! It didn't make any sense. Not to me. Nor, I told her, would it to anyone.

"Is that it? You care about what other people think?"

"No, of course not—"

"Are you sure? Are you sure you don't want to be able to say to those junkies you hang around with, Bob and Bill—"

"Bart and Brett – and they're not—"

"—well, whoever the hell they are, don't you just want to be able to tell them that you have knocked me on the head with your club and carried me off to your cave? Isn't that it? You want me to *belong* to you?"

"No, I want us to belong to each other."

"Don't you get it, you jerk! I don't want to belong to anybody. And I don't want anyone belonging to me. Not at the moment. Right now, I am coming out of a relationship that has been slowly dying for – well, almost since it began. Look, maybe it does look weird that I am still living in the same apartment as Miller. But who cares what it looks like. *You* know it's over between him and me, and it's just beginning with us. And anyway, I've told you already that as soon as I can get my shit together, I'll move in with Noreen or something, but Andy you have to understand this: I am not ready to commit to anyone else. Not yet. You just have to take this for what it is."

"What happened to 'I totally like you'?"

"It has got nothing to do with my totally liking you. Jeez, haven't I shown you how I feel this weekend? But you have to care about me enough to give me some fucking room and not be obsessing all the time about your own insecurity. You have to show me that you can be that – that – giving."

Giving? Did she say 'giving'? Me?

*

134

Remember what I said before about our emotional weather? How for the most part it was gloriously sunny but then, every so often, out of the blue along would come some tumultuous storm that would send us running for cover? So it was, late that Sunday morning in Pound Ridge. But as ever, the clouds would pass and by the time we pulled back into Grand Central, it was all one-liners and holding hands again, and everything was forgotten.

Well, no, not quite forgotten. As I changed the cat litter – after nearly two days away you could smell it long before I had got a key into even one of the six locks – and then settled down to my usual Sunday evening diet of sitcom reruns, I turned it all over in my mind again. And I kept on coming back to the question of commitment. She had told me in the coffee-shop that she didn't want commitment, but if only I had said what I'd really wanted to say when she made the comment about the missed opportunity to see Jerry Seinfeld, might that not have shown her that I wasn't afraid to put my feelings on the line? And if I'd done that, what might she have said in return? And if we had both declared undying love for each other – a stretch but, in the mood we were in, not impossible – how might that have shaped events from then on? Wasn't this just like it had been the very first time she'd told me she was planning on moving away from Miller and I'd been so feeble in my response?

And wasn't it true that on the one occasion when I had just beaten my chest and swung from the vine, when I had just gone out and made all the arrangements for the weekend without asking Peggy, had she not agreed, without hesitation, to play Jane to my Tarzan? Wasn't the lesson I had to learn, clear?

Or was it? Boldness, yes, I must be bold. But what about patience? Didn't I need that just as much? To be boldly patient; how did you do that?

In the end I was so tired I gave up trying to square the circle and fell happily asleep reviewing my – mostly – fabulous trip to Pound

Ridge. Featuring Rob and Laura, Benjamin and Mrs Robinson, Doris and Rock, Bing and Grace, Tarzan and Jane, but, starring, above all, Peggy and Andy.

Really, quite a weekend.

CHAPTER 11

LONDON, SARDINIA, RICHMOND UPON

THAMES, 1999

Poor Jerry Seinfeld.

As my conversations with Donald McEwan testify, I seem to have blocked out almost everything about Peggy when I returned to London. And, along with her, I rejected just about anything that might in some way be connected to her. Jerry Seinfeld was one such blameless casualty.

When they started to run his TV show in Britain, the early adopters, of which the advertising world is full, were quick to get in on the act. Pretty soon they were all talking about Jerry.

"Have you seen that 'Seinfeld' show?" they would ask, hoping, of course, that you would shake your head, so that they could feel smugly confirmed in the knowledge that their trendiness was greater than yours. They seemed to particularly like Kramer and occasionally I would catch some young copywriter or art director ruffling his air and sliding across the floor in an attempt to demonstrate just how hilarious he had been in last night's episode.

At such times, instead of doing as I usually did which was to try to ingratiate myself with the agency youngsters by pretending to like whatever they liked – and thus show how agelessly 'cool'

I was – I would walk sniffily by. This being so out of character with my usual simpering, I would then invariably catch one of them muttering "What the fuck's the matter with him today?" If only they'd known. (If only *I'd* known.)

"Actually, you little prats, it's not just about today, it's about my whole fucking life. You see, I once lived in New York and I met this girl called Peggy and I was fucking insane about her and she liked Jerry Sein—" But, of course, for a thousand and one very good reasons, I would never have said any such thing, not the least of them being that I didn't really have any understanding of why I was behaving like this. It was one of those visceral reactions in which the brain is completely bypassed. All I knew was – in my water – that I didn't want anything to do with Jerry Seinfeld or anyone who was anything to do with him.

And so determined was this refusal to admit the world of Jerry into my consciousness that I barely knew who any of the characters were, and I only knew about Kramer because two young idiots in my department, having discovered him and been desperate to be the first people in London to use him in a commercial – which would involve meeting him, *a bloke off the telly!*, not to mention getting an all-expenses-paid trip to LA – came into my office one day and tried to flog me a script for a Cornish Pasty with Kramer and wotsisname the postman in it.

They soon wished they hadn't.

"Are you fucking deranged? A Cornish Pasty with a couple of actors from an American sitcom no-one has ever heard of—"

"Yes, they have."

"Apart from anything else, do you have any idea how much American actors cost?"

"Yeah, but you're always telling us not to worry about things like that, just do the most creative thing we can."

If there was one thing I hated, it was being told what I'd told someone.

"Yes, but I also expect you to have some fucking common sense! Just get out of here will you!"

They needed no second bidding, but in their anxiety to escape, they'd left their 'work' on the table. I crumpled the script up, charged towards the door, and threw it after them.

"And take this shit with you!"

So that was my general disposition vis-à-vis Jerry Seinfeld and all those who sailed with him, and it may provide some explanation for my actions when I finally arrived back in 'New Pemberley', a little less than fresh from my trip to Cannes. It was about ten in the evening I suppose, the girls were in bed, and the South African nanny was sitting on the sofa in the open plan kitchen stroke living room – quite separate from *the drawing room* as Alison insisted on calling it, which was reserved for special poncey occasions – with her feet tucked under her arse, painting her nails and watching the telly.

Having tried to find – unsuccessfully – something to eat in the fridge that wasn't in some way chocolatey, and having settled instead for drinking some tasteless Mexican beer – all we had – I slumped down on the sofa next to her – but not too close – and picked up a copy of 'Hello' that she must have been reading, and absent mindedly scrutinised the lovely home of whichever Z-lister had graciously invited me in so to do. Without looking up, and just to pass the time of day, I casually asked the South African nanny what she was watching. The answer, as I am sure you have long since deduced, was 'Seinfeld'. Normally, that is to say pre-Polaroid of Peggy, that would have prompted a neuro-transmitter to have got in touch with a synapse or the other way around or something like that and, without my registering any conscious thought, I would have got up and left the room. But on this occasion, now that Peggy was back on my radar, I suppose the neuro-transmitters, synapses etc had got the message – if they hadn't heard, who would have? – and I looked up at the screen to see what was going on. And what I saw was Jerry talking to someone whom he called Elaine. Which I found very confusing because I could have sworn the person he was talking to was someone called Peggy.

I concentrated harder. I got up and walked over to the screen and dropped on to my haunches to have a closer look. I could hear rustling and barely suppressed harrumphing from the direction of the sofa as the South African nanny – *Anneke*, that was her name! – wriggled about trying to see around my head which was evidently blocking her view. I made no effort to accommodate her – this was important, for fuck's sake. Annoyingly they kept cutting from one shot size to another so I could never get a long enough look at Elaine/Peggy's face to be absolutely certain. I ran out into the hall and opened my suitcase and dragged crumpled shirts and worn underpants and grubby espadrilles and half the rest of the stuff out of it trying to locate my Ozwald Boateng suit, which was buried at the bottom. Got it! Out came the jacket, and yes, in the inside pocket I found the Polaroid of Peggy.

I ran back in again to see someone called George and that Kramer person now occupying the screen.

"Come on, come on," I muttered, adding some impatient foot tapping. I caught Anneke flashing one of those supposed to be secret employee looks – doubtless tomorrow she would be telling her nanny mates all about it at the post school-run session at Starbucks.

At last Elaine/Peggy came back on and I checked from the Polaroid to the screen and back. No, it was not as I had first feared. (Yes, feared – jealousy, as always, trumping generosity.) Incredibly, I had already computed the possibility that this must have something to do with Miller and that under his evil influence Peggy had done a gamekeeper turned poacher thing and switched from casting to cast – but eventually I was able to convince myself that this Elaine was not actually Peggy herself. She had the same black tumbling hair, the same Jewish/Italian New York looks, the effervescence and the sudden smile but her features were just a little sharper – maybe that little touch of could-be Puerto Rican wasn't there – her hair was a tad straighter, her manner slightly more direct.

But, on the other hand, she was, in essence, Peggy to a tee. This Elaine woman or whatever her real name was, was so much like Peggy it was impossible not to be reminded of her. I sat there, clutching the Polaroid, utterly transfixed.

So transfixed, that I barely registered the commotion coming from the hall – "Ouch! Fuck! Who the hell left this bloody suitcase here – bugger, bugger, bugger – I've laddered my tights!" – and didn't notice Alison come up behind me. It was only when Anneke, clearly sensing imminent war, scuttled out of the room, that I looked up and saw her.

"Good evening Andrew," she said coolly and then, as she looked down at the Polaroid of Peggy in my hand, her tone dropped another few degrees to icy. "Gosh, I'm sorry. Am I interrupting something?"

Of course, I had another of those just-been-caught-watching-bestial-porn hot flushes – it's just not possible not to feel guilty as hell at such moments – and then tried to cover it up by saying something totally not to the point like, "Oh hi Alison – had a good week?"

"Yes, thank you," said Alison, turning sharply on her heel, "I've had a simply marvellous week."

I wasn't entirely sure what she meant by this, and I wasn't at all sure I wanted to know.

*

Alison reappeared in the kitchen a few minutes later, having repackaged herself in slobbing about the house wear – only jeans and tee-shirt but appropriately labelled – and poured herself a glass of Sancerre. She had a look on her face that did not augur well and although I could hardly have failed to notice that relations between us were going ever more awry, I wasn't quite ready to admit to myself that our marriage was in the last chance saloon. (Even if an objective view might have been that it wasn't so much in it, as half way out of the swing doors and about to be deposited on its arse in the dusty street.) I tried – though to what purpose other than the maintenance of a quiet life I have no idea – to sue for peace.

"How's the basement going?"

This was genuinely meant to be a nice, neutral, unthreatening, completely unloaded question to which – rather like a wildlife programme on the telly – no-one could object. But, having been completely wrapped up in my own world, I had not yet quite come to realise, despite all the evidence that was there for me to see, where Dougal-call-me-Doug fitted in to things. Alison, on the other hand, knew only too well, and assuming that even I couldn't be quite so self-absorbed as not to have noticed – she always underestimated me – interpreted my 'how's the basement?' question as being a particularly snide means of getting at her.

"If you want to know about Doug and me, what don't you stop trying to be so bloody clever for once in your life and just ask?"

Well, clearly – clear even to me who would much rather not have seen – there was now no need to ask.

Some men – and most women probably – faced with this de facto confession of guilt – quite a bit more than de facto really – would have just said get the hell out of here and never darken my door again. In the modern world, where no-one quits the marital home until the judge has assured them that their slice of the cake – their very big slice of the cake – and the cake stand – and at least half of the cake forks – are now unchallengeably theirs, these might just be empty words, but at least you might have the benefit of some kind of catharsis from just saying them.

I, however, typically, didn't say anything nearly so decisive. I just gawped. And I can't say that I found gawping in the least bit cathartic. I don't think feeling utterly empty, as I did, is quite the same thing. I also remember looking at Alison and thinking how incredibly beautiful she looked. A bit late to start appreciating her perhaps, but there you are. And I felt an overwhelming sadness. Despite everything I just wanted to take her in my arms and cuddle her. It might have been proof of that old saying about only realising what you've got when you've lost it. Or maybe, and I think this is nearer the mark, it was just sentimentality.

"So what do you want to do?" I asked when I eventually spoke.

Now it was Alison's turn to confront the truth of the situation. And if she'd come in to this conversation with a clear idea of where she wanted to come out, her confidence in whatever plans she'd had, appeared to falter.

"I don't really know," she said, and suddenly looked rather small. In that instant, the whole tenor of the conversation changed. All the confrontation and bitterness seemed to evaporate. Now we were equals again: two lost souls – just talking figuratively of course, I still didn't do souls – trying to see a way forward.

During this conversation we'd been standing on either side of the kitchen island. Now Alison walked around and sat on the edge of the sofa cradling her glass, and I picked up the bottle and another glass and perched next to her, topping her up and pouring myself a drink too. There we sat, side by side, in silence. And then it seemed as though, whatever the outcome was going to be, we had both decided we wanted to park it for the time being and leave all the ghastly possibilities of splitting up and telling the children and dealing with fucking lawyers and deciding which of us would be lumbered with Spot and all the rest until some other time.

In that odd spirit of sudden comradeship, I told her all about Cannes.

"Legga," she said, "What an arsehole!" 'Legga' was an old nickname for Vince (Dutton, rhyming slang) that had fallen into disuse since, in his more exalted status of recent years, he had become a tiny bit self-important and refused to answer to it.

And she also said, "Lucille! Huh! Didn't I always tell you she was trouble?"

143

And she had, many times. I'd always shrugged it off as one good looking girl's instinctive dissing of another. But now that I thought about it, I realised how right she had been, not just about Lucille, but about so many things professionally, and how much I would miss that, when, as seemed inevitable, the break eventually came.

In fact, it didn't come for many months. We soldiered on – for the usual reasons. For the sake of the children. To avoid the heartache. Because, you never knew, we might find a way back. And because too, we had a family holiday booked, three weeks in a stunning – and stunningly expensive – villa somewhere just south of the Costa Smeralda in Sardinia. It was booked and a hefty deposit paid, and we weren't going to get that back. And perhaps, just perhaps, three weeks in the Sardinian sun might begin to heal the wounds.

So we left it there. I said no more about Doug, asked for no promises as to future conduct, fought no duel. I even sat through a couple of meetings about 'snagging' the now all but completed basement conversion and, pretending, for some unearthly reason to be civilised, even congratulated him on having done a damned good job, which, by the way, he had. Even if introducing Doug on to the scene had – or would soon – cost me my marriage, I had the consolation that, even after the lunatic overruns on costs, we would, when you calculated the increased value of the house, still come out well ahead. And, yes, even in the midst of all this turmoil, I made those calculations and derived some comfort from them.

What Doug must have thought about me, I cannot imagine. If maybe seeming just a touch nervous at times, he certainly played his part in this little tragicomedy well enough, which can't have been easy because Alison must have told him that I knew, if not everything, then all that I needed to know. What can he have thought was going on in my head? Perhaps, being not just creative, but a properly qualified professional, an architect – *Dougal Harris RIBA* – he had a dim view of admen and thought not a lot went on in my head, which as regards Alison and him, was just about the truth of it. One thing I worried about a lot was missing 'Seinfeld'. (Or rather the scenes with Elaine/Peggy.) I really wanted to be able to sit and watch it with Anneke but I was terrified of being caught by Alison. I don't think I would have been nearly so nervous if it really had been bestial porn that I'd wanted to see.

At the end of July, we set off en famille in two huge Mercedes taxis bound for Heathrow, before struggling aboard a plane to Sardinia. It was the five of us; Alison, Florence – who made it explicitly – and expletively – clear that she didn't want to come and would far rather hang around with her mates in Whiteleys, our local mall – India, revelling in her role as angelic goodie goodie by comparison with Florence, Anneke and me. Spot had gone into kennels that were about as expensive as the Sardinian villa. I was rather hoping Anneke might bring some 'Seinfeld' videos with her but she didn't.

The holiday went as most such holidays do. Sunbathing, sunblocking, swimming in the pool, shrieking in the pool, bitter tearful arguments about who had first dibs on the floating poolchair – I usually won those – expensive meals in supposedly family restaurants where the kids turned their noses up at everything they hadn't had a million times before at home, family games of tennis which never got past thirty love before somebody stormed off in a huff, reading – or pretending to read – whichever three for the price of two novels we'd picked up at the airport Waterstones on the way out, and desperately looking for some way to engage India whenever she uttered her nine-year-old's mantra: "I'm *bored*!" This happened increasingly as the holiday progressed (*progressed?*) because Florence had met some little local oik who was staying two villas down, and spent as much time as she could doing fuck knows what with him, thus making herself unavailable for relentlessly teasing her sister, which treatment you might have thought would have upset India, but which, for some unfathomable reason, she seemed to prefer to being left alone.

And I, not being able to find enough to distract me – despite all of the above – could not fail to do some serious thinking. (I dare say

145

that Alison – stretched out on the other side of the pool, face down on the sunbed, bra unclasped, head and copper hair hanging over the end so she could read her book positioned on the ground below, Cutler and Gross shades on, aluminium foil nose piece defying laws of gravity and still in place – was doing some serious thinking too, but though we managed a fair copy of exchanging pleasantries, the one thing we were never going to do was reveal any of our serious thinking to each other, so I cannot report on anything of consequence that she may have had under consideration.)

One subject I did a lot of poolside pondering upon, and not before time you might think, was my attitude towards them – Alison and her chap, I mean. Or, should I say, my lack of attitude. For was it not odd that I simply didn't care? Wasn't I supposed to? And yet the thing was that I seemed emotionally unaffected by it. I had no issue with Alison, and, apart from the fact that I'd always thought that Dougal-call-me-Doug was a bit too full of himself for my liking, no issue with him either. I willingly conceded that I hadn't been the most attentive of husbands – not a drunken philanderer, but often preoccupied with work and what have you. And I saw too that, as we'd drifted on, we'd both really just been going through the motions rather than having a fulfilling marriage. The passion of love, it seemed, had been displaced by the cool objectivity of reason. And it seemed perfectly reasonable to me that Alison should take up with someone else. I didn't forgive her, because it didn't require any forgiving – I didn't feel that I had been offended. And as for where this taking up with Doug should lead, well, I could see it going either way. If our situation – let's stop calling it a marriage – could be sustained, then for the good of the children, and of the finances, and to avoid all the upset that a divorce always seems to bring, then why not? And if not, and we would go our separate ways, which, as I've indicated, I suppose I thought more likely, then I would just have to deal with it.

But then I thought about Miller, and my insane jealousy of him.

And how different my feelings had been in that menage à trois from the way they were in this one. And realising that, when roused, I was just as capable of whacking a glove across the face of a love rival as the next idiot, it just made my passivity about Alison and Doug seem all the more significant. The desperately sad but inescapable fact was that I felt – or didn't feel – as I did, because Doug wasn't a love rival. You have to be in love to have one of those.

Towards the end of the holiday, the parents of the little local oik, feeling, I presume, that some sort of Italian good form dictated they should acquaint themselves with the family of their son's new playmate, asked us all over for a barbecue. (If barbecues are what they call them in Italy.) To my pleasant surprise, they all seemed terribly impressed with Florence. Gabriella, the mother seemed to adore her and the Hollywood-casting aged old granny could hardly stop herself from pinching her cheeks. And when I saw Florence actually carrying out serving dishes of salads and fruit from the kitchen, it was all I could do to stop myself from enquiring if her body had been inhabited by extra-terrestrials. (This was the kind of jolly banter that I frequently indulged in with the girls, despite being constantly told by Alison that what I found passably amusing they experienced as mortally wounding.)

Lucca – il papa – pulled me to one side.

"'Ere," he said, "You liker no?"

And he held up an as yet unlit joint.

"I, er, tike it from Georgio's roomer." (Georgio was the oik.)

"Oh," I replied, trying not to appear shocked, and thinking I needed to get Florence out of this den of iniquity, A.S.A.P.

Then Mario had a fit of undisguised glee; laughing, coughing, spluttering, bending double, literally slapping his sides; he was beside himself at having made such a terrific joke.

"No, no, juster kiddin' Undroo. But you liker, no?"

What could I do? Look like a prig and tut-tut him away, or try not to inhale and pretend to enjoy it?

The trouble was I only had to look at a joint these days, and the party in the meat packing district, and all the paranoia that came with it, and all the soul searching that came after it, came flooding back.

So, whether I did a Bill Clinton or I didn't – and I didn't but neither would I do much more – it was but a short hop from the Costa Smeralda in 1999 to Manhattan twenty years before.

*

It was a Thursday again, it was late August, just after we had returned, still together but no closer, from our holiday in Sardinia, and in Donald's basement it was sweltering. The window was open, but no cooling breeze came through, and the sun beat down on us ferociously; it must have been hot because, for just about the only time I could remember, the heatless real flame gas fire was actually switched off.

For once I wasn't late, because I had come with a real purpose. My mind was beginning to clear, and I wanted to talk to Donald about something in particular. It was the joint I'd had with the oik's dad – or the nervous couple of puffs I'd had at the joint – that had set this train of thought running.

I had taken Donald through the story of the photographer's party more than once in the past, although, given that he'd told me that I'd never mentioned Peggy to him until this latest round of sessions, I can't have said anything to him about the day after, when I'd sat in the diner near my apartment, wondering whether my feelings about her were as real as they seemed, or whether my crush was only so intense because it was just another manifestation of the heightened sensations that just being in New York seemed to induce. Since the joint in Sardinia, when I'd been transported back to the meatpacking district, I had gone on to thinking about that Sunday in the diner, and I now had to go through it all with

148

Donald, because the question I wanted to ask flowed directly from that. And the question was this:

"Do you think that the reason that this business with Peggy has taken such a grip of me now is that it's a kind of an echo of the feelings I had then?"

"Well, when you recall anything – any feelings – from the past, it's an echo of sorts isn't it?"

"Yes, but I mean more than that. If my feelings for Peggy at the time were sort of in extremis because of the whole New York experience, then is the echo I am feeling now going to be that much louder than it normally would be?"

Donald got on my train of thought.

"And reverberate more?"

"Exactly. And reverberate more."

"Well, I suppose it might."

"You see, what I need to know is whether these feelings … this sense I have about Peggy now, can be relied upon. If I am going to try to find her, I mean. I need to know that, don't I?"

I doubt if Donald actually held his breath then or that I held mine, but there was suddenly a palpable sense in the room that a line had been crossed. Until I said those words, at that moment, I don't think I had consciously articulated – even to myself – that I was going to set out to find Peggy. Looking back, it seems that it was inevitable. But with so many things in life, at least in my life, the logical conclusion to a sequence of events is never clear until it's reached. So often I have felt – after the event – as though I have been tip-toeing blindly up a see-saw, not realising, even as I was taking that fateful final step, that the balance was about to irrevocably shift.

And my question was answered. Whatever the reason for the strength of the echo, the Polaroid of Peggy was calling to me, and I was going to answer. Just as I had sat in that diner and turned things this way and that, but concluded that whatever the whys and wherefores, the bottom line was that I was still mad about the girl, so I had now reached the same conclusion again.

"Do you have any idea where she is?" asked Donald.

I laughed.

"Now you come to mention it, not a clue."

"So where would you start?"

"No idea."

"You're not worried about where this might lead? What about Alison? Your family?"

I thought about that. For about ten seconds. And then, by way of a reply, I just shrugged. I wasn't worried about the effect it might have on Alison. Our relationship may have once been romantic but now it was entirely pragmatic. My children, yes, I had concerns about them, of course I did. But I would cross that bridge when I came to it. It was extraordinary. A few moments ago, the notion of looking for Peggy was hardly a notion at all. Now the idea seemed set in stone.

"And what about Peggy? Supposing she doesn't want to be found?"

I thought about that too. For about five seconds. Then I heard her say, "I totally like you." And I remembered the windows-of-the-soul moment in the second best room in the Gardner Inn in Pound Ridge. And I remembered that the one time I had played Tarzan, Peggy had been more than willing to be Jane. (And I remembered all the other times when I'd just faffed about, and how she had followed my lead then too.) No, I wasn't worried about her not wanting to be found.

"And what about her family? She's probably got one. She may have a husband and children. What about them?"

I didn't need to think about that at all. One thing I would never deny – not that anyone would ever challenge me on this score – is that I am ruthlessly selfish. When there is something I think I want, I go for it, and I don't stop for long to think about who might get hurt in the process. Cuckolded husbands I wouldn't give a fuck about. Devastated children might be more of a problem but I'd find some sort of specious rationale – they're better off out of an unhappy marriage, that kind of thing – that would allow me to sleep sweetly.

And if I'm not exactly proud of that, neither am I particularly ashamed. It makes me, I would venture to suggest, just like most people.

So there I was. On the E to P-ometer, I would have had to admit, the glass was falling. Marriage disintegrating, career on the skids, mental health debatable.

But on the plus side, I had, at last, a direction of sorts.

'I know where I'm going.' Well, I thought I did.

'I know who's going with me.' That, I didn't know.

'I know who I love.' Well, I thought I did.

'And my dear knows who I'll marry.' Yes, well at this point, quite apart from the fact that I already was married, my dear may well have forgotten she ever was my dear, so that was possibly a little premature.

PART TWO

CHAPTER 12

NEW YORK, 1979

I clung to the idea that Peggy would throw her lot in with mine even though she had made her immediate intentions – or lack of them – clear enough. I had a mental picture of her arriving at my front door, a suitcase bulging with her clothes in one hand, her favourite potplant in the other, and a cardboard box of her old LPs under her arm. But then my mind's eye would switch channels and I would see myself sorting through my mail and finding an envelope in her handwriting which, when opened, would turn out to contain the old Dear John letter. Unbelievable, I told myself, it's been less than twenty-four hours and she's already forgotten your name. Ha ha ha. My head resounded with hollow laughter.

Yes, as ever, I was constantly veering between wild unjustified optimism and expectation of the absolute worst. When I wasn't trying to decide between Fiji or Rio for the honeymoon, I was thinking that Peggy and Miller must have made it up and that the carryings-on in the second best room at the Gardner Inn had been permanently erased from her memory. And all that was going on in the ten minutes it took me to ride the subway up to the office on the Monday morning after we got back.

I hadn't even got my feet under my desk when I was being bombarded with enquiries.

"Did the guide book come in handy?" enquired Laverne coyly, as I passed reception. Obviously, I hadn't covered my tracks to Barnes and Noble as well as I'd thought. Then it was Brett and Bart's turn. They put their heads round my door to invite me over for a Monday morning conference.

"So, man," asked Brett or Bart, drawing deep, "did you manage to get the royal sword out of its sheath?"

"Yeah man," added the other, "did you go down on one knee? Or both."

SFX: uproarious laughter interspersed with violent coughing. I didn't particularly take to these smutty references to my weekend of the purest love, so I made some po-faced reply – which only increased the uproar/coughing – and went back to my own office.

As I sat down, the phone rang. It was Peggy. I asked her to hang on for a moment, said a silent prayer – to whom or for what I didn't know – got up and locked the door, and then picked up the receiver to find out what the score was today.

"Hi Andy."

"Hi Peggy."

Sort of nil-nil so far. Nothing to indicate which way this was going to go.

"Andy, um, I am going to be a bit tied up for a couple days so I'm not going to be able to see you, you see I have—"

Uhuh. Here we go then. I was already ahead of her. "—I have to make arrangements for my wedding with Miller."

"—I have to see my brother, Marv. He's in the city tomorrow and he wants to take me out. And its crazy busy down here today – detergent panic! Don't know what time I'm going to get out of here. But we can get together Wednesday if that's okay with you."

A wave of relief swept over me. Completely illogical, of course. Bald spots notwithstanding, to the objective observer there would have been no earthly reason for me to feel so insecure. But old habits etc., and when you're totally doolally about a woman who is, technically, still co-habiting with another man, it is hard, even if you have just spent a weekend away together, to be totally sure of your ground. However, custom dictated that I should appear unconcerned.

"Wednesday? Hm. Might be something I'm doing ..." – pause while I rustle papers to simulate sound of turning diary pages – "... on Wednesday. Let me check."

"Look if there's a problem, don't worry about it. Maybe next wee—"

"—no, no, no! Looks fine after all. Wednesday it is then."

Never play poker with a woman. (Mother, wife, girlfriend, daughter, whoever.) No matter how small – or big – the stakes, they always know when to call your bluff.

Or maybe, it's just me.

*

As it turned out, Wednesday was another of those days that might have been better if it had never happened. We went to see the new James Bond movie, 'Moonraker', and frankly, wished we hadn't.

"I prefer Sean Connery," I said, over coffee at a place next to the cinema.

"So do I," said Peggy, "Rog doesn't do it for me." And it was the last thing we agreed on that night.

Another of those sudden cloudbursts? Well, a nasty squall anyway, and all because the subject of Peggy's name came up again. We hadn't discussed it since the very first date.

"The last movie I saw at this place, I also didn't like," said Peggy, "'Ice Castles'. You see that? Yuck. Schmaltz-eee!"

Now, the theme song from 'Ice Castles', as you may recall, was 'Through The Eyes of Love' by Melissa Manchester, and I had had cause to think of it that very day, because I had spent my lunch hour in a record store on Sixth Avenue, having gone there with Brett (or Bart) because he wanted to buy something by the Sex Pistols. (Or The Clash was it? – anyway one of those punk bands that I could never stand, but which I had occasionally self-consciously attempted to pogo to at parties because everyone else was doing it.) So, while he looked at one end of the store, I was idly thumbing through the female vocalist section at the other, looking particularly – and probably not entirely coincidentally – through the Peggy Lee section. There, I discovered, she had just released a new album, and on it was a cover version of 'Through The Eyes of Love'. So, not unnaturally I told this topical tale to Peggy, who said in response, "Oh, really."

Her indifference took me aback. Wasn't it ever so slightly romantic that I should have spent my lunch hour choosing to look through the records of her famous namesake, and what's more, wouldn't you have expected the very title of the song – 'Through The Eyes of Love' – to have made my Peggy just a soupçon, well, gooey-eyed?

But not a bit of it. Quite the opposite, because her next words were, "God, I hate that song. It was worse than the movie. Gush, gush, gush." And then she actually put two fingers in her mouth, just to make it absolutely clear, if I hadn't yet got the message, that 'Through The Eyes of Love' made her want to vomit.

Objectively – ah, our old elusive friend, objectivity again – why should that honestly held opinion, to which she was perfectly entitled, cause my hackles to rise? And yet, totally irrationally, they did. Not all of my hackles perhaps, but certainly the odd one here and there. And, as a rising hackle always will, it came together with its fellows to form a sub-conscious impulse that made me want to get her going, just a tiny bit, in return. There was no real malice aforethought, m'lud. How could I have even known that bringing up the subject of her name again would do the trick? Surely, it was only natural that talking about the other Peggy Lee would lead me on to this:

157

"Er Peggy, just tell me, all kidding aside, what is your real name?"

Peggy, who was having a double malted milk shake or something equally disgusting, and battling to suck in this mess, released the straw, and looked up at me, black-brown eyes gleaming. Alright, they seemed to be saying, let's play!

"I told you, it's Brenda."

"Yes. Brenda. Very funny. Peggy Lee, Brenda Lee, very funny. What's next? Vivien Lee?"

She frowned a little and yet half smiled at the same time, as if she couldn't quite believe what she was hearing.

"Why is it so important to you?"

"Ah! So it isn't Brenda!"

"I never said that. What I said was, 'Why is it so import—"

"Yes I know what you said – " (Can you sense the tension ratcheting up a little?) " – but I think you're just playing games."

"Playing games, huh?"

"Yes, playing games," I repeated back to her but the challenging way she had first repeated it back to me made me slightly less sure that she was. (Told you – never play poker with a woman.) But by now, I was committed.

"And the thing is, I just don't understand why. Okay, it might have been funny for five minutes, but why would you want to have the advantage over me—"

"Have the ad-vaaaan-tage over you?" Right, so now we were into the taking-the-piss-out-of-accents stage. The gloves were coming off.

"Yes," I said, evenly, determined to remain cool. "Why else would you not want to tell me what your real name was? And—"

"I have. It's Brenda."

"—and why would you want to have the advantage over someone who you are supposed to – to – to … "

"To what?"

"To totally like, that's what!"

158

A pause. I looked at Peggy, holding her gaze. Not exactly with a smirk on my face, but expressing a certain satisfaction that I had made the decisive point. But Peggy wasn't done. She looked back over her double malted milkshake, her eyes holding mine just as steadily.

"And why, if you feel as much for me as you say you do, would you not be happy to call me by whatever name I wanted to be called?"

Hmm. Touché. But the fight was still in me. I sprang back to my feet, did a forward roll, picked up my sword, and turned to face her again.

"It's not that I'm not happy to call you by whatever the fuck you want to be called – it's – it's—"

"Yes, it's what?"

"—it's – it's a matter of trust, that's what it is! If you love someone—"

"Love?!"

Shit. Why had I gone there? Still, no way out now.

"Yes, love. Well, that's the question, I suppose" – suddenly I spotted a chandelier I could launch a new attack from – "Yes, that is the question. Is it love? Because if love isn't about trust – absolute trust – between two people, then what the fuck is it about?" (I had no idea what I was talking about, but I liked the sound of it.) "And if you can't even bring yourself to trust me with your real name, for God's sake, then what hope is there for us?"

I stood there, legs apart, the tip of my sword at her throat. But somehow, in the blink of an eye, she rolled away, and was back on her feet again.

"And if you trusted me, you wouldn't keep asking me some bullshit question which has nothing whatever to do with love! If you trusted me you would know I had my reasons for whatever I said – and you wouldn't keep doubting me!"

That's how it finished. With one of those ridiculous 'if you trusted me/no, if you trusted me' to-ings and fro-ings, a pointless, no-score draw. We paid the check – Peggy insisted on putting in her half, making some sort of point I suppose – and we left. There was a bit of an awkward silence as we walked, arm not in arm, to the subway station, but before we parted to go in our different directions, Peggy reached up and kissed me, and then, after a sheepish grin from me and a reciprocal one from her, she disappeared.

So, as seemed to be the pattern, we sort of kissed and made up at the end, but those kinds of tit-for-tat spats, as ridiculous as they are and as this one certainly was, when you're not really arguing about the thing you're arguing about but because of some bruised feeling on one side or the other that gets completely forgotten in the heat of it all, well, they do, eventually, add up and take their toll.

One thing was for sure. I wasn't going to go near the question of Peggy's name again. Peggy or even Brenda or whatever she wanted to be called would do – would have to do – from now on.

*

Peggy and I were, at this point, and for a few weeks after, in some sort of limbo. In popular usage, or at least the way I understand it, that basically means stuck in neutral with wheels spinning but no forward motion. Interestingly however, according to Wikipedia, the word derives from the Latin, 'limbus' which means edge or boundary, referring to the 'edge' of hell. And that, I would say, is a rather more accurate description of the way I felt. We had briefly become lovers at the Gardner Inn and I did, on two or three occasions, manage to cajole Peggy into repeating the experience, neon-lit, in the bedroom in my sublet. But she would never stay the night, which meant she went back to her flat with Miller, which meant in turn, to my mind, that, in a sense – the very important sense that she lived with him – she was more his than mine. And that I found intensely frustrating. Why the idea of having someone exclusively reserved for you – of you being her one and only – matters so much, I really don't know. Maybe Peggy was right when she talked about me wanting to bop her on the head with a club and carry her back to my cave. Maybe it really was just some leftover primeval instinct. But, whatever the reasons, I found the situation very hard to deal with. And, in my place, who wouldn't have?

Patience, yes, I could see the need for that. Mustn't put any pressure on. More chance of the kitten coming down from the tree if you don't frighten it with the fire brigade. But patience was never my long suit. Not that boldness was either. Although, boldness wise, I couldn't see many options anyway. About the only thing I could have done would have been to call her bluff and tell that if she didn't agree to come and live in my cave right now, I was going to stop playing and take my club home with me. And, as we all know how I am with the bluffing thing, we were, as I began by saying, stuck in limbo. Does it seem like I'm going round in circles? Exactly.

If there were a science called emotional physics – which some snake oil salesman somewhere probably claims there is – it would be a basic law that frustration, unless released, slowly converts into anger. Overall, Peggy and I were still having a terrific time when we were together, and I was as convinced as ever that she was the one, but still this incipient anger was bubbling under – and when you start to show even the tiniest bit of anger, the other person gets angry back. That was probably a factor in our contretemps across the double malted milkshake, and it all came to the surface again, a couple of weeks later.

The surface in question was red clay. The red clay of the Public Tennis Courts at Riverside Park on 96th Street.

One day, having a drink after work, Peggy and I were discussing what we might do at the weekend, when some young preppie type, pushing past us on his way to the bar, heard his name called out and, swinging round to see who was doing the calling, narrowly avoided swiping me with the tennis racquet that was sticking out of the backpack he was carrying over his shoulder. He quickly apologised, and I replied with something to the effect that it really wasn't a problem, I'd probably have done the same, they were bloody awkward things to carry, tennis racquets, weren't they? Then off he went and I turned back to Peggy, who said, "You play tennis? You never told me that. We should have a game."

I was more than a little surprised. It had never crossed my mind that Peggy would be the sporty type. Maybe it was the fact that she was so lightly built, or maybe it was just that she was a girl – sorry about the sexist stereotyping – and a Jewish girl at that – and the ethnic stereotyping – but, as I say, it had just never occurred to me. I was, always have been, a big fan of most sports, and an enthusiastic if less than brilliant participant in one or two but I had never once discussed the subject with Peggy because, well, you don't with girls, do you? Or maybe you do now, but this was 1979. Or maybe other people did but not me. Anyhow, we hadn't.

"Blimey," I said, "Who are you? Chris Evert?"

"No," she said, "I'm left handed. I'm more your Martina type."

If I was surprised before I was shocked now. Of course, Peggy was making a fairly routine joke, yet there was something in her tone that told me she was only joking up to a point. Not only did she play tennis, but she clearly believed she played a pretty useful game. And as I had never heard her say a single boastful word – she was much more given to self-deprecation than making even the smallest claim for herself – I could only think that she must be right. Quite amazing. A few moments ago I'd never even contemplated the idea of Peggy on a tennis court, now I was thinking she might be good enough to – to – well, yes, beat me. Heaven forfend! However, a challenge had been issued which no Englishman worthy of the name could refuse. And so the problem of what to do at the weekend was solved, and battle joined. Peggy made a call the next morning, and a court was booked for Saturday afternoon at three.

I had brought my racquet with me from England, though never had cause to use it in New York until now. I found it buried in the back of a cupboard, a wooden Slazenger, the sort of thing that

Bjorn Borg used, still held tight in its press. A racquet press! These days the very idea of one sounds as prehistoric as a flint headed axe. For those who have never beheld its wonders, think of a small, square wooden picture frame without a front or back. The press had two of these, positioned flat, one above the other, and between which you slotted the tennis racquet head, before tightening the adjustable springy screws at each corner which held the thing together. The idea, I think, was to prevent your wooden racquet from warping and to keep your strings of catgut – e.g. made from an animal's intestines! – tight. And not only does it sound archaic, but when you carried your racquet in its press you bore the whole weight of its history. It weighed a ton. If, like the preppie type in the bar, you had swung round with one of those sticking out of your backpack, you could have taken somebody's head off.

Dressed in an old white cable knit sweater I had dug up from somewhere, and an ancient pair of Dunlop Green Flashes (long before they were fashionable again) but wearing black socks, because I couldn't find any white ones, I found my way to Riverside Park. Personally, I think it's pretty bad form to fall about laughing when your opponent walks on to court, but it didn't stop Peggy.

She, on the other hand, was dressed immaculately – and very prettily I had to admit – in a sweet little white tennis dress with her black hair swishing about in a ponytail. And in her hand she carried one of those, then revolutionary, Prince aluminium racquets with the huge heads – huge when compared with my wooden jobbie, actually still commonly used in 1979 but soon bound for the museum. Yes, it was to be Smith and Wesson versus bow and arrow and we all know what happened to the poor bloody Injuns.

It got worse. We began to knock up and the very first ball she hit to me – massive backswing, almighty thud, perfect weight transfer – had so much top spin it bounced straight over my head. I picked the ball up and casually – as casually as I could – I looped it over the net on her backhand side. Thwack! Back it screamed, and just as I was getting my feet in position to return it, the ball suddenly dipped, hit the ground and then reared up and over my head again. A topspin backhand as well as a forehand! You have to be very carefully taught to play one of those. I looked up at her, then back at my little wooden Slazenger and smilingly shook my head as though our mismatched weaponry was the problem. But I had already seen enough to know that she could have been playing with a pool cue and still got the job done.

Even so, slightly miffed at the reception she had given me when I walked onto court, slightly angry at the continuing impasse over her living arrangements, slightly aghast at the prospect of being beaten by a GIRL, and being anything but *slightly* competitive by nature, I did not feel inclined to just chuck in the towel.

I decided to fight fire with – lobbing.

Lobbing – to hit the ball high in the air rather than straight across the net – is an entirely legitimate shot in tennis. Except when it's not. And when it's not is when you are lobbing not to win the point but in order to slow the game down, to take the pace off the ball so your opponent's timing is out, to wind him, or in this case, her, up to the point where she loses her rag and her concentration and makes lots of damned fool mistakes which, having been made, lead to even more, and thus to eventual, humiliating defeat.

That was the plan. It wasn't very British but history shows there can be exceptions – usually when the British are involved. The trouble with the plan was that you have to at least be able to get racquet on ball in order to be able to lob in the first place. I think you can imagine how often I was able to do that.

At the end of the first set, the score of which I have no intention of divulging, Peggy sportingly offered to swap racquets, an offer which I bad temperedly refused. In the second, during which she was obviously taking it easy – and thus irritating me even more – I did manage to lob the ball on the odd occasion, giving her the opportunity to demonstrate what a fine overhead smash she had.

About the only points I 'won' were due to me insisting the ball was out, when a blind man without a stick would have known that it wasn't. (Peggy, even more annoyingly, if such a thing were possible, refused to argue, and accepted whatever I said.)

After two of the most one sided sets of tennis that can ever have been played, we sat down on the chairs at the side of the court, me puffing like Thomas the Tank Engine, her still as fresh as a daisy. Somehow I had to find a way to stop my teeth from grinding, to find a way to say well played, to simulate some sort of pretence of good sportsmanship – either that or look an utter tosser.

So I turned to her to mumble, as best I could, my grudging congratulations, and she just burst out laughing. In the mood I was in, and knowing me, I could have easily responded by swearing at her and storming off in a pathetic, self-defeating paddy. (I have done it often enough.) But, thank the lord in whom I do not believe, for once I did not. She just looked so bloody fabulous, was radiating such good humour, was so obviously making light of the whole ridiculous situation and not just fun of me, that I could hardly fail to see the funny side too.

And that was Peggy for you. Or rather, that was Peggy for me.

*

And then at last, breakthrough. As though that moment of joy after the tennis was the catalyst, as indeed it may have been, Peggy called me one morning, a couple of days later, to say that she guessed I ought to know that she'd spoken to Miller, that she'd packed up her things and that she was moving into Noreen's that evening. And no, she said in response to my scepticism, there was no chance of her changing her mind. This was really it.

Frustration released. Wish fulfilled. Love victorious. For a while, that's really how it seemed it was going to be. And when she finished the call by asking me if I'd like to come to New Rochelle the next

Sunday to have lunch with her family, well, it was all I could do to prevent myself from calling Mavis and telling her to get herself a hat and climb on to the next plane over.

Lunch in Nooroeshel! We were going to be Rob and Laura all over again.

CHAPTER 13

LONDON, 1999

It was September, most of us were back from our summer holidays, and it felt, as it always did, as though we were at the beginning of a new school year. If we weren't wearing freshly cleaned and pressed uniforms and carrying satchels of newly covered exercise books with our names written on them and underlined in three different colours, there was still a sort of natural impetus, a feeling that this was the time for great new projects to begin, that pages could be turned, that the future started now. Fitting then, that *my* great new project, the hunt for Peggy, should be about to get underway. But although I was about to turn my attention to that, I had other fish to fry first.

I looked through the wide vertical blinds that hung down over the glass wall of my office and across the corridor into another very similar one. This office, newly constructed over the summer (which involved some expensive remodelling of the creative department's offices to accommodate it) was almost a replica of mine, but not quite. (Very deliberately, and at my insistence, not quite.) It was about twenty per cent smaller and instead of having the epic views of the Fitzrovia street scene which my office, as estate agents like to say, 'enjoyed', it faced a rather forbidding 'well' in the middle of our building, and its occupant looked out at a meshing puzzle of pipes, or, if she was nosey, into other offices, which, on winter nights, if their tenants forgot to close their blinds, might reveal that all human life was there.

The she-occupant in question was, of course, Lucille Wood, now officially my deputy. She didn't have a sign on her door to prove it, because advertising agencies don't do 'status' in quite that way. But they certainly do it – business class or scum class airplane seats, company credit cards or not, own office or open plan desk, and, in this case, the lesser position and proportions of Lucille's office compared to mine.

However, I was well aware that small countries had been known to build mighty empires so I was keeping a careful eye on things. I didn't imagine her ambition would stop at being deputy anything and, from what I gathered, she and Vince were still an item, or, as the office wags had it, 'she was getting her Legga over'. In other words, she would be in his ear at every opportunity and wheedling away to get him to do goodness knows what.

Faced with the prospect of an enemy alliance I had decided to make some political arrangements of my own. We had a youngish woman account director who went by the uninventable name of Atalanta du Vivier. ('Hattie' to her pals.) Hattie was a statuesque bottle blonde Oxford graduate. (Despite Bradley, Williams and Dutton's own unimpressive academic qualifications, we only went for the best. It made us feel better, E to P wise, to have Oxons and Cantabs stacked up on our mantelpiece.) Hattie had the urban yet posh accent that marked her out as having been to one of those London private schools that teach self-possession to A level – actually, the very same school that Florence and India attended, a coincidence which, when discovered, gave us a sort of natural kinship – and which I could then exploit. My Machiavellian plan was – well I wasn't quite sure what it was – but I figured that getting Hattie into my camp might prove useful, and, when somebody left, and we needed a new account director on the cereal business that we'd won earlier in the year, I lobbied, subtly, but, in the end, successfully, for her to get it. I also made sure that she knew that I had. Q.E.D. she knew she owed me. Though Will had now left, Lucille was still working on the business and so Hattie and she would be spending a lot of time together. At the very least, I reckoned, one or two titbits of useful intelligence might come my way.

But to Lucille in person, I was the very essence of avuncular charm. I was so relieved, I told her, to have someone to help me out with my executive burden. If there was anything I could do to help her in any way at all, she wasn't to hesitate to ask. And would she like to take over the responsibility for this account? And that one? And maybe this other one, but only of course if she felt she had the time? And pretty soon, I had managed to lumber Lucille with all the most unrewarding accounts, and all the most unimaginative clients that we had, while I retained nine tenths of the plums. And the tenth that I gave her, I was pretty sure, had worms inside it somewhere.

With Lucille now buried deep beneath this avalanche of work, my days were relatively free and I could turn my attention to the pursuit of Peggy. The problem was, as I had indicated to Donald McEwan, that I didn't have a clue where to start.

I closed my office door and I took out a piece of paper with the intention of making a list of the facts that I knew. (I ought to explain here that my handwriting is appalling; it would make a doctor with the DTs blush. Even I can't read more than about two words of it, so, in a case like this, I take extra special care and am very deliberate about the whole process.) I carefully centred the piece of paper in the middle of my desk. I ironed it flat several times with the heel of my hand, and then I finally took up my ball point pen. But, just as I was poised to write, I decided it wasn't good enough for the job and called the faithful Julia to come in, whence I instructed her to go forth and find me one of those flashy fine pointed Stilo type things that art directors and designers like to use. And I wanted a brand new one. Black only would do.

Eventually she returned with the required implement, but would only leave the office having first volunteered, as forcibly as she could, to write – whatever it was – for me, as she obviously anticipated that at some point she would have the job of typing it up and thus having to decipher the indecipherable. Eventually, I managed to usher her out of the door.

I carefully removed the cap of the brand new arty pen and then, with a little flourish, I set it to paper. I wrote: Name, Last Known Whereabouts, Date of Last Known Whereabouts, People Who Might Know Her, Whereabouts of People Who Might Know Her.

This seemed like a very sensible methodical start.

Then I filled in the gaps under the headings. Under Name, I carefully wrote, P-e-g-g-y L-e-e, almost mouthing the words with my tongue hanging out as I went, much as a seven-year-old practising their handwriting would. I sat back and reviewed my handiwork. Hmm, Peggy Lee. Very nicely written. I could even read it. But was that her name? Really? Thanks to Peggy's adamant refusal to abandon this ridiculous game that she'd started, I was never able to establish to my one hundred per cent satisfaction whether Peggy really was her proper given name, or just a nickname. So. I was forced to concede that the Peggy bit might be in doubt, and I put a question mark by it. With the 'Lee' though, I felt I was on solid ground, so I gave it a big tick.

I moved on. 'Last known whereabouts.' Damned good question. What were her last known whereabouts? I wasn't absolutely sure. Her last permanent address that I knew of was the apartment she'd shared with the loathsome Miller, but I had the distinct impression that it had been his apartment and would have been in his name. So all I could safely put was Manhattan. Then I added New York. I then added a comma and New York again, as in New York, New York. Then, after a few more moments cogitation, I put U.S.A. But, in all honesty, that didn't seem likely to narrow the possibilities down.

I moved on again. Date of last known whereabouts. That, at least, was easy. 1979, I put in big, very carefully drawn numbers. I then sat back and thought about the last time I'd seen her. The night of the Robert Palmer concert, that was it. Which was – when? August. Yes, almost certainly August. So I added a little dash after the 1979 and wrote A-u-g-u-s-t. I then wasted about twenty minutes reminiscing about that last evening before being woken from my daydream by some juicy oaths issuing from the street below. I stuck my head out of the window to see what was going on and found out that it was a dispatch cyclist who had been riding the wrong way down the street having an altercation with an elderly pedestrian who'd been foolish enough to be using a zebra crossing at an inopportune moment. I shut the window and, once more, bent myself to the task at hand.

Next heading: People who might know her. Hmm. Well, Miller obviously. Mill-er. I pressed so hard writing M-i-l-l-e-r that I tore the paper. Annoying, but that's twenty years of pent-up jealousy for you. I then added P-r-i-n-c-e, before, with a change of mind and mood, I crossed that out and replaced it with P-r-o-n-s-k-i. I dotted the 'i' with a flourish, more of a stab perhaps, making another hole in the paper. Take that, Mill-er!

I moved on. I thought hard. Oh, yes, Noreen! N-o-r-e-e-n. But Noreen who? It was something vaguely Irish I seemed to remember. Began with a – a – Q! Quigley, that was it. Or, wait a mo, was it Quinn? Or maybe, it wasn't a Q at all. Maybe it would come back to me – I'd leave it until later.

Let's see, who else? I sucked on the Stilo. There was her boss in casting but for the life of me, I couldn't remember the woman's name. Complete blank. And I'd barely spent five minutes with any of the other girls in casting – my default position with any girls in any office anywhere was to flirt, or try to, and I could hardly flirt with Peggy's workmates, could I? So I'd hardly exchanged a word with any of the not-Peggys. And besides, that was all I had ever known them as: not-Peggys. Couldn't see that being of much use if I tried to get Interpol involved.

Who else? Bloody hell, there had to be somebody else. We hadn't lasted for long but we'd managed five or six months. Surely, we hadn't gone around in such a bubble that we'd never spoken to anybody else – or had we? Perhaps we had. There was Bart, I suddenly remembered, and Brett, but before I got down so much as the first stroke of a B, I realised that, even if I could find them, their brains would be so addled they probably wouldn't remember me, let alone Peggy, or even that the year 1979 had ever taken place.

I put the pen down and pressed my fingers to my temples, as if gripping my head would force something out of it. I twirled around in my office chair. Clockwise. I twirled back. And then back again. And then, on my second anti-clockwise twirl – or possibly my tenth – I caught Julia staring at me from her desk on the other side of the glass wall. I stopped abruptly and smiled. As you do. Julia smiled back – a smile of pity I would describe it as – and then, with a slight shake of the head, got up and walked away to the coffee machine or somewhere. With her out of the way, I took the opportunity to take on one of my favourite office challenges. How many rotations of my office chair could I manage with a single push? Using feet only, mind. No hands allowed. Strict World Officechair Twirling Championships rules applied.

Important to keep straightening up your head, like ice-skaters doing one of those mental spins. Position feet together and at the right angle – 45 degrees to the side – for maximum leverage, grip arms of chair with hands, lean slightly forward and GO! One rev-o-lut-ion comp-le-ted, two rev-o-lut-ions comp-le-ted – good speed still being maintained, we'd definitely get to three, maybe even four, or maybe, just maybe, the holy grail of office chair spinning, FIVE! – "Talk us through it, Andrew. When did you feel the record was on?"

And then in barges Vince, the bastard! I was slap bang in the middle of my third rotation, feet tucked up and arching my back for perfect body shape and minimum drag, when in he strolls without so much as a by your leave.

I forced the toes of my chocolate brown Todt's hard down on to the floor and ground to an inelegant halt.

"Haven't I asked you to fucking well knock when my door is closed?"

"Oh yeah, right mate. Sorry. Deep in thought, were you? Immersed in the mysteries of the creative process?"

I answered Vince with a grim little smile, invited him to park his ever widening bottom on the Eileen Gray, and cordially asked him to state his business. Oh, yes, and I screwed up the piece of paper, aimed it at the wastebin and scored a basket. I hadn't managed to get as far as Whereabouts of People Who Might Know Her, but I didn't honestly feel that 'No sodding idea' merited recording, no matter how beautifully cursive my script might be.

*

I left the office early that night – with the most burdensome bits of my in-tray now weighing Lucille down, there wasn't a lot of reason to stay. So as not to encourage my staff to follow my feckless example, I told Julia in a loud voice that I was going out to do some research – old habits die hard – and exited the building. But instead of going directly home, I went to HMV in Oxford Street, made for the video department and purchased series 1 to 6 of 'Seinfeld'. (At this point, series 7 to 9 had yet to be screened in the UK.) I used the company credit card, of course. As far as HMRC were concerned, watching 'Seinfeld' was an essential part of my job.

I had planned to take the videos home to watch them – that is to say, sit there mooning over Julia Louis-Dreyfus, who, I had discovered, was the actress playing Elaine/Peggy – at the earliest opportunity. But as I wedged the Porsche into a parking space between a couple of Lexi, I realised this might excite a little comment, so I left them in the car and decided it would be less riskily done at the office. (What risk, you might ask, given that the state of marital relations at New Pemberley was at an all-time low, at least until tomorrow, when it would probably be even lower? So I wanted to gaze adoringly at a few old videos – where was the harm in that? None at all, you might say, indeed it was my inalienable right, but, as we've discussed before, it is perfectly possible to know you're as innocent as a lamb and to feel bang-to-rights guilty at one and the same time.)

Instead, it still being early, I wandered in to the house, hoping to spend a bit of the old quality time – I hate that expression – with the girls. Florence, hips gyrating, was busy spreading half a jar of Nutella on a slice of cholla – must have been her Jewish genes coming through – while wearing headphones attached to a portable CD player from which Ricky Martin and 'Living La Vida Loca' were leaking so annoyingly loudly that India, who was trying to watch a cartoon on Sky, kept shouting at her to turn it down – a perfectly reasonable request I thought, but Florence, of course, couldn't – or wouldn't – hear a word, no matter how high the pitch or the increase in volume of India's voice. Anneke, meanwhile, was busily laying the table for the girls' dinner which like every other day – as Alison insisted it should be – was as green and leafy as any nutritionist would advise, but which would be left three-quarters uneaten by Florence and India, who had either a) already stuffed their faces with Nutella etc as Florence was now doing or b) would, having begged to be excused from the table, immediately go off and eat five bowls of sugary cereal. To complete the scene, Spot was sitting on the sofa – from which he was expressly forbidden – scratching his balls furiously, quite heedless of the propriety of so doing in the presence of impressionable young girls. In other words, it was early evening much as it always was in New Pemberley, and nobody seemed the least perplexed by this little tableau, except possibly me, who wasn't usually around to witness it.

"So how was school?" I said brightly to Florence, leading, as usual, with my chin.

No response. I said it again, louder.

Still, no response. I walked around the kitchen until I stood squarely in her eyeline and said it again, louder still.

"WHAT?" she yelled back. I gave it one last, very loud, shot.

Florence took off her headphones just long enough to look at me blankly and say "Alright" in – well, now that I thought about it, in exactly the same bored monotone that I used to say it to my parents. Then she put her headphones back on and gyrated out of the room and up the stairs.

I didn't have much better luck with India. I went to sit next to her to share in her cartoon watching experience, trying to think desperately of a question to ask other than, "How was school with you then?" But absolutely nothing came to mind. In India's case it did at least elicit more than a one word reply. She couldn't quite manage to tear herself away from the telly to the extent that she could turn and face me, but she was able to report that she was to be in the junior school play – it was usually some kind of musical – that would be put on towards the end of the Christmas term.

"What's the name of the show?"

"Can't remember."

"Good part?" I asked.

"I'm an old Jewish woman or something."

Really? Was it some sort of nativity play they were doing? I was never quite comfortable about my half Jewish children doing overtly Christian things, but I wasn't going to make a fuss about it.

"Do you have any speaking lines?" I asked.

A shake of the pony-tailed head.

And that concluded the interview. A second later she sprang up and ran out to greet Alison, whose key she heard turning in the lock of the front door. Then I heard Florence thundering back down the stairs to do likewise. I couldn't help but sit there in front of the telly despondently wondering why my entrance earlier hadn't elicited the same response. I turned to Spot who continued to scratch his balls and I couldn't fail to see that sometimes that was the only option.

A few seconds later Alison walked into the kitchen with a daughter hanging on to each arm.

"Andrew," she said cheerfully – and therefore, suspiciously, "we have something to ask you?"

We? I knew when I was about to be stitched up and I was about to be stitched up now.

"Oh really?" I said, as neutrally as I could manage. "What would that be?"

"We-ell," she said, casting a conspiratorial look at first India and then Florence – both affectionately clutching her arms tighter by way of response. "You know Dougal, the architect?"

Did I know Dougal the fucking architect? Was she fucking mad? What the hell – but even as all this was rushing through my mind, though not yet out of my mouth, Florence let out a peal of laughter and said, in a fake, very proper voice, pretending to mimic Alison, "Dougal the architect! Oh, Mummy really."

Now, what the hell did that mean? Well, I'll tell you what I thought it meant. In fact, I was bloody certain what it meant. It meant that Florence knew that Dougal was much more than a bloody architect, that's what it meant. I was aghast. I looked across at India? Did she know too? Surely not, she was only nine, but I could see a look in her eyes that told me that even if she didn't know whatever Florence thought she knew, she too knew that architecture wasn't the only string to Dougal's – Doug's – whoever he was's – bow. She might not have known the grisly details or have any idea what the grisly details might be, but she knew. (And later I thought about all the kids of divorced couples in Florence's class, and thought well, why wouldn't she know?)

"So," I said, grim faced, "what?"

"Well," continued Alison, still upbeat – impressively indefatigable in a way – "Dougal's family has a little place in Scotland—"

"It's so beautiful, Daddy," interrupted Florence, "Doug showed us the photos."

Did he, by George? When was that I wondered?

"And they've got wild ponies on their land," said India.

On their land? Not in the Gorbals, then.

"Anyway," continued Alison, on the sofa now, sitting up straight, legs together, and brushing her skirt down, a mannerism of hers when she was getting down to business. "Dougal has very kindly asked Florence and India and me to stay there over half term, and we wondered if you'd mind."

"Half term?" I said, "But they're only just at back at school."

"Yes, but we have to organise flights and stuff. You know how it gets booked up."

"Oh please Daddy, please say we can go."

What were the options? Have a blue fit and make myself look a complete shit in front of the children. Or accept defeat.

"I'll think about it," I said, making a pointless effort to play for time, but we all knew that Alison had done all the thinking already. Later that night, of course, I cornered her upstairs. She was in the bathroom taking her make-up off.

"What the fuck was that all about?" I demanded. "Couldn't you at least have had the decency to have asked me on your own?"

Alison stopped looking in the mirror, then sat on the edge of the bath, and looked up at me sadly. And kindly I think.

"Look Andrew" she said quietly, "I'm sorry if it seemed like you were being manoeuvred—"

"Seemed like!"

"—but if I'd asked you on your own you'd have just gone ballistic and said not at any price."

Which was probably true.

"And I could have taken them without asking you at all. I could have just said I'd been offered the place by a friend and I wanted to have some girls-only time."

Which was also true.

"But I wouldn't do anything behind your back." She paused, slightly sheepish. "Well, not this anyway."

Then she looked up, held my gaze for a moment, and tears began to well in her eyes. Was it an act? How can you ever be really sure? But I didn't think so.

"Andrew, Doug wants – no, *I* want to sort this out properly. It can't go on like this. I want to be with him and I'm sick of all the secrecy."

"When was that then?"

"For fuck's sake Andrew, just for once in your life can you stop being such a bloody smartarse?"

Well, we both knew the answer to that one.

She took a tissue out of her bag, dabbed her eyes, and breathed slowly out.

"So I thought, a few days in Scotland would be a chance to see how we all got on as, as …"

"As a family?"

"Well, in a way, yes."

"Except you're not a sodding family are you? Not without me. It'll be my family and – er – Doug."

Now it was my turn to start getting teary. I paused for a moment to compose myself – or rather to prevent myself from falling on the floor in a grovelling heap.

"And what if your little half-term trial doesn't work? What if he doesn't hit it off with them?"

"Well, it won't be the end, I don't suppose. But it'll be a pointer. If he can't make it work, he's not the guy for me."

"They're not easy you know."

"They're as easy and as difficult as any kids. He knows the score. I have two children. We come as a package or not at all."

"So is that the plan?" I asked, feeling utterly dejected. "You and Doug and the girls? What about me?"

"No," she said. "That is not the plan. They'll have a home with me if they want one – and with Doug – maybe – eventually – if it works out. And I presume, they'll have a home with you. You're their father, not Doug. They'll share their time between us. I don't know how exactly, but we'll find a way. If we want to, that is. And I do."

The weird thing is that even when, like me, you have accepted that love – on both sides – has long since flown out of the window, and you have, you think, been prepared for all of this, when it comes it still comes as the most profound shock.

As sorry for myself as I was feeling, I still couldn't bring myself to blame Alison. Instead, as people always do in these circumstances, I reserved my ire for the third party – in this case, the architect overseeing the extension of my basement and the demolition of my marriage, Dougal-call-me-Doug. Not being consumed with raging jealousy didn't prevent me from feeling thoroughly fed up with him and I could have cheerfully knocked his cocky block off.

And no, the joke wasn't lost on me. I could see how ironic it was – how entirely poetically just – that I should feel so wretched, when, just like Doug, I was myself preparing to chase after another man's wife – also assuming Peggy had a husband. But would this sobering experience, and the prospect of the even more sobering ones yet to come – the breaking up of the family – the loss of my home – all the horrendous collateral damage of separation – give me pause for thought?

I think I can best answer that question with another: Would Spot stop scratching his balls?

CHAPTER 14

NEW YORK AND NEW ROCHELLE, 1979

"Love the neckties, man," said the tall, black, shaven-headed, zootily suited, and very, very cool sales guy in Barney's. "Love the neckties." (In my moviemory he is wearing wrap around shades, but he was working in the middle of a big store on Sixth Avenue, half a block from natural light of any kind, so he can't have been, can he?)

The ties to which he was referring were being worn by me. Two of them. At the same time. It was my latest fashion statement, and, I have to say, probably my greatest ever single moment as a fashion icon. I had risen one morning and questioned, perhaps in the manner of Einstein suddenly coming up with E=MC squared, one of the fundamental precepts by which humankind has always lived. Why, I asked, should a man be restricted to one tie?

And for a few weeks thereafter, during which period this all-time highpoint of my fashion life was reached, when this black guy from New York paid tribute to my convention busting sartorial breakthrough – and no, I don't think he was gay and coming on to me – yes, I say again, I wore two ties tied around my neck at the same time. (If you want to try this at home, you wear an open-necked shirt and have the knots tied along side each other but separated, an inch or two below the collar. But do take care: the effect on the casual passer-by, as my experience showed, can be devastating.)

My two ties made quite an impression on Brett and Bart.

"Man, whatever you're smoking, we want some too," they said, and I am not altogether sure they were joking.

And when Peggy saw me desporting this look one day in the office elevator she smiled, shook her head and muttered "So what's wrong with the other one?" – a reference to the old joke about the Jewish woman who gives her son two ties and then still manages to take offence when she sees him wearing one.

I smiled briefly and nodded back to indicate I had 'got it' and then she added, as she stepped out on to her floor, "You coming like that on Sunday?"

I have never been quite sure whether she was deliberately provoking me to do so, but, as you have doubtless guessed, that was the effect it had. I did, of course, give a lot of thought to exactly what I would wear for my first meeting with Herb and Barbara, who would, I was by now pretty convinced, become my parents-in-law someday. And yes, I did hum and hah about whether the two tie look would be entirely appropriate for a New Rochelle optometrist – I had made sure I was fully briefed – and his former elementary schoolteacher wife. But Peggy had assured me that Herb was not a guy averse to shaking his fist at the establishment and that her Mom (Mom? Never could get used to that, she'd have to be Mum to me) would always go along with whatever Peggy said. In the end, as I prepared for another trip on the New Haven line from Grand Central, I told myself that the best way I could present myself would be to be the real me, a guy who didn't always run with the crowd, who marched to the beat of his own drummer, who conformed to these and all other hackneyed old clichés about not being a conformist, and that right now, that meant wearing two ties. And so, early on that fateful Sunday morning, I looked myself in the eye in the bathroom mirror, hummed 'My Way' while I tied my two knots, and then, confident that I had made the right decision –

reasonably confident anyway – set off for the subway and lunch with the Lees of New Rochelle.

*

If I did harbour the odd doubt about the universal appeal of the two tie look, that was mainly due to a rather untimely meeting with Todd Zwiebel. As I have said, Todd, the far sighted American who had seen Madison Avenue potential in me, had now climbed to the very top of the greasy corporate pole. The Chief Creative Officer of the World or The Manatee as Bart or Brett had, one bong filled day, decided he should be called (to explain: Manatee=Seacow=CCOW=Chief Creative Officer of the World) usually sat in his magnificently situated office on the north west corner of the executive floor, the fifteenth of the McConnell Martin building, which had the very finest views of Madison Avenue as it extended uptown. And it was at this gorgeous panorama that he could normally be found gazing while pontificating upon where he should go for lunch or by what time he could slip away to his summer place in the Hamptons, or his winter one in the Adirondacks. Or whatever else it is, that those at the very top of the corporate greasy pole in America have to pontificate upon.

On this day however, the day I wore my two ties and saw Peggy in the elevator, the Friday before the Sunday lunch with the Lees, the Manatee was not in his office but floundering round the creative department looking to pressgang any unwary uncreative types he could find into working the weekend on a campaign for a brand of shampoo, which its Vice-Prez for Marketing had personally informed Todd, would be washed right out of McConnell Martin's hair unless a brilliant new TV spot was forthcoming PDQ.

Todd, having risen as high as he had, was not in the habit of deferentially knocking on his acolytes' doors and thus barged straight in to Brett or Bart's office just after bong time. (Which, any day of the week, was more or less any time.) Fortunately, in readiness for just such eventualities, the bong was always positioned behind the door and out of sight to the casual entrant, and the fan switch was always within reach of Bart or Brett's hand. Moreover, either because he was so preoccupied with the imminent departure of the shampoo account or with the problem of what time to get the limo round to take him to whichever of his weekend retreats he wanted to go to or because he had never familiarised himself with the fragrance of marijuana – which seems unlikely – Todd, incredibly, seemed not to notice anything amiss, aroma-wise, when he walked in on us.

Yes, us, because I was there as well as Bart and Brett. He did however notice my two ties, at which he looked askance, before enquiring whether any of the three of us wanted to avail ourselves of the career opportunity of a lifetime by spending the weekend working on the said shampoo spot.

"Sure thing," said Bart and Brett, pretty much in unison. "Saturday, Sunday. Whenever. Anything to help out."

Which comment, I have to say, shocked me to the core until it quickly dawned on me that you didn't hold down a reasonably well paid job when you spent half your supposedly working day smoking weed, unless you were prepared to bend with the wind when the occasion demanded it. I, however, bearing in mind my lunch invitation, could make no such offer.

"What about you, Angus?" asked Todd.

"Andrew," I said.

"Yeah well whatever. Can McConnell Martin count on you, Andrew, like these fine fellas?"

"Well, normally Todd I would say yes, like a shot, of course I would and I can definitely do Saturday, no problem, but Sunday, I'm afraid, I'm, er, tied up."

The Manatee gave me a look so wounded, it was as though I had personally driven a speedboat straight over him, and the propeller had cut him to pieces. Then pride helped him stage a partial recovery.

"Well Andrew, it is Andrew isn't it? I'm kinda surprised at you. Especially given all the personal interest I have taken in you—"

"Yes, and you know how much I appreciate that Todd, but it's just that this Sunday—"

"Yes, yes, I know, you have more important things to do than to help out on one of McConnell Martin's most important clients. Well, half a job is not really any better than no job at all, so you needn't worry about Saturday either."

And with that the Manatee swam off, but not before giving an approving nod in Bart and Brett's direction and taking one more swing at me.

"And why the hell are you wearing two ties? This is Madison Avenue, not the fucking Kings Road you know."

After that my relations with Todd Zwiebel were never quite the same again, and the two-tie look, however big a hit it was with Barney's high priest of dude-ness, may well have contributed to the shortening of my days in New York.

*

Herb met us at New Rochelle station in some kind of Pontiac, one of those huge, overpowered, underperforming boats, a 'sedan' – truly my very favourite American word, one which they have never succeeded in exporting but which, for me, immediately conjures up images of the fantastical American cars that I grew up goggling at in the 'Observer Book of Automobiles'. (One of a series of pocket sized reference books that little English boys pored over in the fifties.) This sedan was of much more recent vintage but still as enormous and American as tradition demanded. Herb seemed to be a jolly sort of chap, greying crinkly hair, horn rim glasses – from the family firm I presumed – and of medium height and build as the TV cop shows have it. If he noticed my two ties or anything else about me, he made no comment during the wallowy drive back to the house which was in a wonderfully named street for an optician to live in – sorry, optometrist, the distinction between which he would later explain – called Overlook Road.

Barbara, who also had crinkly hair (but less grey) also wore glasses – I expect they gave themselves a discount. Hers were sort of butterfly shaped which rather fitted with the way she fluttered out of the house, apron on, to greet us. I had half expected Peggy's younger brother, always referred to as Marv, to be there too but he apparently had more compelling things to do than give the once-over to Peggy's latest.

In we went to the house, which was exactly as I expected it be, unfussily decorated in not quite the latest style and generally very 'homey'. I loved it. I got the tour, saw the enormous kitchen with the humungous fridge, the den with the Lazy Boy and the TV – massive by the standards of the day – and the cable control that, this being 1979, was still attached by a wire; and outside there was, of course, the now rusting basketball hoop fixed above the ga-*raage*. It was all there, and like I say, I loved it. I had no problem at all in imagining future little Williamses running about here.

We finally ended up back in the 'lounge-room' where we had now been joined by Peggy's grandmother about whom I had been gently forewarned.

"She's a little deaf," Peggy had said. "Well, no, maybe a lot deaf. And she's kind of in and out of it, if you know what I mean. She probably won't say a whole lot."

Herb introduced us.

"This is my mother Betty Lipschitz. Ma, this is Andy."

"Hello, I'm Betty Lipschitz, Herb's mother. I've heard a lot about you Miller."

A little embarrassed laughter followed. Personally I wasn't too thrilled but I was a big boy and she was a muddled old lady and

185

obviously I had to laugh along with the rest of them. Peggy did try to put her straight but I wasn't optimistic that she'd succeed.

Then a beer was thrust in to my hand – yes, a Miller – please, no, not that, but what could I do? – and, as is the custom on these occasions, we all stood around wondering what to say. During this little hiatus it occurred to me that neither of Peggy's parents looked the slightest bit Chinese. (And neither for that matter did Betty Lipschitz.) I couldn't really see that much behind Herb and Peggy's glasses but I scrutinised their eyes for any signs of almond-shaping and it seemed to me that all four looked much rounder than Peggy's. Were hers some kind of genetic throwback to the Li days in the Ming dynasty? As much as I liked the idea of the Beijing shtetl, I was finally forced to conclude this had been just another of Peggy's little stories. At least, I thought, I wouldn't have to explain any Chinese connection to Mavis.

The silence didn't last for long – the two ties soon worked their magic.

"That's quite a look you have there, Andy," said Herb. "That what they're wearing in the Village these days?"

I heard Mavis tut-tutting in my head when I realised I would be Andy to the whole Lee family as well as to Peggy, but as the only alternative was to say something ridiculously stuffy, I made a silent apology to Mavis and just addressed the question.

"Well, maybe soon. Could happen," I said, thinking of the black fashion guru in Barney's. Who knew: there might be mannequins wearing two ties in their window this very minute.

Herb and Barbara looked at me blankly. Then Peggy enlightened them.

"He's British so he doesn't like to come right out and say it, but he means it was all his own idea."

"Really," said Barbara. "My!" Which could have meant anything from wow, how incredibly avant-garde of him, to, just who is this lunatic my daughter has brought into my home?

"Well, I think that's terrific," pronounced Herb. "I like a guy who blazes a trail!" And with that, we were ushered into lunch where, not unnaturally, spectacles became a topic of conversation.

"Get those in London?" asked Herb, pointing at my own glasses with a fork, as Barbara served up a pot-roast or something else suitably American. (I was too keen to make a good impression to worry about food, and I have no proper memory of what we ate.) I nodded to indicate that yes, I had purchased my glasses in London.

"Whadyapayforem?" he asked through a mouthful of whatever it was.

Barbara frowned disapproval at Herb asking such a direct question.

"What? What?" demanded Herb. "We're in the business. He knows that. You told him we were optometrists right?" Now he waved his fork at Peggy.

Americans, I realised, aren't keen on knives at meals except for cutting, and I self-consciously looked at my own knife and fork filled hands and quickly set the knife down at the side of my plate, not wanting – two ties notwithstanding – to look anything but one of them. Peggy confirmed that, indeed, she had informed me of the family interests in optometry, and then, after a bit of discussion about the relative costs of spectacles in New Rochelle and London – "Course, it's another story in Manhattan, right Barb? They charge what they like there" – and then the previously advertised explanation of the differences between an optometrist and an optician, not forgetting that an ophthalmologist was different again, during which I really'd? and is-that-so'd? as many times as I decently could, and after I had complemented Barbara on her wonderful cooking and accepted her offer of second helpings without, as I've said, having the slightest idea of what I was eating, we got to the dessert, which was probably apple pie or key lime pie or whatever else it is Americans give you.

At this point, or maybe it was with the coffee, the photograph

187

albums came out, and I saw pictures of Peggy at six months, Peggy at two, three and four, Peggy at seven at Marv's fifth birthday party, Peggy at thirteen in braces, Peggy dressed for her high school prom – "New Rochelle High, fine school," Herb threw in – Peggy in her gown and mortar board at her graduation ceremony from NYSU – "Remember that day, Herb?" reminisced Barbara, "Such a pretty town, Binghamton" – and then the album was hastily shut by Barbara on a shot of Peggy with some bloke who I didn't get a proper look at, but who, I had a nasty suspicion, might have been Miller.

Then Herb had the bright idea of showing me round New Rochelle and away we went, Barbara driving, Herb acting as tour guide. (Mrs Lipschitz stayed at home.) Herb put particular emphasis on the sights on Quaker Ridge Road which, coincidentally, included 'Lee's Eyeglasses, serving New Rochelle since 1965'. The Pontiac idled, and the windows descended electrically – still, in 1979, a rather exotic touch to me – while we examined its rather faded charms.

"Barb and I have been thinking," confided Herb, "the place needs a facelift. And you know what?" We waited, all agog, to find out what. "I think maybe we should have a more modern name. Isn't that your line, Andy? Can you come up with something?"

My heart sank. For this was a challenge I clearly couldn't refuse, and yet, as every person whose profession is vaguely 'creative' knows, there is nothing more guaranteed to dry up the well of inspiration than a request for some instant brainwave by a friend or rel. Well, no, there is one thing, possibly. And that's when the request is from the rel of a very particular friend, whom, one is hoping, may ultimately become the very closest of rels themselves. I said I would give it some thought, and then unsuccessfully racked my brains while we drove home.

Then came afternoon tea, not a meal, I think, the Lees of New Rochelle were used to having but clearly added to the agenda in honour of my Britishness, and for which Mrs Lipschitz, whose appetite, unlike her hearing, seemed not to have been diminished by the passing years, rejoined us. As I was passed a piece of Barbara's homemade strudel – or as near as she got, it was Betty Crocker – I happened to get around, as, of course, I would eventually, to the subject of 'The Dick Van Dyke Show' and Rob and Laura having lived in Nooroeshel.

"My!" said Barbara again, in response to the news that I had seen this on television in England – or maybe to the news that we had television at all in England. And then she said, presumably following some subconscious showbizzy train of thought,

"Herb, did you tell Peggy that you were going to be Tevye?"

Herb protested that Peggy's young man didn't want to hear about all that stuff and then without drawing breath gave us chapter and verse on the upcoming Temple Israel (their local synagogue) Dramatic Group's production of 'Fiddler on the Roof', in which, despite his protestations that they should 'give one of the other guys a chance', Herb had been cast as the leading man.

"That's terrific, Dad," said Peggy dutifully. But, touchingly, I thought, she was obviously genuinely pleased for him too. And thinking I should say something, and, seeing it perhaps as an opportunity to underline my own ethnic credentials, I said, "Mazeltov!"

This provoked another succession of "My!"s from Barbara as she grappled with the previously mentioned conundrum for all American Jews: how could anyone possibly be English and Jewish at the same time? And then, as Herb drew our attention to the particular difficulties that the role of Tevye presented, particularly when there was less than six weeks to go until opening night – "We'll never be ready – the director's a meshugannah!" – it became clear that this interest in the performing arts was not some passing fad of his but a lifelong passion. (And, my paranoia never being far from the surface, I couldn't help wondering if this didn't mean Herb hadn't enjoyed a bond with Miller that he and I could never match.)

"Always wanted to tread the boards," he told me. "No

complaints. None at all. Been as lucky as a man could be, all things considered. And if any young fellah asked me for my advice on being an optometrist, I'd say sure go ahead, it's a fulfilling – a worthwhile! – job for a person to do. But, if I'm honest, if I had my time over, it'd be the roar of the greasepaint every time."

"I guess you can tell that from the kid's names," put in Barbara.

Ah, the names. Perhaps the mystery was about to be unravelled. Or perhaps not, because Barbara looked suddenly crestfallen and I caught Peggy glaring at her – as sharp a look as I had ever seen her give. Clearly Mom hadn't been authorised to go there. And then, out of nowhere, Mrs Lipschitz, who wouldn't have known whether authorisation had or had not been given for anything, piped up.

"You know it was me who called Peggy, Peggy."

I cocked my ear. So perhaps we really were going to get to the bottom of this at last. I thought I detected Peggy catch her breath. She began to interrupt,

"Andy doesn't want to hear all this—" but unlike Barbara, Mrs Lipschitz was too deaf or determined to be stopped.

"It was fifty-three, I think. Or fifty-four. Anyway, Leonard – my husband – Herb's father – a good man – usually – but, so who's perfect? – he loved Peggy Lee. The singer I mean. She had a big, big record that year – 'Black Magic', you remember?"

Did I? I wasn't at all sure. It certainly wasn't on my list of instantly hummables. But I nodded along anyway. I wanted to know where this might take us.

"Anyway, it was Peggy's first birthday and I hated that name he'd given her" – she nodded disparagingly in Herb's direction, who shrugged as if to say, 'Please, what can you do?' – "so I just called her Peggy one day. She was too young to understand anything – not one – maybe one – I don't know, but she laughed, and laughed. And I don't why, but then everyone started doing it, calling her Peggy, and it just stuck. Even he gave up and called her Peggy."

I waited. But that was it. I suppose I could have asked the direct question, but Peggy's fierce look to her mother would have been enough to convince me – if I hadn't known already – that might not be wise. So Mrs Lipschitz was allowed to sink quietly back into the memory of life with Leonard in fifty-three or fifty-four or whatever else it was that went on in her lightly pinkly rinsed head.

After a few seconds or however long it took for a settled view to be reached that Mrs Lipschitz had now completed her contribution, Herb once again warmed to his theatrical theme.

"Yup," he said, "you know who my hero was: Sir" – emphasis on Sir – "Laurence Olivier. What an actor! What a per*former*!"

I nodded sagely. And he was British too. Clearly a point in my favour.

"You like the theatre, Andy?" Herb demanded.

I did so want to please him, but, knowing the next question would be "What's your favourite play?" or, worse, "What have you seen recently?" and bearing in mind the only time in living memory I'd set foot in a theatre had been to see the horror show that was Uncle Vanya relocated to modern day Nicaragua, I said, "Yes, yes, you can't beat the theatre, but me, I'm sort of more of a movie guy."

"Oh! The movies! Love the movies! I'm not one of those theatre snobs, no sir. Know my favourite movie, Andy?"

Was I supposed to?

"'Gone With the Wind', Andy! '*Gone – With – the – Wind*'! Greatest movie ever made, bar none!"

Peggy seemed to have had enough by now, and with a rather unsubtle wow-is-that-the-time? glance at her watch, drew proceedings to a close. But, before we finally said goodbye, Herb consulted me once again about the possible renaming of Lee's Eyeglasses.

"We-ll," I said, rather desperately, as the Pontiac lurched to a halt, back again at New Rochelle Station. I was about to add nothing more inspired than something like 'I think you should stick to Lee's Eyewear – it has authenticity', when – drum roll! – something came to me. Suddenly I felt totally confident. "How about 'A Better Look?'"

"A Better Look. Hmm." Herb rolled the words around his tongue. "A Bet-ter Loo-ook."

"You see," I said, "It has a double meaning. 'A Better Look' as in the way you can see things through your new glasses. And 'A Better Look' as in the way you *appear* in your new glasses."

Peggy looked at me almost admiringly. I actually think she was impressed. Almost as impressed as I was myself. And Barbara, well, Barbara's predictable "A Better Look. My!" did seem to accentuate the positive.

Herb, however, begged to differ.

"I dunno," he said. "Probably okay for Manhattan. But a bit too cutesy for New Rochelle. Well, great to meet you, Andy. And Peggy, be sure to make it over for Fiddler, and bring Andy with you if you want."

"Hey, and Andy," he shouted after us as we disappeared into the station, "be sure and wear those two ties if you come. The rabbi'll love it. He'll write a sermon about it – 'The man with two ties' – sounds like it's straight out the bible."

We could still hear him chortling as he started the engine and drove back to Overlook Road.

*

I wasn't quite sure what to make of any of it.

1. What was that last remark meant to mean? Was he taking the mickey? I consulted Peggy as the train wound its way back to Grand Central.

"Taking the what?"

"The mickey. Don't you say that here? You know, 'pulling my leg'?"

"Pulling my what?"

"Oh for goodness sake. Don't you say that either?"

"Yeah. Just pulling your leg."

I looked at her. I had my answer. Like daughter, like father, I supposed.

2. Had I made a good impression? I consulted Peggy again.

"Well, they didn't threaten to cut me out of their will."

"That's the best you can say."

"Well, what do you want? A partnership in Lee's Eyeglasses?"

"Actually, I didn't think 'A Better Look' was that bad."

"Uhuh – too cutesy."

"You think so too?"

"Just pulling your leg."

3. The name business was really bugging me again. It had something to do with Herb's Thespian connections, but what? This time I didn't consult Peggy. Unlike her mother or her grandmother, I wasn't going there.

Then the light bulb came on and the Marv business fell into place. Herb had a thing about actors. Marv was obviously short for Marvin. Turn Marvin Lee around and you got Lee Marvin. Bingo!

But then I came back to Peggy. If Brenda was her real name, and she'd already told me that, why had she been so quick to cut Barbara off? And, wait a minute, Brenda was a singer's name wasn't it, not an actor's? So how did that fit? But then maybe Herb's showbiz fascination extended to singers too. And Peggy was also a singer, remember. But then we had definitely established Peggy was a nickname so it didn't need to fit the pattern. Somehow, I couldn't help feeling I was missing a trick. I was sure all the pieces were there, but I couldn't make the jigsaw fit. I just couldn't work it out. And I never did.

*

Are you impressed by my desisting from tackling Peggy on the question of her name again, despite my itching curiosity? Are you congratulating me on my newly discovered restraint and maturity? Or are you thinking, well, she's finally left Miller and she's introduced me to her parents, so that's the two steps forward – any moment now comes the giant stride back?

Well, you're half right.

It was as we were leaving Grand Central that I did, thoughtlessly, to some extent, overreach myself.

"Why don't you come back to my place?" I asked Peggy. "My place is closer to the office than Noreen's" – she lived in Brooklyn – "and if you don't want people to know about us, not that they don't already," – add raffish grin – "then we can go in separately tomorrow."

Peggy, who was carrying the remains of the pot-roast, or whatever it had been, in a Tupperware container that her mother had forced upon her, stopped in her tracks and stood there on 42nd street, shaking her head. I walked on for a step or two without realising she wasn't with me, then when I saw, I turned and I did, quite literally, take a stride back.

"What?" I said. "What have I said now?"

"Didn't we have this conversation, the last time we came back through Grand Central?" she asked.

"No" I said, not – not for the first time – catching on.

"Yes, we did Andy. I told you I wanted some space. I told you I am not ready to belong to anybody. Weren't those my exact words?"

Actually, I wasn't quite sure those were her exact words, but I didn't think this was the moment to be pernickety. I accepted this had been her general drift, so I said, "Um, well I suppose but—"

"But what?"

"But I am not asking you to belong to me. You are sleeping on the couch at Noreen's, it must be bloody uncomfortable. Whereas – at my place," – I tried a bit of leavening humour –

"you have a whole double bed – well half – and a nice friendly pussy cat to welcome you."

It didn't leaven.

"Space, Andy, space! It hasn't been a week since I moved out! Space and time! That's what I am asking for."

"They're the same thing – Einstein says."

"What?"

"Oh for fuck's sake, Peggy, lighten up. Okay, so sleep on the couch, get a cricked neck – fat lot of space you'll have there."

She slowly shook her head, looked to the skies, and finally walked on with me. Then we got to the subway, and waited in silence for the 5. I got out at Union Square to walk down to my place, and she went on to wherever she had to get to in Brooklyn. Before I got off I thanked her for a great day, searching her brown black eyes for some sign I was forgiven – even if I wasn't quite sure what I was supposed to have done. She made that expression of smiling exasperation that was the sign I was looking for and I gave her a quick kiss and stepped off. She turned to give me a little wave of her fingers and that was the end of our day.

I walked into my apartment, winced at the smell from the cat, but did nothing about it, just kicked off my shoes, tore off my two ties and threw them in the corner, and flopped onto my back on the bed.

Belonging. Belonging. It always seemed to come back to that. Once again, I asked myself, was she right? And yes, in a way, I had to concede she was. I wanted to belong to her. And her to me. Was that some kind of implied ownership, which didn't sound very nice at all? Well, yes, again, I supposed, if you were being completely honest, it was. But wasn't that what everyone really wanted? Wasn't that what being married was about? And yes, I did think she was absolutely gorgeous – didn't she like that? – and yes, I wanted to show her off and tell everybody she was mine. (Might have been the earliest known reckoning on the E to P scale, had it been in my head at the time.) And then again, of course, I could see that was all totally pointless and absurd and who gave a fuck about what other people thought. But you do, don't you?

That, as I have since come to realise, is the thing with the E to P scale; it means two tenths of fuck all, but, in the face of all the science, that is still not nothing.

I turned on the telly to my favourite Sunday night re-run channel. You've guessed it. It was 'The Dick Van Dyke Show'.

CHAPTER 15

LONDON AND RICHMOND UPON THAMES, 1999

"Adultery," said Harriet Braintree, pouring coffee from a silvery jug into a dainty white china cup, "well, it's a rather old fashioned idea, isn't it? As far as the law is concerned anyway. Sugar?"

I sat in the parqueted and Persian-y carpeted, leather-bound book lined, Georgian table and chaired – repro, I'm sure – meeting room of Hardy Wiggins, solicitors and commissioners for oaths since 1822 or some such. Through the window came the chirping of the little birdies who shared Lincoln's Inn Fields with all the lawyers. They added an extra top note to the tinkling of the cash registers which mugs like me kept going non-stop.

"You see, Andrew – may I call you Andrew?" Harriet didn't wait for an answer. "Today, adultery is not considered to be a cause of a broken marriage so much as a symptom. So, no, in answer to your question, it doesn't really make a blind bit of difference."

Harriet – I presumed I should call her Harriet if she was going to call me Andrew – was a pencil slim, not unattractive woman, (mid-forties I should have said), with short dark bobbed hair and a slight hint of an unplaceable Northern accent, who, despite laughing easily, had the brisk authority of a headmistress. She rather reminded me of Mrs McIver, capo dei capi at Florence's and India's school, the main difference being that Harriet had that extra sheen that you only get from a cool half a million (and up!) a year.

My question had obviously been whether Alison's infidelity – another ludicrously anachronistic word – would in any way affect what the settlement might be. As you see, we had quickly got to the nub of the matter.

"Oh," I replied. "Yes, I thought that was probably the case. Just thought I'd ask."

Well, no harm in asking was there? This was only an exploratory meeting to see if I liked the cut of Harriet Braintree's jib – and probably for her to check out if I was good for the £450 an hour – but we'd might as well cut to the chase, mightn't we? Once the decision to separate has been made – or made for you – you are, unless a devout Catholic or something, bound to be contemplating divorce. Then the next thing is to ask your mates if they know anyone, and as three-quarters of them have been divorced themselves, they do. Then they all tell you that their bloke was an overpaid waste of space but their wife's chap was a bloody crafty sod and, if they were you, they'd go to him. Or her. Quite a lot are 'hers' by the way. Then, if you get more than two votes for the same crafty sod, you have a winner. Harriet Braintree got three votes, so it was a no-brainer, and what's more, she came with the added reassurance of me having seen her name mentioned in the press. She'd saved some superannuated pop singer from having his Filipino maid turned fourth wife get away with half the royalties from his back catalogue, so that couldn't be bad could it? My only concern was that I wasn't a high enough roller to get any serious attention from her but, as Geoff had said – he was one of her referees, that is to say his ex had successfully squeezed his pips – £450 an hour is £450 an hour wherever it comes from. So here I was with Harriet, drinking her coffee, eating her chocolate digestives – I had two, they were free, the only thing from her that ever bloody was – and contemplating a much reduced future.

It really is quite extraordinary how romantic divorce isn't. All sentiment is squeezed out before you can say 'list of assets'. The moment you start to give legal force to the notion that love has gone out of your marriage forever, then you turn all your attention to making sure the silver doesn't disappear after it. Of course, that's not you. It's the process. It's the lawyers. They have a vested interest in making sure you fight for every penny. The longer they're holding your coat, the more £450s there are to charge. No, it's not you. It's never you. It's them. It's her. But it's never you.

"So," I asked Harriet. "How do we start?"

And her dapper assistant, Colin, appeared out of the ether, with letters of appointment to sign and billing addresses to take, and I was on the one way street to singledom. Meanwhile, somewhere else in London – very possibly in the building right next door – Alison was with her chap, doing the self same thing and emptying the Williams coffers by another £450 an hour. Only knowing Alison, I'd have bet a whole packet of chocolate digestives that she'd have got her chap for less, and that he – or she – no, it would definitely be a he – would turn out to be better than mine.

I was definitely right about the last bit, although I am sure Alison thinks exactly the same.

*

October in Richmond. Leaves fluttering into the little well outside Donald McEwan's basement window. Me staring blankly at them. With my new find-Peggy project to focus on, I no longer wanted to waste time on long bouts of introspection and I was at the point when, if I'd stuck to the pattern of previous rounds of Donalding, I might have been expected to ask for the bill, before buggering off into the Surrey sunset until the next mini-crisis occurred. But, with the drama of divorce soon to be played out in all its gory detail, I thought it might be a good idea to keep Donald hanging about in the background. I was bound to get upset and I would need someone to pass me a tissue from time to time.

Eventually, I pinpointed one little thing that was very slightly bugging me, although I knew we could discuss it until the cows not only came home but had their supper and got into their pyjamas and started counting sheep – would cows count sheep? – could cows count? – before I got any kind of proper answer. So very slight was the degree of bugging that I had already almost forgotten what this little thing was, and was instead so fascinated by the possibilities of sheep-counting cows, that it was all I could do not to consult Donald on the subject of bovine numeracy. Even to me however, this didn't seem like the best use of his time – or, more to the point – my money, so I eventually got back to the pre-cow problem.

"Donald, there's a bit of a paradox that I can't quite square."

"That's in the nature of a paradox, isn't it?"

I narrowed my eyes or whatever you do when you're thinking 'you see it's not just me, you can be a bit of a clever clogs yourself despite all your WASPy Scottish wisdom.'

"Yes, well, it's this guilt I feel."

"Ah yes, guilt." Donald brightened up. Guilt was meat and drink to a trick cyclist after all.

"I mean, as soon as I even think about looking at the Polaroid of Peggy or watching 'Seinfeld'" – we had, after my mandatory late arrival, wasted the first twenty minutes of the session while I explained the significance of all that – "I feel, well, I feel like a schoolboy being caught having a wank and yet—"

"And yet—"

"—and yet when I think of all the havoc I might be wreaking – which you have been kind enough to point out – when I go looking for Peggy, you know, barging in on her life, pissing off her husband – if she's got one – screwing up her family – if she's got one – doing all that, well it doesn't make me feel guilty at all."

"I see."

"Do you? Because I don't. I mean why do I feel guilty about something totally trivial and yet don't really give a fuck about doing real damage?"

"Perhaps what you think of as guilt is just a fear of being caught."

"Well, what else is guilt? Isn't it the little voice in your head catching you at it?"

"Let's see now. How about: the uncomfortable feeling that flows from a genuine sense – an inner conviction – that what you're doing is wrong. Of course, what you're doing might not be wrong at all, and you only have that conviction because of some silly idea you've absorbed – like having it drummed into you as a schoolboy that masturbation is bad."

"Yes, yes, well never mind the last bit. I don't recall it ever being drummed into me that I mustn't look at Polaroids or watch 'Seinfield'. Quite the reverse with 'Seinfeld'. No, let's stick just with what guilt really is."

"Okay."

"So, tell me, when I have this feeling looking at the Polaroid of Peggy or watching 'Seinfeld', is that just a fear of being caught or does it come from an inner conviction that doing these terrible things is wrong?"

Donald laughed.

"Do you know what Donald? You're a bloody genius. I don't feel guilty about all the really big, bad things I might be doing and now you've convinced me that I don't really feel properly guilty about the little things either. So basically, thanks to you, I have no guilt. Isn't that exactly what a shrink is for?"

Another session successfully concluded. Another bit of clever dick repartee to round things off. So glad I didn't start on the 'cows' thing.

And yet, underneath, I did have this uneasy feeling that I had touched on something that might actually matter. One of these days, I might even have the guts to face something seriously.

*

I am not going to get into the awful business of what happened when we told Florence and India. No matter how much they thought they already knew, and however many of their friends and classmates had been through it already, they weren't, they couldn't have been prepared for the reality. Because no-one ever is. Life, as they knew it, was going to be systematically dismembered and the pieces rearranged. And who knew how? Kids, as we all know, like routine. They like what they know – to the point of watching 'Grease' or 'Thomas the Tank Engine' or 'Wallace and Gromit' again and again and again until they can recite every word from first to last and back. And then they'll watch it again. And if you've ever so much as tried to offer a child a meal that they haven't eaten at least a hundred times before, you'll know how much they don't like what they don't know. The idea that children are better off out of an unhappy marriage seems to me to be dubious at best. My bet is that, given a choice, most children would rather soldier on with mummy and daddy at war than live in the cold peace of the post-divorce settlement. But the thing is, they aren't given a choice, are they? Or at least Florence and India weren't. As much as we might try to soften the blow, and, because we aren't complete and utter bastards, we really did try, it was still basically a case of sorry, chaps, but you can either like it or lump it. So they lumped it. (And even when the children of a divorcing couple are grown up and living away, invariably they still don't like it, because, whether five or twenty-five, the message they are being sent is the same: that the world, as they've always known it, isn't worth saving. You've just taken all the souvenirs off their mantelpiece and smashed them to smithereens on the floor.)

Before the day that I would much rather forget, when we sat the girls down and told them how it was going to be, Alison and I, needing to sort out the details of what we would say to them, had decided to treat ourselves to lunch at The Ivy. I suppose we thought it less likely we would start shouting at each other with all those high rollers around. (Lest you are concerned I might have given something away that I would later want back, let me reassure you that no sooner had Julia told me the booking was made, than I had her get Harriet Braintree on the blower to give me precise instructions on what I safely might or might not commit to. And I believe I'm right in assuming – and I'd certainly bet a pack of chocolate digestives on this as well – that Alison had had the same conversation with her chap.)

"So," I mumbled through a mouthful of Bang Bang Chicken, "we are going to tell them that it's nobody's fault, but that Mummy and Daddy don't love each other any—"

"No, we don't need to say that."

"What then? That Mummy and Daddy love each other, but aren't in love any—"

"Don't be absurd, Andrew. They're twelve and nine. They won't have a clue what the difference is. We'll just say we haven't been getting on terribly well and we think it would be better if we lived apart for a while."

"For a while? Oh shit!" I'd spilled some Bang Bang Chicken on my tie. (Paul Smith.) I started to dab at it feebly with the San Pellegrino dampened end of a napkin – or serviette as Mavis would have called it, and which we, now, certainly wouldn't, how bloody daft is that? – but I was obviously just making things worse.

"Oh, for God's sake, let me do that," said Alison, and reaching to take over, she took the napkin out of my hand with one hand, and, with the other, pulled the tie halfway across the table – and me with it. It struck me that this instinctive wifely assistance was just like old times. And, since she had me by the throat, possibly just like new ones.

After that, we went off the subject for a bit, but I got around to it again, as the waiter brought the main course. (Steak tartare and pommes frites for me, some zero calorie salad for her.)

"So when you said, 'for a while', does that mean you're thinking it might not be permanent?" I ventured.

"No, not really," she said, absent-mindedly taking one of my frites – old habits die hard. "I mean I'm not thinking it won't be permanent. I don't know, suppose I thought it might soften the blow."

"Fair enough," I said. And then, "Oh for fuck's sake Alison, will you stop eating all my bloody chips! If you wanted chips why didn't you order some of your own?" (Old habits really do die hard.)

Eventually we agreed on the following: that we would tell Florence and India that for the time being Daddy would be moving into the spare room – I wasn't giving up my rights to the house just yet – that eventually Mummy and Daddy would be living in separate homes, but they, Florence and India, would have homes with each of us and that they could come and go whenever they pleased – seemed unlikely but they might be seduced by the prospect of power – that they would see just as much of us as ever they had before – which in my case, at least, could hardly be an exaggeration as, to be honest, it had never been that much, and for Florence, well, would it really matter anyway, because how much can you see of anybody through a slammed door? – and that, although it might seem a bit strange to begin with, we would all be much, much happier in the long run.

Well that was the plan, and we all know what happens to plans. As I've said, details of the actual conversation en famille – pretty much the last we ever had en famille – and possibly the first – will remain unrevealed. Apart from two small details which say a lot and nothing at the same time.

First, India wanted to know about what was going to happen to Anneke. Alison and I looked at each other blankly, because, bizarrely, this was one pretty crucial detail we had completely overlooked. After a silence, Alison played for time by saying that it was wonderful that India was thinking of other people – which remark might, at any other time, have brought forth a snort of derision from Florence but, on this occasion, very movingly for me, just saw her put her arm around India – and then added that we would discuss everything with Anneke just as soon as we had finished this family meeting. Which, of course, we would have to. It occurred to me, as I am sure it would have done to Alison, that this question of what, precisely, the arrangements for the nanny were to be, really was going to force us to focus on the exact details of all our living arrangements rather than just deal in airy fairy platitudes about sharing homes and whatnot.

Second, they wanted to know about Spot. Here, calling on my many years of experience as family Snap champion, I managed to get in first. I told them how much I loved Spot, as they all knew, but I knew Mummy loved him just as much, maybe even more, so if Mummy wanted to have Spot to live with her, then I would grin and bear it. This was such a magnanimous offer that Alison could hardly be seen to refuse it. Thus I made myself a self-sacrificing hero to the girls. Thus, I could ensure that I could hang up my pooper scooper at last. And thus I proved I could still earn a little of Alison's grudging respect. When things with Doug settled into their inevitable routine and when the novelty of that routine eventually wore off, I was fairly sure she would look back on my adman's smart-alec incorrigibility with at least a little nostalgia. Or then again, possibly not. But at this dismal lowpoint in my life, I needed to grab at whatever straws of consolation I could find.

*

Anneke wasn't the slightest bit surprised by the news or in the least bit fazed. But then, why would she be? Probably half her nanny mates had been in the same situation.

Anneke being not just South African, but Afrikaans, did not speak English as a first language. (I'd once made a remark to Alison about her muscular calves being ideal for trekking which

205

hadn't amused Anneke, because, unfortunately, she'd overheard it, and it hadn't amused Alison because I had obviously been taking note of the nanny's legs.) With her slightly limited vocabulary and her flat, vaguely guttural accent this could sometimes give the impression she was a little brusque. But on this occasion her unintended directness had the doubtful benefit of making me face an unwelcome reality.

"So," she said, "wool thet mean the girls wool be with Elison mainly during the week" – we insisted all our staff call us by our first names – "end they'll be wuth Endrew for lark, one night a week, and, lark, every other weekend? Thet's how ut usually sims to work. Except thet wuth Thelma's people (another Afrikaans nanny and family) the Ded's always away so thet doesn't always heppen. And the Ded of the kids Vera (another Afrikaans nanny) looks after, he's got a new girlfrind end the kids don't lark her so they don't spend much tarm with him arther."

Yes, I suddenly saw, this was very probably what it would be lark, and I didn't care for the sound of it at all. Didn't lark his girlfrind? What if I had a girlfrind and Florence and India didn't lark her?

"Well," said Alison, seeing the evident dismay which must have been registering on my face, and nipping in before I started hatching a plan to kidnap the girls and take them back to the ancient family shtetl in Lithuania, "we don't quite know what the arrangements will be just yet, but you may rest assured Anneke, that your job is perfectly secure."

"Oh thenk you Elison. Bar the why, ken you till me if ah well git a rarse, you know, for working unn two dufferent homes?"

I looked at Alison, Alison looked at me, and we both looked at Anneke, who looked back at us both, eyes as big as dinner plates, the very picture of just-off-the-farm naiveté.

That's the great advantage of being someone in Anneke's position. You might just be being bloody cheeky and, quite deliberately, be taking a right liberty, but you can get away with it because no-one can ever be certain beyond a reasonable doubt that you're guilty of anything worse than the not very heinous crime of lack of subtlety in a foreign language.

Besides, unless we wanted to recruit a replacement – 'family in throes of self-destruction seeks experienced etc.' – we just had to grin and bear her.

So Alison thanked her for taking the time to speak to us, I uncorked the first bottle I could lay my hands on, and my soon to be ex-wife and I sat in gloomy silence, quaffing long and deep.

I once asked a friend of mine, who'd been through it all, if he had a word of advice about getting a divorce.

"Yes," he said, "don't."

I doubt that it will have any more impact on you than it had on me, but, for what it's worth, I pass his advice on.

*

Not surprisingly, given all the turmoil in my life and in my head at this time, my spirits, as you may have noticed, were up and down like a yoyo. Like a yoyo that was a lot more down than up.

My humour wasn't improved by my failure to make any headway in my search for Peggy. I tried calling McConnell Martin in New York but HR wouldn't give me the time of day beyond telling me that even if they had been permitted to pass on any details of past employees, which they most definitely weren't, their 1979 records weren't computerised and, if they existed at all, were probably archived on microfiche in an underground vault.

Then, after re-reviewing all the remaining evidence, or lack of it, I decided that it might just be worth going down the New Rochelle route. But how? We were still really in the relative infancy of the internet in 1999 and although BWD had its IT geeks, I didn't think it would be wise to ask for their help. Doubtless the news would soon find its way back to Geoff and Vince, something I would not, for obvious reasons, have welcomed. I was certainly not up to speed myself and preferred conventional methods, so I called international directory enquiries. (Remember them?)

After an age spent listening to a lot of whirring and beeping I found myself transferred to 'Information' somewhere in New York. My first stop was Lee's Eyewear but I couldn't get the name of the street off the tip of my tongue. It turned out not to matter. I was assured there was "presently no record of any organisation of that name, sir" anywhere in New Rochelle. Nor of a Herb Lee, or a Barbara on Overlook Road, one street name I could not fail to remember. So either they had moved away or, it sadly crossed my mind, had died. I asked about a Marvin Lee at the same address – perhaps he had inherited the house – but got the same answer. I even tested the operator's patience further by asking about a Peggy or a Brenda Lee, because, well, you never knew, but, of course, I did know and I turned out to be annoyingly right.

I did get the number of Temple Israel, the Lee's synagogue, and called to find out if they could put me in touch with Herb or Barbara but the first World Trade Centre attack in 1993 and other terrorist scares had already cranked up the security paranoia to the point that no Jewish organisation would divulge the details about anything to anyone without a thorough background check and certainly not to some bloke calling from a strange and distant land – as anywhere abroad is to most Americans; and as it certainly was to the elderly, clearly deaf volunteer (surely, they couldn't have been paying him) who was manning the Temple Israel phones when I called.

So after all that, I was not an inch further forward, and couldn't imagine where I went from here, short of getting on a plane and traipsing the streets of New Rochelle with my Polaroid of Peggy in hand. Even in my present distressed state of mind, that sounded a bit extreme.

And then, just when I was feeling that life was all P and no E, when I could see my own thoroughly miserable reflection in the bone dry bottom of my once much more than half full glass, the good fairy came calling. And she came in the delightfully unexpected guise of Vince.

Never have I enjoyed a meeting with Vince more; not, anyway, since he went from being best mate to treacherous bastard. He marched into my office with all the usual Aussie bluster, and yet there was a certain je ne sais qantas missing, which suggested to a seasoned Dutton watcher such as I that, somehow or other, his navigational skills had failed him, that he was deep in the brownest of water and that he needed me to provide the requisite paddle. Immediately, I perked up.

The problem, it transpired, was that the client on our now-not quite so new seven million pound cereal account had decided that he did not, after all, care for the saintly Lucille's campaign for his not-actually-chocolate chocolatey thingies and indeed, in the absence of Lucille or any of her underlings coming up with anything in its stead, was cutting up a trifle rough. The client, a fat Mancunian called Mick Hudnutt, had even gone so far as to suggest that I, who was still, after all, the ECD of BWD should get personally involved. This, I gleefully surmised, would have got right up Lucille's turned up nose, and she, no doubt, perhaps in the aftermath of a bout of beauteous lovemaking with Vince, would, in the charming manner of a professional footballer when clearing his nose, have figuratively pressed a finger against each nostril and expelled the blockage all over his hideously hairy chest. I was so taken with this image that I found myself quietly weeping and Vince, given my recent topsy turvy emotional history, was moved to enquire if everything was alright. (Proving, I suppose, that somewhere, lost in his ever-increasing bulk, he still had something vaguely like a heart. But I was fucked if I was going to give him credit for that.)

"Yes, thanks Legga," I said, wiping my eyes on my Ralph Lauren sleeve – not really my brand, but it was the only clean shirt I could find that morning. Alison had been neglecting her laundry duties of late.

"My name's Vince, mate," said Vince without a lot of matiness in his voice, thus foolishly acknowledging that my cheap shot had got home. I thought his reaction was definitely worth a bonus point for me, if not two.

"Yes, sorry Vince. Got into a bit of a time warp there."

Vince didn't seem convinced, but in his current need, was in no position to pursue the point.

"So, mate, you going to help us out or not?"

Oh, was I! Was I ever! I was going to take hold of Mick Hudnutt's not-chocolate chocolatey dooberries and turn them into the most gloriously desirable bits of nutritionally useless rubbish that any four-year-old ever threatened matricide over. I would show Vince and Lucille and Geoff and all the rest of the twatting doubters, that I, Andrew Williams, was still the man!

That night, I burnt the midnight oil. Not, it's true, labouring over a breakfast cereal campaign. But I worked my way half way through series 1 of 'Seinfeld'. And, despite constantly hitting the pause button so I could drool over Elaine/Peggy, I did, after a while, get into the rhythm of it. Not for the first – or the last time – in my life, I found myself catching on about ten years after the event.

CHAPTER 16

NEW YORK, 1979

"I'm off to meet Miller for lunch," said Peggy.

Yes, those were the words that rocked my world, that sowed the seeds of our destruction, that I completely misunderstood. That was the stick, the wrong end of which I not only got hold, but on to which I hung like a pitbull with lockjaw.

What happened was this: I was coming out of the elevator on the tenth floor to see if Peggy wanted to grab a sandwich, but just before I turned the corner into the casting department, I heard her speak. I wasn't sure who she was addressing – her boss or Noreen I assumed – or in what context she was speaking. I didn't stop to think there might be some perfectly innocent explanation. I didn't stop at all. I turned tail and disappeared back into the elevator and thence to my floor, where I made straight for Brett or Bart's happy hideaway. I walked in, said not a word, and spent the next however long staring mindlessly out of the window at the little yellow cabs stop-starting their way up Madison, while Brett and Bart consumed their usual lunchtime tiffin – something or other on rye with extra bong.

"Hey man, you okay?" solicitously enquired Bart or Brett. "You need a little TLC?"

"Or maybe a lot of THC?" added Bart or Brett, setting off the usual hacking and spluttering which signified their utmost merriment.

"Do you want to go out and get shit-faced?" I asked them, suddenly feeling ready for action.

"When, tonight?"

"No," I said, "right now." And I got up and walked out of that office, grabbed my jacket from my own, swept past Laverne, and into the down elevator and out of the McDonnell Martin building, with Bart and Brett struggling to keep up.

We walked into a bar where I spent the rest of the afternoon and most of the evening ordering, in a very loud clear voice, a Bud or a Coors or a Rolling Rock, making the point to no-one but me because no-one else would have grasped it, that I was ready to get shit faced on any beer they had so long as it wasn't a fucking Miller. And after each beer, I picked up a shotglass and chucked an eye-watering, lip-crimping rye whisky down my throat. And I insisted that Brett and Bart did exactly the same. Then, at about ten, one of them said something like, "Lesh go sheebeegeebee," and we staggered out of the bar, managed to hail a cab without falling under the wheels of the passing delivery trucks, and, with the aid of a little pidgin French and some would-be sign language, just about made our instructions clear to the non-English-speaking Haitian cab driver to head for the Bowery and the New York club de those jours. Brett and Bart claimed to be regular patrons and they must have been telling the truth because, astonishingly, despite our condition, unfit for any purpose, the bouncers let us in. There was a band called Bad Brains playing, not famous for the catchiness of its tunes, but a perfect choice for my state of mind, and I pogo'd the night away, drinking ever more, so pissed that my meat-packing-party paranoia was temporarily suspended and I puffed enthusiastically on any joint that was handed to me. At about one or two in the morning, I noticed there was a chirpy girl with spiky green hair somewhere in my orbit and I asked her, or tried to in the deafening noise, if she had a boyfriend called Miller.

"WHO?' she screamed back.

"MILL-ER!"

Finally understanding, but understandably baffled, she shook her head, and I said,

"Fine, you'll do for me then."

And that was the end of our conversation and the beginning of a not very wonderful thing.

*

This all took place about five or six weeks or so after Peggy and I had been to New Rochelle, which meant that she had now been sleeping on Noreen's couch for a month and a half or so. A long time to have a cricked neck but she showed no new interest in cohabiting with me. I was no closer to capturing my elusive quarry.

Never the less, we'd been having a pretty good time. In July and early August, as is typically the case, it was often so oppressively close and unbearably hot that even the strongest antiperspirants threw in the towel. (Subway to be avoided at all costs.) But the New York summer still had plenty to offer.

Sometimes, Brett and Bart and Noreen and Peggy and I went off as a little group. This infamous fivesome first came together the weekend we went to Fire Island. Christo, a gay art director at the office (originally Christopher, of course) who spent from May until September in nothing but tight white tee-shirts (and jeans!) to show off his muscly tan, occasionally popped in to join the bong throng and one day casually mentioned that he was off on a two week shoot in Hawaii – "Nice job!" opined Brett or Bart – and that his summer cottage near Cherry Grove was going to be empty if any of us fancied using it. It hardly needs saying that we had all had our hands up quicker than Nazis at a Nuremburg rally and with so much competition for the place, we decided to share it; so Christo threw us the keys, gave us the address and apologised for the mess we were going to find.

Knowing Fire Island's reputation for hedonism of a particular kind, Bart, Brett and I decided we might, when catching the rays on the Cherry Grove beach, be giving an impression that we didn't want to give, and so decided it might be desirable to have some female company along. Peggy was keen but didn't want to be the only girl, so Noreen was roped in, and one sunny Saturday we set off on the Long Island Railroad from Penn Central to Sayville, then crowded into a cab to the dockside and finally climbed aboard a ferry to Cherry Grove which was overflowing with people and the sheer joy of being out of the hot, stinking city. The atmosphere was so exuberant that some passengers – we happy few amongst them – broke into song as we made the short trip across Long Island Sound, singing – and I kid you not – YMCA. A ridiculous pantomime, yes, but this was 1979, the same year it came out, so not quite yet – if very nearly – the cliché it might seem today.

Christo's place turned out to be a little, boxy, clapboardy sort of place, just as you might expect, which backed directly on to the beach. (In America, I learned, and as I've touched on before, almost everywhere turned out to be just like you'd expect, because you'd seen it all in the movies.) There was one main bedroom, which Peggy and I, being the only established couple, got – the sort of taken-for-granted arrangement which I always thought was so unfair when I wasn't in a couple – and a smaller one with a single bed, which Brett and Bart chivalrously granted to Noreen. I can't tell you a lot about that Saturday night – a barbecue of sorts, a starry, starry sky, Donna Summer and the like blaring out from boomboxes all along the beach. Or maybe that was just the soundtrack I've added to my moviemory of the night. Much to our guilty delight, Peggy and I came across several items of Christo's that he might have locked away if he'd known he was going to have guests in his bedroom, but despite thinking back to that conversation over the lemon cheese cake, or possibly because of it, I didn't suggest we try any of them out.

A sultry night was ended by blinding sunlight pouring in through the uncurtained window and the squawking chorus of sea-gulls scavenging for breakfast. I reluctantly disentangled myself from Peggy, and searched for and eventually found my underwear – I didn't want to casually stroll into the 'loungeroom' in the altogether and frighten Bart and Brett, sprawled out on the slightly soiled white sofas, into thinking I'd gone all Christo on them. As I was closing our bedroom door, I met Bart or Brett coming out of Noreen's room. Inevitable I suppose.

We all went to a beachside restaurant for lunch expecting to eat something fishy but they had some kind of Sunday special advertised as a 'pig roast'. Not the most inventive product description I'd ever read, but certainly to the point.

"You know I'm strictly Kosher," I said to Peggy.

"Oh, me too," she replied, and we both had the pig. Another piece of evidence, as if I needed any, that we were totally in tune.

We caught the late ferry back, the setting sun slanting across the crowded deck, where the atmosphere was a little quieter and more reflective but no worse for that. Here my moviemory is a medium two-shot of Peggy and I, our arms around each other's waists, staring straight out, and then a cut to a wider reverse shot from a helicopter, so that you can see that what we're looking at is the wake behind the stern as the ferry cuts through the spangled evening sea. The helicopter then climbs ever higher until it takes in the whole panorama and the ferry looks no bigger than a toy boat in a bath. Alright, I admit, I may now be describing the scene in slightly more technical detail than spontaneously comes to mind, but it's not so very far from the way I remember it.

*

215

Then, another time, Christo suggested we all go off to Studio 54. We were extremely doubtful that we'd be allowed in, but Christo thought he knew the secret.

"Just wear your two ties," he said to me, and he turned out to be right. We hovered around the edge of the crowd outside the door, and the guy in the shades with all the power of Nero at the Coliseum took one look at me and we got the thumbs up. Much back slapping from Brett and Bart, and many 'way to go's' accompanied my triumphant entrance – and better still, the odd 'who's he?' from the envious unwanted still stuck out in the unwelcoming street.

There was a whole crowd of us that night, all the usual crew plus a couple of pals of Christo's, a South African designer who looked more like Frank Zappa than Frank Zappa and his dinky blonde model girlfriend. It took us about twenty minutes before we could get one of the dancing gay barmen in their satiny shorts to serve us – it was the full flamboyant New York bartender act – mainly because we couldn't make ourselves heard over the amyl nitrate powered shouting and whooping and bloody annoying blowing of whistles that accompanied whatever already foundation wobbling track was being played. My two ties only had so much door opening power though, because they wouldn't let us in to any of the VIP and Very VIP lounges that the real movers and shakers hung out in.

Still, it was fun. I demonstrated one or two of my devastating disco moves to Peggy, who gave me that look that says 'Hmmm, interesting,' but which actually signified that the only reason she wasn't scurrying back to her seat was that she wouldn't have been able to force her way through the sweating, squirming mass of bodies that pressed from all sides.

Later, fairly drunk and in some cases stoned, and high also on the fact that we had actually got into Studio 54, we went back for more drinks to the South African designer's place which, of all places, was on Roosevelt Island, a tiny patch of land in the middle of the East River, recently reopened for residents after years of use mainly as an asylum for the insane. ("Roosevelt Island!" said Bart in wonder, having not caught up with the news, "You mean people actually live there?") To get there, you had to take the newly installed cable car by the 59th Street Bridge, and just being in a cable car in Manhattan seemed so wild that it could only add to the intoxication of the evening. On the balcony of the Roosevelt Island apartment, Peggy and I watched the reflection of sun in the mid town skyscrapers as it rose, while Frank Zappa – who else? – filtered out from the room behind us. Another evening, another moment, that you don't forget in a hurry.

*

And somewhere around this time too, there was the evening when, in one of those decibel packed bars that we used to favour after work, Bart or Brett happened to find out that Noreen's family came from somewhere called Manville in New Jersey, a place name which he recognised because he had a cousin who had once been ten pin bowling there. And one thing led to you can guess exactly what, and, goodness knows how, we all ended up in the Manville Bowl, a place about as far removed from Studio 54, in terms of all that was hip and cool and right-on as it was humanly possible to get. But in terms of having a rollicking good time, maybe even better. No stars to fuck at the Manville Bowl but plenty of beer to drink and carbs to eat and laughs to have. I didn't, by the way, and wisely, you may think, sport the two-tie look at the Manville Bowl.

And interspersed with all of the extra-mural activities of our newly formed group were romantic – yes, corny to say so, I know, but that's the right word for it – evenings when it was just Peggy and me. Evenings when, despite the pervading presence of Eau de Feline, we would just spend our time watching whatever schlock telly was on and then by amusing ourselves in my lumpy bed. Or maybe we'd have a cheap Italian or Mexican or Polish meal – in

217

the Lower East Side there was no cuisine of any ethnicity that was unavailable and all available for a knockdown price – and just chit-chat our way through the evening with an ease that, viewed from so many difficult years distant, seems all but impossible to imagine.

But sometimes at the end of these evenings Peggy would opt for Noreen's cramped couch rather than my lumpy bed, and I can't say I always accepted her decision with perfect grace.

*

One Wednesday – the week after the trip to Manville, I think – on what had been one of our now pretty regular film nights, we were, as usual, conducting the post movie post mortem in one of those nondescript coffee houses that we always gravitated towards after the main attraction. I can't remember what the name of the film was or whether either or both of us liked it or not, so I think we can safely put it in the neither here nor there file. I do remember Peggy suddenly dismissing the movie from the conversation by saying, "Hey Andy, you remember my dad saying he was going to be Tevye. Well, they're doing it next Sunday and he asked me if you wanted to come see it with me?"

Her face was bright and eager. It was clear she genuinely wanted me to come. And so, it seemed, did Herb and presumably Barbara. It would mean I was being invited back to meet her parents for a second time. All this, you might think, boded well. My policy of bold patience (or patient boldness) was apparently paying off. I was being invited into the bosom of the Lee family, and for a second time too. I had had my first audition and I must have passed. But did my heart lift? Well, yes, but maybe not as far as it should have done.

It wasn't just that the prospect of watching an amateur production of 'Fiddler on the Roof' performed by the members of a suburban synagogue made me worry that I'd soon be thinking that Uncle Vanya in contemporary Nicaragua wasn't so bad after all. And neither was it the deflating sensation, one I've experienced many times in my life, that when you finally seem to be in sight of getting what you really, really want, you find don't really want it at all.

No, what this was about, at least in part, was a battle of wills. And we were locked in stalemate. She just wouldn't give in. And I wouldn't give up. I hadn't been constantly pressing her to come and live with me and the cat, nor pushing the probably more saleable line of looking for somewhere else to live with me but without the cat. Yet somehow, on some telepathic level, that was the message I know I was insistently transmitting. And you can fairly accuse me of handling this totally wrongly, of being my own worst enemy, of simply not backing off enough to give her the time and space that she kept saying she wanted. Surely, I should have seen, that in the scheme of things, four weeks on Noreen's couch, or even four months, was nothing to get worked up about. Notwithstanding the inconvenience and irritation to me of this arrangement, we were, as I have just described, having a pretty terrific time, were we not?

And you could also ask, if it meant so much to me, why I didn't just say stuff this patience lark for a game of soldiers and go all out for the boldness? Why did I not go off to a jewellers one lunchtime, buy an engagement ring, take her for a candlelit dinner and flip open the box between courses? I suppose one answer is, that for all my supposed ardour, and the long term possibilities I entertained, and the Tarzan and Jane flights of fancy, I wasn't yet ready to go that far.

(But I will say this in my defence. Wasn't Peggy, in spending so much time with me, in sleeping with me a little more than occasionally, in twice inviting me to meet her parents, and yet also making such a business of declaring her need for independence, sending out slightly mixed signals?)

Finally – except was it really, really finally? – there was Miller.

Yes, she had at last quit that particular hearth and home. And reassured me a hundred times that the embers of their one-time romance had grown so cold in the grate that they couldn't have been revived if you'd thrown a tanker load of petrol over them and chucked in a lighted blow torch. But what about all those boy meets girl, boy loses girl, *boy gets girl back* stories? Such things happened. So, from my perfectly reasonable, utterly paranoid point of view, for as long as Peggy wasn't safely stamped as my property, and preparing the fricassee of hairy mammoth in my cave, why shouldn't such a thing happen again?

All that was why, when I said in reply to Peggy's second invitation to New Rochelle, "Brilliant. Yes, I'd love to come", I may have said it just a little – a tiny bit – wearily.

And it was why, when I overhead Peggy saying she was going for lunch with Miller, it was a racing certainty that two and two would add up to anything but four.

*

I awoke looking up at a moulded (and probably mouldy) ceiling with peeling yellowy paint and a single naked light bulb hanging from it, thankfully unlit. I had no idea where I was or how I had got there. It seemed that I was lying on someone's bed but, again, it was a mystery as to whose. I tried to turn my head to see if there was anyone else present who might be able to offer some useful clues but a series of violent explosions in what, I would guess, was my cerebrum, advised against sudden movement. In between the explosions, I could detect the sound of rain beating against a window and those were the only signals my brain seemed capable of receiving until there was a click and a blinding flash.

"Turn the fucking light off." Not perhaps the politest way to greet a stranger.

"So, you avake," came the reply, husky, feminine, mittel-Europeanish by the sound of it.

At last the pennies, began, one by one, but very slowly, to drop.

It was probably not a stranger after all. It was almost certainly the girl with the green spiky hair, who'd turned out be German, and whose name was – fuck knows. Had she told me? Had I asked her?

"Not vonting to be pogoing now, Andrew, yes?" she enquired and then laughed.

Yes, I most certainly did not want to be pogoing or doing anything more strenuous than staying stock still, exactly where I was. As to how I had got there, I dare say you can fill in most of the blanks yourself. But, very briefly, in case you think that's my job, I'll cover the bases:

Pogo-drink-snog-pogo-puff-pogo-grope-pogo-drink-puff-leave-snog-grope-walk-drink (brought it from club) walk-puff-snog-snog-snog-jog (interest rising) arrive (here) climb-climb-climb-climb-rest (now I was beginning to remember – this was what they called in New York a cold water walk-up, and a sodding long way up too) climb-climb-unlock-unlock-unlock (not many for a New York door) and – the usual. Actually, it wasn't that usual, at least not for me, whatever impression I might like to give to Bart and Brett, and neither do I want to demean – still can't remember her name – by claiming that I didn't enjoy myself with her or suggest that she wasn't a very sweet girl with a nice bod whose number I wouldn't, at a different point in my life, have been very pleased to take.

But Peggy, whose face suddenly floated into view, she was not. Jesus H. Christ, what had I done? No, forget the question mark. !!!!!! (No question was ever more rhetorical than that one.)

I fell out of the building – which turned out to be miles across in the Lower West Side, practically by the Hudson and not nearly such a smart address as it is now – and into the very, very damp street down which Noah could easily have floated. The rain continued to cascade down, and as I had not had the foresight to equip myself with a raincoat, hat and umbrella before going off on my drink and drugs and dancing and doing it with a stranger binge, the huge fat drops plastered my ever thinning hair to my scalp and ran in rivulets down my forehead and my face, and down the upturned collar of my second hand Hawaiian shirt – did I mention that? Not very punk but purchased from a store in Hudson St, v. cool at the time – and meanwhile my shoes squelched their way through puddles the size of Lake Superior.

As I aquaplaned my way across town, my brain at last began to re-engage, and I realised today was a working day, and what is more, that I had a deadline to meet on the print ad I was supposed to be writing for the newest rust bucket out of Detroit, the producers of which had, in their wisdom, chosen to employ an advertising agency who, in their turn, relied upon the lightning wits of people such as Bart, Brett, and myself. More fool them, you may say, and it would be hard to disagree, but still, good manners decreed that the agency, and therefore, I, should have something to show. That being the case, and, taking into account my deteriorating relations with Todd Zwiebel, and that this job was at least two weeks overdue, I decided that I would have to head for McDonnell Martin rather than take the preferred road home.

Leaving a small pond in the elevator, and a river of drips as I passed the ever supportive Laverne – "That another new look, Andrew? Think I preferred the two ties" – I eventually reached my desk, and sat shivering in the freezing cold of my air-conditioned office. On my desk was a handwritten note, short and to the point: 'Where the hell are you? Bring your stuff straight to meeting. Nick.' Nick was Nick Moreno, my immediate creative supervisor. And there was a PS, cryptic and rather menacing: 'This matters!'

I looked at my watch. Fuck, it was nearly eleven and I had barely half an hour to think of something. The art director who I was supposed to be working with on this particular brief was Christo, but, frankly, he was a dead loss at coming up with anything resembling an idea, and it was always understood that when on a job with him, the writer came up with the thought, and Christo, having, it had to be admitted, a bloody good eye, would tickle it into visual shape. In other words, if I didn't have a brainwave rapidamonty it would be my fan that the shit would be hitting.

Any writer, of whatever kind, will tell you that the only thing that really gets the creative juices flowing is fear of the rapidly approaching deadline, and so it was that day. The three muses popped into my office on cue and presented me with a stunning idea which – you would have thought – fitted perfectly with the brief. This was, according to the briefing document with which I was mopping the rain off my head, to highlight the quietness of our new compact's engine. (Compacts – e.g. vehicles slightly less enormous than last year's ludicrously over-sized models – were, following the latest oil price hike, all the rage in '79.) And my inspired solution to the problem, my knock-em-dead headline for the ad, was: 'Do you have a bee in your bonnet about compacts?'

Complex, I will grant you, multi-layered, but utterly brilliant. It addressed the number one consumer concern – as shown by reams of research – that smaller cars with smaller engines made for a noisier, and therefore less desirable, driving experience than the six litre monsters that American motorists had always had before, and would really much rather have now. Do you see? A bee in your bonnet. As in a persistently worrying idea. But also: As in a noise coming from your engine. How fucking clever was that! (In case you insist on answering that question, and doing so by saying something like 'not fucking clever at all, just obscure and totally dreadful', I would say, while conceding the basic point, that sometimes when striving desperately to be creative, the totally dreadful and the fucking clever can be easily confused. Anyway, at this point in proceedings I had no such doubts.)

Suddenly, all worries about my unforgivable disloyalty to Peggy were forgotten. Self-flagellation would cease. Non-stop patting on the back from Todd Zwiebel would follow. That was always the way for me, and I am sure I am not alone. I got such a rush from having an idea I thought was really good – in advertising that's your fundamental raison d'etre – that any pain I was feeling about anything would instantaneously evaporate. The trouble always started when I realised that it really wasn't that great an idea after all. Then I would be plunged into despair quicker than a butterfingered trapeze artist.

So this was what preceded the moment when I ran into the creative review meeting with my piece of paper and my brilliant line written on it. I hadn't even had time to speak to Christo beforehand so it was new to everyone in the room: to him, to Nick Moreno, to the account men, who, first thing in the afternoon, were due to meet the client. And also there was the Manatee himself, who, completely unexpectedly, had descended from Mount Olympus for a second time in as many months, quite possibly, one could not help but surmise, because the rust bucket manufacturers were exhibiting the same signs of itchy feet as the shampoo charlies. (This, I felt, shed light on the cryptic PS.) Still, not to worry. The greater the agency's need, the greater my glory would be.

"So," began Nick Moreno, who had never trusted me, being a hard bitten Italian American from New Jersey, and for whom, therefore, it was an article of faith that all Englishmen were faggots, "tell us what you got."

And so I presented my brilliant idea and waited for the metaphorical thunder of applause. (And, it might not be too much to hope, perhaps the odd literal ripple.) But there was no metaphorical thunder. No literal ripple. Not a single palm slapped another palm, not in reality nor as a figure of speech. Instead, there was a mystified silence. At the very most, there might have been the tiny susurrus of air movement brought about by collective furrowing of brows or dropping of jaws.

Sensing, a trifle anxiously, the possibility that my audience might not have grasped all the subtleties of my brilliant idea, I went through the aforementioned rigmarole about the various implications of bees and bonnets. The account men looked at each other, Nick looked at Todd, Todd looked to the heavens, and Christo looked at me with the expression of a man on a plane who's just looked out the window and noticed the wing's dropped off.

Then Nick said, clearly enjoying the moment regardless of the fact that we had less than a couple of hours before the now distinct possibility of walking naked into the conference chamber, "Well, let's see now. Number one. In America, the part of a car that covers the engine is called a 'hood' and not a 'bonnet'."

"Number one?" I squeaked back, thinking 'there's a no.2? Because no.1 alone has just totally screwed me.'

"And number two—" Nick paused for effect.

"Number two, there is no such expression in America that I have ever heard of—"

Here he paused again, and looked around the room just to make sure he was not unique in this deficiency. He wasn't.

"—there is no such expression as 'a bee in the bonnet'."

Ah.

I walked out of the meeting with my head held as high as it could be – not that high – and to the accompaniment of Nick saying to Christo that he shouldn't worry, they'd get someone else to work with him through lunch. He didn't even bother to ask me to have another go, even on my own, when, given the urgency of the situation, they would have been grateful for any half-baked idea from the doorman. And he didn't even bother to say to me directly – not that he needed to, but still – that I was being stood down. (On the grounds of my hopelessly, incurable, effete Englishness.)

I couldn't even face Brett and Bart. I thought of turning to the one I loved for consolation – for who else should you turn to in such circumstances? But then the night's misdemeanours suddenly swung back into view, and I slumped forwards onto my desk in a miserable heap. Never mind two ties. My next fashion statement would be sackcloth and ashes and those spiked metal garter things that those Opus Dei chaps are supposed to wear. And, if that didn't work, I might do a bit of thrashing myself with chains, too.

I did wonder about something though. And that was this: given that only an hour before, when under the illusion that I'd had this brilliant idea, I'd succeeded in putting my unfaithfulness to Peggy completely out of my mind, was I feeling quite as sorry as I was telling myself? Or was I just feeling sorry *for* myself?

I didn't like to think I was quite that shallow – I hadn't come to accept my true flawed self as I have today – so I took a fateful decision (and, as you will see, stuck to it) to ensure that I took full responsibility for my errors.

In other words I was in a hole, and I called in a JCB.

CHAPTER 17

LONDON, 1999

"Eebahgum."

It was Frank Connor, BWD's financial director, speaking.

I looked up, startled. Frank was from Dagenham originally, and had never quite managed to lose the accent. I hadn't been paying a lot of attention but I couldn't imagine why he'd suddenly broken into broadest Yorkshire.

"Pardon?" I said.

"E-bit-da," he said very deliberately, and then stopped to make sure I had taken it in.

Ah, not 'eebahgum' but 'ebitda'. Well, that explained that then.

"For goodness sake, Andrew, do listen. You asked me to help, so you might do me that courtesy. Ebitda is what it's all about. You've got to have your Ebitda before you can start."

I think he started to notice my eyes glazing over again. He got more animated. "It's an acronym, Andrew. For a formula. The letters stand for the things we base the value of a company on. E-B – earnings before, I – interest, T – tax, D – depreciation, blah, blah, blah …"

Frank didn't exactly say blah, blah, blah, but he might as well have done. Like all creative types I regarded the bean counters as even lower in the pecking order than the suits – unless I needed them to sign my expenses or something, then I prostrated myself before them – and I could never be bothered to clutter up my brilliant mind with tedious figures. The only reason I was with Frank was that Harriet Braintree insisted I provide her with an accurate picture of my financial situation and for that I needed to know what my stake in the company was worth. Frank was the guy who could tell me.

Before I had started to get hold of this stuff about my 'net worth', Harriet had been at pains to warn me to play with a straight bat – "No hiding the Rubens in the attic, Andrew, no secret bank accounts in Lichtenstein, ha ha ha." And being the wuss I am, the type who goes cold at the very thought of the old bill or the taxman or anybody else knocking on the door at the dead of night, I dutifully complied. As far as this part of the exercise went, that meant not succumbing to the temptation to have a quiet word in Frank's shell-like. Harriet's warning was not to be ignored. "Believe me, Andrew, they'll know if you're playing ducks and drakes."

So while Frank tapped away at his calculator, muttering about multiples and cash flow and other such impenetrable financial rhubarb and wrote down lots of numbers with his fountain pen and made his careful computations, I wandered about his office, checking out the view – nothing to write home about, facing into the well like Lucille's – looking over his shoulder at the silver-framed photos of his wife and children – nothing to write home about either – and keeping my mouth shut like a good boy.

After an eternity Frank waved me back to my seat, and wrote something down, which I presumed was the amount he'd arrived at, on a post-it note which he very deliberately folded in half before pushing it across the desk towards me. (Why do people insist on doing that? Do they think they're in the Mob? Did Frank think I was wearing a wire? The door was shut, we were on our own, why couldn't he have just told me?) I went to pick the post-it note up, but he clamped his hand over mine, and then lamented over the amount we'd overpaid for the design company and the losses that had been haemorrhaging from the PR outfit.

"If it hadn't been for them – and salaries, over budget again this year – and the renovations – paid through the nose if you ask me – it would have been a fair bit better. Be that as it may, we have a total company value of fifteen and a half, I would say, which makes your share …"

He released my hand and leant back in his chair, with a smug look on his face as if he were personally responsible for my good fortune. I opened the folded post-it note. £4,680,000 was written in his careful hand.

"Crikey!" I said, "Really."

"Give or take."

"Give or take?"

"Yes," said Frank, breaking into a huge grin. "Depends on how much you give and she takes."

Well, if his jokes had been original he wouldn't have been a bean counter.

*

That's right. Four and a half and change. Oodathunkit. Little Andrew Williams, yeah, Mavis and Sid's boy, hasn't he done well? I fairly bounced back up the stone steps which led into Hardy Wiggins.

But, curiously, perhaps because she was jaded by the value of the back catalogues of superannuated pop stars, Harriet Braintree did not seem that impressed.

"Yes, Andrew, I know it sounds like a lot – and, please do not misunderstand me, I am not for one moment suggesting it is not a considerable sum, but you'd be amazed at how a divorce – if not properly handled – can, well, can cause a fortune to dwindle. There are all sorts of things to take into account. To begin with, there's CGT."

CGT! Of course. How could I have been so stupid as to forget it? Possibly because I had no idea what it was. Some sort of sports car perhaps? A modern variation on a drink before dinner? But I didn't have to ask for an explanation because Harriet took my ignorance for granted.

"Capital Gains Tax. Won't be enormous, you've had the company for ten years, so you'll get the full taper relief."

Full taper relief? Sounded depressingly sleazy or rather appealing depending on your point of view.

"You'll still have to pay about ten per cent on any profit you've made, which I'm guessing will be most of that. So, that's going to be somewhere around the four hundred thou mark."

Four hundred *thou*! Not enormous? Not exactly a handful of coppers either. Still, I reasoned, it could be worse.

Which it soon was.

"And then, there is the little matter of the original partners' agreement."

Now what was she on about?

"You don't remember? Gosh, you artistic types are all the same." I presumed this was an attempt to bracket me with the superannuated pop star. I wasn't sure whether I should be flattered or insulted. "You see, according to what I've seen, there was a clause in your original agreement that none of the founding partners could sell their shares on to a third party without the written agreement of the others."

"Oh. Is that bad?"

Harriet snuck a look at me over her half-moons which suggested that she may have been doing the superannuated pop star a disservice.

"Well, realising your asset – getting your money out – might not be straightforward. But let's cross that bridge when we come to it – hmm?"

Something very unpleasant had just hoved into view.

"Do you mean that me laying my hands on what is rightfully mine depends on the say so of Geoff Bradley and Vince Dutton?"

"Technically, yes, it may, but I do have my doubts that an agreement like that would stand up in court. Still, court is a place we'd prefer not to go, Andrew."

We moved on to the rest of my stuff. The bottom line was this; I had my house, then worth about £800,000 – today goodness only knows, I only know *I* couldn't afford to buy it – except that it wasn't my house, it was ours. Ours being Alison's and mine in about equal part, say a quarter each, and the Woolwich Building Society's who were in for around half. Then there were the contents – again split between Alison and me – and worth about sixty thousand, top whack. I had some shares and investments outside of BWD, maybe worth four hundred thou on a good day. Then came the barrel scrapings such as the nanny's second hand VW – the Porsche and the Jeep were both owned, or rather leased, by the company.

My basic salary at BWD was – yes, a fair screw I won't deny – one fifty at the time, and, on top of that, dividends from my company shares, had, last year, been the same again. So that was three hundred. Yes, yes, I know, very nice work if you can get it. Well, I'm not going to try to justify it because you can't, and isn't it terrible about the poor nurses, and I'm sure that if I hadn't had the luck I'd had, I'd be wearing a bandana and chanting revolutionary slogans and lining up at the front of the barricades to lob a Molotov cocktails at the likes of me. (No, of course I wouldn't, I'd be right behind the guys lobbing the Molotov cocktails and making jolly sure I didn't get caught.)

Anyway, it was what it was. And when you looked at everything together surely it wasn't at all that bad? Wait a mo, it was even better than that. Almost forgot to mention my pension. There was six hundred thousand plus in that. Harriet Braintree, however, was a hard one to please.

"You see, Andrew," she said, "it looks like quite a bit, and on top of that we have to take account of whatever Alison has to throw in the pot, but the bulk of it, much the greatest part, is tied up in the company. And your pension almost counts against you, because it will be included in your overall worth, but you can't get at it, until you're old enough to take it, can you? And yes, your income is nothing to sneeze at, but goodness knows, so are your outgoings, you've only got to think about Florence and India's school and uni fees for the next however many years, and all the maintenance there'll be—" (yes, thank you, Harriet, as if I needed reminding) "—so, well, what I would say is, despite the success of your firm, and really, well done on that, I never knew advertising was such a wonderful business, I really would be thinking about cutting your cloth, if you know what I mean."

I gave a grim smile to confirm I knew what she meant.

"Oh and Andrew, before you leave, I think Colin has your account ready. Much less painful to settle things little by little, I always think."

Not that much less painful, I thought, not at four fifty an hour.

When I left Hardy Wiggins the boing in my bounce had all but gone.

*

I wandered around the flat looking at … I didn't quite know what. I'd taken it all in in about the first ten seconds but had the idea that protocol demanded I seem to make a more thorough examination. I opened and closed a few kitchen cupboards and pretended to check out the central heating controls.

"Bit of work and it'll look like a pretty good deal," said the young estate agent showing me round. "New carpets, lick of paint. All the basics are here."

All the basics were three bedrooms – one really far too small – plus bath, kitch, recep. It would just about do, it was in Bayswater which was close enough to the house and the girls school, and they were asking two seventy-five which, it seemed, was about manageable. If you're wondering how a man with a cool four million and a bit share in an advertising agency could only just manage two seventy-five, so was I, but that was what my accountant – who had already been twice divorced himself – was telling me. (His piece of divorce advice was, "Remember the bad times, Andrew, remember the bad times.")

Once the solicitors had got involved, the pace of the divorce had picked up. It just seemed sensible to get it over with. I could have hung about New Pemberley for a bit longer but it was no fun trying to maneouvre your way past your wife – as was – as would soon officially not be – on the stairs without touching. Not that I wanted to touch her, any more than I suppose she wanted to touch me, but the deliberate avoidance just pointed up all that we no longer were to each other.

It was clear that Alison was going to get the house – there was no way I was going to push the girls out of the only home they could remember – so that meant I had to go. I thought about renting but couldn't see the point. I suppose I could have taken a bit more trouble, seen a few more places, but whatever I had been shown would have looked pretty shitty compared to what I was leaving, and besides, I just wasn't in the mood for enthusiastic house hunting. So, I offered two five five, got it for two sixty, and one windy midweek day in October – there was no way I was going to manage this without some serious caterwauling if the kids weren't out of the way at school – I lugged a couple of suitcases of clothes and a few books and whatnots stuffed into a cardboard box down the steps and waved goodbye to Anneke, who choked back a tear and very nearly set me off too.

But heigh ho, onward and upward, one door shuts – well that's what you try to tell yourself, because really, what the fuck else is there to say?

*

Mooneys – no, not the cult, different spelling – had their London office in one of those faceless little streets around Holborn. (Handy for all the solicitors clustered around the nearby Inns of Court, I suppose.) They occupied the top two floors of a building above a shop that sold umbrellas. I pressed the buzzer by the brass plaque on which their name was inscribed, the door clicked open and up the winding, lino'd stairs I climbed. Mooney's was an American outfit, not as big as Pinkerton's, but they had this branch office in London, and Harriet Braintree, had, via a couple of intermediaries – dealing with people like this was far, far beneath her – pointed me in their direction. She hadn't known quite what to make of my original enquiry – "Private investigators? Surely, we know all we need to about your wife's er – activities" – and I really couldn't be bothered to properly enlighten her. I just gave her the bare bones: said it was nothing to do with Alison, but that I was just trying to trace a missing person and I thought she might know someone. I hadn't known quite what a private investigator's would look like – probably expected something like one of those places you see in forties films with S. Spade or P. Marlowe etched on a glass door – but it turned out to be grey carpet tiles and tired pot plants and anonymous wooden laminated desks, modern and dead, the sort of look that BWD might have had if Frank Connor had been in charge of the design.

My appointment was with someone called Keith Lyons, who turned out to be a balding, paunchy chap, an ex-Met D.I. he told me – I immediately decided he'd probably never made it higher than sergeant – doubtless getting one of those bloated police pensions that I'd read about – and whose most notable feature was that he supported his weight on his knees on one of those funny ergonomic chairs with no back.

"Slipped disc," he offered by way of explanation. "It's a bastard."

By 1999, I had long since given up smoking and almost everyone I knew had too, but Keith Lyons was still keeping the flag flying for the terminally stupid, and we went through the usual palaver of him offering me one, me refusing, him saying 'Mind if I do?' and me lying that I didn't. Eventually, after he'd got a good couple of lungfuls of carcinogens down him, he turned to the business at hand.

"So tell me what you know about this person. Let's start with the basics.

Name?"

"Um, Lee."

"First name or last name."

"Oh, last name."

He wrote Lee down on a form.

"First name?"

"Ahah, well there you have it."

"Sorry?"

"Well, she's known as Peggy."

Before I could stop him, he'd written Peggy down on the form. Then looked up, frowning. Something had just dawned on him.

"What? Peggy Lee? The singer? She shouldn't be too hard to find."

"Er, no, not that Peggy Lee. This is another Peggy Lee. And that's just a nickname."

"Ok – ay. And her real name is?"

"Er, Brenda."

"Brenda? Brenda Lee? Like Brenda Lee – the other singer?"

"Yes."

"But not that Brenda Lee, am I right?"

"No. I mean yes, not that Brenda Lee."

"Ok-ay." He stubbed the cigarette out, and crossed out Peggy and put Brenda.

"Only, that may not be her name either."

"Sorry?"

"Well, it's a bit complicated. She told me Brenda was her real name but I think she may not have wanted me to know."

He laid his Bic on his desk, breathed out, and leaned back. I winced because he'd clearly forgotten he was in an ergonomic chair without anything to support him from behind. He'd got to the critical point where he was about to topple on to the floor, when, with a supreme effort, he managed, with the use of his core muscles, and a bit of urgent arm whirling, to halt the momentum and force himself forwards again. Can't have done his slipped disc any good at all. Having survived this crisis, he lit another cigarette. (A Piccadilly tipped, I noticed; hadn't seen one of those since they built Stonehenge.)

"Forgive me, Mr Williams—"

"Please call me Andrew."

"Er, very well, Andrew. So, she didn't want you to know her name. What makes you think she'd want to be found by you now?"

"Well, yes, someone else asked me something similar."

"Sorry?"

I was about to mention Donald McEwan's doubts when I thought better of it. I wasn't sure that an ex-Met detective would read the right things into me seeing a shrink.

"I'm just sure that she would."

"Alright then. Let's move on."

We then covered what my relationship with her had been – blood relative, no – husband, no – boyfriend, just about – and how long it had been since I had last seen her.

"Twenty years."

"Any contact since?"

"No."

"Do you have an address?"

"Do you mean postal or e-mail?"

He raised his eyebrows, implying, I thought, something along the lines of, ooh, I say, get you, very up to date.

"Okay then. Postal?"

"No."

"E-mail?"

"No."

Another, even more drawn out ok-ay, this time stretching it to another syllable: ok-ay-ee. And another Piccadilly tipped.

"Telephone number?"

"No."

"Mr Williams – sorry Andrew – is there anything you know about this lady, apart from the fact that her name is Lee?"

"Well—" I began, and then went through the list of enquiries I made myself, the fruitless enquiries at McConnell Martin, New Rochelle Information, the Temple Israel Synagogue, all that I had done until my search had run into the sand.

I looked up at him with spaniel eyes.

"So that's why I've come to you."

He leaned forward on his ergonomic chair – he wasn't going to make the mistake of going backwards again – and said, as sympathetically, I think, as he could:

"Look, Andrew, I can see you've got a bit of a bee in your bonnet about this lady," – a horrible feeling came over me when he said those words but I couldn't work out why – "but it's not a lot to go on, it really isn't."

He was obviously tempted to draw a line under things here but seeing my crestfallen face – or possibly the prospect of a few days fees slipping unnecessarily away – he said,

"Alright, let's try again. No point in asking you if you know her social security number I suppose?"

I shook my head. No, no point, not when—

"What about her date of birth?"

Not when I didn't even know that. I shook my head again. The best I could do was,

"I think her birthday's in February. She was an Aquarius, I remember that, I'm a Sagittarius and we definitely discussed that. But she never had a birthday when I was with her you see. And she was two years younger than me, so that would make her date of birth, the year I mean – fifty-two or fifty-three, one or the other."

Keith Lyons, and he was an ex-Met detective remember, so this can't have been easy for him, was clearly beginning to have serious doubts about the ethics of taking my money.

"Andrew, I'm really not sure you wouldn't be wasting—"

Suddenly I remembered something from New Rochelle.

"Wait a minute, I can tell you where she went to school! It was New Rochelle High. And where she went to college – she went to NYU, I saw her graduation picture. There was some little town – it was called, wait a minute, Bamington, or Bingleton, something like that. That any help? Must be. Don't they always have those year books at schools and things in America?"

Keith Lyons still looked unconvinced.

"It's a long shot. We don't have her name and they probably wouldn't release the information even if we had."

But a long shot was good enough for me.

"What sort of money are we talking about here?" I asked eagerly. I could see the cogs whirring behind his eyes; he'd given me every chance hadn't he? But if I was really determined to open my wallet and let him empty it, what was he supposed to do?

"£500 a day," he said. "That's our standard charge. Say three days work. Not as much as four I shouldn't think. Plus VAT. Thick end of two grand I suppose, all up."

Actually, now that I thought about it, and given Harriet Braintree's advice about cloth cutting and my accountant's equally sanguine view of my situation, this wasn't nothing. But hell, I wasn't going to stop now. If I abandoned my search for Peggy, if I didn't have the prospect of finding her to distract me, well then, my immediate future looked a pretty dismal prospect. So, in for a penny, in for the thick end of two grand.

"Okay," I said.

"Okay," he said, and produced another set of forms for me to

238

sign. Then he said, "Silly me – almost forgot. Don't suppose you've got a photo of – er – this Peggy Lee, have you?"

"Oh, yes," I said, "I forgot too. How stupid was that!" And I reached into my pocket and pulled out the Polaroid of Peggy.

Keith Lyons looked at it.

"Hmm," he said, which I assumed was a grunt of approval. "Blimey, I haven't seen one of these for years. A Polaroid I mean."

It was odd, but despite all the times the Polaroid had been in and out of my various pockets and my office drawer and wherever else, the fact that it was a Polaroid as opposed to any other kind of photo hadn't really crossed my mind. In 1979 Polaroid cameras were the only way to get an instant picture and they were – or we thought they were – at the very cutting edge of technological advance. Twenty years on, not that long really, and they were museum pieces. I looked at the Polaroid, with its strange little white frame, and remembered how we used to look at those things just after we had taken a shot, and wait for the chemicals inside, whatever they were, to do their stuff, and for the image to gradually, magically materialise out of nothing and how we used to wave them about in the air or to hold them flat against the heat of our bodies to speed up the process – or so we thought.

"Can I keep that?" asked Keith Lyons.

"No," I said, "you can't." There was no way I was letting it go.

So we photocopied it and, since it was already slightly faded, he had a rather muddy image of Peggy to send off to the States, if that, as I presumed, was his plan.

It was bucketing down when I got outside Mooney's offices, and I had another strange frisson – some unlocated, undefined impression – from the past. I ducked into the umbrella shop and bought one, then put it up, and walked, despite the weather, all the way back to Fitzrovia. I let all the taxis splash past me, without once trying to hail one.

I wanted time to think and what I kept thinking about was the

239

moment just now, when I'd looked at the picture of Peggy and the way that it had registered for the first time that it wasn't just any kind of a photo, but a Polaroid. And I couldn't help but think how fitting that was. It was of another time, and now it dawned on me, as it never had before, at least not in that way, that she was too. That we were too.

But as soon as I walked through the doors of BWD I shut the idea out of my mind. I was too far down the line to let it take hold.

*

I was once interviewed by someone, some arse licking trade journo, who asked me about how I dealt with 'the tyranny of the blank sheet of paper'. It is rather a good phrase, one I'm quite sure he'd nicked from someone else, which neatly points up the pressure you are under when you have to think of something and your mind refuses to engage. There the blank sheet of paper sits – or now the empty computer screen – and stares back at you accusingly. Despite being blank, it doesn't say nothing. It screams 'useless, empty headed, talentless idiot' at you. You're being paid to do this, and you can't think of a damned thing.

I was reminded of that conversation as I sat in my office late one night, a couple of weeks after the joyous day when Legga – I rarely now thought of him as anything else – had come grovelling to me, begging for my help with the cereal account. A fortnight on and I had bugger all.

I have always found that my most inspired ideas come to me within the first few seconds of first hearing of whatever project it is that I have to think about. In that first instant, I seem to have the vital flash, make the lateral connection, that, in advertising, and other things like it, is an 'idea'. I have never been a deliberator, someone who carefully weighs the options before reaching the considered decision. (As you may have noticed.)

The problem with this method, or lack of it, is that once the first few seconds have passed, and nothing jumps into your mind, a tiny worm begins to wiggle away inside. It's that little worm of self-doubt, and it has a nasty habit of feeding on itself, and yet getting bigger and bigger, until it fills your mind so completely that all you can think of is that you can't think of anything. This is the way it was with the chocolatey dib dabs that weren't made of chocolate at all.

At the end of one day after another I left my office with nothing but a waste bin overflowing with screwed up pieces of paper defaced only by aimless doodles – mostly of Legga and Lucille being attacked with various instruments of torture – and the next morning I would march in determined that today would be the day, but every day the little worm wormed away and it wasn't. Although it was imperative that this piece of work – which next year must sweep all before it at DADA and Cannes – was seen to be mine, I was not so proud that I wasn't ready to share a little bit of the credit. (A very little bit.) So after the first fruitless week, I called on all sorts of underlings to help me. It's usual to work in pairs – copywriter and art director typically – so I lost no face in doing this. Experienced old hands, up and coming middle-weights, callow novices, I gave them all a crack. We considered all the tried and tested possibilities: endorsements by sportsmen, mini sit-coms, cartoons with jingles. At one point, we – whoever it was and I – came up with a combination of all three: a cartoon version of Sylvester Stallone, in some sort of supposed-to-be funny situation in which he's down on his luck until he has a bowl of this stuff. Rather like building a house by putting the roof up first, this was all put together *after* we had come up with the line for the jingle: 'They're choccy, Rocky'. (We'd tried 'Be a choccy jockey' but that led nowhere, and 'It's just like chocci gnocchi' seemed to be not just inaccurate, but slightly beyond the cultural reach of the average British toddler.)

'They're choccy, Rocky' may not have been much better but so desperate was I that I even ran it past Lucille to see what she thought. Her patronising 'well you never know, there might be something there' – she couldn't get the smirk off her bloody face – swiftly confirmed what I'd known all along.

The deadline was looming – there was a meeting scheduled for the next day with the increasingly tetchy Mick Hudnutt – and I had all but given up the ghost. I had already thrown the problem open to the whole department, thus giving up the key credit of personal authorship even if I still could have – and most certainly would have – claimed that it was my generalship as creative director that had made all the difference. But there was still nothing to take credit for. In fact, so bare was the cupboard of ideas that I'd had Julia scrabbling on her knees to see if she could dig 'It's choccy, Rocky' out of the waste-bin.

It was ten o' clock in the evening and gradually the useless disloyal tossers in the laughingly mis-titled creative department – all of whom owed their entire careers to my selfless care and nurturing – had, one by one, crept out as if they had homes to go to. Which, unless you called my new hideous little flat a home, I did not. So, utterly bereft of inspiration, I slumped there in my lonely office, watching more episodes of 'Seinfeld'. I was midway through series four, which meant I reached the episode where the characters – including Elaine – have a competition to see who can last longest without having a wank. (Or whatever the slang is for the female version.) Two things occurred to me. First, what genius that they could make the plot perfectly clear yet never refer to masturbation explicitly so that it could be broadcast on American prime-time television. Second, that, given my present personal situation, had I been a character in the show, I wouldn't have lasted past the opening credits.

I finally left, too late even to get to a pub, and made for the cold comforts of Bayswater, and when I awoke the next morning, I was as heavy hearted as when I had gone to bed. Mick Hudnutt and humiliation were only hours away. As the clock ticked down, the governor and the chaplain – in the shape of Vince Dutton and Hattie du Vivier – came to escort me from the condemned man's cell. Neither were in the mood for giving me any last words of comfort. I'd asked Julia to get 'It's choccy, Rocky' typed up again and told them that it was all we had. I offered Vince – I was so defeated I was back to Vince – a feeble, "Sorry mate, best I could do", in the hope, I suppose, that there was still a little sympathy to be squeezed from twenty years of friendship, but if there was, it was undetectable to me. And Hattie, whom I'd been carefully grooming to be Mata Hari, was now terrified that Mick Hudnutt was going to take his bowl of cereal elsewhere, and that she, as the agency person in charge of the account, would be left with no account to be in charge of. She clearly held me accountable.

We left my office on the slow march to the meeting room. There were no chains around my ankles but there might as well have been, and trying to think of anything but the fate that awaited me, an image of Kramer bursting into Jerry's kitchen drifted into my mind. Wait a minute. I stopped. Wait a cotton picking minute! And there, a few paces from the door, with the sound of Mick Hudnutt's Mancunian vowels already grating, I turned to them, the blood suddenly coursing through my veins once more. I was suddenly so pumped up I felt like Henry V rousing the troops at Agincourt.

"Just get in there and keep him talking. Say anything. Talk about the football. Talk about the weather. Anything you fucking like. I'll be back in ten. I've got it. I'm telling you, I have fucking got it!"

One last lingering look at their doubtful faces – O ye of little faith! – and I was off back to the creative department. Now where were those two idiots who'd done that cornish pasty script?

CHAPTER 18

NEW ROCHELLE AND NEW YORK, 1979

Herb was word perfect. He had exactly the right number of yibbys and dibbys, biddys and yubbys, and dums and bums. And, by the time he was finished, I was pretty well yubby dibby biddy perfect myself.

If he'd been machine-gunned to death and had his head impaled on a stick on the way to the Temple Israel Community Centre – anything less and he'd have insisted on carrying on – I could very probably have stood in for him, because he'd spent the whole afternoon going through his script with me, checking off every word and every syllable of every whatever it is that a yubby, a dibby and a biddy is categorised as.

*

On Herb's big day, when he would become the Tevye by which all future Tevyes in New Rochelle productions of 'Fiddler on the Roof' would be judged, I had, as before, taken the train out from Grand Central. It had been agreed that I should be there in time for lunch – leaving plenty of time afterwards for the food to digest and the excitement to build. This time I travelled alone. After the girl with the green spiky hair, I had decided that I should give

Peggy a bit of that space that she so craved. More to the point, having made up my mind what I was going to do, I needed time to screw up the courage to do it. So when Peggy said she was wanted to spend the Saturday night before at her folks place I offered no objection. Sunday would be soon enough.

It was Peggy herself who picked me up from the station, and that was a slight shock. I had never seen her drive before. None of my contemporaries had a car in Manhattan so to see anyone I knew at the wheel would have been strange, but Peggy was so slightly built that, though all those cheap ethnic meals we'd been having certainly seemed to be filling her out, she seemed dwarfed behind the wheel of the enormous Pontiac. For all that, it gave her a kind of assumed authority – she was the captain of the ship. I found that vaguely odd – perhaps it was a touch of old fashioned chauvinism – but I felt at a slight disadvantage somehow, and because of that, perhaps I tried to compensate by being assertive. Which was exactly the opposite of the way I had planned to be. Or maybe that had nothing to do with it. Maybe I was just nervous. Who wouldn't be? I had come to confess all. To throw myself on her mercy. To be honest. To be contrite. But it went wrong from the start.

"Peggy," I said, "there's something I want to talk to you about."

"Well, there's something I want to talk to you about too."

"I think I know what that is."

"You do?"

She glanced sharply at me, braked suddenly, skidding a touch – yes, it was raining again, and we pulled over to the side of the road.

"You've been seeing Miller, haven't you?"

"What?"

"I know you saw him the other day for lunch – if it was lunch you were having."

"WHAT?"

I had started off down the wrong road, and now I didn't know

245

any way off it. And even as I spoke, my completely absurd, hysterical jealousy of Miller was fuelling my sense of self-righteousness.

"Well, you're not the only one who can carry on like that."

"Carry on? Like that? Like *what*? Are you crazy?"

Good question. But I ignored it, and blundered on.

"I went out with Brett and Bart the other night. Same day you had lunch with Miller."

"Oh, really?"

"And I met someone."

"You *met* someone?"

Now we had got to the heart of it. And at last I had the sense to change tack.

Or rather, confronted by the immediate problem of explaining the inexplicable, the bravado just fell away.

"Yes, well, I'm sorry. I didn't mean it to lead – well, where it led. I got really drunk – and stoned – I was upset about you seeing Miller. It got out of hand. I know that's not an excuse. That's what I wanted to say. I'm sorry."

Peggy sat with her hands on the wheel and it seemed like an age before she spoke.

"You really are a total jerk, Andy. A total jerk. I don't know how you knew I saw Miller but you know what, it was just to give him his fucking keys back. Sure we had lunch. I lived with him for two years – he never hurt me – I mean not physically– *he* never cheated on me – I'm not just going to never speak to him again."

Of course, put like that it sounded as reasonable as it was.

"I'd better go back to New York."

"No. That'll just upset everything with my dad. He's put so much into this. We'll just – I don't know – pretend, I guess, for the day."

In a series of rapid, angry movements, she restarted the car, put her foot on the gas, yanked on the wheel and lurched back out into the traffic. I reached out my hand and put it on her arm. She shrugged it off, and in a voice choked up with tears just said, "Andy, will you please just fuck off." It wasn't a question.

We drove for a few minutes in silence and then, as we waited at a red light, the wipers arcing to and fro, I said, "So, if it wasn't about Miller, what did you want to talk to me about?"

She shook her head slowly from side to side; utter disbelief.

"If it wasn't about Miller? – Jeez, you never let go do you? You know what Andy, forget it. I take it back. There is nothing I want to talk to you about!"

When we got back to Overlook Road, we managed to put on a pretty good show for Herb and Barbara – rather like, now I think about it, Alison and I did for Glenda and Vic – and, likewise, when her grandmother appeared. But whenever we were briefly alone, Peggy made sure she stayed well out of touching distance. With the atmosphere as it was, I was actually quite grateful to be seconded to the post of Herb's rehearsal buddy.

Well, I can hear you saying, you have no-one to blame but yourself. Who doesn't know that confessing to infidelities is the quickest way to becoming single again? And why exactly did you confess? Why does anyone confess? Not for the benefit of the person who's been betrayed. It's not their slate you're trying to clear. You confess because you want to be absolved, but, in doing so, you put doubt in their mind they will never entirely be free of. No, if you're going to be unfaithful, man up and carry the burden of your guilt. If you can't live with your imperfections why should you expect anybody else to?

So, in summary: I had fucked up royally. And then made it ten times worse. Out of jealousy, impetuosity, stupidity I had managed to make the girl who had totally liked me and about whom I was just as bonkers as ever – well, I had managed to make her what? Doubt me, yes, no question about that. And, very probably, almost inevitably, reject me out of hand, forever.

The ninety-nine per cent of me who was always convinced the

247

sun would sooner or later fall out of the sky could see no way out. But the last little bit of me that carried my one or two, leftover, incurable optimist genes – personally I'd never been big on the chosen people thing but we had got out of Egypt hadn't we, despite four hundred years of the Pharaohs – still saw little Williamses with dark wavy hair and brown black almondy eyes running about somewhere in the distant future.

*

I'd bought the Sunday edition of 'The New York Times' before I left New York, but its overblown bulk sat on the empty seat beside me, every one of its umpteen sections still pristine and unread. I had a lot to think about that day, and not just about my imminent confession to Peggy. Given the hash that I was to make of it, you may find it hard to believe that I'd given it any thought at all, and it's true that, as I looked distractedly out of the window and the soggy glories of a rainy New York State rushed by, my mind was on something else entirely; something else, perhaps, that I should also have been telling Peggy about, but which had been such a surprise, I needed time to properly gauge my own reaction first. At about 11.30 a.m. on Friday, it had come straight out of left field – literally, you might say, if I'd been sitting facing South. And which, it may not surprise you to learn, I absent-mindedly calculated – somewhere between the stops at Mount Vernon East and Pelham – that I had been. Seeing as the desk in my office faced downtown, more or less, it would have been to the left of me that the Atlantic Ocean and, therefore, England lay.

England. It was weird how little thought I had given it since I had been in New York. As I was to do with Peggy when I got back to London, I had wiped it from my mind. I had the occasional call to Mavis and Syd and I exchanged the very infrequent aerogramme – remember those? – but in 1979, three thousand miles was still three thousand miles. And then suddenly Laverne burst into my office and told me there was a phone call for me from London but that I should take it in Nick Moreno's office. The weirdness of that last part – I had never felt welcome in Nick's office and certainly, following the bee/bonnet fiasco, not now – immediately put me on trouble alert but, as I drew little hangman figures on the steamy train window, it occurred to me that I may well have missed the true significance of that.

My immediate fear, typically I suppose, had been that some disaster had befallen one of my parents but when I rushed into Nick's office it turned out to be nothing to do with Mavis or Syd.

"It's Stuart Price," said Nick, as he passed me on the way out, carefully shutting the door. I blinked after him – it did not compute. Stuart Price was my old Creative Director in London, with whom I had got on reasonably well, but no more than that, and from whom I had not heard a word in the nine months or so I had been in New York. What could he want? And then it turned out it wasn't just Stuart on the phone, but Gerry Morgan as well, then not quite at the dizzy corporate heights to which he would later scramble but still at some serious executive level and not the sort who would normally bother himself with the likes of me. So what could *he* want? All very odd, and just to compound the strangeness, this was a conference call, probably the first I'd ever had. That, I thought as I sat there, must be why we were in Nick's office, because he had the kind of phone that could cope. (Again this was '79, still in the electronic stone age.)

But now, on the train, I thought maybe that was wrong too. Maybe Nick Moreno had been in on the whole thing, maybe the Manatee had too, maybe it had been their idea in the first place. Because what Stuart had wanted to tell me was that one of the Creative Group Heads in London – below him but above common or garden copywriters like me – was leaving, and that since this guy had, as one of his accounts, the tyre business which I'd had some writing success on, they wanted to know if I might be interested in coming back to London to take his place. And when, stunned, or at least, extremely surprised and, inevitably, flattered, I'd asked how soon, Stuart had said, the sooner the better.

I asked for a day or two to think about it and Stuart paused and then I heard Gerry's voice, speaking directly to me for the first time. He said, yes, of course, that would be fine. And then we said our goodbyes, and I retired to Bart and Brett's office to consult with them.

"Shit, man," said Brett or Bart, "would that make you like, *management?*"

"I suppose so," I replied.

"Wow," said Bart or Brett, "fucking A. Hail to the chief."

And of course, that was an important part of it. Something I couldn't ignore. The crucial first step from humble serf to squire's overseer actually gave me a shot at a proper career, and although I had never thought of myself as the ambitious type, now, when offered the opportunity, I saw its advantages.

I kept turning all this over in my mind as the train clattered on. In the end I decided that it might have been this way: a hole had appeared in London that they needed to fill quickly and that Stuart had concluded I might be the peg to fit; protocol meant he had to get Gerry to call New York to ask for their permission – hence his involvement. New York – Todd and Nick – slightly disillusioned with me, to put it mildly, would obviously have done nothing to stand in my way. Or alternatively, Nick and Todd had been in touch with London to say I wasn't cutting it, and London just happened to have had a hole to fill. Either way, I had the political savvy to realise that I probably didn't have a lot of options. New York didn't want me and London wouldn't like it if I threw what was, after all, a real promotion, back in their faces.

Thing was, I really didn't want to go back to London. Did I? And what about Peggy if I went?

*

The rain had finally stopped when we all climbed into the Pontiac for the ten minute drive to Temple Israel. Though it was August, Herb was wearing a scarf wound around his neck to protect his throat and he had brought with him a small glass of something with honey in it, to sip on the way. No chances were to be taken with the leading man's vocal chords. He was in the front passenger seat with Peggy at the wheel – possibly I thought to avoid having to sit next to me. Barbara and I sat in the back, on opposite sides, with Mrs Lipschitz sandwiched between us in the middle. We drove in silence all the way apart from the spasmodic glglglglglgl coming from Herb and his glass.

Mrs Lipschitz had, in fact, not spoken a word to me or to anyone in my presence since her sudden entry into the conversation over tea on my previous visit. She had maintained her silence throughout lunch today, and all the way through the afternoon. Now, completely unexpectedly, just after we pulled into the Temple Israel parking lot – Herb had a special place reserved, close to what was to serve as the stage door – she tapped me on the shoulder, and apropos of absolutely nothing at all, produced one more revelation.

As we climbed out of the car, she said confidentially to me, as though we were still having the same unbroken conversation about names that we'd had before, "Herb, he was always crazy with names. What's wrong with Lipschitz, that's what I'd like to know? Is Lee so much better? Was it worth all the trouble and money to change it?"

And that was it. Not another word. Thinking about this during the first act, I realised that she had finally nailed the lie about the Li's of the Beijing shtetl. As regards the Lipschitz v. Lee question, I thought, on balance, that I was with Herb.

*

The show was a smash. All that Herb could have wished for. I sang silently along with every word and he didn't miss a

251

biddy or a bum. When Tevye's daughters Tzeitel, Hodel, and Chava – who, I estimated, were variously played by girls (?) of about sixteen, twenty and forty-two – started to sing their big number, 'Matchmaker', both Barbara and Mrs Lipschitz looked questioningly at Peggy and me, and Peggy, determined to give nothing away, smiled sweetly but gave no encouragement to them. Nor to me.

When they started on the second or third chorus – the bit about finding a find and catching a catch – I tugged at Peggy's sleeve and gave her a little smile, but she remained totally non-committal. Or should I say that in the act of being non-committal she managed to give me to understand that the non-part was the only bit I needed to be taking note of. After that, I gave up, went on mouthing my diddys and dums and applauding and cheering as required.

I don't know how many fiddlers have been on the roof of the Temple Israel Community Centre since – more than a few I suspect – but I don't suppose there have been more curtain calls than the first night (of four) Tevye was played by Herb Lee. (Also of Lee's Eyeglasses, serving New Rochelle since 1955.)

*

The trip back to New York was everything you would have expected. Trappist monks wearing gags could not have been less talkative. Peggy stared out of one window, and I stared out of the other. As it was pitch black outside neither of us saw anything but the reflections of our faces. Hers grimly set, mine blank, empty, pretty much devoid of hope.

We walked to the subway in the same silence in which we had travelled on the train, and when the five arrived at the platform, Peggy held out her arm by way of indicating that I should get on first. Then when I did, she took a step back, and the subway train pulled away without her. I left her standing there, not following the exiting train with a turn of her head or even just her eyes, but staring dead ahead.

*

Another Sunday evening. Another lonely beat on the Lower East Side. I bought a couple of slices of pizza on the way from the subway to my apartment, found a beer in the fridge and turned the telly on. I looked around for the cat and not seeing him I concluded that he must be out prowling the streets. (In all the time I lived there, I never found out how he came and went.) I was, for once, rather disappointed not to see him. I would have been grateful for any company that night. But it was just me and Rob and Laurie and little Ritchie. As I might have known, the comedy rerun station had been doing its scheduling in consultation with the gods, and had put on back-to-back 'Dick Van Dyke Shows' with the specific aim of making me feel even worse.

It worked. I wanted another beer, but found I'd had the last one in the fridge, so I went across the street to the bar with the neon sign that used to light up my bedroom. It was a kind of old fashioned place with a local clientele, which at that time, unlike today, meant not especially young or well heeled. They served a bit of food – a burger or a burger was the usual menu choice, and they played a bit of music – nothing too loud or radical. It was, in short, just a regular bar. And wouldn't you know it, the gods had followed me there. I was sitting there swigging a Schlitz or a something but definitely not a you-know-what when I picked up on the music that was quietly filtering though the sound system.

'The Best is Yet to Come' sang Peggy, in that inimitable silky whisper.

You can take something like that in one of two ways. A sign that somewhere at the end of the long dark tunnel there may yet be a chink of light. Or you can decide it's just cruel, bitter irony – fate spitting in your soup.

I went for option two.

*

On Monday morning, I got to the office early and tried to clear my head. What, I was trying to calculate, would my position be if I didn't take the London job? I could see the upside of the offer but I just wanted to think it all through, one more time.

The terms of my work permit meant that McConnell Martin New York weren't free to fire me. I had something called an L1 visa which meant I could only work in the US for the company that had brought me into the country – if they wanted to get rid of me, they had to send me back to where I came from, or arrange a transfer to another office. That gave me some bargaining power, I supposed, although I couldn't quite see what. If I just dug my heels in and said no, sorry, I'm not going, they could obviously find a way to make my life uncomfortable: move me to an even smaller, even less fit-for-human-habitation office than I already had, give me really crap work to do or none at all, get on my case every time I was a minute late coming in or getting back from lunch. In other words gradually turn the thumbscrews tighter until I resigned. (I am sure that would count as constructive dismissal in the UK today but I doubt such a concept existed in America in 1979 and perhaps not even now.) And, if I were to resign, then the work permit situation would work against me because I wouldn't be free to get another job unless I had a Green Card – the holy grail pursued by every foreign worker in the US. Although I had started my application, it would be at least a year before the Department of Immigration, the wheels of which ground exceeding slow – and then some – decided to officially anoint me with the glorious title of Resident Alien. And then, and here was the Catch 22, only if I stayed with McConnell

Martin, because they were the sponsors of my application. Without them, I'd have to start the whole balls aching process again. What it all boiled down to was that I would be taking an enormous gamble if I quit and would probably be forced to make money by doing casual work in bars or restaurants. And even if I could find such work, what sort of people would hire me? By definition lawbreakers and exploiters of illicit foreign labour. Doubtful if such employers had progressive employee benefit programmes.

Even so, and despite realising that the proprietors of Lee's Eyeglasses might take a dimmer view of a potential son in law whose prospects were so much reduced, I might have been prepared to risk all if Peggy was there to come home to after a twelve hour shift washing dishes.

But that was clearly not to be the case. And it was made even clearer when Noreen walked into my office with a message from Peggy saying she had rented a flat of her own.

"Oh," I said, further depressed by this unsurprising but still unwelcome news. "Where?"

"I think it's up to Peggy to tell you that − if she wants to."

Ah, I thought, she knows. She *knows*. And waited for her to leave. But she hung around just long enough to change her mind and say, "It's 94th and Riverside. A studio. It's tiny but it's real cute. Okay for one person."

I then − as you do − spent about an hour deconstructing that for any hidden nuances of meaning. I considered the details of the address and what it implied. It was diagonally across the city, on the extreme far side of Manhattan from my place on the Lower East Side, her NW to my SE. So you could interpret that as meaning she was putting as much distance as possible between us. On the other hand it was on the Upper West Side, her old neighbourhood, the place with which she was most familiar. So it was only natural she'd choose somewhere around there. But, being her old neighbourhood, it also meant that one of her near neighbours would be Miller.

And then, there were its dimensions. A tiny studio, okay for one person. From that, one could only infer, it was not big enough for two. Nice of her to point that out. Real cute. Her very words.

And then I wondered whose message that really was. Peggy's or Noreen's? Hell has no fury etc except, possibly, when it's the best friend of the woman scorned, who, let's face it, has been known to take a certain pleasure in stirring the pot.

Not that any of that much mattered when you weighed the facts of the case.

I did spend the next couple of hours, almost until lunchtime, searching for any sign of a silver lining but the cloud over my career in New York remained unyieldingly black. So at around one, I asked Laverne to put an international call through – my line didn't allow me access for anything so exotic – but when I finally reached Stuart Price's PA, she told me he was already gone for the day. If I was the type of person who believed in signs, I might have believed I'd seen one there, but, as I think I have made clear, I'm not that type of person, and all I thought was, what the hell, I'll call him in the morning, and I'll think I'll go to the deli and get my favourite mortadella and provolone on rye with dill pickle, mustard *and* mayo and take it into Bart and Brett's office and have my lunch with them.

I was going to miss those ridiculous New York sandwiches, as thick as a whole flight of doorsteps. And, call me sentimental if you like, but I was going to miss Brett and Bart too. Perhaps I had already caught those weepy Americans habits and wasn't going home a minute too soon.

*

I did call Stuart Price the next morning, he said how delighted he was, and I tried to sound appropriately pleased in return. Then he said, that for reasons of internal departmental politics, he didn't want the news getting out for a few days, so could I please keep schtum. (He wasn't Jewish but, like lots of advertising people, he liked the odd bit of lingo.)

Then I asked for an appointment to see Todd Zwiebel, and was, a few hours later, summoned to appear on high. When I got there, Nick Moreno already had his fat Italian–American bottom on Todd's sofa. (As Bart or Brett commented, when I popped in to see them afterwards, he was probably planning for the day when he could take the office over for himself and send Mrs Zwiebel the traditional Mafia 'message' wrapped in newspaper: 'The Manatee – he sleep with the fishes'.)

I explained to Todd that I'd had this terrific offer from London – like he didn't know! – and I didn't feel I could turn it down. He said he understood, but how upset he was, and I tried to sound appropriately sorry in return. Then I mentioned how Stuart Price had emphasised the delicacy of the matter.

"He asked me if we could keep it schtum."

The Manatee, looking very confused, said, "You Jewish, Andy?" And then turning to Nick Moreno as though he, of all people, might provide an explanation. "Andrew Williams – that's a Jewish name?"

Then he turned back to me, and his final words were, "English *and* Jewish. I never got that."

*

A week or so passed. The lid had been successfully kept on the news of my departure, and a date had not yet been fixed for my flight home, so I was still going through the motions of being a copywriter in New York. A very hot and sweaty New York. September had arrived, but any cooling rain seemed to have gone with August, and steaming, sticky summer was back, as they say, with a vengeance. Who had offended it may have been unknowable, but like a schoolteacher keeping the whole class back, it was taking it out on the whole sweltering population.

I was never much of a diary keeper but I had noted down the date of the Dr Pepper concert in Central Park, the one with Robert Palmer, to which, weeks before, I had – emphasis on 'had' – arranged to go with Peggy. It was on Thursday, a couple of days time. I'd had the tickets tucked away in my desk for ages and now I was in a quandary about what to do with them. I liked Robert Palmer, but not enough to go on my own and I didn't really know who else to ask. In the end I went to Brett and Bart and said one of them could have the other ticket, but they would have to decide amongst themselves who the lucky guy was to be. They hit upon the inspired idea of playing a best of twenty-five series of 'scissors, paper, stone' to decide – each leg of the twenty-five to be the best of five games. As these things do, news of the event got around, and Christo, Noreen, Laverne and I, along with at least half a dozen others were packed into Bart and Brett's office, on the Wednesday evening, the night before the concert, for what they had now decided was a World 'Scissors, Paper, Stone' Series and for which they had made special souvenir posters, which were now plastered around the walls of their office. (Really wittily done too, much better than their ads.)

Excitement was reaching fever pitch when, Bart or Brett, I forget which, came storming back from a 12–7 deficit to take five legs in a row and make it twelve all. Beers were in full flow, the bong was on the go, Noreen was massaging Bart's shoulders, Christo was fanning Brett with a towel – or it could have been the other way around – and they were all set for the decider. And then there was a knock on the door, everyone held their breath – this was not the moment for anybody from management to walk in, and they didn't. It was Peggy.

"Not interrupting anything, am I guys?" she asked. And then she looked at me and said, "Do you have a minute, Andy?"

Chapter 19

London, 1999

The two idiots sat on the edge of the Eileen Gray sofa as I scribbled changes to the Cornish pasty script, the first one being the replacement of any reference to Cornish pasties with non-chocolate chocolatey breakfast cereal.

"I thought you said our script was shit," said one of them, the mouthier of the two, who clearly felt that, as I seemed to have resurrected their idea, he had gained some kind of higher moral ground. Without bothering to look up, I lobbed a grenade and blew away the ground from under him.

"It *was* shit. Cornish pasties, traditional English food being eaten by trendy New York TV star. Pure borrowed interest."

"What?" asked the second idiot.

I put my pen down, and decided to give them a sixty-second lecture on the difference between a good idea and a bad one.

"Leo Burnett said—"

"Leo Burnett? You mean he was an actual person?" asked mouthy idiot.

I gave him one of my best, what *do* they teach kids at school these days? withering looks. (Not that it wouldn't be a strange sort of school that taught its pupils about one of the fathers of the modern advertising industry and founder of the massive international agency that bore his name.)

"Leo Burnett said," I repeated, "that no ad should have 'borrowed interest.' The idea should flow from the 'inherent drama' of the product."

"What?" asked second idiot again.

"Your script was shit because the idea did not flow from the inherent drama of a Cornish pasty—"

"What would the inherent drama of a Cornish pasty be then?" asked mouthy idiot.

"—whereas my script—"

"*Your* script?" said both idiots simultaneously.

"Whereas *my* script is a great idea because it flows from the fact that Jerry Seinfeld's kitchen always has loads of cereal on display and he himself loves cereal. That is not borrowed interest – that, my friends, is inherent drama." (I wasn't entirely sure that Leo would have agreed with me on that point but as he was long gone to the place where there is no drama, inherent or otherwise, I had no fear of being contradicted.)

"Yeah, but all you've done is replace Cornish pasties with this chocolatey cereal shit."

"So little and yet so much," I said, getting back to my scribbling. "Although that, in fact, is not my only masterstroke."

"Newman is out," I pronounced, putting a line through the postman's part, "and Jerry is in." As I spoke I stabbed an unneeded full stop after his name, for added effect. "There! It's just Jerry and Kramer. JULIA! Come and type this up. Half a dozen copies. And don't spare the horses."

"Jerry Seinfeld!" they both shouted, as Julia rushed in to collect the silk purse that I had just triumphantly wrought from their sow's ear. "How much is *he* going to cost?"

"Haven't I told you before? Don't worry about the money, just concentrate on having a great idea. When will you chaps learn!"

"Did you know," asked less mouthy idiot as he slunk from the door, "that Jerry Seinfeld turned down a hundred and ten million dollars from NBC to do another series?"

Of course I didn't know that, and the acquisition of said knowledge might have given me second thoughts, as perhaps it should, but, as I've explained, first thoughts are my stock in trade, and I had a meeting to go to and Mick Hudnutt – not to mention Hattie and Legga and especially, Lucille – to impress the fuck out of.

As I raced back to the meeting room – it was Kurosawa if memory serves me right – with a sheaf of scripts in my fist, I did, I have to admit, detect, somewhere in the ether, another of those mysterious shadows cast from the past. (Déjà vu of bees and bonnets probably, if only I had bothered to dig deep enough.) But as I stood outside straightening my tie – purple, Memphis, highly collectable – before making my grand entrance, all I could think about was how I was going to knock 'em so dead they would rue the day they had doubted me. Of course, there would have to be an afterlife for them to do that which I, being a confirmed atheist, did not believe in, but never mind that, you get the idea. Besides, if it meant Legga and Lucille spending eternity rueing the day they doubted my brilliance, the notion of the afterlife might prove so attractive to me, I'd be forced to change my mind about it.

*

We waited for the emperor Mick Hudnutt to adjust his toga and give his verdict. I didn't have much doubt my ingenious offering would get the thumbs up but you never know with clients. (Here's a crossword clue I once made up – it may not have been that original – after a potential award winner of mine had been strangled at birth by some philistine of a Marketing Director: *An unmentionable expletive, with the character of a client, three times over. No lie. A second person is added. 4 letters.*)

"Well," said Mick, "Yeah, interesting. Very interesting. Tell me again about how the Kramer thing works, you know, the twirling you were talking about."

So I read the script once more, adding – with a demonstration – the tiny, yet surely DADA and Cannes winning embellishment I had come up with while the meeting had actually been going on. This meant doing an impersonation of Kramer but since I was now on to series seven, I had him – hairstyle excepted, of course – pretty much off pat. Kurosawa had a shiny maple floor – was Maple particularly Japanese? – and, as I was wearing leather soled Church's, I could do the Kramer slide into Jerry's kitchen without too much difficulty. My late added stroke of even more genius was to have him twirling and whirling and somersaulting as well – you could do anything with special effects if you paid a geek enough money – to signify his never previously experienced delight at the taste of the chocolatey thingummies that weren't chocolate at all. I didn't demonstrate the actual somersault but my twirl and whirl went off well I thought.

"Yes, yes, not bad," said Mick Hudnutt, now apparently convinced – apart from one proviso. "I assume you've checked the money out." He looked now in the direction of Vince and Hattie. They were the sober, responsible suits, not one of the off-with-the-fairies creatives like me.

"Well …" said Hattie, looking at Vince, desperately.

"Well …" said Vince, looking at me, threateningly.

"Well," I said, "I always say, have the great idea first, then let's worry about the money—"

"Well, that's all very well for you to say, but—"said Mick Hudnutt.

"But," I cut back in, "we'll be talking to his agent the moment this meeting's over. Two things you may be absolutely certain of are – one, that Jerry Seinfeld knows a good idea when he sees one – and two, that money is not the first thing on his mind." Yes, I thought, we can be absolutely certain that money is not the first thing on the mind of a guy who turns down one hundred and ten million dollars.

Really, I mused, thrilled with my own clever-dickery, I could have stood in for the PM at PMQs. I had just answered an impossible question by deflecting it with the pure, unchallengeable truth. And yet not answered it at all. Delusions of grandeur perhaps? Can't be ruled out. They are generally held to be a sure sign you have lost the plot, and looking around at all the open mouths facing me, I had an uneasy feeling that the general view was that I very possibly might have done. I made my excuses and bade sayonara to Kurosawa.

*

I told Julia that I was taking the rest of the day off and promptly did. I drove to Florence's and India's school, hung about outside for an hour – pretending to read the paper, trying not to look suspicious – and waited for them to come out. Then I bribed them with promises of Frappacinos and the like and took them off to Whiteley's to see the only film that seemed vaguely suitable, something called 'Inspector Gadget'. I called Alison, brushed aside the 'what about their homework?' complaints and dedicated myself to perfecting my future role of indulgent, divorced dad. India and Florence sat on either side of me at the cinema, each clutching a carton of popcorn the size of a dustbin, and played their parts to perfection. India didn't complain that it was a boy's film and Florence wasn't snotty about it being a kid's film. I can't say 'Inspector Gadget' did it for me, but I didn't pay that much attention. I spent quite a lot of the movie with rather blurry vision looking from one to the other thinking that not everything about my marriage to Alison had been such a disaster after all. When we got back to New Pemberley, we all told Alison we'd had a lovely time, and I think we all meant it. Alison did her best to look happy about it, but somewhere behind her eyes you could see she felt the little stab of hurt that the left out parent always feels. And which you never quite get used to.

A little later, before being banished back to Bayswater, I went to

India's bedroom to read her a story, and Florence joined us, as she seemed to like to. Half way through whatever it was I was reading, India interrupted me to ask, out of the blue, "Are you having a party for your birthday, Daddy?"

I had completely forgotten – or with that peculiar gift I seem to have, managed to obliterate – the fact that my birthday was almost due. I would be fifty in less than a month. I didn't feel a lot like celebrating for all sorts of reasons, and age is only a number and all that, but if you pretend to ignore those really big birthdays they just loom all the larger, so, half meaning it, I said oh yes, I was sure we'd do something.

"Okay," said India. "I think it's the week after we do our school play. You haven't forgotten about the play, have you?"

"No, of course not," I said.

But of course I'd forgotten that too. I quietly took out my phone and sent a text message to Julia reminding her to call the school to check the date – there was no way I was going to ask Alison and put myself in the wrong – so that she could put it in my diary. Then I returned to the story. I did my best to sound interested in what I was reading but I was badly distracted.

Fuck. Fifty. FIFTY!

*

"We've had an offer from Alison's solicitor," said Harriet Braintree to me over the phone. It was not yet eight in the morning – say what you like but she obviously put in the hours – and she wanted to know if I'd like to come in to discuss it. "I'm free for an hour at nine, if you are," she said.

Anything to avoid the welcoming committee that I knew would await me at BWD, so I Porsched myself straight around to Lincolns Inn Fields. Once I was settled with a cup of coffee in one hand and a croissant in the other – I made a mental note to have all meetings

at Hardy Wiggins this early, as they seemed to offer the best value –
Harriet got down to the nitty gritty.

(Before I invite you to get down with her, a couple of asides.

1. You may want to skip all the tedious detail – I only wish I
could have done. But if you like to have all the facts, here they are.

2. I refer you back to the E to P scale and my earlier notes. They
may need refining. One of the flaws in the whole E to P theory, I
have come to realise, is that you can only feel Pity if you feel you are
better off than the person you are judging. When the mighty fall,
but only fall to a level that most mere mortals could never hope to
achieve, you don't feel Pity, you remain totally Piti-less. That may
be your position after you have read the details of Alison's proposed
settlement, as I still seemed – I stress *seemed* – to be doing okay, a
lot better than Stephen Wilkinson probably was. But Stephen, if
you're reading this, can I cheer you up by telling you it gets a lot
worse?)

"Here we go, then," said Harriet, putting her specs on. "What
they are asking for is the house – completely paid for, furnishings
and contents – less your personal effects, of course, maintenance
for the children and some contribution towards household expenses
– and a million and a half in cash."

Yes, of course, inside I went *how much? In cash?* No problem there
then, I'll just check my pockets to see if I've got it in loose change.
But I tried to maintain a poker face, though I have no idea why as
there was no-one there to bluff. It just seemed the thing to do.

"It's not that bad," said Harriet. "Let's set aside the maintenance
side of things for the time being – we can argue the toss about that
later. With all your assets – share of house, shares in your company,
pension, other stuff, you're theoretically worth around five five, give
or take."

(I was about to repeat Frank Connor's feeble joke, but thought if
I'd heard it before, then she certainly would have done.)

"So," she said, tapping her pencil on some notes she had in

front of her, "according to their figures – and we have no reason to doubt them, do we? – Alison has her bit of the house, about a hundred thousand in savings and about a hundred and fifty in her pension fund. So that's about half a million. Sixish between you."

The figures were beginning to become a bit of a blur. I was wondering if the superannuated pop star had had a better grasp of things. Harriet wasn't finished either.

"The house and the million and a half make about two point three. That's about thirty-eight per cent. Which isn't that cheeky for an opening bid – and, of course, we'll say a million five is far too much."

My mouth now full of croissant, I raised my eyebrows questioningly, hoping she might tell me what *wasn't* far too much. She obliged.

"If we're not going to mess around playing silly buggers, we'll go back with seven hundred and fifty thou in cash and see if we can settle for a round million. With the house that's around thirty per cent all up which sounds pretty reasonable. But …"

The inevitable but.

"But they're only doing it this way because they know getting the money out of your company may not be straightforward. Basically she wants a nice clean payoff without any hassle and to achieve that, she's willing to take a little less than she might get. Look, theoretically, you're left with a total pot of three and a half million, maybe a tad more. Which doesn't sound too bad."

No, it didn't sound too bad.

"But £600,000 is stuck in your pension fund, and you have to negotiate with your partners over the rest. How are your relations with them? People can be funny you know. You may be getting on famously but when they think you're negotiating from a position of weakness, they may try to take advantage."

Indeed. And when you're not getting on famously, they certainly will.

"Still, all in all, my advice would be to see if we can work with this."

Well I wasn't paying £450 an hour not to take her advice, so I did. I agreed that she should call them back and haggle. Not that we would ever use a word as indecorous as haggle. Meanwhile, I would talk to my partners.

I drove back to BWD with certain issues relating to non-chocolate chocolatey breakfast cereal to discuss and a lot more besides.

*

"Take a seat, Andrew," said Geoff and I did as obliged and sat in one of the cappuccino brown Corbusier leather chairs he had chosen for his office. He, being BWD's CEO and thus the man who would have to deal with our clients' top brass, had gone for a modern but slightly more sober style of decoration than I had. Had a couple of nice abstracty paintings too – while he was working his way round from the seat behind his glass desk to take a position half sitting on the front of it, I wondered if the A in EBITDA stood for art, or whether the pictures on his wall would one day disappear home in the boot of his Beemer. (636 coupe.)

I hadn't even made it as far as my own office before the announcement came that the main event on this day of reckoning was to take place immediately. I'd called ahead to Julia to tell her I was on my way in and she was waiting for me in reception with a concerned expression and a message that Geoff and Vince needed to see me urgently. Not exactly a surprise though I had thought I was a little senior to be abruptly summoned to the headmaster's study. Perhaps that little blow to my pride set me off on the wrong tack from the start. Or maybe I would have been arsey anyway. I suppose I usually was.

Vince was already there, seated on the matching sofa, serious face, leaning forwards. Body language wise, they were both telling me, as if I needed to be told, this was not a day for larks.

"Not going to muck about," said Geoff. "Total fuck-up yesterday. I spoke to Mick Hudnutt myself last night. Spent two hours licking his arse – not a pleasant business, but needs must. I begged him – begged, Andrew, I'm hardly exaggerating! – to give us another chance and Vince has spoken to Lucille and she has got the whole creative department trying to come up with something. He's given us seven days. My bet is the business is already as good as gone."

"Seven fucking million," added Vince.

I felt, as you always do, and never being averse to a bit of combat – providing there is no prospect of actual physical pain – that I had to mount some kind of defence.

"It was – it is – a fucking good idea."

"No Andrew," said Vince. "It was a fucking insane idea. We've been fucking up since the day we won this account. Remember? That first bloody meeting that you refused to come to? Do you? And ever since, we've been on the back foot. We've bombed out one time after another. And then – then I come to you and ask for your help, you sit on your fucking arse for weeks and then at the last minute, come into the meeting like some fucking demented whirling dervish," – he didn't like my whirls? That hurt – "and come out with this madness."

"Why didn't you stop me?"

"Stop you! I tried for Christ's sake. I kept looking at you," – had he? – "but you were away, gone, unfuckingstoppable. And okay, I'll admit for a moment you had me half sold," – ah, so he had liked my whirls – "but I didn't think even you would be so fucking idiotic as to offer up Jerry fucking Seinfeld – to a client who is already getting ready to fire us – without at least finding out if he might do the job first."

He sat down, suddenly looking defeated – the sort of look they hang you for in Australia. I almost felt sorry for him.

"Well, we don't know he won't."

That seemed to perk Vince up. More like the old Legga.

"Oh but we do, Andrew, we do. We put the call through to his agent last night – while Geoff's on his knees with Mick Hudnutt – while you've fucked off who knows where – and Hattie says you could hear the fucking guy pissing himself all the way from New York."

Somehow that didn't sound like the sort of thing that girls who went to Hattie's school would say, but I didn't pursue the point.

"So, anyway," said Geoff, picking up the reins. "Things really can't go on like this."

The question hung heavy in the air. How would things go on?

"Look mate," said Vince, softening – apparently. "We know you've been under a hell of a strain lately."

"Divorce is never easy," put in Geoff, "as I know only too well."

"So we think a bit of a rejig might be in order."

Now we were coming to it. And, as far as they were concerned, this is how it would be:

First, I would become chairman of the company which wasn't the promotion it might sound like, because we'd never had a chairman, never seen the need for one, thought it was a pointless, stuffy, needless title and had always taken the line that it would be much cooler and more modern and more shirt-sleevey, and would sound slightly more groovily collaborative if we made a point of *not* having a chairman.

Second, I would take charge of overseeing our planned expansion into Europe. Planned? By whom? Nobody had ever mentioned it to me before.

Third, and now we were down to the short strokes, I would relinquish the title of Executive Creative Director forthwith – while remaining a key creative role on some accounts, whatever the hell that meant – and Lucille would take over with immediate effect.

My first thought was that they obviously hadn't just been

planning this since the meeting yesterday afternoon. My second was that if I wasn't going to have the big creative job and that I was to be handed some meaningless title in its place, they'd soon – possibly already had – get round to the idea that my earnings should be commensurately reduced. With my massive maintenance expenses coming up, that did not sound like an attractive idea. My third thought, consistent, I think, with the first two, and which I spoke aloud, was, "Fuck you."

Perhaps, you will think, given the weakness of my general negotiating position, I should have been more diplomatic. They could, given there were two of them to one of me, simply outvote me on this and force the issue. And, thus far, I had not even touched upon my very pressing need to get some of my money out of the company, for which, of course, I needed their cooperation. So you might say I talked loudly and carried a small stick, which, I believe, is the opposite of what you are advised to do.

"When I think of what I've done for you guys! Nobody had ever heard your fucking names before you got hold of me."

They looked at me and each gave me their take on the 'yeah, well that was then, this is now' look.

I brushed down my trousers – no crumbs, force of habit, jeans actually, 501s – and stood, ready to leave the room.

"Look, Andrew," said Geoff, "this isn't going to go away. And there's another thing."

Another thing?

"Hate to bring it up but you're going to be fifty in a few weeks."

So. It wasn't just about the meeting yesterday. Or even the last few months. Ageism was not yet a crime against humanity in 1999 or even a term anyone used but I, as ever, was in the vanguard of the trend.

Geoff warmed to his theme.

"Look it's not being fifty per se that's the problem, obviously."

Obviously.

"But it marks a point doesn't it?"

"Well would you mind getting to it?"

"The point is," he continued, determinedly unruffled, "that we, BWD I mean, always need to look new and fresh. That's what advertising is about, isn't it? We've got to keep moving the business forward. You've got thirty per cent of it. You have a big interest in that."

"And Lucille, mate," added Vince, "yeah, sure she had a few problems with Mick Hudnutt but who hasn't? She's got the right profile. New century coming up, mate, it's a changing world. She's young and she's a woman."

"Yes, well, 'shes' very often are women," I said, "and really, Legga, we all know your position on Lucille."

Cheap. But fair enough in the circumstances.

"We want to do this in a civilised way," said Geoff, having the final word. "So you can have a bit of time to think it through. If you don't like the way we've put it, you've got two weeks to come up with a different version. Sorry, Andrew, but that's it."

As he said, that was it. The fight went out of me. Not that it had been much of a fight – my pike to their nuclear warhead. All that was left to me was to try to make the best of things.

I did have the presence of mind to realise that this was not the moment to discuss my need for the divorce money and to realise that I should wait and pick my moment. If I could force myself to be sufficiently charming I might be able to make them feel a little sentimental about the past ten years. Perhaps then, I could leverage a slightly better deal out of them.

Out of those treacherous bastards? There was more chance of Jerry Seinfeld saying he'd do the job after all.

*

I sat in the Porsche, stuck on the Hammersmith flyover, not being soothed by something I couldn't name oozing out of Classic FM. My first reaction on leaving Geoff's office had been to call Donald McEwan to ask him if, by any chance, he could find time to see me. Being the thoroughly good egg he was, he'd said he could squeeze me in in an hour, and not feeling like sitting in the back of a cab twiddling my thumbs, I'd decided to drive myself. So now I was drumming my fingers on the steering wheel staring up the arse of a smoke belching artic from the Ukraine. Then the phone rang. And, just when you think things can't get worse:

"Hi, Mr Williams, Keith Lyons here. Mooneys. Um, look, drawn a bit of a blank I'm afraid. Heard from my colleagues in the States. Just not enough to go on."

"Oh. No luck with the school thing?"

"Nah, no way – well, no legal way – of getting the info."

"NYU?"

"And why me?'

"Eh? Oh – no – NYU – New York University. She went there. I told you, remember?" (He obviously didn't. Probably taken no notice in the first place.)

"Sorry. Bad line. Didn't catch you properly. Nah, same there. So, unless you've thought of something else …"

It briefly crossed my mind that they might send a man to China to have a route around the Beijing hall of records but I just dispiritedly said, "No, nothing."

"Rightio then. I'll send you the bill. We did actually go to four days so … with expenses … and VAT … that makes £2742 and two point … ah bollocks to all that … just call it two seven forty. If you could settle it within the fourteen days as per the terms of our contract."

How decent of him. A full two pounds taken off the bill. And thank you and goodbye. The artic hadn't moved. The phone rang again.

"Hello, Andrew? Harriet Braintree. Just spoken to your wife's people. Not being very helpful I'm afraid. They'll come down to the house plus a million and a quarter in cash but they won't budge beyond that."

Like they always tell you – like I told you – the other side's lot is always better than yours.

"So, what do you think?"

"Well, it's still less than thirty-five per cent, and if we dig in, our bills …" – she meant her bills – "…are just going to, you know …" Yes, I did know. "So, I think, yup, let's do it."

So, even more dispiritedly, I said yes. Then Colin came on the line. And you know what he wanted. (I cannot bring myself to repeat the actual figures to you without bursting into tears.)

The traffic in the lanes on either side of me started moving. Then a huge bloke appeared round the side of the artic, lumbered around to the back, opened a door, hauled his enormous backside inside and reappeared about a minute later carrying a sign which he clipped on to the back of the truck. He shut the door, turned to me and shrugged, then disappeared round the side again, leaving me with a clear view of a big red triangle. If your European Highway Code's not up to speed, that meant, in any one of forty-seven official languages, that the Ukrainian artic had conked out.

I checked my watch. I was now so late that even by my standards I was late. I called Donald, apologised – as ever, of course, not a murmur of criticism – and eventually found a slot in the passing traffic so I could pull out and eventually, when I reached the Hogarth roundabout, turned around and headed back. Oh, Donald did say one thing. He gently asked me if I could settle my bill which, I knew, was way overdue. By my soon-to-be ex-wife's, by Harriet Braintree's, and even by Keith Lyon's standards, it was miniscule, but even so. There was only one thing for it: another session of 'Seinfeld', or more accurately, of

Peggy/Elaine. (Jerry himself, I was beginning to have issues with again.) Back to the office and more of series seven.

*

Series seven, episode six is, as all 'Seinfeld' aficionados will know, seminal. Out of the one hundred and eighty episodes, all of which I have seen at least once – and at various Peggy/Elaine moments have stopped, fast backwarded, rerun, paused again, checked from screen to Polaroid for the particular signs of likeness that a certain camera angle in certain lighting will create, and then rerun again – it is possibly my all time favourite. Number two is 'The Contest', the story about masturbating, about which I have already waxed lyrical and which (American) TV Guide ranked number one on its list of 'TV's Top 100 Episodes of All Time'. Number three is the double header about 'Schindler's List', the plot of which is just too complex to go into here, but, take it from me, is another masterpiece. And number one is series seven, episode six, 'The Soup Nazi'.

'The Soup Nazi' is a story centred on a man who sells soup which is in such demand that he feels able to deal with customers who dare to question him in any way – by asking for instance, if they can have the free bread that the previous customer just got – by sending them away with a flea in their ear, and no soup. It is hard to imagine anyone behaving with such high handed arrogance in real life, except possibly the creative directors of advertising agencies – much like me. Realising that I might have been a Soup Nazi myself may have made me particularly fond of this episode. But the main reason it tops my list is something else, something only a handful of viewers, or possibly less, will have noticed, since the moment which I got so excited about is literally that, a moment, and it happens during the end credits.

I first noticed it on the day I returned from not having been able

274

to fight my way through the traffic to get to Donald McEwan's. It was some time after one when I walked back into my office, and I immediately drew all available blinds – didn't want Julia, Lucille or anyone else staring through the glass walls at me – and locked the door. Then I took out series seven and starting watching episode five, which is where I was up to. I may not even have given my full attention to episode five, as I was feeling so bloody sorry for myself. Not only was I beginning to realise how well founded Harriet's advice to pay attention to my cloth cutting had been, but those one or two vestigial eternal optimist genes were being tested to destruction. The only tiny bit of flotsam I'd had to cling on to in my ocean of misery was the idea that I might somehow be able to track Peggy down, and now, following Keith Lyons depressing call, that too seemed to have drifted out of reach.

And then I watched episode six, and they continued the gags into the title sequence as they always did in the later episodes. There was a little street scene running under the titles, not that the scene has anything do with it. It was one of the titles themselves that caught my eye. For there, on screen, for about half the time it takes to blink, is a credit for the most minor of the minor characters. It says: man in soup kitchen – Miller Prince.

The tiny piece of flotsam instantly floated back into my hand. Miller Prince – the *Miller Prince.* For surely, it must be he. I knew enough about the acting world to know there could be only one. If you are called Miller Prince and there is already a Miller Prince treading the boards, then you must, by union rules, call yourself something else. So this must have been him, and for once, the very thought of Miller Prince did not fill my throat with bile. Instead, as though I had been reintroduced to the twin brother stolen from our cot at birth, I felt a huge surge of goodwill towards him. For if Miller Prince had been in an episode of 'Seinfeld' made in 1995 – I checked the dates on the cover, and that's when it was – then there was a good chance he was still at work – or trying to be – in 1999.

And that meant that he would be a member of SAG – the Screen Actors Guild – and that there must be some way of tracing him. And Miller Prince had lived with Peggy Lee for two years had he not, so you never knew, he might, just might know what her real name was or have some other tiny clue as to where she might be.

I reran 'The Soup Nazi' to try and work out what the 1995 Miller Prince looked like – out of shape, I hoped, and bald, not that there's anything wrong with that – but there was no way of telling him from any other man in soup kitchen. Anyway, it mattered not. What I had to do was trace him. To get a number, to speak to him.

"Julia," I yelled. "I need you."

And I told Julia that I'd had a new idea for the non-chocolate chocolatey breakfast cereal and that I needed her to speak to our TV production department, and that I needed to trace a little known American actor called Miller Prince. By five that afternoon, they had the name and number of his agent in LA. The agent's shocked tone of voice told me he was stupefied to receive a call enquiring after an actor who no-one had ever heard of, but he quickly recovered himself to tell me what an amazing talent Miller Prince was and how much sought after and all the usual bullshit. But after I had sat through that, and told him that I would need to speak to Miller personally before I could take the matter further, and refused to contemplate any alternative, he had finally relented, and said he would call Miller and ask if he was willing to give me his number. Twenty anxious minutes later and the agent called back.

I took a deep breath and dialled Miller Prince.

Chapter 20

New York, 1979

"I totally like you," said Peggy, not, as you will recall, for the first time.

We were squeezed onto the corner of a table in the same manically busy, deafening bar we'd been to on the day we'd first met in the elevator. Not the best place to have an important conversation, but looking back, it seems like an appropriate choice to have made.

She said it, just after the waitress had brought us our drinks, in response to the question she had just posed herself.

"Guess you're wondering why I wanted to see you?"

And when I nodded, she said that there were a couple of reasons, and I asked, as was expected in such an exchange, "Well what?"

And she said, "Well, first…"

And then she took a sip from her orange juice – she'd flatly refused anything alcoholic – before, once more, giving me the line which, on the day I die, will be engraved upon my heart. (Always assuming I have one – as yet unconfirmed.)

The obvious thing at this point, you might think, would have been to enquire as to what the second reason might be. But I was so elated, so thrilled that the black clouds had just, totally unexpectedly, cleared and that the promised land had suddenly come into view,

277

that I leaned across to kiss her and, in doing so, tipped her orange juice all over her.

I looked around desperately for a napkin to wipe it off her tight floral dress – a strange choice, she usually wore her clothes looser – but, when I finally located one, she wouldn't let me touch her, and it crossed my mind that that too was a bit odd, but then, when she took the napkin out of my hand and did it herself, I thought I was probably imagining it and put it out of my mind. In any event, my mind was already racing and full of the possibilities that Peggy's return to my arms might present.

"Well, I've got something to tell *you*," I said.

She looked up from wiping her dress, slightly alarmed.

"Not like the other thing you told me, I hope."

"Er, no." Somehow, in the euphoria of finding myself totally liked again, the girl with the green spiky hair had gone clean out of my mind. But now, she and all that she represented, was back. I knew there was no point in going on with the rest of what I had to say, unless I dealt with this.

"Look, I am so sorry about all that. There was no excuse."

"Yeah, you said all that before."

"Yes, well, I meant it. Have you forgiven me?"

"Forgiven you? No, I don't think so. I haven't forgotten it, so I don't see how I could have forgiven you. Never understood how you could separate the two."

"Oh" I said, trying to get my head around all this. "But if you totally like—"

"I guess I've decided not to think about it. Hoping we can just kind of move on. Might be a mistake, I don't know, but in the circumstances—"

I'd really stopped listening at the point when she said we were moving on. No, it wasn't forgiveness, but neither was my stupidity to be held against me. Or, at least I was to be given a second chance, And as there was absolutely no danger of any repeat offence – I would confidently swear that on any future Lee-Williams's life – I was very nearly, as good as, home-free. So having decided we'd put my infidelity to bed – so to speak – I carried on as though we'd never discussed it.

"No," I interrupted her, "this piece of news is nothing like that."

And then I told her about all the phone calls to London and my upcoming promotion and return to the London office. And then I said, "Look Peggy, I know this is a bit sudden, but the thing is, you say you totally like me, and believe me, I totally like you back, no, more than that – I fucking love you." There, I'd said it, if not quite as romantically as I might have done. "And Peggy, I know all the stuff about you needing space and time, but why don't you come with me and" – I almost said 'marry me' but, perhaps, it has subsequently occurred to me, fatally, I stopped short of that and went on – "we could get a flat in London and have the most amazing time. You'd absolutely love it there."

"Wow," she said, looking confused – astonished but also perplexed. "I wasn't expecting that."

"Well," I said, "What do you think?"

"I don't know. I really don't know." She frowned and then looked up at me and smiled, but with a tinge of sadness. I couldn't work out what that meant but I didn't have time to ask her that, or what her second reason might have been either, because, at that exact moment, the noise in the bar got even louder and in burst Bart and Brett and Laverne and Noreen and Christo and all the rest all simultaneously screaming at the tops of their voices that, after much heated argument about the permitted level of hand flatness and several hotly disputed appeals, the World 'Scissors, Paper, Stone' Series had been awarded to Bart, but that Bart, that most gracious of victors, had given the ticket for the Robert Palmer Dr Pepper concert back to Brett.

"Sorry boys," I yelled, "but neither of you can have it. Peggy's coming with me after all."

And what could Peggy do but go along with that, and being, as they say in the States, the stand-up guys they were, Bart and Brett just laughed it off and ordered more drinks all round.

"But I tell you what – if you can't be there, you can have the next best thing."

"Yeah, really," Bart or Brett, yelled back. "Like what?"

"You," I screamed over the din, "you will be able to see exactly how much fun we had, the very next morning. Or on the night itself, if you would like to hang around outside. Because I shall be recording all the key moments on my faithful Polaroid."

*

From the bar of limitless noise, where we had stayed for a good part of the evening and got in some fairly serious drinking – apart from Peggy who had remained steadfastly abstemious, not that I took much notice of that because she was never much of a drinker – we went en masse down to another bar in the West Village that was a particular favourite of Christo's and from there, wandered – a joint or two being passed around as we went, not that I had more than one or two very tentative tokes – to a restaurant in Mott Street in Little Italy. It was one of those places where you imagined that if you climbed on to the lavatory seat and felt behind the cistern above, you would find a Beretta taped there, so, as well oiled as we were, we had the sense to behave and not upset the locals. Neither the decor, the waiters, nor the menu made any concessions to modernity. So after one or other of the house specials, spaghetti and meatballs or Veal Parmigiano of course, and a few straw bottomed bottles of some rasping Sicilian red, we emerged once more into the still steaming Manhattan night. I asked Peggy if she wanted to come back with me, and she said, sure, why not, what's the worst that could happen. (Ironically, as recently occurred to me, the very advertising line that Dr Pepper was to use many years later.) This what-the-fuck kind of response was so un-Peggy like – she was usually so decisive about things one way or the other – that I remember having contemplated whether I shouldn't ask if she was absolutely sure she wanted to come. But I was so absolutely sure that was what I wanted, I wasn't prepare to take the risk of her changing her mind. So we hailed a cab, shouted arrivederci to the others and they shouted it back – yes, of course, we really did, we were young, stupid, drunk and in Little Italy – and then climbed in, fell back on the sticky plastic seat and bumped our way over the potholes and home.

That night was the last I spent with her in my apartment on East 9th. Once again I have a moviemory. This time the camera is outside my first floor window – second floor, of course, in the States – so I suppose it must be on a crane or something. It is looking in through the window and with the pink neon light from the bar across the street blinking on the ceiling, and the ceiling fan whirring above us, there we are, Peggy and I, modestly covered you will be happy to know, under the solitary white sheet that was all we needed in the heat of that night. Peggy is lying on her back, asleep, her face peaceful and serene. And I am beside her, but not asleep, leaning on my elbow, looking down at her, just looking, unable to believe my luck. After the horrendous mess of things that I had made, incredibly, unbelievably, against all the odds, I was still in the game.

In the morning, over coffee, I asked her again about coming to London. The cat, for some reason pretending to be domesticated, sat by my kitchen chair, tailed curled under its bottom gazing up at Peggy as though it was as interested in her answer as I was. Perhaps it thought that if she said no, I might change my plans and stay, an outcome I doubt it would have welcomed.

"I'll talk to you about it tonight," said Peggy, and refused to say more.

*

A mild hangover allied to demob happiness ensured that I avoided anything that might be called work that day. News of my imminent departure may not have been generally known but the powers that be were, of course, fully up to speed and no new projects were coming my way. So there were only the odd bits and bobs to clear up and neither bit nor bob received any attention. All my energy, such as it was, was focused on the Dr Pepper concert tonight. And, more so, on the life changing conversation with Peggy that would come after it. I was already imagining the cosy little flat in Camden or Maida Vale or Islington or Notting Hill – South of the Thames might have been Outer Mongolia as far as I was concerned – that we would soon be sharing. I reminded myself to remind Peggy to get an international driving license so that she too could drive the company car that I had by now convinced myself I would be entitled to in my new management position.

The concert was due to begin around seven and I was going to meet Peggy in reception after work and we would go straight on to the show. Seeing as she was still wearing the same orange juice stained dress she'd had on the previous night, she was going home at lunchtime to change. I, on the other hand, had come dressed and fully equipped for the evening. Being far too warm for two ties or even half a tie, I had gone for a slightly James Dean look – white tee-shirt and Levis, which did, it was true, carry overtones of Christo and therefore possibly the overtones that Christo carried. Still it was bloody hot, it was 1979, and I was secure enough in my own sexuality – wasn't I? – not to be put off by that. I had decided to take with me and sling over my shoulder a non-matching and slightly retro denim jacket just in case – unlikely in the extreme – the night temperature dropped below that of a smelting furnace. Remember, this was a time when it was said that whether you wore your earring in your left or right ear – not that it mattered to me as I no longer wore mine – or clipped your keys on to one side of your jeans or the other, it meant you were giving away tell tale signs as to which team you played for, and I'd heard said, even whether you batted or bowled. (I always kept my keys in my pocket.) It did cross my mind that if I slung my denim jacket over the wrong shoulder I might be giving off signals I definitely didn't want to. This was the kind of thing I worried about that morning and I did think of checking with Christo but I knew that if there was such a thing as a wrong answer, he would give it to me on purpose. I also wore the jacket because it had a couple of really big pockets which meant I could carry my flat Polaroid camera in one pocket, and in the other a pack of ten spare units of Polaroid film, requisitioned that morning, free of charge from art supplies in the basement. I planned to document this very special night in detail. We would have lots to show all those little Lee-Williamses of the future.

By around two I was chomping through another of those monster New York sandwiches in Bart and Brett's office when Laverne came rushing in to announce London was on the line again. The conversation turned out to be brief but significant. Stuart Price told me that they had been asked to pitch for a new piece of business at very little notice, and, being a bit short-handed, they were wondering if I would like a crack at it. (This was the rather casual way he phrased it, but I realised, of course, that it really wasn't open to me to refuse.) From a work point of view, I could see that it was a terrific opportunity but when he told me that they needed me back in London to take the brief at 9 a.m. on Monday morning, I swallowed hard. 9 a.m. on Monday in London was 4 a.m. in New York, and if I was to get through the Monday morning rush hour traffic from Heathrow that meant I would have to catch the very earliest of the redeyes. Working backwards I saw that would necessitate leaving Manhattan by around 8 p.m. to make it to the airport. So, by my instant reckoning, plus/minus three days and six hours was all that was left of my great American adventure. Stuart confirmed this when he told me that they had booked me a ticket for the 22.45 TWA flight. As I said, I'd never had a choice in the matter. And, as international companies always do in these situations, he told me not to worry about any notice period on my apartment or shipping my stuff or my removal expenses because all that would be taken care of, and oh, there was one other thing, now what was it, oh yes, they'd put me up in a hotel – somewhere pretty decent he was sure – until I found somewhere to live. Then he said how much he was looking forward to having me back in the London office and he rang off. I'd barely managed to get a word in, let alone work my way around to asking about a company car.

Reeling at the suddenness of this, and still trying to calculate the implications, I reported back to Bart and Brett. An ad hoc emergency leaving committee was instantly formed containing all the usual suspects and it was decided that Saturday night would be party night and that party night would continue into Sunday and that a recovery brunch would be held prior to the cab collecting me to take me to the airport. I was instructed, therefore, that I would have to pack by Saturday afternoon. Many 'fucking A's, 'way to go's and high fives were involved in the making of these arrangements. A celebratory bong was then lit, the puffing from which I declined to participate in. Apart from my usual nervousness, I was determined to keep my head straight for the negotiations ahead with Peggy. I didn't expect – though I didn't dismiss the possibility – that she would be ready to join me for Sunday's flight – but wouldn't that be fucking marvellous! – but we still had a lot of ground to cover, literally and metaphorically. I called down to her office to give her the top line on the news but she wasn't back from her trip home to change, and then I decided it was best left until we met to go to the concert, so I didn't call her back. Within minutes, it seemed, the news of my lucky escape – for that was the way it seemed generally to be perceived – had spread half way round the building and I spent the rest of the day fending off envious well wishers from every department. My back was sore from all the slapping and my address book full of the numbers of people I barely knew. If a tenth of the people who said be sure and keep a place for me when I come to London actually turned up, I would have a full house for the rest of my life. No, a mistake there. *Peggy* and I would have a full house for the rest of *our* lives.

*

We met downstairs in reception and walked up Madison and across to Fifth Avenue and then up to Central Park. I didn't want to appear over excited when I broke the latest news – she still hadn't actually said in so many words that she would come to London, though, by now, I'd convinced myself that Mavis and Syd, mainly Mavis, would soon be running the rule over her – so I decided that the best tactic would be to wait until we were in our seats and then coolly and calmly go through it all.

She looked absolutely gorgeous. She had changed into a plain bluey-green cottony sort of summer dress – with big buttons I remember – and although I had never thought of her as a particularly voluptuous girl, I noticed how that night she seemed to give the lie to that. I told her how wonderful she looked in the dress and she gave a despairing little laugh and said she'd just had to go out to buy it because she couldn't get into anything she had. And I repeated that I had never seen her look better. And I hadn't. Her black hair was shiny and bouncing about like in all the shampoo ads (another moviemory possibly, I admit) and there was a glow about her that just made me think, delirious and deluded as I was, she doesn't just totally like me, she looks exactly the way people say you're supposed to when you're in love.

My plan to speak to Peggy before the concert was, as you will have guessed, rendered useless by the fact that from the moment we got into the open air amphitheatre, we couldn't hear ourselves think. First there were records of Robert Palmer blaring out, then roadies learning to count and ritual drum bashing and hideous feedback and then the support band came on – unmemorable but fingers in your ears loud – and then, as the sun set and night took over, on came his band, and finally Robert Palmer himself. Earlier in the year he'd released an album called 'Secrets' and most of the set was taken up with playing tracks from that. You might remember a couple of them. Afterwards, quite a few had an ironic resonance for me. 'Too Good to be True', for instance. And a song written by Todd Rundgren that Wikipedia says reached 54 – the age, coincidentally, that Robert Palmer died – in the Billboard Charts. It was called 'Can we still be friends?' Ouch. And, of course, they finished, and replayed during their second encore, the song that I always associate with Robert Palmer, and particularly with that fateful night; 'Bad Case of Loving You'. Ouch, ouch, ouch.

Then it was the ritual towel around the neck and 'thank you New York, I love you' and we were being jostled out with the rest of the crowd into the Manhattan night, gratefully grabbing those free ice-cold Dr Peppers as we went.

*

I'd taken lots of Polaroids during the evening – went through all ten in the pack in the camera and all but one of the spare pack I'd brought along from art supplies. Most of them were useless because there were no zooms on the lenses of those cameras and we were miles from the band, but I got the girl who was sitting next to us to take a couple of Peggy and me. We waited with that special mock-horrified anticipation that always preceded the moment when the image on the Polaroid finally revealed itself and, of course, ritually groaned in despair when our fears were confirmed. I have not the slightest idea whatever happened to any of those shots. Probably got left in the dark in a cardboard box that was moved from attic to attic until one day it was heaved on to a skip and thence into some landfill.

Eventually as we got further from Central Park and the dispersing crowd got thinner and thinner, we found a bar, thankfully air-conditioned, to save us from the heat and humidity which, that night, must have broken all records.

I ordered Peggy a fruit juice, again she refused anything alcoholic, and myself a beer. I didn't care which kind, and that wasn't just because of the heat. By now a Miller held no more significance for me than any other brand. Then Peggy said she'd been thinking over what I'd said, but I held up my hand to stop her. There was something about the angle at which she was sitting that made me convinced that I had to use the final Polaroid there and then. So I asked her to take off the cardie she had by now wrapped round herself as protection from the freezing air conditioning – as ever, feast or famine – then got her to turn this way and that, readied the flash, made my final adjustments, and – go on then, smile! – took the shot. A shot of Peggy – a Polaroid of Peggy – in the bluey-green dress with the big buttons. Then I put it into the pocket of my denim jacket to warm it up against my body so that it would develop quicker. And then I told her that before she said anything more, there had been some developments at the London end, and I told her what they were.

"Sunday?" she said. "Are you serious?"

"Look, I know it's not ideal but can't we go, and then get your parents or someone to send—"

"What? No, Andy, no."

"Okay then, if you think that's impossible I'll go and when you're ready you can foll—"

"Andy, please. Will you please just – stop."

One word – one syllable even – 'Stop.' There was something about the way she said it, an abruptness, that really struck home. In

287

that instant the cold truth dawned. That bit of me, the overwhelming majority of me, that knew nothing ever went right in the end, had been proved right all along. And the hoping against hope bit of me which had insisted everything was ticketyboo and that my ship was coming in and that everything was coming up roses had got everything right except that it was coming up weeds and my ship had sunk and everything was anything but ticketyboo.

"Look, Andy," she said and must have seen how crushed and bewildered I was, because she reached across and put her hand on mine. A horrible, well meant gesture of sympathy or compassion or pity or whatever which only served to confirm my very worst fears. As if any confirmation were required. It repelled me. I pulled my hand away and looked at her. Hard. Challenging her to piss all over my parade just like she was obviously going to.

She gathered herself to deliver the coup de grace.

"Andy, I can't do it. I've thought about it. I really have. Maybe at a different time – if things were different – but now – no. I'd be all on my own Andy."

She looked at me imploringly.

"What the hell are you taking about?" I said. "I'll be there. We'll be together. That's the whole point."

"No, Andy, no,"

"I mean if you're worried about getting a job or work permits or something I'm sure the agency will help us work it out. Or I dunno, we'll get married if we have to."

There I'd said it, but again, perhaps not quite as romantically as I should have done.

"If we have to?" She sat back and laughed. Bitterly? Ironically? I really don't know. Seems probable now but at the time I was too busy with my own misery to observe all the subtleties of her performance.

"Look, Andy ..." She seemed as though she was beginning again and was setting herself to say something when she stopped,

288

and said once more, "No. No, I'm sorry, but you have to go to London and I have to stay here."

And then, she stood, leaned across and kissed me one last time on the lips, and walked out.

*

I went home and went to bed. I must have done because that's where I woke up but I remember nothing of that evening after she left. Perhaps the blocking out was already beginning.

Today, Friday, was to be my last at work in America. I knew that, somehow, I would have to put on a show. For half an hour I sat at my desk, trying to collect myself, still, I think, crazily clinging on to the smallest of hopes that Peggy might walk into my office and say it had all been a terrible mistake. Then I got a call from Noreen, this time sounding sweetly sympathetic, saying that she had a message from Peggy, but, mercifully, going straight on to tell me what the message was so that the smallest of hopes weren't allowed to get any bigger. Peggy wouldn't be in today, she said, she'd gone to New Rochelle for the weekend, and had asked me please not to get in touch, she was sure I would understand. I wanted to scream no, I do not fucking understand, but didn't and just said, thanks Noreen, and then I fixed a smile of sorts, and, setting myself to the simple but impossible task of getting through the day, I went out to face the world of McConnell Martin New York one last time.

Despite the temptations of the bong, and Brett and Bart constantly urging me to loosen up and have a valedictory hit, I stayed well away. I couldn't imagine or rather, I could imagine only too well, what sort of dark places I might be taken to given the state of mind in which I already was. Alcohol, for whatever reason, I deemed a different matter, and made no attempt to resist being dragged off at lunchtime for the made-up-on-the-spot tradition of downing farewell daiquiris made with every fruit in or out of

289

season. Bart and Brett and the rest had by now clearly decided that the party on Saturday had begun a day and half early and I was only too happy – happy in the sense of it being a euphemism for contentedly intoxicated – to go along.

They were mindful enough of the proprieties of employment – since I was leaving I couldn't have given a monkey's – to return to the office in mid-afternoon, but not with the intention of actually working. Instead they disappeared for an hour before summoning me once more, this time to an impromptu gathering around Laverne's desk in Creative reception, where they produced a huge leaving card they had dreamed up and produced exquisitely as is the rule in advertising agencies. The idea was rather convoluted – too much dope, almost certainly – and based upon bees. Both the notions of buzzing off and being under bonnets were included, though I forget quite how. It really didn't matter – they all thought it was as funny as fuck. Everyone had signed it, including the Manatee himself, and even, in a very perfunctory way – Good luck, Nick – that shit, Moreno. Everyone, that is, except for one person. I hardly expected her name to be there – I consoled myself with the thought that her disappearance to New Rochelle meant she couldn't have signed it – but that didn't stop me from scouring the card, back to front, top to bottom, looking for it.

I wasn't allowed to be morose – not visibly anyway – for long. Christo had been out to buy a big cake of some description and then bottles of wine were being uncorked and little plastic cups brought out, and Bart and Brett both stood on a desk and demanded silence, and, between the two of them, they managed to make a semi-coherent speech with all the usual mildly deprecating but good humoured references to Limeys and Brits that the occasion demanded. And they threw in one or two nice things about me too which, despite my determination to keep all feelings in lockdown, I could not fail to be touched by. I had never felt so popular and yet so utterly alone.

Then there was the usual 'speech, speech' stuff and I was required to reciprocate, and even as I stood on the desk and did so, I found myself scanning the edges of the packed crowd to see if Peggy had crept in. But there was no sign of her. Then Bart and Brett and the rest of the team gave me a present: they had clubbed together and bought me a bong of my own. Try getting that through customs, they shouted. I did hide it in my suitcase and bring it back to London, but like the Polaroids – all but one – it was lost in the proverbial mists of time.

With the general sense that all pretence of work had been abandoned for the day, the party drifted on for the rest of the afternoon. At one point, I escaped back to my office, just to make absolutely sure that there was no possibility that she hadn't come in while the party was going on, and left a note or card. She hadn't.

*

I strapped myself into the seat of the 747 and gratefully accepted the complimentary glass of champagne from the nice TWA lady. I stretched my legs out, luxuriating in the unfamiliar space of my Business Class seat – it may well have been the first time I had been thus privileged. I was still feeling pretty pissed from the leaving party that had only ended when I was finally pushed into the cab by Bart. Or was it Brett?

We had all gone on – and on and on – from the drinking in the office on Friday to one bar after another and then ended up squeezed into Noreen's apartment in Brooklyn. I had actually slept on the famous couch, part of it anyway, as I'd had to share it with Brett. (Bart, I discovered in the morning, had, as it were, revisited Fire Island – it must have been him that night too unless they were taking turns – and spent the night with Noreen.)

So where had we got to now? Some time late on Saturday morning, not that it mattered, because we just carried on where we had left off. Day merged into night, Saturday into Sunday – couldn't tell you where I slept – until, late on Sunday afternoon, enough sense forced its way into my consciousness to tell me I had a plane to catch. So all back to my place, clothes and bong slung into my case – tennis racquet and press and a few other dearly beloved items to be shipped on later – a tearless farewell to the cat and I was on my way. I actually got out the door and was on the sixth and final lock when I realised I'd left my passport inside. I was wearing the denim jacket – I'd hardly taken it off since Thursday – and went to put the passport inside one of its pockets when I found it was full of the Polaroid camera. In an unaccustomed act of generosity – which I ever so slightly regret, as the model I had, a brown SX70, now goes for a good few bob on eBay – I took it out and handed it to Brett and Bart as a parting gift, suggesting they fight over it later. Then into the cab – and the plaintiff trumpet of Chuck Mangione on WGBO or some other jazz station, which always seemed to be playing in every cab you took, and which I came to think of as *the* sound of New York, and which played me out of Manhattan as the driver plunged us into the Holland tunnel.

And then check-in, customs, take-off and the lights of the skyscrapers disappearing away into the distance.

Nicely sozzled – a second glass of champagne topped me up perfectly – I was ready to sleep. I hadn't taken the Polaroid of Peggy out my pocket since I put it in there to warm, the moment after I took it. With that special gift of mine I had managed to forget all about it. And it stayed there until Alison found it, almost twenty years later.

CHAPTER 21

LONDON, 1999

"Yes, this is Miller Prince."

I might have expected the voice to have matured, but I remembered how it had struck me as being so rich and deep on the day I had rung his doorbell. (Before running away.) He sounded just the same to me. Voices never really change.

"Well, er, Miller, my name is Andrew Williams. I think your agent may have told you I was going to call."

"Yes, excuse me, but don't I know your name? Aren't you the guy who was a friend of Peggy's?"

So she'd mentioned me to him. Well, why shouldn't she have done? In a sense that made it easier, though having invented this story, I felt, absurdly, that I had to maintain the fiction until I could work my way out of it.

"Peggy's?" I said trying to sound as I though I wasn't quite sure who he meant.

Then he made it even easier.

"I thought I recognised the name when my agent called me. And then – as soon as you spoke, I kind of knew." No, voices never change. He paused and then picked up again, but sounded slightly deflated. "You haven't called about a job have you? Don't worry about it. Nobody ever does these days."

293

When I'd first spoken to the agent and sniffed the truth about Miller's career – or rather, had it confirmed, because, let's face it, what else could 'man in soup kitchen' mean? – I won't pretend that, in a kind of E to P scale way of thinking about things, I had been entirely displeased. Frankly, I hadn't been that upset that my ex-love rival, the actor who had gone up for the shaving gel commercial, he of the supposed granite jaw and rippling pecs, was not the most sought after actor in Hollywood. But hearing him now, who could not feel a little sympathy? Perhaps, given the sorry mess I was in, it brought us closer together.

"Yes, look Miller, sorry about all the subterfuge. I needed to speak to you. I've been trying to find Peggy. Do you have any idea where she is?"

"Yeah, I guessed it might be something like that. No, I don't. Why are you looking for her?"

Yes, well, obvious question. And hard to answer. I doubt I could have given a sensible explanation to myself.

"Oh, just for old times' sake."

Another pause, and he said, "Well, sorry I can't help you. Good luck."

Fuck. Another dead end. And with nothing left to lose, I took one last shot in the dark.

"Look, this may sound, um, a bit strange, but do you happen to have any idea what her real name is?"

He immediately brightened up. He chuckled, only word for it.

"You mean she wouldn't tell you either?"

Hearing that, it sent me the opposite way of course. If it was possible I became even gloomier.

"No, I kept asking and she kept making up things which I realised couldn't be true, and I kept on about it, and then, I don't know, it got to the point where she wasn't going to tell me, come hell or high water."

"Tell me about it."

"You too?"

"You have no idea!"

Adversity, as they say, makes strange bedfellows. Now, we were the best of friends.

"Yeah, but—" he said.

Yeah, what?

"She once left her passport lying around."

What!

"And you saw her real name?"

"I did. Look, er, Andrew, I don't know why the hell I should help a guy who tries to steal my girl and rings my doorbell and then runs away. Jeez you looked like a jerk" – he'd seen me? – "but okay, I'll tell you. To be honest, I have no idea what the big deal was, but people are funny about names aren't they?'

Yes they are Miller. People are funny about names. Names like Miller Pronski. I myself – never mind. Now what the fuck was her name?

"Anyway, it was Vivien. I don't know if that's going to help you any, but it was Vivien."

Vivien? Wait a minute. Hadn't we – hadn't I—

"Okay pal, well I have to go now. Gotta living to make. Not the living I planned, but what was it John Lennon said? Anyways, I got a share in a little store in Santa Monica. We sell soup. If you're ever round here, you should come in – we're real nice to our customers." Another chuckle. "Nice talking to you."

"Wait," I said, "thanks. And look, please take my number, you know, just in case you think of anything else."

He said that he couldn't think what that might be but he took my number anyway and the two old love rivals holstered their guns and said goodbye.

Vivien! Old conversations floated up from the deep. The one in the coffee place after we'd seen that awful film. 'Ice Castles' – that was it. Vivien had come up then. I'd suddenly connected it with Lee – different spelling of course – and she … and she … That was right, she'd had that funny expression on her face, the half-smile half-frown, as though she couldn't quite believe what she was hearing and I'd thought what she couldn't believe was me refusing to let the matter drop, when in fact what had got to her was that I had guessed right. Shit! And then I was back in New Rochelle again with Herb and all that smell of the greasepaint stuff, and, of course, hadn't he told me his favourite film had been 'Gone With The Wind' – starring Vivien Leigh, doh! – and that his favourite actor was Sir Laurence Olivier? And I'd thought he'd just said that to make an effort at some silly British connection with me. Which he might have done. But the clue was there. Larry had been married to Vivien Leigh! And then I thought back to the train journey home to New York that day, and the vague idea I'd had that all the clues were there, if only I could piece them together. And they had been, and I hadn't! And then the phone rang.

"Hi Andrew, this is Miller Prince again. You know what, I did remember something. A couple years ago, a guy came in for some soup, and I recognised him from way back in New York when I'd been with Peggy and we got talking and he said he'd run into her and she'd said something about being married to a dentist. He mentioned the name of the place she said they lived, been trying to think but I can't remember. Jersey somewhere, that rings a bell. But I'm pretty sure he said the dentist's name was Davis."

"D-A-V-I-S or I-E-S?"

"I don't know. That's all I can tell you."

And that was all he told me, and he rang off once more, and we never spoke again, and I never again saw his name in the credits for anything. But I remember thinking, as I twirled joyfully around in my office chair, that I sincerely hoped that he would end up with a chain of stores selling soup and that he would retire a very rich man. And I swore to myself that the next time I was in New York –

or maybe in New Jersey! – which I planned on being very soon – I would buy myself a beer, make sure it was a Miller, and toast his health. Miller Prince. What a guy!

Then I stopped twirling, called Keith Lyons, told him what I had, and asked him to get on to it immediately.

"How are you spelling Vivien?"

"How many ways are there? Never mind. However Vivien Leigh spelt it."

"Who?"

"Vivien Leigh, the actress. 'Gone With The Wind'. Married to Laurence Olivier."

"You don't happen to know how—"

"No, I don't. Aren't you supposed to be a detective?"

"And Davis – I-S or I-E-S?"

"Don't know."

"First name or last."

"Don't know."

"Well, it's something I suppose."

Something! Compared with what we'd had before, it was fingerprints, DNA and a signed confession.

"It'll be another two days. Five hundred per plus VAT plus expenses. The usual."

Yes, fine, whatever, will you please just get the fuck on with it?, was the gist of what I said in reply.

*

Half term had come and gone weeks ago. Florence and India had been up to Scotland with Alison and Doug and had returned depressingly enthusiastic about what they'd found. If you believed half of what they said, Doug's 'little place' was the size of Saudi Arabia, the wild ponies were more adorable than Bambi, and his mother Lady Harris – Lady Harris – whose presence on earth, let alone at the little place in Scotland, I had not been previously aware of, had a double first in twinkly-eyed granniness. None of which bothered me half so much as the news that Doug had been "sooooo fun" and was "like a really amazing like rider" and oh, a whole lot of other stuff, which all amounted to the same thing, namely, that they were being carefully softened up for the moment when Doug would become a de facto second dad. Or worse than that, a de facto dad in residence. Because I would have bet my house – sorry, I no longer had a house, so my cramped, miserable, poxy Bayswater flat then – that Doug would be moving his pipe and slippers into New Pemberley before the ink on the decree nisi was dry.

But, what really, really got my goat, was that, just as I was heading back out into the wintry night after I had dropped Florence and India off after a not very successful outing to the McDonalds in Whiteleys – Florence had said she was far too old for a 'Happy Meal' and then grabbed the free plastic Tarzan from India's and refused to give it back – Alison casually said to me, "You know this show India is doing at school next week? Well, she's asked Doug if he'd like to come. I hope you don't mind."

"What? Really Alison, I don't think that's appropriate."

"What do you mean, not appropriate?"

"Well, I mean surely it's for the parents."

"Not just parents. Other people can go to. Grandparents. Friends. Anneke's going."

"Yes but not, not – you know – I'm India's father and it's not his place."

"That's what he said you say."

"Well, I've said it."

"Well, you'd better tell India then."

"Okay I will."

But of course, I didn't. So that was that would be that then. Me sitting in some excruciatingly uncomfortable folding wooden chair, side by side with Doug for an hour and a half, watching India being an old Jewish woman – probably with no lines – in a school nativity play. I think that's what they mean by the phrase, exquisite torture.

*

Geoff leaned forward, elbows on his big glass desk, hands clasped, looking almost as though he were in prayer. If he had been asking for divine guidance it should have been to help him see how to deal with a repentant sinner. I hoped for mercy. I had just come, if not exactly cap in hand – I quite often favoured a Borsalino style fedora in the winter months, but never a cap – then with as much humility as I could muster, to ask for their assistance in resolving my divorce issues. Geoff pondered my request, with or without help from above, before announcing that the one he really needed to commune with was Vince who was back on his spot on the cappuccino Corbusier sofa. He asked if I would give them half an hour's grace while they considered their response and, as I was banking on millions in return, I gladly obliged, not exactly knuckling my forehead on the way out, but if I'd known the proper technique, I very well might have done. I think I can fairly claim to have wiped away all traces of my previous stroppiness.

When I shuffled back in, hoping if not for forgiveness then for pity – I really didn't give a damn about the sentiment as long as I got the money – I saw that Frank Connor was also there. Geoff – it always began with Geoff when the stakes were high – wasted no time.

"Here's what we're prepared to do. Number one, you accept all that stuff from the other day – you being chairman, Louise becoming ECD and all the rest. And – and you put up a decent show – around the office – with 'Campaign' – with clients – of pretending you like it. Number two, and we can't go further than this right now, we can't raise any more money than this even if we wanted to, Vince and I are prepared to buy half your share in BWD – which still leaves you fifteen per cent."

Okay, I thought, half of four point six and a bit was two point three and half a bit. One and a quarter to Alison left a million plus for me – minus a bit of tax – cash in hand. Plus, I still had fifteen per cent of BWD.

But then I realised Geoff hadn't finished. With a look at Vince he resumed, "We'll give you a million and a half for half your share."

"Eh? But Frank said—"

"Yes, we know what Frank said. But – in no small part due to your own personal contribution, Andrew – Mick Hudnutt looks like he's taking his business elsewhere. That'll reduce the valuation – you could tell your old lady that – sorry, ex-old lady – it might help, but, even if it doesn't, that's as far as we're going."

So, no forgiveness, no pity, no sentiment at all. Just business. Sorry Tessio, it's not personal, it's business.

At least, that allowed me to get up off my knees.

"I could go to court. Have the agreement broken."

"You could try."

"Sell my share to someone else."

"If you can get the agreement broken."

"And if you can find a buyer for a minority share," Vince threw in.

"I could borrow against it."

"And pay the interest." Vince, again.

"I'll take two."

"One point five. That's it."

"One point eight."

Geoff just shook his head. I finished the meeting with a deep breath and the short announcement that I would get back to them, and then I left Geoff's office with as much dignity as I could manage.

Treacherous bastards.

*

I could have just phoned Harriet Braintree, but I needed to get out of the office. So, once more, I was sitting in the refined atmosphere of the Hardy Wiggins meeting room, the air heavy with the perfume of today's seriously expensive flowers. No idea what they were, horticulture was never my strong point.

We'd discussed all the options and none looked particularly enticing. Protracted court battles, escalating costs with no guarantee of a positive result – "no such thing as an open and shut case, you know, Andrew, and yours isn't open or shut" – and even if we won, I had to find a buyer, and the buyer would be bound to want my entire share so I'd have to find a decent income from somewhere to pay the eye-watering maintenance costs Alison's lot were asking for. Let's face it, I would hardly be able to go on working at BWD, after the bitterness of a legal battle, whatever the result.

Or I could go to a bank and try for a loan but what did I have for collateral except shares in BWD that might not be saleable? And, even if I got the loan, there would, as Vince had helpfully pointed out, be the interest to pay. Probably lots of interest given the difficulty of realising the value of the shares. All of which led Harriet to say that in her opinion, their offer, though not generous, might, given the strength of their bargaining position, have been even smaller.

"Fuck them." I said.

"Hmm," she said, "I'm afraid to say that at this point, it rather looks the other way around."

I thought that was about as predictable as Frank Connor's give and take joke.

Only hers wasn't a joke.

*

I couldn't tolerate the thought of going back to the office and seeing their faces – doubtless, suitably grave on the outside but laughing like drains behind the masks – so I decided I would call in later with my capitulation and I drove home. When I got there, I found a letter from the bank lying on the floor. 'Dear Mr Williams,' it said, 'We notice that your current account is overdr—'. That was as far as I got. I screwed it up and chucked it in the bin. I decided a sandwich and a cup of tea might make me feel better, but the milk in the fridge was off and the bread in the bin was mouldy. So I got into the Porsche and drove to M and S in Bayswater.

Before I went in, I sat in the car in the insanely expensive car park – I noticed things like that now, parking charges, and the price of a pint of milk and a loaf of bread, none of which, previously, I would have given a second thought to. I stayed in my seat looking out through the windscreen at all the Mercs and the Lexi and the customised people carriers – this was one shopping mall where Mondeo man was rarely seen – because I needed a few minutes to take it all in. Or to make sure that I hadn't been taken in. On the journey back from my meeting with Harriet Braintree, I had gone over all the figures in my head, and I simply could not bring myself to accept the fact that I was now brassic – as good as, anyway. I decided I needed to sit there calmly – I put on Classic FM and got a nicely soothing string quartet – and go through all the figures again on a piece of paper.

I found a biro hidden by some old sweetpapers in the gearstick 'console', and I looked in the glove compartment and all the other cubby holes for something to write on. Nothing. So I went through my jacket pockets. Outside waist pockets, nothing. Inside pockets, nothing. I tapped my outside breakfast pocket, not that I ever put anything in it, not since I stopped the foppish silk handkerchief thing which I'd briefly favoured, and – wait – yep, you've guessed it, there was the Polaroid of Peggy. I thought back. Yes, must have worn this suit when I'd been to see Keith Lyons.

For a moment I sat there considering my dilemma. Could I bring myself to tattoo Peggy's back with crude financial calculations? Would this represent some kind of symbolic desecration? Would it somehow curse Keith Lyons' renewed search? I may be the unbeliever's unbeliever, but it's damned hard to shake off all superstitious pottiness. I hesitated. But Peggy lost. No time like the present I decided. I had to face the truth, however unpalatable it was. And Peggy would be fine. She would stay smiling as sweetly as she has done for twenty years, diplomatically looking the other way.

In the debit column, I put one and a quarter to Alison plus four hundred thou to pay off the house and, on top of that, lawyers fees, Mooney's fees, even Donald McEwan's fees, and a bit for contingency. Let's call it one and three quarters to be on the safe side. Then in the credit column, I put the one point five I was getting from Bradley and Dutton – no first name terms here – minus, say £150,000 tax so call it one point three five. Plus – and, being so much reduced, it felt more like a minus – I put a hundred and forty thousand which was about all I had left of my other (not BWD) shares since I had taken that moronic accountant's advice and sold the rest to buy my flat – why, oh why, hadn't I rented?! (If I could ever afford to pay his fees, I'd fire the twat.)

Bottom line? The real, no punches pulled, look if you dare, bottom line was that I was about a quarter of a million in the red, and I would now have to get a mortgage on almost the entire value of the flat to be able to pay Alison. Alright, maybe my contingency allowance was a little generous, and, yes, I still had my fifteen per cent of the agency and I still had my pension. But there was no prospect of cashing in on any more of BWD and I couldn't get at my pension until goodness knows when. And anyway, how was I ever going to be able to afford to retire?

Stephen Wilkinson, are you watching now?

*

My mental arithmetic having been proved faultless – how I wished all those Maths Teachers who'd despaired of me had been right – I locked the car and went, reeling, into Whiteley's. I think this was when I was tipped over the edge. The prospect of penury can do that to you – financial worries are the number one cause of suicide I've been told. As you'll have realised – unless you think this is a very drawn-out suicide note you're reading – it didn't have that effect on me. But I do think my already shaky grip on reality was prised a lot looser. Looking back, you would have to say that no sane man would have carried on as I was about to do. The defence rests.

I was making my way towards Marks and Spencer, when I noticed there was a long queue going somewhere, and when I asked one of the queuers what she was queuing for, she informed me that it ended at Books Etc – a now defunct chain of booksellers – and that there was a celebrity book signing there. And who would the celebrity be? Monica Lewinsky. I joined the queue.

You see what I mean. Why on earth would I have wanted a copy of 'Monica's Story' by Andrew Morton, signed or otherwise? Let alone spend the next two hours queuing up for it. Which I did. Temporary insanity at the very least. Monica, by the way, turned out to be a charming young person, and after we had exchanged pleasantries, she signed, I paid and I received my receipt. (Hand written, because the Books Etc computerised till, perhaps unable to cope with the demand of 'Monica's Story', had packed up.)

Another possible sign of madness is getting rid of your shrink at the very time when you obviously need him most. After I had dumped my shopping on to the passenger seat – my plastic bag from Marks, and my signed copy of 'Monica's Story' – I made two calls. One to Geoff, as brief as I could make it, and, even as I spoke, silently cursing the black night in Mayfair when I'd teamed up with him and his little, fat Aussie mate. And a second to Donald McEwan, asking to see him as soon as I could. I didn't tell him on the phone but I had made up my mind this was to be our last session – and so it was to prove, for several years anyway. Accommodating as always, Donald said he could fit me in, first thing tomorrow morning.

*

For once, for about the only time in living memory, I was on time. Possibly because I was now obsessing over money – or the lack of it – and I had very belatedly realised that time was money, and that it might be Donald's time but it was very definitely my money. (And please don't mention the twenty quid I had pointlessly lashed out for 'Monica's Story'. Don't expect consistency in the unhinged. Besides, it was a book. Which meant I could – and most definitely would – say it was 'for research' and claim back the cost from BWD. That, I think, is what you would call 'method in my madness'.) Donald, being Donald, made no comment – perhaps in case that would have implied fault on my part for my previous unpunctuality, and that would have meant going against his never-judge policy or perhaps because it was just his unfailing good manners.

I sat down on the throwover of my usual threadbare armchair, still with my coat on. Not a coat in fact. A Schott black leather jacket, the kind of thing I might not have worn when out in New York in '79. Particularly if knocking around with Christo. It had a furry lining of some sort which I was very grateful for, as December had that day decided it was winter, the central heating – if there was any – was struggling, and the heatless gas fire was living down to its reputation. Donald, being a hardy Scot, of course, made do with an old cardigan.

I began by bringing him up to date on all things divorce wise, and BWD wise, which meant money wise. And then I explained, with profuse apologies and with genuine regret, that as far as cloth cutting went, I would have to, very reluctantly, trim him from the finished item. He nodded, and said he quite understood. All this had taken no more than five minutes.

"Of course, I'll pay you for the full time today," I said.

"Och, no need for that."

"No, no, I absolutely insist."

"Well, we still have forty minutes. Is there anything you'd like to say?"

Of course, I couldn't think of a thing. I really hadn't felt the need for serious soul baring since I had embarked on my search for Peggy. Having decided on that, I had a purpose and a plan – of sorts – and they were just the kind of distractions you need to avoid self-examination. And today all I'd been focused on was saying a sad goodbye. On the other hand, he was right, there were forty minutes left – only thirty-six now – and I was paying for every one. So I racked my scrambled brains and alighted on something I'd read in 'Monica's Story' the night before. (I wasn't sleeping brilliantly and I had ploughed through it until about four.)

"You know about this compartmentalisation business?" I enquired. "You know this thing where Bill Clinton is supposed to be able to shut off all this impeachment stuff completely so he can concentrate on not nuking Iran."

"Yes, I've heard about it."

"Do you buy it?"

"Not sure."

"Do you think I could be like that?"

"Are we talking about your suppressed memories of Peggy again?"

"What else?"

"I tend to think people remember what they want to remember," he said.

"And forget what they need to forget?"

"Yes, but I said 'want' and you said 'need'."

"Easily confused," I said.

And he smiled and agreed they were.

"Haven't we talked about that before?" I said.

"We've talked about most things before," he said, and smiled again.

And for once, maybe another first, I didn't even try to find a riposte, and have the last word.

And that's how we left it. Memories suppressed. Compartmentalisation. The nature of guilt. Want or need. These and many other questions we had mused over and reached no conclusions about. This is what you get when you go to a shrink. Or it was what I got. That and the pleasure of spending time and arguing the toss with a really nice and very wise man. And, although as I have said, I was not at this time, acting entirely, or even remotely, rationally, neither was I sinking into the depths of depression, writing suicide notes, plunging into the bottle, or sticking rolled up fivers into my nose. And I did know people, a few of them, who had done all of those things. So, all in all, I would have to say, it was money well spent, even accounting for all the hours, and it was many hours, that I had wasted being late.

"Be careful," he said kindly, as we shook hands at the bottom of the steps that led up to the road.

But did I listen?

CHAPTER 22

LONDON, 1999

I drove back towards the office, but I felt rather melancholy knowing I wouldn't be seeing Donald again. I had a half-baked idea that doing something vaguely pastoral might improve my mood. Not being able to think of anything else, I drove to Westbourne Park and told Anneke I was going to take Spot for a walk. For a minute I thought she was going to tell me that she would have to call Alison and check to see if it was alright, but she just shrugged and went to get his lead. As Spot and I walked away, she said she probably wouldn't be there when I got back, but the cleaning lady would let Spot back in. Then she signed off by saying she would see me at the school for India's show. Fuck, I thought, when is that? But I didn't want to ask Anneke, in case it got back to Alison.

When I got back to New Pemberley and had handed Spot over, I noticed, as the cleaning lady shut the front door, that something had changed. It took me a while before I realised what it was. Or wasn't. It wasn't New Pemberley anymore. Fresh black glossy paint – applied by Doug? – had obliterated all evidence of my little joke.

My first thought, as I climbed back into the Porsche, apart from remembering to open the windows to get rid of the lingering dog odour, was that I really must make a point of discussing with

Donald what the psychological significance was, both for Alison and me, and, of course, for the children, of the de-New Pemberlisation of the old family home. But then I remembered about the cloth cutting. Missing him badly, I decided not to go to the office just yet, but went instead to Soho, and spent the afternoon at Groucho's. It was, I realised, the first time I had been there since I had got so pissed on the night we won the seven million pound cereal account and fell over and tore my trousers. Groucho's had a lot to answer for. I spent half the afternoon in there, not seeing a single soul I knew, and getting ever more fed up, until, as the darkness fell at the ridiculously early time it does in December − "Fucking Scots farmers," I said to the bloke behind the bar who, being something foreign, was mystified by this remark − I decided there was nothing for it but to go back and hide in the office. At least I could get on with seeing the remainder of 'Seinfeld'. (I had, prior to getting to grips with 'Monica's Story', being treating my insomnia with huge knock-out doses of Elaine/Peggy. I'd seen the rest of the episodes in series seven after 'The Soup Nazi', all of series eight, and I was now half-way through the ninth and final year.) On the way out of Groucho's, the guy behind reception, who I sort of knew, shouted something to me.

"Sorry?" I asked.

"Happy birthday," he said.

I froze. Surely it couldn't be … And, even if it had been, how the fuck did he know? I had reached the point where I was actually having to check the date of my own birthday, but relief was at hand.

"Yeah, saw − the er 'big one' − was coming up next week. And I just thought I'd do the friendly thing," he said.

Yes, very friendly. Thank you. But I think you'll find I've another fifty years to go before the big ONE! No, I didn't say any of that apart from the thank you − not out loud anyway.

"Yes, and the reason I noticed the date is that your membership dues − well, they're a bit overdue, ha ha."

Ha ha. So not just being friendly then. A gentle reminder. I thanked him again. More cloth cutting to be done.

*

A couple of hours later, and I was getting seriously stuck into series nine. The smell of death was obviously in the air – I refer to the death of my career – as nobody seemed to be coming near me. The action was all around Lucille's office these days. On my way in I'd overheard someone say that Mick Hudnutt would be in first thing tomorrow morning – presumably to see what new miracles had been wrought on his troubled account – and all the young guns were rushing in to show her their brilliant ideas.

Still, looking on the bright side, I was on to episode fifteen, 'The Wizard', which was particularly interesting to me because Elaine's boyfriend refers to them as an inter-racial couple, thinking that she is Hispanic. This rather reminded me of the slightly Puerto Rican like features that I have sometimes ascribed to Peggy, so I froze the frame as this point and spent a few minutes checking Julia Louis-Dreyfus for cheekbone height and eye-almondiness, and then referring back to the Polaroid of Peggy to see how they compared in regard to these criteria. (Are these any criteria of Hispanicness? I really don't know, but for some reason I thought they might be.)

At exactly this moment, Julia finally did stick her head around my door, to tell me it was nearly six, she was going in ten minutes, and had I forgotten something or other, but I was so wrapped up in my review of Elaine and Peggy that I missed whatever it was that I might have forgotten. A minute later, she was back again. Some chap called Keith Lyons was on the line.

Another moviemory. And another freeze frame. And this time it's me in it, eyes wide open, terrified.

That's how I see it. That's what I remember. Feeling as though time had stopped and knowing that when it restarted, I would discover that my last even semi-realistic hope of finding Peggy had gone. Or possibly, just possibly, that this insane pursuit might, against all the odds, finally be leading somewhere. As with job applications or exam results or football scores, I wasn't at all sure I wanted to know the answer, because for as long as I didn't know, the little guttering flame of hope still burned. Then I unfroze and picked up the phone.

Almost forty-eight hours to the minute after we had last spoken – but not quite – Keith Lyons had called back to say that his American colleagues had located a Dr Myron Davis – they call dentists doctor over there he told me – living with a Mrs Vivien Davis in somewhere called – wait a minute, he had it there – Tinton Falls, New Jersey.

Tinton Falls? Where the hell was that? Never mind – there were maps. (And yes, he charged me for the full two days.)

Perhaps I should have waited, but I couldn't. I peered at the address and telephone number he'd given me, and I picked up the phone and dialed. The usual wait, then that particular American ringing tone, once, twice, three times – come on, be in – four ti— "Hello?"

It was her. I was sure it was her.

"Er, hello, is that Peggy – er Peggy Davis?"

"Ye – es. This is Peggy Davis. Who's speaking?"

"Andrew – I mean, Andy Williams."

A pause. I could almost hear her memory rewinding.

"Andy? Really? Andy Williams? How – how'd you get my num—"

And then, just then, just as we were getting going, Julia burst in again.

"Andrew, I just told you. You've got to get to the school for India's show. Seriously, if you don't leave right now, you'll be late."

"What! Why didn't you – oh shit. Peggy, look I'm sorry, something's come up. I have to go. Can I call you back later?"

"Sure, I'll be here. Is everything okay Andy? You sound pretty hassled."

311

"No, no. Well, yes, but I'm fine. I'll call you later. Bye. Bye Peggy."

I picked up my car keys and ran.

*

Of course, I was the last person to arrive. I tore into the school hall turned theatre for the night and all the heads turned towards me. Little sibling heads, doting grandma heads, the less than impressed head's head, and the familiar shaking reddy-auburn head – 'absolutely typical' was the message it unmistakably conveyed – of my very, very soon to be ex-wife Alison. With a stream of excuse-me's, and I'm awfully sorry's, and oh gosh, I'm afraid I didn't see your foot there's, I made my way to my appointed place, and yes, being the last one in the party to arrive, I was indeed stuck next to sodding Doug.

He greeted me with the condescending smile of the victor.

"India's really excited about this," he confided.

"Doug, I know you're new to this sort of thing, but she's got a walk on part in a Nativity Play. I think I know my own daughter and I wouldn't have said that it had her in a lather of excitement."

"A Nativity Play?" he said, and burst out laughing. "Hardly."

"Not a Na—"

"And she's got a lot more than a walk-on. She's got a lot of lines."

Lines? But when I asked her –

"She's Golde."

One of those shadows from the past flitted by again.

"Golde?"

"Tevye's wife. 'Fiddler on the Roof'. Do you know it?"

The house lights dimmed as he spoke, thank goodness, or he would have seen the various expressions of confusion, embarrassment and deflation that must have been competing for space on my face. I racked my brains: had India told me about this?

312

Had I not been paying attention? Both entirely possible, though I couldn't recall anything specific. But however this oversight had occurred, it mattered not. I had missed a unique and an almost certainly never to be repeated opportunity to bond with my daughter. The hours we could have happily spent, me playing Tevye while she honed her Golde. I could have wept for the lost dibbys, yubbys and biddy, dum, bums. And worse than that, Doug, this impostor, this cuckoo in *my* nest had obviously been allowed into India's confidence and now even her *heart*. Had she not specifically asked for him to be allowed to attend?

I tried to cheer myself up by concentrating on the show. You have to be pretty bitter and twisted not to be charmed by a bunch of nine-year-old girls wrestling with their Christmas show. The missed entrances, the faltering notes, the whispered prompts just add to the oohing and aahing gaiety of it all. India, as it happened, made a very respectable job of Golde. And the little girl who played Tevye, who, beneath her stuck-on beard, I recognised from India's endless party-going as being an American girl called Cameron, made a decent fist of him too. (I think Herb shaded it, but it was close.) Halfway through the first act, during a scenery change that went slightly awry, precipitating general audience titter and a break in my concentration, I suddenly remembered my truncated call to Peggy. It had completely slipped my misfiring mind.

I decided I would go outside in the interval – this would have the added bonus of relieving me of the pain of having to sip a beaker of warm Pinot Grigio standing next to Doug – and phone Peggy from there. But when I checked in the many pockets of my Schott jacket, not one contained my phone. In the rush to get here, of course, I had left it on top of my desk. I could see it sitting there now – oh shit! don't tell me – I frantically checked my pockets again. Oh bugger. Bugger, bugger, bugger! Yes, it was sitting on my desk alright – on top of the piece of paper on which I had written Peggy's number in Tintin wotsit. And that meant I wouldn't be able to call her when I got home either. Or call her from anywhere until I could get back in the office tomorrow morning. And by that time it would be the middle of the night in Tonto, which meant I couldn't try until lunchtime – and who knew, she could be setting off on a lone round the world yachting trip tomorrow, and I might not be able to speak to her for a year.

The end of the first act came with tumultuous applause from the audience. Even by the normal standards of over the top parental encouragement the bloke on the other side of me seemed to be giving it a lot of wellie and threw in a couple of whistles too. I turned to see who it was, and I recognised him as Cameron/ Tevye's dad, Hank or Hal someone, who was, if memory served, something in the city. Spotting another opportunity to avoid having to engage with Doug, I gave Florence a big kiss, a wave to Anneke, a nervous smile to Glenda and Vic – Jesus, was everyone here? I half expected Spot to pop up from somewhere – and made some sort of neutral facial expression in the direction of Alison who returned same. Then I attached myself to Hal or Hank and took my beaker of Pinot Grigio with me.

"Cameron is really very good," I said.

"Why thank you," he replied, "Imogen was real special too."

"India," I corrected him. And then for no better reason than to fill in the awkward silence that followed, I suggested, not really meaning it, that Cameron was certainly talented enough to get work in commercials. And that, of course, reminded him I was in advertising and that led to the inevitable discussion, now joined by his wife Margot – long accent on the 'oh' – about what ads I was doing that they might have seen. So I mentioned one, and Margot said yes, she'd seen it, but in such a way that told me she clearly hadn't understood a thing – possibly, I privately concluded, too esoterically British for her. So then I tried to think of something I was doing that an American might be able to relate to, and that is how, little by little, the conversation led on to the non-chocolate chocolatey breakfast cereal and the Jerry Seinfeld connection.

"Oh," said Margot, "my brother is a friend of his agent. He says he's a really nice guy."

That was all she said. She didn't make it clear whether her brother had said the agent was the nice guy or whether it was the agent saying it was Jerry, and I didn't ask because I wasn't taking much notice at the time, or I thought I wasn't, but I remind you again of my fevered state of mind. As you will shortly see, this little throwaway remark lodged in my unconscious and in that unstable environment grew into something else entirely. But we shall come to that. In the meantime, the curtain rose on the second act, India and her nine-year-old chums iddle-diddle-daidle-daidled their way through the rest of 'Fiddler on the Roof', the curtain came down, the audience stood and cheered, and Doug and I quickly found ourselves locked in a fierce competition to see who could clap more loudly. (Hal/Hank's half time efforts were paltry by comparison.) Determined not to be outdone, I also yelled out "Well done, Indeeyah", which, judging by her own pained expression and the admonishing "Da-ad!" I got from Florence, may have been a gesture of support too far. Afterwards, we all – Florence, India, Alison, Glenda, Vic, Anneke, Doug and I – went off to some mentally over-priced supposedly wood-burning pizza place. This had apparently been arranged in advance but nobody said a word to me until we were actually leaving the school. Even so, given that I simply had to win my rutting competition with the interloper stag, aka Doug, it was essential that, when the bill arrived, I was seen to be the big-hearted generous Daddy of them all who picked up the tab. There are times when cloth cutting, however advisable, is a secondary consideration.

When we left – all of the others going back to no-longer-New-Pemberley, and me to miserable Bayswater – I told India for the hundredth time that she had been better than Judy Garland, better than Emma Bunton, better than anyone who'd ever set foot on a stage, before giving her one last big hug, and a matching one to Florence. And then I watched them all disappear laughing and joking into the night, with Doug clearly the cheerleader, or so, in my depression and sense of exclusion, I was determined to believe.

That night, I hardly slept at all. I finished 'Monica's Story' and with nothing else to read, and the rest of 'Seinfeld' series nine unreachable in my office along with my phone and Peggy's number, I just lay on my bed and brooded. My fiftieth birthday was on Monday, now just four days away. And, to compound my unhappiness, it dawned on me that neither Florence nor India had asked me at the restaurant what I might be doing to celebrate. In fact, neither had said a word about it since that one conversation when I had been reading India a story, weeks and weeks before. How ironic, I reflected bitterly, that the only reference to Monday had been made by Alison who'd drawn me aside to say that we had things to discuss and to make sure, whatever I did, to drop by the house after work.

*

Fuck them I thought. Fuck them all. Fuck Geoff and Vince and Alison and Doug and Lucille and Mick Hudnutt and yes, to my eternal shame, I probably thought fuck Florence and India too. And then came the thunderbolt, and the flash of lightning that enabled me to see what I must do. And what I mustn't. I wouldn't ring Peggy back. No, I would get on a plane and fly to Tumtum and knock on her door and speak to her in person instead. And I would do it on Monday – that was how I would celebrate my fiftieth birthday, that would be my birthday surprise! For several minutes I must have just lain there, marvelling at the wonderful simplicity of my idea. All my problems answered in one. I no longer felt the burning resentment against all those who had slighted me and brought me low – how could I feel anything but goodwill towards anyone when I would, so soon, come face to face with the face of which I dreamed? At that moment, I think I very probably felt as excited and as thrilled with the brilliance of my idea as I had on that day in New York when I had coined the line, 'Do you have a bee in your bonnet about compacts?'

But then the awful spectre of cloth cutting started to cloud my mind. I wasn't at all sure I had enough money in my account to pay for the ticket. No, thinking back to the screwed-up bank statement, I knew that I hadn't. I had credit cards, yes, but with all the bills that I still had to settle – shit, why on earth hadn't I let Doug win the rutting contest at the wood burning pizza place? The money that had cost would have got me a couple of hundred miles past Dublin at the very least.

And then I remembered that I had a *company* credit card. And then, somehow, I made a sudden leap, as the creative mind will, to something else entirely, at first seemingly quite unconnected. I remembered Margot's brother and his friendship with Jerry Seinfeld's agent. Hadn't she said that either Jerry or Jerry's agent was a really nice guy? She certainly hadn't said that one of them wasn't. In fact, the more I thought about it, the more it stared me in the face that they both must be really nice guys. If Jerry was a really nice guy would he have a nasty guy for an agent? And if his agent was a really nice guy would he have a nasty guy for a client? (Yes, the earning power of a client who could turn down a hundred and ten million might have a bearing there, but I chose to ignore that.) So here we have two really nice guys – one of them, it was true, who it was reported – third hand – had pissed himself over the phone from New York. But how did we really know what he was laughing about? Maybe it had nothing to do with the idea of Jerry appearing in a British commercial for non-chocolate chocolatey thingummies. A really nice guy like that probably had a really good attitude to his staff, and maybe the office gofer, who would be encouraged to go ahead and express himself at all times, had just cracked the funniest

317

joke ever and that was what made Jerry's agent piss himself. At four in the morning in Bayswater with nothing else to cling on to, you certainly didn't want to rule it out.

And did Margot not have a direct line to these really nice guys? She just had to call her brother. And did I not have a direct line to her? So wouldn't it be true to say that last night, by the most amazing coincidence – now, here, really was a reason to believe there might be some divine force out there – I had been given a direct line to Jerry's agent and thence to Jerry and that they both, according to all understanding, were really nice guys. And given that, Mick, what I am telling you is that there is now a real opportunity to pull off the astonishing coup of having Jerry Seinfeld appear in a commercial for non-chocolate chocolatey wibbelys and I am personally flying to New York over the weekend to handle the negotiations.

Madness, you say, sheer madness. Yes, I say, yes, but members of the jury, that is my point.

*

The cold light of day sometimes reveals the flaws in plans hatched in the middle of the night, but you have to be of a mind to see them. Whereas, by the time I was turning the Porsche out of the Fitzrovia traffic and into the car park under the BWD office early on Friday morning, I had totally convinced myself of the rightness of all I was about to do. In Dr Pepper terms, what was the worst that could happen? I would fly to New York, not have a meeting with Jerry or his agent, but fly back and report that I had. I would explain that, unfortunately, as nice as these guys really were, they could not be budged. It wasn't about the money, and Jerry really loved the script but he just didn't want to do any commercials. I had tried and failed. I had gone the extra mile, the extra three thousand miles in fact, but to no avail. Could I really be blamed for that?

I had thought everything through. First, I would write a brief document to distribute at the meeting – documents always add weight to the most negligible of propositions. I chose as a title: Seinfeld Reborn. Then I added a question mark. Seinfeld Reborn? Better. 'Never over-promise' is always a good rule when you're trying to sell something. Then I bunged in a bit of jargon filled rhubarb about how appropriate the 'Seinfeld' idea had always been for the non-chocolate chocolatey doodads and some sort of vague itinerary for my trip. Obviously getting a hearing would be tricky but I reckoned that if I was able to get this piece of paper in front of Mick Hudnutt, they would have to hear me out. I called Julia in, asked her to type it up – triple spaced for extra weight – run off half a dozen copies, put them in binders with shiny plastic covers, all the usual bullshit, and threw in some dire threats of a gruesome end if she breathed a word to anyone. Then I asked her to book me the first available business class flight to New York, and a really nice hotel room somewhere – if everything went to plan I might even be doing some entertaining – and also to check out which room the meeting would be in. It turned out to be Twain, always, as it happened, my preferred choice. This was because several of his sayings were painted on the walls, which at least provided something interesting to look at when the meetings got as tedious as they invariably did. There was one in particular that I would point to when I was trying to flog something to a nervous client: 'A person with a new idea is a crank until the idea succeeds.' I decided I would use that today as the soaring finale of my oration. "That person," I would tell them, looking Mick Hudnutt straight in the eye, "is me!" I could see the heads nodding already.

At five past ten, I walked into Twain unannounced and sat down. I was still the Executive Creative Director so they could hardly insist that I left but the hostility and suspicion from Lucille, Hattie, and Mick himself was palpable. (The various client and agency underlings just mimicked their superiors.) Vince, who I had been forced to sit next to because the only vacant chair was there, looked daggers at me and was in the process of sending me a warning note – I was close enough to get an idea of what he was writing – when his PA, Maxine, came running into the room and mumbled something into his ear about an urgent message from Geoff. Then she slipped him a folded note which he opened surreptitiously but which I, by pretending to drop a pen on the floor, and then reaching down and rising up again at a certain angle, was able to get half a butchers at. I thought it said something about a try-out but I couldn't have sworn to it. Then Vince folded the piece of paper, stuck it into his pocket, apologised to Mick and left. He forget to pass me his warning note, but he flashed me a ferocious look on the way out which did just as well.

Nevertheless, his early exit gave me an opening and I jumped straight in. I insisted on pushing 'Seinfeld Reborn?' onto the agenda there and then, distributed my document, and made my pitch. It was received in hushed silence. Or stunned stupefaction, to put it another way. But as sceptical as he might have been, what could Mick Hudnutt say? Particularly as I made the specific point that, as it was I who had failed to check out Jerry's availability and price in the first place – always good to chuck in a mea culpa if you can – the agency would be picking up the tab for the trip. Job done. I left the room as abruptly as I had entered and turned off my phone as I went. I had no intention of letting anyone call me to put a spoke in my wheels.

My flight was booked for the next afternoon, Saturday, and exhausted from my sleepless night and to avoid seeing anyone from the office, I intended going home for the rest of the day. I walked around to the hole in the wall to get some cash before getting back into the Porsche, but when I put my card in, the machine refused to pay out. My account was completely empty and by now, probably seriously overdrawn. But I needed money. I felt in the pockets of the Schott jacket – very unlike me to wear the same thing two days in a row but I had – just to make sure there weren't a couple of crumpled tenners somewhere, but all I came up with was the receipt from Books Etc for 'Monica's Story.' The good news was, of course, that it was convertible into cash, if I could get to accounts, but I couldn't afford – or thought I couldn't – to run into Geoff or Vince, so I decided to wait in the car until lunchtime, when I thought most of the agency would probably be out. So I tipped back the seat and had a snooze in the car until, just after one, when I sneaked back in, and successfully made it to the accounts floor. But then I realised that twenty pounds wasn't going to get me very far. I thought about getting an advance for my trip but I was worried that the accounts girl might ask someone for authorisation and that might turn out to be Frank Connor who might tip off Geoff or Vince, and that my whole elaborate scheme would begin to unravel.

This was what lay behind my decision to do something I hadn't done since I was as young and callow as the two idiots. With hindsight it looks a questionable decision as, indeed, it would have done with any foresight, but, having said that, I should emphasise once again my general loss of plot, in the context of which it was made. I had, you see, the jolly wheeze of doctoring the Books Etc receipt and fiddling my expenses. This wouldn't have been possible if I'd been given the usual printed receipt but, having received a hand written one – in a strange mauvey, blue biro – I had been gifted an opportunity which I now lacked the common sense to miss. 'Monica's Story' cost, as we know, £20. My idea – not in the least original, and one with which you yourself may be familiar – was to slip a '1' in between the £ and the 2, thus making the cash-in value of the receipt £120. To accomplish this deception successfully, it was essential to use exactly the right colour and the same style of writing as on the original receipt.

But where to find the right colour of mauvey-blue? I looked on Julia's desk. Royal blue. Navy Blue. But no mauvey-blue. I slipped into Lucille's office. No pens on her desk at all. I went from desk to desk throughout the creative department – on a Friday lunchtime as empty as the Mary Rose – and found reds, greens, blacks and every shade of blue except the mauvey-blue I wanted.

There remained only one desk to check – that of mouthy idiot. And there I saw it. A cooler head, a more calculating fraudster might have thought to palm the mauvey-blue biro and remove to his own office before committing his crime. But I, impatient and careless, and simply not thinking, opted to slip the '1' in right there. Not easy though: I bent over the desk, checked the writing already on the receipt, did a couple of practise '1's on a piece of paper lying on mouthy idiot's desk, then pressed the receipt firmly down with one hand, and went to make the clean downward mauvey-blue stroke with the other. But just as I did so, I sensed a sudden presence, and head jerking up and pen-holding hand jerking with it, I saw mouthy idiot standing beside me.

I did not doubt for one moment that mouthy idiot was the perp of many similar felonies for his expression said nothing if it wasn't 'I know exactly what you're up to, mate'. And that being the case, I suppose I could have given him a sort of 'honour amongst thieves' wink before casually strolling out. But instead, embarrassed and flustered, and with his laughter ringing in my ears, I pushed past him and fled back down to accounts. I handed in my receipt to the girl behind the little window who looked at it with obvious suspicion, hardly surprising given that the '1' had a pronounced squiggly aspect, more like a tadpole than a numeral. She stared me in the eye, challenging me to come clean, but I held my nerve, claimed my £120, and since I was a partner in the firm, she could hardly refuse to pay out.

I went home and found an envelope on my doormat. Inside were the tickets for the 3 p.m. Saturday BA flight to JFK and a voucher for the Helmsley Hotel on 42nd St. All as requested. Thank you Julia. I made a point of not checking my phone messages, and took the phone – the landline as we now call it – off the hook. I made a sandwich (with my freshish M&S bread), and passed the afternoon and evening watching the remaining episodes of series nine – including the two part finale, which, I learned from the video cover, had been seen by seventy-six point three million people when it was first broadcast the year before in the States, and had been written by Larry David – an authentic genius in my opinion – who'd returned to the show specially to do it. I felt rather sad when it was over. And yet, also, an odd sense of – what? Closure? Didn't seem very appropriate if it was, because, surely, I was on the verge of a new life-changing, beginning.

I took a shower and tried to sleep. And now, feeling much calmer, with my preparations all in place and nothing to stop me, I slept long and deep. In the morning, I awoke, packed a few things – should I take a tie? two ties? – and carefully checked I had Peggy's address and number, and the Polaroid. I certainly didn't think I would have any difficulty recognising her but I just thought I should have it with me. Superstition again I suppose. Nonsensical. Primitive. Aren't we all?

First thing in the morning I went to Tower Records in Whiteley's and bought a couple of Greatest Hits CDs for the journey. Peggy Lee and Chuck Mangione, just as you'd expect. A few hours later I was in the back of a cab on the way to Heathrow, my Walkman CD player switched on, Chuck's magic trumpet floating through the headphones.

Track 1. 'Feels So Good'.

CHAPTER 23

TINTON FALLS AND NEW YORK, 1999

I sat humming along to Peggy Lee (who else?) oozing out of the sound system – 'The Best is Yet To Come' (what else?) – in the rather splendid vehicle I had hired from Avis on 43rd St, just around the corner from the hotel. It was by no means their cheapest model but I was on company business. So I was on the company credit card. Besides today, after all, was my fiftieth birthday. And if making it to half a century isn't an excuse for pushing the boat out – or in this case a nifty blue Mercury Cougar – then what is?

I had just pulled onto the side of Galloping Way, Tinton Falls, New Jersey, not quite bang opposite to, but giving a clear view of, the rather imposing home of Dr Myron Davis and his wife Vivien. (It appeared there was gold in them thar teeth.) I had been up early to make the supposedly hour and a bit trip but, having had to fight my way through the midtown rush hour traffic to the Lincoln Tunnel, and then work out what or where the New Jersey turnpike might be, and then get onto the I-95 (South but so easy to go North) and then make sure I didn't miss the exit for the US 9 (which I did) and then – oh never mind, I got there in the end, even if it did take twice as long as it should have done.

But as it happens, the delay served my purposes. It meant that it was not likely that I would arrive before Myron left for work –

assuming he didn't now spend his days on the golf course which to judge by the splendour of his house he very well might – and that I would be able to ring Peggy's bell without running into him. And my long, inadvertently circuitous, journey had provided the opportunity to listen to all of Peggy Lee's Greatest Hits. (Even Peggy Lee wasn't called Peggy, by the way. Or even Lee. She was born Norma Deloris Egstrom in 1920. And, as the whole world knows, she wasn't, curiously, the only star of her generation to have been a Norma first.)

The song for which Peggy Lee is most famous is, probably, 'Fever', recorded in 1958, and although it was on the CD, it's not my favourite and I fast-forwarded through it. There are two Peggy Lee tracks of which I am particularly fond, and 'It's Been A Long Long Time', playing now as I sat in Galloping Way, and which I'd filled the Cougar with a good half a dozen times on the way from New York, is one of them. Of course, at that moment, it would have been doubtful if there were any song ever recorded by anyone which would have resonated more.

I checked my watch. Twenty past nine. There was a car parked on the street right outside their front door – or rather next to the beginning of the long pathway that ran from the street through the perfectly mown 'front yard' to the door itself. A visitor of some sort I presumed, but I couldn't contain my jumping heart much longer, so I took a deep breath, turned the other Peggy off, and walked up the path and rang the doorbell.

I waited. Only a few seconds in reality, I'm sure, but it was one of those occasions when so much seems to hang on the outcome that any waiting is simply unbearable. And then the door swung open, and for a moment, I swear, I literally stopped breathing. Corny. Clichéd. Mills and Boone. But I can't think of any other way of putting it.

I looked at her. Gawped would probably be more accurate. It was unbelievable. She looked exactly the same. Exactly. The same tumbling black hair, the same flawless skin, the same sweetheart lips, the same brown black almondy eyes, the same slight suggestion of a mischievous smile playing around the corners of her mouth. And she stared back at me. Neither of us spoke. Neither of us seemed to know what to say. And, then at last, she said, "Excuse me, do I know you?"

For an instant, the most appalling thought went through my head. Were the appearance of unblemished youth and the complete lack of recognition part of the same dreadful condition? And then I realised they were, only there was no reason to be appalled, and there was nothing dreadful about it.

"Peggy?" I ventured, but already knowing the answer.

"Oh my God, you want my Mom! I'm sorry, for a minute there, you – er – you kind of looked – like you thought you knew *me*."

"Well, yes, I did. Only I thought you were her." I paused and looked again. I looked down to my feet. Was the outside floor level lower than inside? Because, now I thought about it, she did seem a bit taller than I remembered. But otherwise – I felt in my pocket and pulled out the Polaroid of Peggy. It was uncanny. Exactly the same – maybe a little less full in the face and a little slimmer than Peggy in the Polaroid, but then she'd been a little bigger in the shot than in the most of the time I knew her. No, it was extraordinary. I showed her.

"Oh my God," she said again. "That's my Mom! Wow! Where did you get that? When was it? Who are—"

"It was 1979," I said, "Central Park. A Dr Pepper Concert. Robert Palmer—"

"Robert who?"

"I'm sorry," I said, "For the misunderstanding, I mean." I thought about Florence. She would have been absolutely horrified to have been compared to a girl of twenty let alone a woman of forty-eight. Still, this girl was obviously a few years older than Florence. How old I wondered?

"No," she said, "No problem. Look, let me go see if my Mom can see you. She's with the physio at the moment," – ah, the physio, must be the visitor parked outside – "but let me tell her you're here. Can I give her your name?"

"Yes, wait, no, look it was meant to be a surprise. Would you mind just saying, I don't know, that – that an old friend is here to see her."

"O-kay. I guess."

She obviously thought it was a little strange – and it obviously was, so I said, "Look, I'm Andrew." No reaction, English guy called Andrew and no reaction, so I'd never been mentioned. "But would you mind not saying that to her? I mean, I'm sure she won't mind – it'll just be more fun."

"Oh sure, sure. I'm Betty by the way." And then she dashed off.

Betty I thought. How nice. Betty after her grandmother, Betty Lipschitz. Then it occurred to me, that meant Betty must be dead, as Jewish people don't usually name their children after living relatives. I was reflecting, rather nostalgically, on to my trips to New Rochelle when young Betty returned.

"Hey, I'm afraid she's real busy with the physio for a little while. She'll be through in about half an hour. Would you like to come in and wait?"

Since we still hadn't established the whereabouts of Myron, I wasn't absolutely sure I did want to go in, so I said, "Look, I'll tell you what, I'll just go and get a coffee somewhere, then come back in half a hour. Please tell Peggy that."

"Oh. Okay," said Betty. "Sure." And gave me a glorious Peggy of a smile, and shut the door.

So I drove around until I found a cafe – it turned out to be a Starbucks, still, it is hard to believe, a novelty to me, as they hadn't opened in the UK until the previous year – and spent the next half an hour of my fiftieth birthday having a cappuccino and observing the citizens of suburban New Jersey. I thought of calling Florence and India – I did feel a little guilty at having suddenly abandoned them – but it was only for a few days, and I couldn't see how I could get in touch without raising awkward questions – where are you? why can't you tell us? – that I didn't want to answer. Besides, it was only for a few days, and I was still angry with them for being so disinterested in my birthday.

Then I drove back but the physio's car was still there, so once again I parked close to, but not right by, Peggy's house; a place from which I could see without being easily seen. I waited – the physio couldn't be long, and sure enough, within a minute or two, I saw the door open and a young woman in a white, nurse-like frock step out. She turned to speak to someone in the doorway – would I at last get a glimpse of Peggy? I did, but not the one I expected. As the physio made the first few slow steps down the path, still half facing the house and talking as she went, I saw a wheelchair push forward over the threshold of the door and stop. And there sitting in it, quite unmistakably, was Peggy, smiling and waving the physio goodbye.

*

There are certain moments in your life when you learn a great deal about yourself. Or so I have heard people say. But mostly, I suspect, what is really happening is that you are simply receiving confirmation of what you have already known deep down for a very long time. I suppose it might be just about possible that, if someone with whom I was living were struck down by illness or injury and forced into a wheelchair, I would be able to find a way to cope. But, as much as I believe that it is the connection of minds that really matters – the wavelength thing – and as much as I believed in the strength of my connection with Peggy, I knew that I could never enter into a relationship with anyone, no matter how I felt about them, if they were in a wheelchair. Callous. Unfeeling. Selfish. Even possibly self-defeating. Yes, maybe, all of those things. But, in that instant when I first saw Peggy in the wheelchair, I knew that there was no point in pretending I could ever do or be otherwise. Even before the physio had reached her car, I had turned the Mercury around and was heading back to New York.

*

Happy birthday to me, happy birthday to me, happy fucking fiftieth birthday to me. I spat the words out as I lay on top of my king-sized bed in the Helmsley. Yes, I was bitter. Yes, I felt sorry for myself. And yes, I could see the ironic, self-damning truth that it was me I felt sorry for and not Peggy in her wheelchair. Ironic alright, but I found it hard to raise a smile. I can usually see the funny side of most things but although – being me – I was already, in a dark corner of my mind, punning away – 'I don't know, maybe we could make it work at a push', that kind of thing – I wasn't even amusing myself.

This period, of lying there fully clothed, feeling nothing but bleak despair and self loathing – I hated myself for abandoning her like this, though not enough to reconsider my position – lasted for at least a couple of hours. But it takes a lot to keep a good man down. Or even me. Gradually, I began to swim around the wreckage, and see if there was anything I could salvage.

And naturally, again me being me, or unnaturally you may think, depending on just how low your opinion of me is, my first thoughts were about what other people might think. Nobody at home knew I was here to see Peggy. Hardly anybody there knew she existed and nobody, except Keith Lyons, had any idea I knew where she was. So I could fly back, stick to my Jerry Seinfeld story, apologise profusely to my children but explain that it was work and that it had to be done – and don't we drum into our children from the first, the primacy of work over all things? – and then just carry on as before, perhaps throwing a grand belated fiftieth birthday. (As grand, at least, as my cloth cutting would allow.) Then I would just

329

block the whole thing out, repress it, *compartmentalise*, and rebuild my life. I should say that I wasn't sure that even I could manage the last bit, and that it might be necessary to re-engage Donald McEwan for a bit, cloth cutting or no.

Having sorted that out, I turned at last to Peggy. I hadn't succeeded in meeting her and I didn't think she could have seen me from the door. So she wouldn't know that I'd seen her. Of course, she would realise I had been the mystery visitor, because, after I hadn't returned to Galloping Way, Betty would have eventually told her my name. But I thought I could see how to handle that without either just leaving things hanging or letting her believe that I was wheelchairist. (Yes, that word actually occurred to me, and I had a brief derisory chuckle, so, as you can see, I was already beginning to feel more like my old self.)

I calculated that I could call her and say I was in New York for a business meeting – I had the whole Jerry Seinfeld thing set up and ready to roll, didn't I? – 'yes, Jerry Seinfeld, remember Pound Ridge? what a coincidence' – and that, having some down-time, I'd thought I would run up to New Jersey to surprise her. But, while off to get a coffee when she was with the physio, I'd had an urgent call to go back for a meeting in New York and I had to fly back to London tomorrow. So, sorry to have missed you Peggy, lovely to meet Betty, regards to Myron, have a nice life. There. All over, and no real damage done. Except the shattering of my dream, of course. But right now, that seemed like the least of my problems. I called room-service, ordered a burger and a beer, and turned on the telly. (No, neither 'The Dick Van Dyke Show' nor 'Seinfeld' were on.) I thought I would allow another hour or so for the imaginary meeting with Jerry Seinfeld and his agent to take place, and then I would call.

Which I duly did. And Peggy herself answered. And, after all the only-to-be-expected stuff – 'Amazing that you came all the way to Tinton Falls' and 'You really thought Betty was me!' and 'Why d'you drive off like that? Couldn't you have waited another ten minutes?' – I told her the story exactly as rehearsed. Or almost exactly as rehearsed. Because, not actually being able to see her in the wheelchair, and hearing that marvellous voice that I'd always loved so much, I sort of forgot all about the wheelchair. And, as we spoke, the years fell away just like people say they do, and it seemed like we had both switched straight back on to the old wavelength and were broadcasting and receiving with such unforced ease, that I somehow got a bit carried away, so when she said, "Why don't I come into the city tomorrow? We can have lunch if you're free," I didn't kill the idea there and then by saying I was catching an early flight or had a meeting, but just offered some half-hearted resistance, saying no, I couldn't possibly expect her to do that, but which she brushed aside by saying in a slightly more serious tone, "No, Andy, there is something I have to tell you."

And then I did picture her in the wheelchair, and another appalling thought came into my head, one I just couldn't shake, which was that the wheelchair was the harbinger of something much worse, and that, what she had to tell me was that this was the last time our wavelength would ever be used. That was one thought I just couldn't block out, at least not at such short notice. So I agreed to meet her at one o' clock at a place called Angelica's Kitchen on East 12th St. (After she'd rung off, it occurred to me that it was not a million miles from my old apartment and I had an idea I might have been there once, possibly even with Peggy. I wondered if there was some significance in this. And then I realised it could hardly be less convenient for Penn Central where her train would come in. I couldn't imagine how she would get to Angelica's Kitchen in a wheelchair. Perhaps Betty was coming with her. Or a nurse? I shuddered.)

The rest of my fiftieth birthday was spent in a deep depression. I went alone to a movie, something that rarely decreases one's sense of isolation, and was so distracted I couldn't have told you the name of the film five minutes after I'd come out. All I could think about was that Peggy was in a wheelchair and how I would never have been able to deal with that, but that Peggy would not be in a wheelchair for much longer and the thought of that was even worse.

In the morning, I did what packing I had to do, picked up a couple of phone messages from reception left by the office in London which I didn't bother to read, paid and checked out but left my bag with the bellboy, went to Times Square and bought a couple of 'I love the Big Apple' tee-shirts for Florence and India – not very imaginative, but they'd probably just dump them on the floor and never wear them anyway – and wandered about until the moment could be put off no longer. Then I hailed a cab, and off I went to see Peggy in her wheelchair for what I supposed would be the first and last time. There had been occasions I had looked forward to more.

*

I did recognise Angelica's Kitchen when I got there. It was one of those organic, no known additive places which had seemed pretty flakey in '79 but which was now packed full of rather well heeled, gluten-free types, mainly women of about Peggy's age. I wasn't concerned about finding her in the crowd though, because, even if I hadn't seen her for twenty years, the wheelchair would surely be a dead giveaway. Characteristically, I was a few minutes late, but, though I scoured the whole place I could see no sign of a wheelchair. I couldn't imagine she would have been and gone, so when I saw a couple of people leave, I grabbed a table near the door. At least when she arrived, the nurse wouldn't have to push her far.

I was in the process of ordering an everything-free carrot juice to fill in time when I felt a tap on the shoulder. I looked around from the waitress to find a woman who was either Peggy or her long-lost twin leaning over me. For a moment I thought it really might be a long-lost twin, because she looked remarkably healthy for a woman who had come to tell me she was about to go off air for the last time.

"Sorry I'm late," she said. "This thing" – now I saw she had a crutch – "kinda slows you down."

So, no wheelchair, no nurse, and as far I could see, no Betty. The possibility of an imminent demise may have been greatly exaggerated. But still a crutch. Could I live with a crutch?

"Tennis," she said, pointing to the crutch. "What can you do?" And then she said, "Oh I forgot. You don't play, do you?" and let out a peal of laughter.

It turned out to be a ruptured medial ligament of the left knee, an injury sustained in the Asbury Park Senior Women's Doubles quarter final when she turned too quickly attempting to run back and retrieve a lob – "didn't you like that shot, Andy, ha ha ha?" – and which had required an op and physio and six weeks sitting around in a wheelchair if she listened to the medics. Not that she did. As soon as they were out of sight, so was the wheelchair.

"Actually, I'm pretty nifty with this thing. Can we order? I'm ravenous."

Throughout this explanation I simply nodded along. I couldn't admit to having seen the wheelchair – not without arousing suspicion that my squealing exit in the Mercury wasn't directly connected to it, because one of the disadvantages of knowing someone who can read your mind is that they know exactly how you think. And that, in turn, meant I couldn't express my intense relief that she wasn't wheelchair bound for life – a life that I had convinced myself was shortly to be no more. An enormous weight had been lifted from me, actually two weights – and even the crutch was only temporary – but I had to keep it all to myself. However, this did have the advantage that I did not have to make the difficult segue, at least not outwardly, from grief to relief and back to the message that I had originally come to deliver.

And so, mightily relieved for both her and me, I began to tell her the whole story: how Alison had found the Polaroid, how that had forced all the buried memories to the surface, how my marriage had disintegrated, how I'd lost all interest in my business, how I'd come to see that I simply had to find her, how I'd tracked down Miller Prince, how he'd provided the vital clue, how I'd flown to America for the sole purpose of declaring my undying love and reclaiming my lost past. And, as though it were Exhibit A, the evidence that proved beyond doubt that my case was unanswerable, I pulled out of my pocket, and lay before her, right by her tofu salad which had just been delivered by the waitress, the Polaroid. The Polaroid with the financial calculations of my divorce on the back, the Polaroid of her in the bluey-green dress with the big buttons taken just after Robert Palmer had sung, 'Doctor Doctor, Gotta Bad Case of Lovin' You.'

She looked at it, with, perhaps, not quite the expression I hoped for. What I sought was some sort of confirmation, a slight nod of the heads perhaps, a determined set of the mouth, a message coming from behind the brown black almondy eyes, something that said she understood exactly where I was coming from, and now that I had shown her the way back, she too was in exactly the same place. But what I saw on her face – a little more lined than I remembered, by the way, but still strikingly pretty – was first, confusion and then disbelief and then something disturbingly familiar. Very similar, in fact, to the look that had come over Geoff's face when I had told him about Peggy that day in the BA lounge at Heathrow, when we hadn't been able to take off for Paris – the look that accompanied the words, 'you need to see a fucking shrink'.

She didn't quite say that though. What she said was,

"Andy. Andy – I'm married. I have a husband. A family. A life – here. Do you seriously expect me to give all that up because you suddenly drop out of nowhere after twenty years? Is that what you thought would happen?"

I said nothing. I didn't know what I thought. I hadn't thought that far ahead. I hadn't thought – period.

"Look," she said, and leaned forward and put her hand over mind, the same well-meant but unacceptable gesture of pity that she'd made in the bar the night she finally ended it after the Dr Pepper concert. "Look, I came here to tell you something. You know, I am really pleased to see you, of course, I am, but even if you hadn't told me all this, even if you had just been here on business, and, I don't know, got my address somehow and just dropped in to say hi, I was going to tell you, you just can't do that. Andy, it's too risky."

Now I spoke. Too risky. What did that mean? She picked up the Polaroid and pointed at herself.

"Didn't you ever think, Andy?"

"Think? Think about what?"

"Think about me."

"Think about you? What the fuck do you think I'm doing here?"

"No, look at me. Not now. In the picture. What do you see?"

"I see you. What else is there to see?"

"What else? Betty is what else!"

"What!"

"Look at me. Didn't it ever cross your mind? Didn't you ever notice I was busting out of my clothes? You knew how tiny I was really. I was pregnant Andy. That was what I was going to tell you that weekend we went to see my dad in the show. Remember that weekend? When you told me the story about that – that girl. And then I was going to tell you at the Dr Pepper Concert. Only before I had a chance, you told me you were going back to London. And Andy, I knew then that was it – there was no way I was going to a strange country where I knew no-one to have a baby with a guy – who – who, oh never mind. It was never going to happen. And even if I'd told you, and made you feel so responsible that you'd stayed here, I knew you'd never have been happy. You had this great offer in London – you were so excited about it. If you'd stayed you'd have resented me and oh I don't know. I just knew – know – it would never have worked."

I still hadn't taken it in.

"Betty is my daughter?"

"No. I mean, yes she is, biologically. But, in every other way, she is Myron's daughter, that's what she believes, that's what she's always been told, and she is completely happy with that. Myron has been a wonderful father to her, just like he has to our son."

It was sinking in at last. I started to ask the obvious questions.

"When was it?"

"Well, um, Pound Ridge. Must have been."

"The first night then?"

"I guess,"

"But how?"

"I think even you know that Andy."

"I didn't mean that. I meant I thought you were on the pill."

"Why? Did you ask? Did I tell you?"

What I wanted to say, but didn't, was that this was 1979, pre-Aids, or before anyone had realised the bomb was ticking, and we all thought condoms were history and every girl was on the pill. Anyway, I didn't really have to say it. She'd been there. She knew. What I did say was,

"So if you weren't on the pill, why did you …"

"Because, I don't know, I got careless. Over-confident."

"Confident about what?"

"Confident I wouldn't get pregnant. I – Miller and I – wanted a baby, and I came off the pill. Tried for a year. Nothing. So I just didn't think it would happen I guess."

Weird conflicting emotions here. Jealous that she'd wanted to have a baby with Miller – still jealous after all these years, as the song doesn't quite go. But absurdly, shamefully proud that I'd managed to get her pregnant so quickly when Miller had tried and failed for so long.

Ludicrously, I tried to claim some moral high ground.

"Didn't I have a right to know?"

"I tried to tell you."

"Not hard enough."

"Maybe. I did what I thought was best."

And bit by bit, all the rest of it came out. She'd thought about an abortion, but decided against it. Myron Davis, whom she'd known slightly for some time, was ten years older than she was, a friend of a cousin of hers, and one night – a few weeks after I'd gone back, I think it would have been – she'd seen him at a party, and, for some reason – a wavelength thing? I winced at the thought – she'd told him everything. (I wasn't sure how many months pregnant she must have been, but I suppose, by then, it would have started to seriously show.) He'd been wonderfully understanding she said – and presumably besotted with her – and within a month had asked her to marry him, offering to bring the child up as his own.

I sat there like the dummy I was. Stunned. Empty. Bereft. I had now not only lost the girl of my dreams but also my daughter by the girl of my dreams. What on earth was there to say? Eventually I tried this, even though I knew it would have absolutely no effect.

"I have two daughters, you know. Florence is twelve, thirteen soon, and India – she's nine. Wouldn't Betty like to know them? How old is Betty by the way? Nineteen I suppose."

"Twenty in March. And yes, I'm sure she would. But to know them, she'd have to un-know a lot of other things, and I cannot see that would do her any good. Or Myron. He doesn't deserve that. There's an old saying Andy, What you've never had, you don't miss. She's never had two sisters. She won't miss them."

No, I thought, but from now on – for the rest of my life, I'd miss Betty. And blocking her out was never going to be an option.

The waitress came to remove our plates – both still completely untouched despite Peggy's claim to be ravenous – and I asked for the check. While we waited for it, I aimlessly said, "Nice you called her Betty. I remember Mrs Lipschitz very well."

337

She looked up and for the first time since the tennis jokes, she laughed.

"Not Betty with a 'y'," she said. "Bette with an 'e'."

I frowned. I didn't quite understand and by way of explanation she sang the title of one of Tevye's big numbers.

"Tradition!"

I still didn't catch on, so she said, "Never mind, you'll work it out." And then, as I handed over the money to the cashier, she kissed me on the cheek and said, "Andy, I'm glad we met today, but please don't ever try to get in touch again."

Then she put her crutch under her arm and limped away. I watched her hobble – but not too badly – up 12th Street, and I couldn't help thinking she was right: she was pretty nifty with it.

And she was right about the 'y' and the 'e' thing too. I did work it out. But not until I was half way across the Atlantic. I was reading a book, or trying to, when suddenly it came to me.

'Bette' I thought. With an 'e'. Of course! And then I wondered what the son was called – Sammy?

And then it occurred to me that I had never got around to asking her about the Vivien thing.

Not that it seemed to matter anymore.

Not that anything seemed to matter anymore.

CHAPTER 24

LONDON, 1999

"Fraud," said Geoff, and I saw nothing in his expression to suggest he wasn't deadly serious, "is a serious criminal offence that usually carries a prison sentence."

We were, once again, and, as it turned out, for the penultimate time, in his office. There was Geoff, Vince, Hattie, Frank Connor and another sleek, grey haired bloke in very pricey looking, Prince Charles-ish, lace-up shoes, whom I thought I recognised, but to whose poker face I could not put a name. I had been summoned here the moment I stepped through the doors of BWD after I had hotfooted it in from Heathrow, having just got off the redeye on Tuesday morning. I had decided that the rougher and redder-eyed I looked, the more likely it would be to add some gritty authenticity to the yarn I was about to spin, and, wanting to get my retaliation in first, I had opened my mouth to speak the moment I had sat down on the cappuccino armchair. But Geoff had held up his hand to silence me and then launched into his barrage of accusations.

"Fraud?" I said. "What are you—"

Geoff held up the 'Books Etc' receipt with the squiggly tadpole. Who, I wondered, was the stoolie? The accounts girl or mouthy idiot? Hard to call.

I just stared blankly – a sort of tacit taking the Fifth – and Geoff screwed up the receipt angrily and threw it in his leather covered (and cappuccino coloured) wastebin. Whereupon, Frank Connor dived into the bin, rescued the receipt and then carefully smoothed it out, thereby sending me the unmissable message that this was hard evidence.

"But the dodgy receipt is just count one," Geoff continued, picking up a shiny, plastic covered copy of 'Seinfeld Reborn?', and showing it slowly around the room, as though the others had never seen it, "And is as nothing – nothing – compared to this!"

"Are you on a fucking suicide mission?" put in Vince. "Not only do you take a totally bogus trip on company money but you put it in writing."

"Bogus trip! Wh––" I started, as though some kind of ancient Samurai honour dictated I had to put up a defence, however futile.

"Oh, please give it a fucking rest!" said Vince. "We knew what you were up to by Friday afternoon."

I began to feel myself switching to the usual default position of a cornered rat: belligerency. But – me being me – I mixed in a bit of casual flippancy too.

"Friday afternoon?" I repeated, as off-handedly I could manage.

"Yep" said Vince, "Hattie got on to it the moment you left the meeting. It was obvious that story about that woman at your kid's school knowing Jerry Seinfeld's agent was just bollocks. As it happened Hattie knows the woman herself. Go on Hattie, tell him."

What? I looked at Hattie. I knew she felt, with some justification admittedly, that my recent behaviour may not have had the most felicitous effect on her job prospects, but had I not been the person who'd advanced her career in the first place? Et tu Hattie? Apparently so.

"I called Audrey."

"Audrey?"

"Mrs McIver – the headmistress."

"Yes, thank you Hattie for clarifying who the headmistress of my own daughters' school is."

"There really is no need to take that attitude," said Vince.

"Oh really. What attitude should I take?"

"Well, you could try lying still so they could put the fucking straitjacket on you."

Geoff stepped between us – metaphorically – none of us would have actually risked mussing our hair – metaphorically – and asked Hattie to continue.

"So I asked Audrey if she'd seen you talking to anyone at the junior school show. I speak to her a lot anyway on pog business."

"Pog?"

"Does it matter? Parents and Old Girls Committee, if you must know. Does fundraising for the school. Anyway, she said she'd seen you talking to Margaux Delancey and of course, I know her because—"

"She's on Pog too?"

"Yes, Andrew. As it happens she is. So I asked her what she'd said and well …"

Hattie tailed off in to silence. What else was there for her to say? What else was there for anyone to say?

Quite a bit, actually. Beginning with Vince.

"You might be interested to know that Mick Hudnutt is no longer a client. He went back to his office after the meeting, and called me at lunchtime," (just when I was squiggling the tadpole, I mused), "to say they'd had enough. Didn't help my digestion, I have to say. He said they needed an agency that didn't have a deranged fucking maniac for a creative director!"

"He said that?"

"Words to that effect, Andrew. And then took his seven fucking million quid away!"

Then it was Geoff's turn again. But first he ushered Hattie out of the room. She was not to be allowed to see the actual pulling of the cheesewire around my neck.

"Right" said Geoff, when the door had closed behind her. "This is how it's going to be. You go on sick leave right now—"

"Fuck knows you need it!" put in Vince.

"—that's permanent sick leave, Andrew," said Geoff. "We put out a press release, some bullshit saying we hope you'll be back soon, and Lucille takes over. In a month or two – providing you play the game – we'll have a leaving party for you. Clients, staff, old friends, press, and you get out with your head held high. At least, it looks like that."

"What about my shares in the company? The money you agreed to pay?"

"Yes, I was coming to that. You have to realise we made you that offer before we'd lost a seven million pound account."

The flippancy was now overtaken by panic.

"You're withdrawing it? You can't—"

"Oh I think you'll find we can." Geoff looked at the bloke in the Prince Charles shoes as if he could provide confirmation, and then I remembered where I'd seen him before – at the company solicitors when we'd signed the original partners deal. (The piggy eyed, thin lipped assassin, here to fulfill his destiny.)

"Still we're not complete cunts, Andrew, so we're just going to amend the terms."

Not complete cunts. I wondered what the degree of incompleteness would be.

"And?"

"Well, we'll continue to pay your salary for six months. And you can keep the cars until that stops. And" – crunchtime, I braced myself – "we're still prepared to pay you a million five …" – bloody hell, that's not too bad – "… but for your whole share."

Sounded pretty complete to me.

"What? That's half what you offered before. And I won't have any income after six months."

"You don't have to accept of course."

"And if I don't?"

"Andrew, we're not blackmailing you."

Meaning they were.

"If you want to take legal advice, we quite understand, and you have some time. We won't call in the police until one."

Well, I thought, I'm not going to beg. But I came close.

"Geoff – Vince – look, I accept I have been acting a bit irrationally and maybe I exaggerated the situation slightly, but I really thought I could sort something out—"

"Andrew, please, you're wasting your breath," said Geoff. "Just answer me one question will you? What the hell did you go to New York for?"

Nothing, I thought, I went for nothing. I came back with nothing. Actually, thinking about Bette, I came back with a lot less than nothing. And now I said nothing and left the room.

*

I went up and straight in to my office, brushing aside Julia's attempts to speak to me, and called Harriet Braintree, giving her the news as matter-of-factly as I could. She'd have heard worse I figured, so I was actually quite surprised when she sounded genuinely worried. (Probably worried that I was going to start querying my bill.)

"Goodness Andrew, sounds like you've got yourself in a bit of a pickle there. I'm not a criminal lawyer of course, and you should probably speak to one. I can get you a name if you like."

Well, I thought, in for £450 an hour, in for – so I called the name she'd given me, who confirmed that I was, indeed, in a pickle, a particularly tart and pungent pickle, from which he could see no easy way I could be easily extracted. He didn't even suggest that I go in to see him – which suggested to me that Harriet had already forewarned him that I was on the uppers of my Todts – and I have to say I was grateful for that. My options were clear. I didn't have any.

I tidied my desk and called Julia in. I told her the official story, but in such a way that I made it clear that I was leaving her to pick the bones out of that. She burst into tears. I really hadn't anticipated that, and I felt quite choked myself. But I did the manly thing, stiffened my upper lip, gave her a hug, and told her I'd be fine, and that I'd call her and buy a bloody good lunch very soon. (Cloth cutting permitting, but I didn't mention that.) And then I picked up my case – photos of Florence, India, and yes, of Alison, already having been slid into the side pocket – took the last nostalgic look around that you always do and left the office of the Executive Creative Director of Bradley Dutton Williams forever. As I got into the lift, I heard Julia shouting that she'd forgotten to tell me something but I didn't want to stop. I just wanted to get it all done and dusted as soon as I could.

When I walked back into Geoff's office for the last time, it was no more than thirty minutes after I'd left it. A good two and half hours before my one o' clock deadline – probably earlier than I had ever been for anything in my life – but, judging by the fact that they were all still there, I don't think that the brevity of my deliberations was any great surprise.

I hardly had to say anything. Geoff told me that everything was prepared and that included a confidentiality clause, strict observance of which was required if I wanted to get all my money, three quarters of a million to be paid into my account today, and the rest in six months time, when I ceased being on salary. I was about to make a protest that I wasn't getting it all now, but then I thought that, one way or another, it was all going to Alison anyway, and that Harriet Braintree would probably be able to work something out with her solicitor. (And it turned out I was right.) So I just nodded along with everything Geoff said and then he of the Prince Charles shoes approached the desk and laid before me a series of legal documents, all with little pencil 'x's on them denoting the places I was to sign. A. C. Williams, I wrote, so many times that it began, after the fourth or fifth time – just like when I used to have to sign batches of traveller's cheques – to look less and less like my usual signature and more and more like the weak efforts of a crap fraudster. Which was fair enough, I suppose, since that is what I was. But it didn't seem to matter to them. Then Geoff signed and Vince signed and Frank Connor witnessed everything and the lawyer nodded his sleek grey head and put the documents away in his brief case.

And then an awkward silence. The burial was complete but the corpse was still standing there. In the end, I just said something completely inconsequential like 'Okay then' and turned and walked out of the door. I thought I saw Geoff make the slightest move of his right arm as though he were going to shake my hand but he quickly saw I wasn't going to respond and he stopped himself. I don't suppose it made me look very big, but I was fucked if I was going to give him the satisfaction. Actually, that moment, the almost snub I had managed to inflict on him, rather lifted my spirits. I picked up my case and left the building rather jauntily.

As I climbed into the Porsche there was just one thing that was slightly bothering me. How come they'd never asked me to be on the Pog Committee?

*

I was sitting outside the school again, waiting for Florence and India to come out, not a little worried about how this was going to go. On the plane I'd had everything worked out; I would need my head straight to get everything sorted out at the office, so I would deal with that first, and only afterwards try to square it with the girls. I didn't try to call them when I landed and left my phone off just in case Alison tried to call me. (I knew she'd be fuming, because I hadn't pitched up last night to discuss whatever it was she'd wanted to talk about.)

As things had turned out at BWD, the direction of my head, straight or otherwise, turned out to be entirely beside the point, so I might just as well have called them from the airport. In fact, in all the turmoil of the morning I hadn't given them a thought. It wasn't until I got back to the flat that I turned my mobile phone on to find an endless stream of anxious messages from Julia, angry messages from Geoff, and Vince, even angrier ones from Alison – none of which were unexpected, and none of which I listened to. It was the same with the answering machine on my landline. But on both, there were calls too from Florence and India, and these completely threw me. The initial ones were quite calm, just wanting to know where I was, and asking me to call back, but they got increasingly hysterical and shrill and heartbreakingly tearful. It wasn't that easy to understand what was being said as they got more and more agitated, but after playing them two or three times, I finally got it. And it wasn't good.

It became clear that the reason neither had mentioned my birthday for so long, and the reason Alison had said she wanted to talk to me at the house were not unconnected. The need for this supposed talk had just been a cover for the surprise party that Florence and India – entirely of their own volition as Alison was at pains to tell me later – had been planning for me. They'd arranged for Alison and Doug to go out, had spent the weekend specially decorating the house with 'Happy 50th birthday, Daddy' banners they'd designed and made themselves, baked and decorated a birthday cake for me, and even cooked a special birthday dinner for the three of us, refusing to believe, as Alison also told me, that I wouldn't come back to the house at some point, even though Alison had phoned Julia first thing on Monday morning and had found out then that I was in America. Despite this, Alison told me, she had been unable to convince the girls that I still might not turn up, and so, apparently, she and Doug – noble Doug – had gone through with the charade of pretending to go out, and sat outside in the car, until finally, at about ten, she had gone back into the house and escorted them tearfully to bed. The only good to have come out of this was that Spot had leaped onto the table overnight and wolfed down the entire cake which, as he didn't vomit it back up, she assumed he'd enjoyed, and which she said – and I did not contest the point – had served me bloody well right. Much of this I didn't find out until Alison took me through every excruciating detail, but I got the gist of it from the phone messages and that was bad enough. I think I can safely say I needed no further discussion with Donald McEwan on the subject of the nature of guilt.

I got to the school before three, and that left me with plenty of time to ruminate on what a completely fucking useless excuse for a father I was. Peggy was clearly right. Given how hopeless I was with Florence and India, Bette was obviously a lot better off having nothing to do with me. Karma is one of the many things I do not believe in but there did seem to be a certain cosmic justice at work here in that, on the same day I had treated Florence and India with such casual, thoughtless cruelty, I should discover I had another daughter and then be forbidden all contact with her.

So I sat there in the Porsche – only mine for another six months and counting – beating myself up relentlessly. Every so often my attention would drift away to something else and then suddenly I would be reminded again of the missed party and the banners they'd made and the cake they'd baked and the dinner going cold on the table – I found out later it was scrambled eggs and baked beans, and the poignancy of that just made me feel even worse – and whenever any aspect of it came back to me, I'd get this sudden physical pain like I'd been hit in the solar plexus, and I would let out an audible squeak of anguish. In the end, I became exhausted by it all and I checked my watch. I still had twenty minutes to wait.

Then, for the first of many, many times over years that have passed since, I reviewed my actions at the office that morning, and wondered if I'd done the right thing. And, although I am an

347

inveterate changer of my mind, and have never bought a single thing without thinking, the moment I am out of the store, that I've made a terrible mistake and, as often as not, have rushed straight back in to demand my money back, I decided I'd come to the right decision. And, in the light of what I knew then, about me, about them, about the situation – and even allowing for the fact that, as things turned out, it was almost certainly not everything – I have never come to any other conclusion.

You might think that they were bluffing, that they would never have risked the publicity that bringing me down so publicly would have brought the agency. But they could have got on the phones and explained all to the clients, even though it wouldn't have looked good. I held no particular sway with any of them – Charles Mullins was long since gone – and, alright, Geoff and Vince might have had to promise a few favours but they had a ready to go replacement in Lucille, who was already bedded in – no pun intended – on a lot of the accounts, so they would have probably have got away with it. And, if I had called their bluff, wouldn't it have been a massive gamble which, if I'd been wrong, would have cost me absolutely everything? Anyway, I think my poker playing abilities or lack of them have been pretty well documented here, and despite the gut wrenching news I would get a few weeks later – yes, incredibly, it turned out my gut was still not totally wrenched – I've always believed that I made the right call.

And, as I sat there in the car, thinking about all that, and confirming to myself the wisdom of my decision, I did feel marginally better. For about five seconds, tops. And then I glanced up, and saw the school buildings, inside which were my two daughters whom I had treated so appallingly, and I felt sick to the stomach once again. I was wrong about Geoff and Vince. They might be treacherous bastards. They might be cunts. But complete cunts, no, not any more. Everything is relative. Once they might have scored a perfect ten. But there'll always be someone who comes along and raises the bar. Or, in this particular field of human endeavour, lowers it. The title was now mine.

*

Eventually they emerged from the school, India first, from the gate reserved for juniors, in the midst of a little gaggle of friends. I saw her looking around and then I spotted Anneke, who had come to pick them up as always. I had completely forgotten that she would be there. I got out of the car and, as I walked towards Anneke, India saw me, ran over, launched herself and gave me a totally underserved hug. I told Anneke that I would wait for Florence, and she left, if a little reluctantly, no doubt calling Alison immediately to bring her up to speed.

India seemed hell-bent on hanging on to me, her arms locked tight, her face buried in my midriff. I didn't know what to do except tell her everything was okay and stroke her hair. It didn't seem a very adequate response. I felt both deeply moved and rather conspicuous. Then Florence joined us, but was much chillier, refusing to be kissed and ducking under my arm when I tried to put it round her shoulder. But that might have just been being twelve and not wanting to be embarrassed in front of your schoolmates, so I didn't say anything until we were in the car.

Then I did my best to offer some kind of explanation. I decided not to give them the bullshit about work that I'd rehearsed, not out of any sudden compulsion to be truthful, but because I couldn't be sure Alison would back it up. Besides, it would become rapidly apparent to them that Daddy no longer had any work. I just said I'd had to go and see an old friend – which sounded totally feeble – and that one day I hoped they would understand – but would they? I doubted it – and apologised profusely for messing up their plans – I hoped that bit, at least, sounded convincing – and that I would try to make it up to them somehow – when all else fails, try bribery. I brought out the 'I loved the big apple' tee-shirts which I didn't imagine for a minute would do the trick bribery-wise, but they were all I had to hand for the time being. India made an effort to look pleased about hers but I was getting no change out of Florence. Then I offered them a trip to McDonald's but Florence said she had homework to do, and then I said, maybe I could pop round and see them later, but Florence repeated the homework line. Knowing Florence's usual enthusiasm for homework, this sounded less than convincing. And when India, perhaps sensing from her sister's attitude that she too should be more distant, said she'd just remembered she had a playdate at a friend's, I gave up. I didn't blame them in the least. In a way, I was pleased their forgiveness wasn't to be earned that cheaply. I drove them home and spent the rest of the day and the evening alone. Lying in bed, I reflected that, inconceivable as it seemed, I had now begun my second half century. Not an auspicious start.

*

I awoke in the morning to my new and empty world. Having no job to go to and no milk in the fridge, I went to a greasy spoon – on that last bit of Queensway that runs up to the Porchester Baths – and ordered a bacon sandwich and a mug of tea. I bought 'The Times' and read it from cover to cover. Tony Blair had received a hero's welcome in Kosovo. Chelsea had won 6–1. I had only the vaguest idea where Kosovo was and wasn't a Chelsea supporter but when you have no job to go to, you find yourself taking an interest in whatever is available. Christmas was in the news because it was less than two weeks away, but I tried not to notice that because I didn't have the faintest idea how or where or with whom I was going to spend it. I did however know with whom I wasn't going to be spending it. Alison had called me the night before to give me the expected dressing down and added that Doug had managed to get a late booking over the holiday at a skiing resort in Val d'Isere – our old stomping piste, as I believe I mentioned at the beginning – and that, in the circumstances, she thought I would understand if they took the girls.

It wasn't news I was thrilled to hear, but I accepted it without any more protest than was necessary to make Alison feel at least a little bad. To be alone at Christmas, seemed, I suppose, like a fitting act of penance. Comfort of the hair shirt if you like.

So there I was: no job, no wife, no house, no money, no Bette, no Peggy, and, just to complete the full set, no Christmas either. Oops, no, not quite the full set, not this year. Because this was a special year, a one in thousand years year. But, no worries, I had that last crappy card too. Nowhere to go for millennium eve either.

You may remember that, at the time, the big story was the millennium bug. All that media frenzy about whether, at one second past midnight, some sort of universal computer glitch would cause jets to fall out of the sky and the world as we knew it to end.

Personally, I was rather looking forward to it.

PART THREE

CHAPTER 25

LITTLE VENICE, 2015

When I came back to England, I reverted to my old habit of repressing challenging memories – or blithely ignoring them – however you like to view it. Too painful to remember or too easy to forget, you pays your money and you takes your choice. There were also my money worries and they inevitably swamped whatever else was going on in my head. Occasionally, listening to some golden oldie radio station, I would hear the Kim Carnes track, 'Bette Davis Eyes', which had never previously had any particular significance for me, but which, now, unavoidably put me in mind of my never to be known daughter, and those almondy eyes that she had inherited. But, after a while, the great gift of compartmentalisation came to my aid once again, and I shoved the whole sorry business into a drawer somewhere in the back of my mind.

I still have the Polaroid of Peggy, and that's in a drawer too, a real one, in a desk in my flat in Little Venice. And if there were a fire in my flat, it would be one of the few things that I would be seriously concerned about saving. You might think that odd after all the trouble it caused me, but all I can say is that it's stuck with me for all these years and I am sticking with it. Of course, I am sincerely hoping there won't be a fire. It's a very comfortable, well proportioned, three-bedroomed flat in quite an expensive part of town, so you'll have worked out that, after the nadir of ninety-nine, I managed to stage some kind of recovery.

When you find yourself in such dire straits as I was in, what you must do is revert to the eternal verities of life. Such as the E to P scale. This might surprise you. It might seem like the wrong sort of instrument to be using when you are down on your luck. But one of the beauties of the E to P scale is that it is a scale of relative values. Providing you can find someone who is worse off than you, you will soon begin to feel a whole lot better.

And if you continue to have doubts about the E to P scale, please consider the name by which it is more commonly known: counting your blessings. Same thing basically, just presented in different ways. Funny, isn't it? One seems like the height of folly, a complete misreading of what really counts in life, and the other is regarded as ancient wisdom. To quote from the hymn:

Count your many blessings, name them one by one,
And it will surprise you what the Lord hath done.

And were you to argue that Ira D. Sankey, who wrote it, wasn't talking about material things, I'd say, well, wouldn't a roof over your head and a full belly count amongst his sort of blessings, and what are they, if not material things? You see: material things do matter, up to a point, even to those who believe in the 'Lord'. It's just a question of which point. One of the things you learn as you get older is that few things in life are as simple as they seem. Life is untidy. Simple answers are for the very young or the very stupid. (And sometimes I am tempted to think that these days we have far too many of both.)

So: you tot up your score on the E to P scale, and if all you've lost are the kinds of things I'd lost, and you still have the air to breathe and a Porsche to drive, even if it is only for another five months and twenty-nine days, you can always manage to find someone who's worse off than you, and as I say, that alone will give you the most tremendous fillip.

So, eventually, after a lengthy spell of wallowing in self-pity, its attractions began to pall and I took the first tentative steps towards re-entering the world of the living. I picked my chin off the floor, pulled myself up by my bootstraps, told myself that what doesn't kill you makes you stronger, walked through the door that opens when the other one shuts and I went to see a few headhunters. Despite my summary ejection from BWD, I still had a name and a reputation in the industry and, as a result, I had an enthusiastic reception from most of them. And likewise from the people they sent me to see. By early March of the new millennium, I was appointed European Creative Director for a huge international agency and I took to it as to the manner born. I stayed with them for ten years, in a series of ever more senior jobs, until I retired in 2010. Being an executive in a big organisation doesn't allow you the freedom that you have when you're running your own place, but neither does it carry the same ultimate responsibility – the buck doesn't stop with you. In fact, in all honesty, it's less about the buck stopping than buck passing and I soon became very adept at it. I flitted from London to Paris and Berlin to Rome, Stockholm to Madrid, Amsterdam to Prague, and I was always on hand when the bouquets were being handed out and always somewhere else when the brickbats were flying. And every year, when June came around, I would be in Cannes, swanning up the Croisette, supping at the tables of whoever was prepared to pay. (Lest I should appear too much the sybarite, may I also add that I had not completely lost my touch creatively and still managed to have the odd idea that picked up a gong here and there.)

But, as easily as I fitted into this new corporate business-class life, it did nothing to soften the blows inflicted by a couple of events that took place within the first few months of 2000. The leaving party mooted by Geoff on the day they kicked me out did take place but not quite as planned. It was decided it should also serve as the official coronation of Lucille Wood – a passing of the baton kind of thing. I was slightly miffed that I was not to be the

356

sole centre of attention, although I could see that it made a sort of sense and went along with it. But a couple of months later, I saw, in the Media Section of the 'Guardian', a big picture of Lucille – looking as luscious as ever – and a long piece about her. A couple of paragraphs in, I read that BWD would no longer be Bradley Williams Dutton but Bradley Wood Dutton, and I found that pretty hard to take. What's in a name? Sometimes, enough to make you go ouch every time you see it.

And then, within a couple of weeks of that, came the event that, as I mentioned earlier, proved that my gut had not yet reached the limit of its capacity to be wrenched. BWD was taken over. Our old employers, McConnell Martin, whose London operation had gradually grown less competitive as BWD had grown stronger, had decided to forget and forgive and pay the price of folding their operation into ours. (Idiotically, I never stopped thinking of it as 'ours'.)

Hattie du Vivier, whom I happened to see at a school fundraiser, and against whom I bore no grudge, not least because I realised, in my bachelor state, that she was really rather attractive, filled me in on the details over a little supper I invited her to. I have to say I bloody nearly choked on my chablis when she told me that it was strongly rumoured that they would be paid £30 million. That would have made my share – the share they paid me one and a half for – worth nine! I naturally took some legal advice as soon as I heard this, but was told the contracts I'd signed were watertight and there was no way I had any feasible retrospective claim. Did they have wind of this before they screwed me? I thought back to the folded piece of paper that Maxine had handed to Vince in Twain on 'Seinfeld Reborn?' day, and my straining to read the message as he opened it. I'd thought it said 'try-out' but now I wondered if 'try' had been more 'sounds like' than the word itself. Still, it made no difference. I just had to suck it up. Treacherous bastards.

You might be interested to know what happened to the treacherous bastards. As part of the deal they both had a five-year earn-out arrangement, meaning they had to stay with BWD for five years – or BWD-MM as it became. After that, Geoff, by then on his fourth wife, bought a vineyard somewhere in France and never worked in advertising again. Likewise Vince, who went back to Oz, and bought some enormous spread on the Hawkesbury river. Sadly I have yet to hear news of him drowning in it. Lucille Wood meanwhile climbed ever higher and last year became the Chief Creative Officer Worldwide of McConnell Martin, the CCOW, the seacow, the new Manatee, sitting, perhaps, in the very same office as Todd Zwiebel once had.

And the others? Julia got married and had twins, Frank Connor dropped dead at his desk, and, according to an edition of 'Campaign' that I recently saw on the shelf of my local newsagents, mouthy idiot now has my old job, Executive Creative Director of BWD-MM London. Hattie du Vivier left but she still works in the business. She's in her early forties now, still single, and still rather attractive. I know all this and a lot more about her, because we became good friends for a number of years, and occasionally more than good friends. I think she might have wanted to put our relationship on a firmer footing despite our twenty-yearsish age difference, but – unfairly perhaps, because I would never quite cut her loose – I have resisted anything more than a fairly informal arrangement. Our dalliance/affair/association, call it what you will, is still, in fact, not quite history, but I'll come back to that in a while.

My relationship with Florence and India wasn't too bad at the beginning, but then seemed to weaken. Alison married Doug and the girls were based with them and, as I travelled more and more, the 'every other weekend' the divorce papers mandated that we spend together, became not so much every other as most other and then some other and so on. But then, after a couple of years, Alison and Doug had a baby – before she got too old I suppose – and, naturally, that changed the family dynamics. Then I found the girls wanted to spend a lot more time with me, and to avoid the place being completely overpowered by the reeking of dope – or 'blow' as I gathered it was now popularly called – I cut back on my overseas trips and spent more time with them. We've had our issues over the years, but nowadays I like to think we're pretty close. Florence is twenty-four and a junior creative in an agency, a career move that was nothing – well, almost nothing – to do with me, and, judging by the number of blokes who seem to be competing for her attention, I'm not the only one who would tell you how beautiful she has become. India is at drama school – Golde turned out to be the beginning of something – and, to my jaundiced eye, is a racing certainty to be the next big thing. She's very striking but in a completely different way to Florence. Whenever I am out with either of them, my chest puffs up with preposterous paternal pride.

Alison and Doug are still together and living with their ten-year-old son, Finn, in the house formerly known as New Pemberley. The other day I was wandering around Westbourne Park, and pressing my nose against estate agents' windows, as one does, and I saw a house identical to ours – theirs! – on sale for six million quid. Didn't Dougal-call-me-Doug do well? I bump into them occasionally and look at Alison, now the stranger that an ex always becomes, and wonder how it was that once, all those years ago, one of us would happily stand casually cleaning our teeth while the other took a pee. It seems inconceivable and at the same time so terribly sad that it all goes to waste. (And I'm not trying to make a smutty lavatorial pun.)

I have not a clue – why should I? – what happened to Keith Lyons. And judging by his skills as a detective, I'm not at all sure he would have either. Donald McEwan, with whom I was to enjoy several more bouts of jousting over the years, died in 2006. I felt the loss of a friend as acutely as I have ever done, and have never seen another shrink. And Harriet Braintree made quite a splash in the papers, when she threw over her practice and went to live on some Caribbean idyll with the superannuated pop star.

As for the American end of things, I'd known about Brett's progress since the mid-eighties. While a commercial he'd been working on was in production, he had, for some reason, caught the eye of the director, who asked him if he had, himself, ever thought of directing. It was odd because I'd never heard Brett say that was what he wanted to do and it had never occurred to me that he would have any particular aptitude for it, but the moment you heard that story, you thought, yes, of course, he's made for it. And he was. After a period of being carefully 'trained on', he moved to LA and within a few years – perhaps because he was a whole landmass away from Bart and the bong – became hugely successful. I ran in to him in Cannes one year and he bought me a very nice dinner. He told me then that Christo had died of Aids in the early nineties, and that Noreen and Bart had got married, and lived somewhere in Connecticut with their three kids.

I have no idea whether Todd Zwiebel or Nick Moreno are dead or alive. After we started BWD, I never heard of either of them again. And neither do I know anything about Laverne, I'm afraid. About three years ago, just before I retired, I went to the West Coast for an international conference, and while I was there I hired a car and moseyed around Santa Monica to see if I could find Miller Prince and his soupery. I found a couple of places which seemed likely, but saw no-one who I thought might be him, so I spoke to the manager of each, and asked if they knew his name. I felt as though Miller had been such a big part of my life and yet I had never met him. But I had no luck. Perhaps there'll be a late flowering of his acting career and I will see his name in some American police series or something like that. And I sometimes idly wonder what happened to the girl with the spiky green hair. Grey haired now certainly – under whatever she puts on it – and spikeless, probably a respectable hausefrau who wears one of those little tweedy hats with a feather and lives in Hamburg or Düsseldorf or Mönchengladbach. (Or is that just half the name of a football team?)

I can tell you a little about Dan and Grace Gardner. I was in Hatchards in Piccadilly only a few months ago, in the travel section, looking for guidebooks for Venice, to which Hattie and I were going for a long weekend in October. (The morning and evening light in Venice in the autumn, Hattie told me – as somebody had told her – was not to be missed, and that seemed as good an excuse as any for going there.) Anyway, my attention drifted away from Venice and Italy and there, amongst the American section, I saw a new edition of Karen Brown's 'Country Inns of the Tri-state Area'. Naturally, I felt the need for a thumb through, and, with a little nostalgic quickening of the pulse, found the Gardner Inn. It was Charlie Gardner who was now responsible for the legendary Bloody Mary's – was he the kid who took our bags up? – but apparently, Grace and Dan, though no longer in the frontline, still kept a weather eye on the place.

And that I think, covers more or less everyone. With one or two notable exceptions.

CHAPTER 26

VENICE, 2015

A couple of weeks before Hattie and I were due to leave for our weekend in Venice, I was walking around Soho, and, in the window of a shop in Newburgh Street, whose customers, I think I can safely say, were usually somewhat younger, I saw a tee-shirt that took my fancy. It was white with the word 'Tourist' printed on it in red, in an elegant sans serif typeface, and below that, in blue, it said 'Touriste', and then below that in another colour it said 'Turista', and below that it said tourist – or what I presumed was tourist – in Japanese, and then in Arabic and so on and so forth. Rather witty and neatly done I thought. Old habits die hard, and I still have an eye, or like to think I do, for an amusing bit of clobber.

I was sporting my new purchase as I sat in an armchair in the reception area of the Hotel la Isole, a smart but not eye-wateringly expensive little boutique hotel in the Campo San Provolo. (At least, not as eye-watering as some in Venice.) I was browsing the international copy of 'The Times' but actually thinking more about how I was going to spend the day. I had just breakfasted alone and was expecting to stay that way as the demands of a sudden influx of work had forced Hattie to cry off at the last minute, and, rather than waste the ticket, I had thought, what the hell, you're big enough and ugly enough – and certainly old enough – why not go on your own?

So there I sat, gazing distractedly at the paper, when I heard someone say, "Nice tee-shirt."

Of course, I knew the voice instantly and yes, my heart leaped. I looked up to find a sixty-or-so-year-old version of Peggy smiling down at me, her black hair shorter, streaked with a little grey – or more probably her grey hair streaked with not that much black, but so what, it looked fine – a few lines, but not that many, around the corners of her mouth and eyes, a silk scarf tied around her throat as women of a certain age seem to think they need. But those were just about all the signs there were of the years that had passed, and, all in all, she still looked pretty wonderful to me.

"What are you doing here?" I said, as you would.

"What are *you* doing here?" she replied, as she would be bound to do. We were like two dancers at an assembly ball, about to do a minuet, making the little bow and curtsey before the music starts. And off we went.

It turned out that Peggy was on a ten-day tour of Italy – Rome, Florence, the Lakes, Venice, the usual – with a group of a half a dozen women friends of the same sort of age.

"Your husband doesn't mind you being away for so long?" I asked, perhaps a tad mischievously, without quite realising what I was fishing for.

She looked at me, slightly sideways. As ever, she had seen right through me.

"Myron's dead. A couple of years ago. Heart attack." Not without feeling but short and to the point. As much as she needed to say. Very Peggy.

"I'm sorry," I'm said, not meaning it. I bore Myron Davis no ill-will – apart from the fact that he'd married the woman I loved and brought up my daughter as his own – but although I wouldn't have wished him dead, I wouldn't have been me – or, I venture to suggest, most other people – if I hadn't immediately considered the possibility that his being out of the way might present a promising opportunity. I asked Peggy if she had time for a cup of coffee. She thought for a moment, asked me to hold on, then went over to some women standing talking to the concierge – all of whom looked, quizzically, in my direction, as if saying, 'what, the guy in the unsuitably youthful tee-shirt?' – before she returned to say that yes, she'd be happy to join me. We wandered over a bridge or two, until we found a place just off St Mark's Square.

While slowly sipping the most expensive Cafe Americanos since the last ones I'd bought in Venice, we ran through the last dozen or so years. You first, she insisted, and she winced in all the right places as I told her about the BWD catastrophe and my divorce and impoverishment – I neglected to mention the part that she'd unwittingly played – and she nodded admiringly when I reached the phoenix from the ashes coda. Then it was her turn.

"Peggy," I said, "before you tell me all the rest, and I know how you feel about – you know, about my – er – my part in all this, how's Bette?"

Rather deliberately, she put down the spoon with which she'd been idly stirring the dregs of her coffee, and looked at me carefully, slightly squinting in the sunlight.

"Bette's fine," she said. "She's married."

"Is she?" I said, not quite knowing what to think about it, but having a vague idea that her wedding was something else I'd missed out on. "How long?"

"Oh," she said, "three years – three years last November."

So Myron was there to walk her down the aisle. Or stand by her in the chuppah. Whatever they did. I was pleased and sorry at the same time.

"And they're fine? Bette and …"

"Bette and David. They're fine."

"Good, that's good."

"They, er, they have a little girl."

I gulped, figuratively at least. So now, not only did I

have a daughter with whom I could have no contact, but a granddaughter too.

"Why did you tell me that, Peggy?"

"I don't know. You asked about her. It was dumb. Sorry."

"No, no, I'm glad you told me. Do you have a picture?"

"Are you sure you want to see?"

Yes. No.

"Yes."

She dug about in her bag and brought out an iPhone. A few seconds later, and a little girl of about eighteen months, with lots of dark wavy curls, was presented to me. I looked for signs of any Williams in her. Did she have my chin? If she did, she would never know.

"She's lovely," I said. "What's her name?"

"Catori."

"Catori?"

"Yup. It's Native American. Hopi. It means 'spirit' they tell me."

"He's – I mean David, he's, er …?"

"Not unless the Shapiros are a long lost Native American tribe, no."

"Hm. Well, it's traditional," I said.

"Right. Just someone else's tradition," she said, anticipating me exactly. Wavelength still fully functional.

She put the phone back in her bag, and then, when I had her attention again, I said, "You haven't mentioned anything to Bette I suppose about, er …"

"No, Andy."

"And you still don't think she ought—"

"No, Andy."

"Okay. Okay." I exhaled slowly, as though somehow that would draw a line under the matter. But it didn't, never has, and, for all my blocking-out, never will. "Shall we go for a walk?"

And, Peggy, keen to get off the subject no doubt, agreed. So we paid and we strolled through Venice and the battalions of tourists in every square, around every corner.

"What language do they speak here?" Peggy asked.

"Mainly Japanese. Some Mandarin."

"No Italian?"

"You still think you're back in New Jersey," I said.

"It's Joysey," she said, "and you've been watching 'The Sopranos' too much."

And that's how it went. The same old banter. Not, I am suggesting, Groucho Marx meets Mae West. But an easy joshing. An effortless sallying back and forth. We could still, after an absence of thirty-five years – bar one organic lunch – carry on like we'd never been apart. We could – it felt to me – still be an 'us'.

And you know what happened next. Well, of course – we were in Venice, weren't we? We climbed across a little bridge, looked down and saw a gondola. I cocked my head in its direction, raised my eyebrows and opened my palms towards her in the little gesture that says 'what do you think?' and she raised her eyebrows, and gave the little shrug that says 'why not?' So in we climbed – me gripping her hand as she stepped over the side and, did I imagine it or was that her hand giving me a reciprocal squeeze back? – and the gondolier gondolled away and we lay back and floated down the little side canals and into the sun spangled Grand Canal and past all the astonishing palazzos and goggled at the dome of the Basilica di Santa Maria della Salute (I had no idea it was called that until I checked later) and floated under the Rialto Bridge and the Bridge of Sighs and anyone who tells you that Venice is not a total mindfuck has no left side of the brain and almost certainly no right side either. And then, when the gondolier indicated we had reached the end of our time, Peggy and I looked towards each other and made more shrugs of agreement, and I waved the gondolier on, and off we went again. And afterwards we went to a little restaurant in a little square which I couldn't find again in a million years and Peggy pulled out her iPhone and texted

366

her friends and we had some kind of pasta and some kind of vino and we stayed half of the rest of the afternoon. And then we got lost about twelve times trying to get back towards St Mark's Square and then eventually joined a queue and went inside and did the tour of the Doge's Palace and marvelled at all the glorious paintings which all seemed to be on the ceilings and none on the walls.

"These people must have had permanently cricked necks," I said.

"It says here," said Peggy, looking at the guidebook, "that, at the height of Venetian power, it took six weeks to get an appointment with a chiropractor."

And then, around seven, we'd had enough of sight-seeing, and we wandered back to the hotel, and, as we went, Peggy put her arm in mine.

Context is everything, and if romance is in the air anywhere, it's in Venice and that certainly can't have done any harm. But I think it was more than that. We were on neutral territory, neither in London or New York, neither of us in a relationship and unconstricted as we never had been before, not even in Pound Ridge. We were in a space uncrowded by anyone we knew – except of course, for Peggy's holiday pals. And, as we walked into my room, I wondered if she wasn't a little concerned about what they might say. As ever, she read my mind, and said in a version of the old line that Vince once gave to me in Cannes,

"What happens in Venice stays in Venice."

*

And that is where it's going to stay. If I wasn't prepared to give away the secrets of the boudoir when we weren't yet thirty, I am certainly not going to describe the goings-on of two people past sixty. All I will say is there was still an 'us'. No doubt you're grateful you've been spared any further details.

In the morning, I managed to persuade the nice chap in

reception to send some coffee and rolls to my room and we had breakfast by the window overlooking a pretty little tributary canal. As we sat in our hotel dressing gowns – one of which, I suppose, would have been worn by Hattie – I asked Peggy, as delicately as I could, about Herb and Barbara. Herb, she told me, had died before I had been back to see her in '99 but Barbara, I was pleased to learn, was still going relatively strong and living in a retirement community in Boca Raton. And then she said, "They changed the name, you know."

"What name?"

"Lee's Eyeglasses."

"Really. What to?"

"A Better Look."

"Are you serious? I thought Herb didn't like it."

"It was my Grandmother. She was the only person he ever listened to. She told him he'd always been a lousy judge of names, and 'A Better Look' was terrific."

I was absolutely chuffed. Good old Betty Lipschitz. No DADA Silver Pencil nor Cannes Golden Lion ever gave me more pleasure. And now that we were back onto names, I told Peggy how I had eventually twigged the significance of Bette.

"Actually, I'm a bit surprised you did it," I said, gradually approaching the topic I really wanted to discuss. "You know, naming your own child after someone famous when—"

"Look, it made Herb happy and by then he was already getting sick. Anyway, I thought it was kind of neat to keep the idea going, and none of Bette's friends would ever know about the other one. Too long ago. And I liked the name, Bette. So why not? 'Course, then the song came out, but that made it kind of cool."

"It was just that, well," I said, carefully tiptoeing towards the point, "knowing how sensitive you always were about your name …"

That sideways look again.

"Yes?"

"Peggy, will you just explain to me what the big deal was about telling me your real name was Vivien?"

"Okay, if you really want to know, there were two big deals," she said. "In the first place, or no, because really it's in the second place, it was because you just wouldn't shut up about it. In the end you could have water-boarded me and I still wouldn't have told you."

"Thought it was something like that. But Miller said you were the same with him."

"Well, maybe I was. Because – in the first place – I always hated the name. Simple as that. Viv-ee-en. Stupid broom up-the-ass English name. Nobody in America – nobody I knew – was called Vivien. Now I think it's just a name, who cares? But when I was a kid I was completely phobic about it. I used to dread other kids finding out. You have no idea."

But of course I did. If there was one person in the world who could understand exactly how she'd felt it was me. And then, I was overcome by a need to confess. If my relationship with Peggy was to mean anything at all, then I could not, in all conscience, have extracted that truth from her, without trading mine. I was about to tell her what no living human apart from me knew.

"Peggy" I said, taking her hand in mine. "There's something I have to tell you."

"You really don't," she said. "Tell me if you want to, not because you have to."

Did I want to tell her? No I did not. But there was no going back.

"No, I do have to tell you."

"Honestly, you don't," she said.

"Peggy, my real first name – no, not my real name, because I changed it legally – but the name I was given at birth was – Cyril."

She looked at me in such a way that, for a moment, I thought she was going to burst out laughing. But instead she went very serious and said, "Which only goes to prove ..."

"What?"

"Love is never having to say you're Cyril."

It was then that she burst out laughing.

*

It was midday, or just before, and I was standing outside the hotel. There was a little gang of porters ready to schlep all the luggage belonging to Peggy and her friends – they had not travelled light – down to the dock at San Zaccaria where they would get the 'vaporetto', the boat that would take them to the railway station, from where they would begin the next leg of their tour. Meanwhile, they were still combing their bills at reception before checking out. The serenity I had been feeling was now tipping into sadness. The last thing Peggy had told me before she left my room – and, try as I might, I could not change her mind – was that this weekend must be treated as a one-off, that we should leave it there. She was terrified, she said, that if we were to stay in contact, sooner or later, one way or another, Bette would find out the truth, and that, she was as convinced as ever, would lead to more trouble than it could ever be worth. Better, she insisted, that we go out on a high note than risk disaster.

With checking out finally finished, these half dozen or so sixtyish American women trooped out of the hotel, none, apart from Peggy, having spoken a word to me, and so not quite knowing whether to acknowledge me or not. Peggy was last, and, as she reached me, she stopped, pushed back her bag on her shoulder so her arms would be free, and then threw them around my neck. And she said, "There are some things that are more important, but please always remember this Andy: You're a complete asshole but I totally like you."

And then she turned around, and giving me a little finger wave over her shoulder, walked off with her friends, in pursuit of the porters. I watched them disappear around a corner, and stayed, staring disconsolately after them, though Peggy was gone and dozens of other tourists were already milling about in the space where'd she been.

As I was about to go back in, the nice chap from reception came rushing out shouting, "Signora Davis, Signora Davis." He was clutching Peggy's silk scarf which she must have left on the desk. As he realised they'd gone, he threw up his arms, turned to me, held out the scarf, and said, "You will be seeing Signora Davis, yes?"

"No," I said, but then thought better of it. "Yes, I'll take it to her."

I took off after her and ran towards San Zaccaria – I hoped. It was only two hundred metres away, but that can be a long way in Venice if you take the wrong turning. Luckily, for once, my nose was a reliable guide, and I saw her just as she was about to board the vaporetto. I shouted and waved the scarf above my head, and, spotting me and the errand I was on, she stopped and walked back a few paces towards me.

"Didn't I just tell you we shouldn't see each other again?" she said, grinning, taking the scarf and thanking me. And then she leaned forward and whispered in my ear, "Seriously, Andy, don't phone me, don't text me. And please, please don't try to find me on Facebook. But," – and here she paused and sighed, as though she were thinking twice about saying something, before going ahead – "if you want, send me an e-mail."

She took a couple of paces back towards the boat, before I halted her again.

"Where to?" I called.

"Theotherpeggylee@gmail.com. One word."

It was more than half a lifetime later but her casual, over the shoulder, delivery reminded me exactly of the way she'd called out 'casting' the day I met her in the elevator. And then I watched her climb aboard the Vaporetto, and a few minutes later, it sailed up the canal.

What caused the change of mind? Had she regretted what she'd said as soon as she walked off with her friends? Had seeing me again, when she hadn't been expecting to, suddenly seemed like a second chance? Did the waving of the scarf above my head seem like some kind of symbolic signal?

None of that went through my mind, as I skipped back to the hotel. No, not literally. Not dignified at my age. But in my head, yes, I skipped.

*

I have e-mailed Peggy and she has e-mailed back and I e-mailed back again and she back to me and it's been going on for a couple of months now, and the last time I even wondered if we might not, at some as yet undetermined point in the future, meet for a few days holiday on a remote little island in the Caribbean or some other place where we might not be seen. In her reply she didn't say yes, let's do it, but neither did she reject the idea out of hand, so you never know. That's another thing you learn as you get older. You just never know.

And that is the story of Peggy Lee and Andy Williams who begat Bette Davis.

CHAPTER 27

(THIS IS REALLY AN EPILOGUE BUT IF I CALLED IT AN EPILOGUE NO-ONE WOULD READ IT.)

When I got back to England, I called Hattie and took her to lunch with every intention of finishing it. But – me being me – I didn't. My weekend with Peggy had sent me the message in screaming dayglo colours that a weekend with Hattie would have been a sad and empty affair by comparison, but once a blocker-out always a blocker-out, and why spend a lonely Sunday when you don't have to? I may not be doing the noble thing but neither am I the married man who keeps his lover dangling on a string by always promising he is about to leave his wife. I have made no promises to Hattie – in fact, I've been quite frank that I want no more than we have already. But, on the other, less conscionable, hand, neither have I mentioned anything about Peggy.

A few months ago, completely out of the blue, I got an e-mail – how he found me I still can't quite work out – from the secretary of the Old Boys Association of my old school. He wrote to tell me they were having their centenary lunch and would I like to go? Tickets were £15 and, for that, I would enjoy a three course buffet lunch (vegetarian option available) with white or red wine, menu enclosed. There would be an address by a former junior minister in a government long since voted out but who was about the most famous old boy the school had ever had. There was a postal address at the bottom of the e-mail to which I could send my fifteen quid, should I wish to accept his invitation. On a whim, I decided that I did wish and sent my money in.

Last week, I went. I chose my wardrobe very carefully, not because I wanted to stand out, but because, now the opportunity really had arrived to show my teenage peers what's what and who's who, I'd decided that might not be a very good idea at all. Yes, I was curious to see who might be there and how their lives had turned out, and no, I probably wouldn't have gone if I'd just done a ten-year stretch for armed robbery, but really, I just wanted to go along, and, in so far as I could, to fit in. I wore a suit, lightish weight wool, a plain navy blue, three button, single breasted, elegantly cut, neatly pressed, white button-down linen shirt, red silk tie, polka-dotted white, black penny loafers. As I looked in the lift mirror on my way out of the converted Regency building from which my flat has been carved, I thought I had done the trick. Thoughtfully turned out – I was always going to be that – but, for me, pretty low key. And I didn't take the Porsche and park it where it couldn't be missed. I no longer have a Porsche, I drive a three-year-old Audi convertible these days, but I didn't take that either. Today I would be everyman and take the train.

I walked into the school hall, a place I hadn't been for well over forty-five years. It still had a familiar smell. Not having a perfumer's nose I couldn't have picked out the ingredients, but at a guess I'd have gone for a distillation of disinfectant and beeswax with a top-note of body odour. As unremarkable in this respect, as the school had been in most. I was offered a name badge. It said 'C.A. Williams'. Someone must have been ferreting about in ancient school archives. I stuck it in my pocket. I hate name badges even when they don't contain a reference to the dreaded C-word. Horrible, nasty plasticky things that ruin the line of a good jacket. People were standing around in clusters, quite a few of them remarkably elderly. I felt quite buoyed up by my relative youth, but I also noticed that I was about the only person under the age of ninety wearing a tie. I'd tried, but fitting in never was my forte.

I found my name on a board and from there, the table at which I was to sit. A few people were already nervously in place, eyes flitting around in the hope of seeing someone they might recognise. None of them seemed to know me. Then I felt a tap on my shoulder and I watched as an enormously fat bloke lowered himself into the chair next me. He smiled half-heartedly and grunted. His name badge said S. Wilkinson. *This* was Stephen Wilkinson, left half for South of England Grammar Schools? I looked closer but saw nothing I recognised. I assumed his Adam's apple was hidden behind the multiplicity of chins.

Naturally – this, presumably, was the purpose of a reunion – we talked. I asked him what he did. Retired, he told me. Laid off a few years ago when the company he'd worked for had gone tits up. Never managed to find another job – now he was sixty-five, he just said he was retired. I was about to make a complete idiot of myself by remarking what a coincidence that was, my also being sixty-five, but, fortunately, a voice from a distant mic insisted we stand for grace.

Over my coronation chicken, I idly asked Steve, as he insisted on being called – predictable yet odd as I had never addressed him as anything but Wilkinson at school – what line of business his old company had been in.

"Cameras and copiers," he said, "used to work for Polaroid. In Welwyn – Herts – like I say, until they went bust."

So, of course, I went off into raptures about Polaroid and the SX70 in particular. Steve looked at me, bemused – I don't think he lived in a world where people went into raptures about anything. When I paused for breath he said, "We had this advert once. It said, 'The Polaroid Generation'. Had a picture of a young bloke with long hair – like we used to have." He stopped, looked at my smooth, bald head and seemed about to make some sort of remark but must have changed his mind because he just carried on where he'd left off. "And a pretty girl – sort of Marianne Faithfull type. This couple, they were about the age I was – we were – at the time. And I've always thought, that was us, the Polaroid Generation. Did you know, at one point, we had eight hundred and fifty people working for Polaroid UK alone? It was the latest thing then, remember? And then, along come all the PCs and digital and what have you, and nobody wants to know. SX70? Bloody museum piece now. Just like us – yeah, that's us, the Polaroid Generation."

I mumbled something about him having a point, and depressingly, I rather thought that he had. Then he said, "Here, you were in advertising weren't you? I saw you once on Kilroy or something. I said to Jane, my wife, I know that bloke. I went to school with him. You had some wacky green suit on."

I remembered the show. And the suit. It was sea-green, slightly turquoise perhaps, very smart. Another Ozwald Boateng. But I didn't think it would mean much to Steve, so I said nothing.

"You always were a flash bastard," he said, and laughed. And, eyeing my dress-down, navy three-button, added, "Still are by the looks of it."

To be honest, although this really wasn't what I'd come for – although, if it wasn't for this, what had I come for? – I was actually quite flattered. Despite my lack of Porsche, I couldn't help feeling this was working out quite well E to P wise.

"Always knew you'd end up doing something like that," Steve said.

"Did you?" I replied, genuinely surprised, because I'd never had a clue what I was going to do.

"Oh yes," said Steve, leaning back, his plate now wiped Fairy clean. "Well, you always were a right clever dick weren't you. And that's what clever dicks do, isn't it? Advertising."

*

Once again, Steve had been right on the money. Because that *is* what we do. And I would be a liar if I said I feel any shame in being either a clever dick or an adman. (Despite being retired and out of the game, I am, still, an adman to my bones.) You see, I really do think admen are genuinely and, in a way, admirably, clever, and, to try to avoid being accused of sexism, may I add here that women – Lucille Wood, for one – can be admen too.

Think about it. You go to a film or a play or watch some telly drama and you know it's all pure fiction and that they're just actors but, if it's any good, you buy into it. It's the willing suspension of disbelief thing, isn't it? But, at least, it's a fair trade. In exchange for the suspension of your disbelief they are giving you laughter or tears and a story. But advertising is pure subterfuge. We're not showing you a funny commercial for the sake of making you laugh – we're trying to get you to part with your money, something most sane people are naturally disinclined to do. And yet still, if it's done well enough, if we wrap it up in a story that's funny or charming or dramatic enough, you'll suspend your disbelief and go along with it. How bloody clever is that? (And before you tell me that advertising never gets you to buy anything, let me tell you that everyone says that, and, if that were true, why would there be any advertising at all?)

No, no-one is more skilled than us in promoting the suspension of disbelief. Not even the purveyors of the 'great' religions. What is faith but choosing to believe in what you cannot know? Ergo, the suspension of disbelief. The religious chaps are clever, I'll grant you, because the promise of an afterlife that you can't prove *won't* happen is a jolly good idea. But admen can't get away with that. With the exception of political ads – and we won't go *there* now – the law makes us back up our claims with some kind of proof. So, can you see what I mean now? We admen really are clever dicks.

Some people, most in fact, while conceding we are clever dicks, will, in the next breath, dismiss us as shallow. When Mavis died, I found some old primary school reports of mine. At the age of seven, my primary school form teacher had written, 'Andrew is a clever boy but needs to be more thoughtful'. See, they had me off to a tee even then, and, clearly, even then, I was an adman in the making. Well, people don't change do they? You are what you are what you are. But don't misunderstand me. I'm not saying you don't learn lessons if they're hard enough. For instance, and bearing in mind the debacle that followed my telling Peggy about the girl with the green spiky hair, although I confessed to her about the Cyril business, I made no mention of my reaction to seeing her in the wheelchair, and never will. I am sure she knows me well enough to know that was exactly how I would have reacted, but she doesn't need to know that was how I actually did. Yes, you can learn. But no, you don't fundamentally change. So, 'clever but needs to be more thoughtful' – yes, to slightly misquote Hovis, it's as true today as it's always been.

But there's a bit of a paradox here. Because, though we may be shallow, don't we admen also touch on what is most profound? Is not the suspension of disbelief, the very stuff of life? Not only for the faithful, choosing to believe in the life everlasting. But for the rest of us too, the people like me who know perfectly well that life is just what happens between two lots of oblivion. And yet, though we know it perfectly well, do we not carry on as if we will live for ever? Isn't the thing we dread most the news that we might have some terminal illness, even though we know that life itself is, by definition, terminal? And what is that if it is not the suspension of disbelief? Except, possibly – definitely – the suspension of sanity.

My other favourite song of Peggy Lee's, the other one that she's really well known for, is 'Is That All There Is?' (Written by two other people I think of as geniuses, Mike Stoller and Jerry Lieber, who also wrote 'Hound Dog.') When you listen to 'Is That All There Is?' you're unable to stop yourself from seeing how it cuts, so unsentimentally, right to the heart of things. Yes, indeed, you say to yourself, that is all there is. Yet, the moment it's over, you carry on as before, living in the fantasy world of the permanently cloudless sky. The suspension of disbelief is something we seem, literally, not to be able to live without.

Are you still with me on all this? Or, are you just shaking your head, and saying, oh do give over, stop being such a clever dick? Really, I don't mind. Either way, I win. (Please spare a thought for Donald McEwan here. He had to put up with this kind of thing for years.)

And whilst on the subjects of advertising and people I think of as geniuses, I have one more little thing to add, one more virtuoso to admire, and then I am going to finish. The chap to whom I am referring was an adman himself – the late Hal Riney.

In the late eighties he wrote some commercials for a wine brand in the States called Bartles and James. In this campaign there are two old boys who, we are asked to believe, are Mr Bartles and Mr James telling us about their wonderful wines. If I recall correctly, they were sitting on the porch of some sort of old fashioned homestead, as they talked to camera. None of this may strike you as being particularly exceptional but it was all so charmingly done and the two old chaps so endearing, that you wanted to believe. Were these two old guys really Mr Bartles and Mr Jaymes? Did a Mr Bartles or a Mr Jaymes even exist? Who knew? Who cared? They were lovely. And even someone like me, a pro, who knew all the puppeteers' tricks, was more than willing to suspend my disbelief. In fact, as I only recently discovered, two actors called David Joseph Rufkahr and Dick Maugg, respectively, played the parts, and a brilliant job they did too. The dialogue was written and delivered in a very humble, folksy way – the very antithesis of selling. It was an incredibly difficult trick to pull off, but they – actors, director, Hal Riney – managed it to perfection.

There is an unwritten rule in advertising that you may steal ideas from any source – movies, plays, books, wherever – but to nick something from another ad is bad form. That, in adland, is plagiarism. It may surprise you that admen have such scruples but I assure you that most do. Anyway, using that rule as a guide, that you may steal from one creative form to use in another, I am now going to steal from Hal Riney's Bartles and James commercials.

The crowning glory of these commercials, is something I have never ever seen done in any other ad. At the very last moment of every commercial in the campaign, Mr Bartle in his humble and folksy way, turns to the camera – the viewer – and speaks. He delivers not the obvious clever-dick advertising line you expect, but smiles gently and says simply and quietly, "Thank you for your support."

When I first saw that I got goosebumps. I loved it. I ran around forcing other people to watch it. To be so seemingly, convincingly guileless. What could be cleverer than that? Did I believe a word of it? No. Yes. Yes. No. It didn't matter. What mattered was, I wanted to believe it.

And so, in tribute to Hal Riney, and on behalf of Peggy, Florence, India, Bette, Spot, Alison, Donald McEwan, the treacherous bastards, mouthy idiot, Bart and Brett, the Manatee and all the rest, I am going to steal his idea.

Thank you for taking the time to read our story.

ACKNOWLEDGEMENTS

So many people to thank for their help in getting this on the road. (In a couple of cases, unknowingly.) Notably, and in no particular order – and with grovelling apologies to anyone I've forgotten – Bill Campbell, Simon Scott, John Bacon, John Donnelly, Dave Waters, Brian Byfield, Graham Nunn, Paul Collis, Hannah Phillips, Laurie Phillips, Sam Evans, Nicola Gill, Peter Bennett-Jones, Lisa Harriman, Geoff Howard-Spink, Daniele Ferreyrol, Joanna Dickerson, the late Dr Derry Macdiarmid, all at the London MeetUp Wednesday night writers' group, and, last but not least, Amy Frolick.

And, for their forbearance, thanks to Amar and the girls and boys of Starbucks, Queen's Park, where much of this was written, and to Ian 'Mac' McArthur on whose boat bobbing in the Caribbean a good deal of the rest was. (Second location marginally preferable to the first.)

Thanks too to John Bond, Silvia Crompton, Daniela Rogers, Annabel Wright – the dedicated publishing pros at whitefox. And to Viki Ottewill for her tremendous work on the cover design. And to Justin Hackney for building the website and for other bits of invaluable techno-help.

Above all, supercharged more-than-I-can-ever-thank-you thanks to the hugely supportive Maureen Lipman and Carol Birch, and to the fabulous Rosie Bowen.

I didn't listen to any of them but I'm sure that I should have done.

SONG TITLES IN THIS BOOK

'You Are the One that I Want'
Written by John Farrar

'Singing in the Rain'
Music: Nacio Herb Brown
Lyrics: Arthur Freed

'Let's Jump the Broomstick'
Music and Lyrics: Charles
Robins

'Love is the Drug'
Written by Andrew Mackay
and Bryan Ferry

'True Love'
Music and Lyrics: Cole Porter

'Let's Do It'
Music and Lyrics: Cole Porter

'Shoulda Woulda Coulda'
Written by Beverly Knight and
Craig Wiseman

'Through the Eyes of Love'
Written by Marvin Hamlish
and Carole Bayer Seger

'If I Were a Rich Man'
Written by Sheldon Harnick
and Jerry Bock

'Tradition'
Written by Sheldon Harnick
and Jerry Bock

'That Old Black Magic'
Music: Harold Arlen
Lyrics: Johnny Mercer

'YMCA'
Written by Henri Belolo,
Jacques Morali, Victor Willis

'Too Good to be True'
Written by Robert Palmer

'Can We Still Be Friends'
Written by Todd Rundgren

'Bad Case of Loving You
(Doctor, Doctor)'
Written by Moon Martin

'Feels So Good'
Written by Chuck Mangione

'Fever'
Written by Eddie Cooley and
Otis Blackwell

'It's Been a Long, Long Time'
Written by Jule Styne and
Sammy Cahn

'Is That All There Is?'
Written by Mike Stoller and
Jerry Lieber

'Hound Dog'
Written by Mike Stoller and
Jerry Lieber

ABOUT THE AUTHOR

Richard Phillips is a writer and radio broadcaster who once lived in adland. While there he worked for agencies in London and New York, and helped create a number of successful campaigns. (And a few that are best forgotten.)

He was born in Brighton and left school at 16 to attend the university of life, from which he failed to graduate.

He is divorced*, has one daughter of whom he is inordinately proud, and a large television.

Richard Phillips, who has a full head of hair, is 47.

*Open to offers.

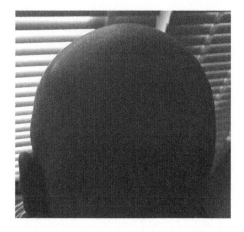